KURT AUSTIN ADVENTURES®
Novels from the NUMA Files®

Clive Cussler's Condor's Fury (by
    Graham Brown)
Clive Cussler's Dark Vector
    (by Graham Brown)
Fast Ice (with Graham Brown)
Journey of the Pharaohs
    (with Graham Brown)
Sea of Greed (with Graham Brown)
The Rising Sea (with Graham Brown)
Nighthawk (with Graham Brown)
The Pharaoh's Secret
    (with Graham Brown)
Ghost Ship (with Graham Brown)
Zero Hour (with Graham Brown)
The Storm (with Graham Brown)
Devil's Gate (with Graham Brown)
Medusa (with Paul Kemprecos)
The Navigator (with Paul Kemprecos)
Polar Shift (with Paul Kemprecos)
Lost City (with Paul Kemprecos)
White Death (with Paul Kemprecos)
Fire Ice (with Paul Kemprecos)
Blue Gold (with Paul Kemprecos)
Serpent (with Paul Kemprecos)

OREGON FILES®

Clive Cussler's Fire Strike
    (by Mike Maden)
Clive Cussler's Hellburner
    (by Mike Maden)

Marauder (with Boyd Morrison)
Final Option (with Boyd Morrison)
Shadow Tyrants (with Boyd Morrison)
Typhoon Fury (with Boyd Morrison)
The Emperor's Revenge
    (with Boyd Morrison)
Piranha (with Boyd Morrison)
Mirage (with Jack Du Brul)
The Jungle (with Jack Du Brul)
The Silent Sea (with Jack Du Brul)
Corsair (with Jack Du Brul)
Plague Ship (with Jack Du Brul)
Skeleton Coast (with Jack Du Brul)
Dark Watch (with Jack Du Brul)
Sacred Stone (with Craig Dirgo)
Golden Buddha (with Craig Dirgo)

NON-FICTION

*Built for Adventure: The Classic
    Automobiles of Clive Cussler and
    Dirk Pitt*
*Built to Thrill: More Classic
    Automobiles from Clive Cussler
    and Dirk Pitt*
The Sea Hunters (with Craig Dirgo)
The Sea Hunters II (with Craig Dirgo)
Clive Cussler and Dirk Pitt Revealed
    (with Craig Dirgo)

CHILDREN'S BOOKS

The Adventures of Vin Fiz
The Adventures of Hotsy Totsy

CLIVE CUSSLER'S
CONDOR'S FURY

GRAHAM BROWN

MICHAEL JOSEPH

PENGUIN MICHAEL JOSEPH

UK | USA | Canada | Ireland | Australia
India | New Zealand | South Africa

Penguin Michael Joseph is part of the Penguin Random House group of companies
whose addresses can be found at global.penguinrandomhouse.com

First published in the United States of America by G. P. Putnam's Sons,
an imprint of Penguin Random House LLC 2023
First published in Great Britain by Penguin Michael Joseph 2023
001

Book design by Alison Cnockaert
Printed and bound in Great Britain by Clays Ltd, Elcograf S.p.A.

The authorized representative in the EEA is Penguin Random House Ireland,
Morrison Chambers, 32 Nassau Street, Dublin D02 YH68

A CIP catalogue record for this book is available from the British Library

HARDBACK ISBN: 978–0–241–63541–4
TRADE PAPERBACK ISBN: 978–0–241–63542–1

www.greenpenguin.co.uk

CAST OF CHARACTERS

National Underwater and Marine Agency (NUMA)

KURT AUSTIN—Director of Special Projects, salvage expert, and boating enthusiast

JOE ZAVALA—Kurt's assistant and best friend, helicopter pilot, and mechanical genius

RUDI GUNN—Assistant Director of NUMA, graduate of the Naval Academy, runs most of the day-to-day operations at NUMA

HIRAM YAEGER—NUMA's Director of Information Technology, expert in the design and function of the most advanced computers

PAUL TROUT—NUMA's chief geologist, graduate of Scripps Institute, married to Gamay

GAMAY TROUT—NUMA's leading marine biologist, also graduated from Scripps, married to Paul

CAST OF CHARACTERS

Naval Intelligence

REAR ADMIRAL MARCUS WAGNER—Head of Naval Intelligence, old friend of Rudi Gunn's

COMMANDER JODI WELLS—Ranking operative at Naval Intelligence, leader of the Arcos mission

LIEUTENANT MASON WEIR—Leader of fire team alpha, Arcos mission

PETTY OFFICER BOSWORTH CONNERS—Member of fire team alpha, Arcos mission

PETTY OFFICER DIEGO MARQUEZ—Member of fire team alpha, Arcos mission

Ostrom Airship Corporation

STEFANO SOLARI—Brazilian aviation visionary, after a successful career as an aeronautical engineer, he launched Ostrom, creating the first international airship line since the days of the zeppelin

LUIS TORRES—Cuban engineer working for Ostrom, loyal to Martin Colon

CAPTAIN MIGUEL BASCOMBE—Senior captain at Ostrom, in charge of test flights, friend of Stefano Solari

Picadors–Cuban Intelligence

MARTIN COLON—Former colonel in Cuban Intelligence, leader of the Picadors, an elite unit tasked with weakening the United States, now a VP at Ostrom Airship Corporation

ROJO LOBO (THE RED WOLF)—An assassin during his time in Cuban Intelligence, Lobo is now a smuggler of pirated goods

ANTON PEREZ—Former colonel in Cuban Intelligence, now chairman of the Ministry of Production, which oversees the production and distribution of Cuban raw materials

CAST OF CHARACTERS

VICTOR RUIZ—Former sub commander in Cuban Intelligence, now a member of the Cuban National Assembly and an up-and-coming politician

LORCA—Former commander in the Picadors, now a high-ranking member of the Cuban Port Authority in Havana

YAGO ORTIZ—Cuban neuroscientist involved in the Havana Syndrome experiments, later recruited by Colon to the Arcos project

ERNESTO MOLINA—Important member of the Central Committee, heads the Counter-Espionage Commission, a sometime ally of Martin Colon

PROLOGUE

CUBA

ARCOS, CUBA

An old Russian-made SUV sped through the tiny Cuban village of Arcos on a humid afternoon. Dilapidated buildings lined the streets. Telephone poles leaned over at odd angles as if they were about to fall. With the sun dropping low, the SUV raced around a curve near the outskirts of town, narrowly missing a wild dog that had strayed too far from the gutter.

Martin Colon glanced in the rearview mirror. The stray dog had spun around and darted away just in time. It was now cowering in the weeds beside an old building beneath faded images of the Cuban and Soviet flags.

"How far to the lab?" a voice said beside him.

Colon looked over at the man in the passenger seat. Ernesto Molina was a politician and a member of the Central Committee in Havana. He was something of a roughneck, willing to throw his weight around and bluster. He was also an influential force, heading up the Counter-Espionage Commission, a group charged with finding traitors and spies. Colon had gone to great lengths to keep him as an ally, but the relationship was fraying.

"Three miles from here," Colon said.

Molina tugged at the collar of his wrinkled, olive-drab field jacket. Like many in the Cuban government, Molina chose to wear a military uniform, hoping to be seen as a leader of the revolution. Colon was the opposite. He wore only civilian clothes, despite being a full colonel in the Cuban Intelligence Directorate and a former pilot in the air force.

"And you're sure the Americans are coming?" Molina asked.

Colon was certain. "My sources tell me a raid will happen any day now."

Molina didn't like this. The specter of American soldiers on Cuban soil was both terrifying and infuriating. He blamed Colon for the danger. "I warned you about this project. The committee has always been wary of it, but I backed you. In return you've taken things too far. Kidnapping an American scientist. Running experiments on human subjects. What madness is this?"

"The American came willingly," Colon explained, offering a half-truth. "The test subjects were political prisoners. Traitors. Your committee would have ordered at least half of them to face a firing squad if I hadn't taken them off your hands."

"You've been reckless," Molina snapped. "And now you have to face the consequences."

Colon remained calm and in control. He was far less worried than his political passenger. And he'd been anything but reckless. "And just what consequences are you talking about?"

"You've run out of rope," Molina said. "We're shutting you down. The materials and research will be moved to a military base where they'll be properly guarded, if not destroyed."

"Destroyed?"

"Yes," Molina replied. "Some members of the committee consider your work an abomination. Others consider it a threat. And now they alone will decide what to do with it."

Colon's jaw tightened, but it was all for show. His informants had told him of the growing unease in the committee long ago. He was prepared for the news. He was prepared for everything.

He glanced to the west. The sun was about to dip behind the mountains. If he was right a squad of commandos from the U.S. Navy would arrive sometime after dark.

"It's a good thing the Americans are coming," he said.

Molina looked at him as if he'd misheard. "Why do you say that?"

"Because I need the world to blame them for what I'm about to do."

With a jerk of the steering wheel, Colon whipped the vehicle to the left. Molina, who wasn't wearing a seat belt, was thrown against a door that hadn't closed securely for years. The door flew open with the impact. Molina went sailing through it and out onto the dirt road. He tumbled more than slid, arms and legs windmilling until he came to rest in a thicket of weeds that had grown up around a wooden fence.

Colon slammed on the brakes and brought the Lada to a stop. Grabbing a pistol, he got out of the car and walked back to Molina. He found him bent and broken, but not yet dead.

"Why?" Molina wheezed, looking up at him. "Why?"

"Because you and the rest of the old men in Havana would waste what we've done on silly mind games or even turn it against our own people. I won't allow that to happen."

"But . . . the Americans?" Molina managed.

"Don't worry," Colon said. "They won't get it either."

As Colon spoke, he could see Molina sliding a bloodied hand with broken fingers toward a holster on his belt. He didn't wait for Molina to reach it. He straightened his wrist and fired one shot into Molina's chest and then a second into his skull. The echoes of the gunfire rang out across an unnaturally quiet landscape. Colon doubted anyone would hear them or come to investigate if they did. This was the *zona de muerte*, a field surrounding the testing facility populated by dead animals left to rot in the sun. It formed a very effective shield. No one came here if they didn't have to.

Holstering the weapon and climbing back in the SUV, Colon reached over to close the passenger door and then put the car back in gear. As he sped off, he glanced into the distance. He could just see the outline of a radio tower silhouetted against the gathering dusk. It wouldn't be long now.

Lieutenant Mason Weir crawled through an overgrown field thick with tall grass as pinpoints of starlight appeared in a darkening sky above him. A special operative in Naval Intelligence, Weir was leading a three-man team toward a small building in the distance. Moving slowly and sticking to the thickest parts of the tall grass, Weir was halfway across the field when he came across a dead horse with no eyes lying in the dirt. He stopped beside the animal, waiting for the two enlisted members of his team to catch up.

The first to arrive was a petty officer named Bosworth Conners. Everyone called him Bosco. "Damn shame to treat an animal like this," he said, studying the eyeless horse.

Weir had seen another dead horse over by the tree line, along with a couple of dead goats and at least one bull. He knew from satellite images that the fields surrounding the small building were littered with carcasses. This one looked the freshest. "Brass wants to know what killed it," he said to Bosco. "Take some blood."

As Bosco got out his medical kit, the third member of the team moved up beside them. "I'll tell you what killed it," Diego Marquez promised. "Radio death ray."

He pointed ahead to a tower rising up behind the flat-roofed building. It was a classic transmission tower made up of intersecting metal rods. Halfway up, a trio of crescent-shaped dishes pointed in different directions, while a red beacon blinked on and off at the top. "Havana Syndrome," he added. "The latest way to melt your brain."

Havana Syndrome was the name given to a raft of neurological symptoms occurring among U.S. embassy staff in Cuba. Each case was different, but most involved a sudden ringing in the ears, pain in various joints, and a feeling of intense heat that seemed to be coming from the inside. More severe problems such as vertigo, confusion, and seizures sometimes followed. Several people had been hospitalized, one with trauma that resembled radiation burns.

The CIA thought the whole thing was nonsense. NSA was undecided and waiting for more data. Only Naval Intelligence considered the issue to be a legitimate threat. And only because they'd linked it to a rogue American scientist named Wyatt Campbell, who had experience with directed energy weapons.

They'd tracked him to Havana. And then to Arcos. And when satellite images revealed a pasture littered with dead animals and a small building giving off excessive amounts of heat, they'd decided to act. Sending Weir and his team to investigate.

Depending on how it ultimately turned out, they were either there to rescue Campbell or to capture him and drag him back to the States in chains.

While Bosco drew the horse's blood, Marquez used a high-tech machine to sample the air. He reported all clear.

Weir nodded and got on the radio. "Mongoose, this is Strike Team," he said. "We're about to enter the snake pit. Building is quiet but not dark. Four vehicles parked outside. No sign of activity. Air samples clear of chemicals and biologics. Confirm we're still a go?"

A female voice came over the speaker in his ear. It belonged to the mission leader, call sign Mongoose.

"You're cleared to enter the pit," she replied. "No sign of military units in the area. We're ready to cut the power and start jamming. We'll stand by to provide backup once you've breached the door."

Weir acknowledged that and turned back to his men. "Bosco, you done yet?"

Bosco had just pulled the needle out. He packed the sample away. "Stored and saved."

"All right, let's go."

Weir led them to the edge of the brush. The building was only sixty feet away. A scan of the structure showed no heat signatures on the outside, which told them there were no guards on patrol or snipers on the roof. It also detected minimal heat coming from within, the opposite of what the satellites had picked up. Aside from a strange hum coming from the radio tower, the area was deathly quiet.

They crossed to the wall, crouching around a door. They still hadn't seen any activity or faced any form of resistance.

"You sure we're in the right place?" Marquez asked.

Weir was sure. He sent a signal to Mongoose and the lights around the building went dark. The interior glow coming from the high mounted windows dimmed as well, but never went totally black. The hum from the radio tower continued.

Looking up, Weir saw the red light still glowing.

"The tower must have its own generator," Marquez said. "Want me to go find it and shut it down? I wouldn't want to get fried when we egress back across that field."

Weir nodded. "Knock it out," he said before turning to Conners. "Bosco, you're with me."

As Marquez looped around the building toward the radio tower, Weir and Bosco pushed through the door with their MP5 submachine guns at the ready.

The hall was empty, but its appearance surprised them. What looked like an old storage facility from afar was decidedly modern on the inside. The floor was polished concrete, the walls made of sterile, high-gloss plastic. Glancing down the hall Weir spied security doors with coded locks. All of it partially illuminated by a set of emergency lights at the far end.

"Definitely the right place," Weir said, studying the laboratory-like setup.

They moved down the hall, coming to the first room and pushing the door open. Despite the heavy bolt and the numerical keypad connected to it, the door swung open with ease.

"Top-notch security," Bosco said.

Weir glanced around. The room was vacant. Not a scrap of furniture or a stray box. It struck him as odd. Before he could say anything the sound of gunfire rang out. Three quick bursts followed by silence and then two more.

Weir hit the deck with Bosco scrambling to the door.

"See anything?" Weir asked.

"Clear," Bosco replied.

With nothing around them suggesting they were being shot at, Weir pressed the talk switch on his radio. "Quez, you taking fire?"

The reply came instantly. "Not me, boss. All quiet out here."

Another round of shooting erupted. This time accompanied by an anguished scream and then a final, silencing shot.

"It's coming from down the hall," Bosco said.

Weir didn't like any of this. It wasn't far-fetched to think the Cubans might execute Campbell or even silence their own people if a raid occurred, but at this point for all they knew it was just a power failure. A common occurrence in Cuba, especially in the heat of summer.

Weir moved to the door and then ducked across the hall into the next room. They found overturned file cabinets and trash cans filled with paper that had been set on fire. The smoke was billowing, and the flames grew hotter as the open door let new oxygen in. All they could do was close the door and move on.

Across the hall they discovered a bank of computers smashed to bits. Lying on the ground nearby were two men in lab coats, each of them bloodstained from multiple gunshot wounds.

"Hamza and Min Cho," Weir said, comparing their faces to images he'd seen in the briefing before the mission. "The Iranian and North Korean scientists who the brass thought might be in on this. At least they were right about something."

Bosco grimaced at the bad news. "Someone's cleaning this place out. If these guys are dead, Campbell won't be around for long."

Weir agreed. "Get what you can from the computers and check these guys for pocket litter. I'm going to find Campbell."

Weir was breaking protocol by spreading his men out like this, but he needed to move fast. Otherwise, the whole mission would be for nothing. Leaving Bosco, he continued down the hall. Smoke was now clinging to the ceiling and dampening the glow of the emergency lights. A spate of chatter from the backup team told him they were on their way, but he was too focused on the hunt for the scientist to join in.

He searched the next room and found nothing. A few steps away he reached a large door. Like all the others it was unlocked. Kicking the door wide, he cleared the room with the MP5 at his shoulder. He saw no sign of danger and stepped inside.

This must have been the main laboratory, he decided. It had shelves filled with equipment and supplies, and worktables loaded down with microscopes, centrifuges, and other high-tech machines. He moved deeper into the room, checking the shadows and the space behind each workbench. Near the back end of the room, he found another body lying face down. He rolled the man over, noticed the scruffy beard and the long nose. "Campbell," he said to himself. "Damn."

Before he could do anything else, the radio squawked in his ear.

"Chief, this is Quez. Something odd out here. This tower isn't hooked up to the main grid at all. Nothing here but broken and frayed cables left over from the sixties."

"You find a generator?" Weir asked.

"Yeah, but it's the size of a dollhouse. Might be putting out three hundred watts. Just enough to light up that red beacon on top."

As Weir struggled to put some meaning to that discovery, Bosco chimed in on the radio call.

"Hate to say it but there's nothing worthwhile in the lab. I forced my way back into the room with the burning trash cans and pulled out some of the papers. It's just empty notebooks and blank sheets."

Weir knew there could only be one reason for this. "This whole thing is a setup," he said. "Get out. Get out now."

A loud squeal hit his ears, telling him his transmission had been stepped on. A second try resulted in the same thing. It meant someone was jamming them.

Weir turned for the door, only to see it slamming shut. He lunged for the handle, but grabbed a second too late. He heard the bolt slide home and saw the coded lock engage. Two hard pulls were enough to tell him it wasn't budging.

As he looked for another way out, the ventilation system kicked on. Streamers attached to the grates in the ceiling fluttered like ribbons as the air began to flow. A nasty scent like an electrical fire quickly filled the room, as if the air conditioner were melting down.

Weir didn't know what the hell was going on, but he knew he needed to get out of there. He swung his MP5 around and blasted away at the glass window in the center of the door. A tight pattern of impact strikes clustered in a circle, but they left only mushroom-shaped dents in what was obviously a bulletproof panel.

"Don't waste your ammunition," a voice said from behind him.

Weir spun and saw only the glowing screen of a laptop propped up on one of the desks. The image of a face appeared on the screen.

"Who the hell are you?" Weir said. "What is all this fun house nonsense?"

Weir was surprised to hear the words coming out of his mouth. It was not his style to engage a target in conversation. He felt as if the peculiar situation had thrown him off.

"It's anything but nonsense," the image told him. *"In fact, I'm about to reveal a truth you'll find hard to believe."*

Weir edged around the first worktable, wary of being attacked while he focused on the computer. He felt a tone in his ears, followed by an odd ringing. "And what truth is that?"

"You've been set up to fail. Your government sent you here. Your Bravo team stayed close enough to observe, but too far away to render any real assistance. Your fire-team members split off one by one, allowing you to come here . . . to this room . . . alone."

Weir found himself getting angry. The smell in the air was bothering his eyes and burning his nostrils. It was worse than the smoke in the hall. He felt like smashing the computer screen but instead found himself answering once again. "Why would they do that?"

"Because you're the final test subject. The last experiment. The human guinea pig. They've known what we were doing here all along. But rather than blow this place off the map they sent you here to be infected. To bring the dust home. Even if you get out alive, they'll prod you and poke you and eventually dissect your brain in a petri dish in hopes of figuring out how we've accomplished the impossible."

Weir tried to reason through the noise in his head. He thought back to the demand for samples. Air, soil, water. Blood from the dead horse. He didn't want to believe it, but there was something familiar in what the voice was telling him. As if he'd already been thinking it himself.

"Someone had to be sacrificed to find out the truth," the voice continued. *"They . . . chose . . . you."*

With each new word, Weir's struggle to process them became more serious. He found himself thinking about Havana Syndrome and then realizing this was something more. But what?

The harder he tried to think, the louder the noise in his head became. He found it difficult to hold a thought. Even more difficult to refute what the voice was suggesting. The noise became pain, and the pain a blinding wall of resistance, impenetrable to any notion other than those coming from the speaker.

Weir fell to his knees. He no longer sensed the metallic smell in the air, nor felt the weapon in his hand or the ground beneath him. His vision began failing. His world shrank, until all that existed was the wave of pain and the voice that cut through it.

"You have only one choice," the voice said. *"Kill them. Kill them all."*

As Weir considered this thought, the wall of pain vanished, falling away like a plate-glass window shattered into a thousand pieces. The truth was suddenly clear. All he had to do was act.

His senses returned in a rush. Feeling flooded back into his hands and feet. Sight to his eyes. He saw the computer screen go dark. Heard the air handler kick off. Watched the fluttering streamers fall slack.

With his strength returning, Weir stood, watching as the bullet-scarred door opened. He heard footsteps in the hall and saw Bosco appear through the smoke.

Bosco cocked his head, looking at him strangely. "You all right, Chief?"

Weir didn't smile or speak. He just swung his weapon into place and opened fire. Bosco fell in a hail of bullets with rounds through both legs and one arm. He remained alive only because the body armor he wore had protected his chest.

Bosco cursed in agony and brought his own weapon around.

Weir fired again. This time holding the trigger down until the magazine was empty and the walls were covered in blood.

With the shooting finished, Weir entered the corridor. He stepped over the body of his dead friend and turned down the hall, pulling and discarding the empty magazine and jamming a full one in its place. He moved slowly and methodically, a single thought playing on an endless loop in his mind.

Kill them. Kill them all.

1

A HUNDRED MILES NORTHEAST OF NASSAU
PRESENT DAY

Captain E. F. Handley stood on the bridge wing of the MV *Heron*, squinting into the distance behind the ship. His dark eyes focused on the line running from the *Heron*'s stern to the dilapidated fishing trawler she was towing.

He grunted a note of displeasure. "We've got a situation brewing."

Handley was a lifelong sailor in his early sixties and the captain of the midsized freighter that made runs between the Bahamas and various American ports. His face was a weathered mix of sun-damaged skin and a bristly beard. It was deeply tanned with a hint of carmine red in the palette. His hair was wild and unruly, a nest of coarse grays that stuck out from beneath an old ball cap, which he repeatedly removed and repositioned in hopes of corralling the bushy mess.

"What kind of situation?" a taller, more kempt individual asked.

Handley looked over at the man in khaki pants and a blue windbreaker. Gerald Walker was not a member of the crew but had chartered the voyage and come along to supervise, taking them to a random spot in the eastern Atlantic, where they'd found the damaged trawler and taken it under tow.

Walker claimed he wanted to take it back to Nassau, but he would allow no radio calls or other forms of transmission, and Handley expected he had another destination in mind.

As a pretense, Walker pretended to work for a big insurance company, but Handley knew an American Navy man when he met one. Walker was too squared away to be a civilian. Too tight-lipped to be telling the whole story. Besides, the trawler was of negligible financial value, cheaper to sink than to save. And then, of course, there were the bodies . . .

"See our towline?" Handley said. "It should be dipping into the water halfway between us and the trawler, but it's pulling up. The sag has gone out of it. The strain on the line is growing."

"Current or wind?" Walker asked, showing he knew a thing or two about towing a derelict.

"Neither," Handley said. "She's taking on water. She's sinking. We're gonna have to go back on board, set up pumps, and see if we can find the leak."

"I can't allow that," Walker said with a firm but polite tone.

The captain propped the ball cap higher on his head. "Something you don't want us to see on that ship, Mr. Walker? Something other than a bunch of dead Chinamen?"

"Dead Chinese," Walker corrected. "And I don't know what you're referring to. That ship was abandoned when we found it."

Handley laughed. "You play all the games you want, Mr. Walker. Meanwhile, that ship is getting heavier and lower in the water. She's dragging us like an anchor, which means we have to slow down or the line will snap. Reducing speed means Nassau is another half a day's sailing. The slower we go, the longer it takes. The longer it takes, the more water that trawler takes on. Forcing us to slow down even more. See where I'm going with this?"

Walker understood the predicament. "You're saying the trawler will be on the bottom before we reach the Bahamas."

"She'll be un-towable long before that."

As Walker pondered the options, Handley took another look behind them. Out beyond the trawler, something new caught his eye. An odd arc of light had appeared in the sky. It looked like the sunrise, but it was nearly dusk, and the sun was going down in the other direction.

At first, he thought it must be a reflection or a mirage. But the shimmering arc of light was moving closer. "What the devil is that?"

The apparition seemed to be approaching in silence—or perhaps just so quietly that any sound was drowned out by the wind and the waves—but as it crossed above the trawler, a humming sound became audible.

An instant later, the arc of light split into four separate orbs. Two of them branched off to the port side, while the others went to starboard. Before long they were circling the *Heron* like a pack of wolves.

"Captain?" one of the crewmen said nervously.

"What is this?" Handley snapped, looking at Walker. "A message from your dead Chinese friends?"

Walker was turning from point to point, trying to keep his eyes on the slowly circling balls of light. They were growing brighter with each pass, leaving streaks on his retina as they flared into spheres of gold and orange.

Walker used his hand as a shield against the light, trying desperately to block the glare. Try as he might, he saw nothing that suggested machinery or equipment behind the light. No wings, nor propellers or rotors, just glowing balls of light slowly circling the ship.

Watching them turn, his heart began to race. He knew things. Things that Captain Handley and his crew didn't. This knowledge chilled him to the bone.

The humming noise grew louder and deeper, becoming a haunting tone, like some aboriginal instrument echoing through the canyons. Walker found his skin itching and throat going dry. He stepped back against the bulkhead, his face now shaded, but lit in oscillating waves from the artificial suns dancing around them.

He scratched at his arm, casually at first and then uncontrollably, soon he was digging his nails into the skin, raking them until he drew blood. His eyes darted around, following the globes. Across and back, across and back. It was dizzying and mesmerizing all at once.

A pair of rough hands slammed him into the bulkhead, snapping him out of the trance.

"What the hell are these things?" Handley demanded.

Walker tried to answer but a shield had gone up in his mind. He tried to force the words through, but the harder he pushed, the tighter his throat cinched.

Realizing Walker had become useless, Handley shoved him aside. He ducked through the hatch onto the bridge, noticing that the lights overhead were throbbing in concert with each passing disk.

A migraine erupted in his head. A tight feeling spread across his chest. "Get off a distress call," he ordered. "Tell them we're under attack."

One of the crewmen was already fiddling with the radio, switching frequencies and trying to get a message out. He was getting feedback and interference on every channel. The noise got worse until a high-pitched squeal and burst of static blew out the speaker and the unit went dark.

The radioman stared at the ruined unit, which was mounted overhead. The microphone slipped out of his hand and dropped, swinging wildly on the looped cord that connected it to the transmitter.

Several lights blew out in sharp pops, like the flashbulbs of older days. The helmsman went still, his face catatonic, his eyes staring into the distance.

Handley pushed past his immobilized crewmen and pulled open a locker. As the door swung wide, his chest tightened again—much like it had during a heart attack he'd suffered three years earlier.

A damned bad time to be having a second one, he thought.

He pushed his thumb into his sternum to fight the pain while reaching into the locker. The first thing he grabbed was an emergency VHF radio. After lifting a plastic shield from its face, he pressed and held the distress button.

A tone confirmed he was transmitting. "Mayday, Mayday, Mayday," he said loudly. "This is the MV *Heron* out of Nassau. We're under attack and request immediate assistance."

He let go of the transmit button and heard only a loud electronic squeal.

He turned the squelch down and tried again. "I repeat, this is MV *Heron*, we're under attack. Our location is—"

A wave of feedback erupted from the speaker as the unit flared hot in his hand. The little LEDs that told him it was generating power. It blazed for an instant and then went dark.

"Damned useless thing."

Handley tossed the radio aside and reached deeper into the locker, grasping for a different piece of emergency equipment. He pulled out a Browning ten-gauge shotgun and ripped off the plastic trigger guard.

Flicking off the safety, Handley moved out onto the bridge wing. The balls of light continued to circle, buzzing past the ship no more than fifty feet away.

Tracking them left Handley feeling dizzy, so he braced himself and waited for another one to come around. As the next sphere appeared from behind the funnel, he raised the shotgun and pulled the trigger.

The first shot either missed or had no effect, so Handley pumped the forestock, reloaded, and fired again as the next orb appeared. A third orb followed the second, and Handley emptied the weapon in its direction. *Bang . . . bang . . . bang.* The spent shells kicked out from beneath the shotgun, the steel pellets blasting their way across the sky.

With the shotgun empty, Handley dropped to one knee. As far as he could tell, he'd accomplished nothing. Worse yet, the pain in his chest had become unbearable. He grabbed at his sternum as the shotgun fell from his hand. As the next orb raced by, he slumped to the deck and lay there.

Standing in the shadows, Gerald Walker had watched the scene play out. The swirling lights continued to orbit the ship, moving so fast they appeared like streaks in the darkening sky.

The oscillating hum continued to haunt him, while slowly resolving into a sound like whispered speech. Confusing at first, like an announcement echoing through a large stadium, the words eventually became clear.

Cut . . . cut . . . cut . . . Loose . . . loose . . . loose . . .

With every sound and syllable the pressure in his head grew worse. His eyes began to sting. Sweat dripped down his forehead. He continued to dig at the skin on his arm.

Cut . . . cut . . . cut . . . Loose . . . loose . . . loose . . .

Stepping back onto the bridge, he found the helmsman unconscious and the radioman digging at his ear, blood running through his fingers. Without warning, the radioman shouted something, ran out onto the bridge, and vaulted over the rail. No life jacket, no hesitation, just a desperate leap into the unknown.

Walker considered following him. The veins on his forehead bulged. Tunnel vision set in. His mind spinning with the circling demons.

Cut . . . cut . . . cut . . . Loose . . . loose . . . loose . . .

It made no sense to him. None at all. And then he thought about the trawler they were dragging to Nassau. He turned to the stern and focused on the Chinese ship. Without a conscious thought, he began walking toward it.

2

Thirty miles away, a two-hundred-and-seventy-foot vessel with a turquoise-painted hull was finishing a hard turn to starboard. The rakish vessel had the name *Edison* stenciled near the bow, directly below a set of twenty-foot-high letters that spelled NUMA, the acronym for the National Underwater and Marine Agency.

As the ship leaned over in the turn, a half dozen people on the bridge braced their legs against the centrifugal forces while gripping various handholds like riders on an out-of-control subway car.

The *Edison* was NUMA's primary training vessel and had graduated well over a thousand officers and crew since coming into service. The inside joke was that crews would stay on the *Edison* until the lightbulb went on and they were ready for frontline duty on one of the many ships in NUMA's oceangoing fleet.

This particular group was a mix of first-time officers and crewmen. They were being molded under the capable hands of Captain Steven Marks. Marks was a twenty-year NUMA veteran with eight years in the Coast Guard before that. He was known to be a stern taskmaster and he pushed the recruits to learn more than they thought they could in the shortest time possible.

"That's two hundred forty degrees," Marks called out to the helmsman. "Rudders to neutral, reduce speed, and be ready for all-stop."

Marks watched the crew act on his orders and nodded almost imperceptibly with approval. He and his trainee crew were practicing a man-overboard drill. The high-speed turn was known as a Williamson turn, which was designed to bring the ship back over the spot where the passenger or crew member had fallen. Viewed from above, the Williamson turn drew a question mark shape on the surface of the water. And the *Edison* had come out precisely on the line she was supposed to.

On the right-hand side of the bridge, up near the glass, a pair of observers watched. One was tall and lanky with a rugged face, deep blue eyes, and prematurely silver hair. The other man was shorter, stockier, with a T-shirt stretched over curved muscles of someone who spent plenty of hours in the gym.

The taller man was Kurt Austin. "You can let go now," he said to the man next to him.

Joe Zavala shook his head. "The way these guys drive? Sorry, I'm not taking any chances."

That brought a slight laugh from Kurt. Truth was, the *Edison* was a little top-heavy. She rolled into the turns with the pace of a sports car but the lean of an old city bus. Still, Kurt suspected the hard maneuvers were over, especially as the vessel reduced its speed.

"Lookouts report," Captain Marks ordered.

Men stationed on the bridge wings, the bow, and amidships were scanning the waters with binoculars.

"No joy on Oscar," the bridge lookouts reported. Similar reports came over the comms from the other lookouts.

It was nearly dusk, a tough time to spot a man floating on the dark sea, but Marks wasn't cutting the crew any slack. "Open your eyes," he snapped. "He's only wearing a bright orange vest."

The *Edison* had slowed substantially now. The plot showed them closing in on the exact spot they'd been at when the drill commenced.

Kurt looked forward, squinting as he studied the sea. A veteran of numerous drills and a fair number of live action searches, he was more attuned than the new crew to techniques of spotting a man against the swells. A quick scan told him they were closer than they thought.

Before he could say anything, the radio began to chirp on the emergency frequency. A signal came through garbled and spotty.

Kurt heard the caller shouting out *Mayday*. He glanced at the captain. "Is that part of the drill?"

"No," Marks said, as he looked over at the radio operator. "What frequency is that on?"

"Channel 16," the radio man said. "Emergency only."

After a burst of static the Mayday call was repeated and some of the words came through more clearly.

"*. . . under attack . . . request assistance . . .*"

Marks looked both aggravated and concerned. They were halfway between Florida and the Bahamas; not the type of waters they expected to hear of someone being attacked. He wondered if it was a prank. He looked at his guests. "Either of you responsible for this?"

Both Kurt and Joe were known pranksters. But this wasn't their doing.

Kurt shook his head firmly and looked over at the radioman. "Is there an ID on the call?"

The radio operator glanced at a code appearing on his screen. "MV *Heron*," he said. "A bulk freighter out of Nassau."

"How far off?"

"I'm getting a locator signal showing her about thirty miles to the south of us."

The emergency tone ceased, and the radio went quiet. But that didn't mean the emergency had ended.

"Captain," Kurt said quietly. "Unless there's a closer ship . . ."

Marks nodded. Both of them knew the rescue drill was over. "Plot a course and turn toward the source of the signal," he ordered. "As soon as it's laid in, take us all ahead flank speed."

"What about Oscar?" another crewman asked, referring to the mannequin they'd thrown overboard at the beginning of the drill.

"He'll have to tread water until we get back."

"Unlikely," Kurt said. "Considering we ran him over a half mile back."

The captain grunted his displeasure, but that's why they trained until they got it right: so that everyone could learn from their mistakes. He grabbed the microphone and switched the output to ship-wide intercom.

"This is the captain speaking. The M-O-B drill is over. We're about to respond to a genuine distress signal. All hands brace for a hard turn and remain at your emergency stations. This time it's not a drill."

The *Edison* cut into another hard turn and began to shudder as it picked up speed.

Thirty miles was a fair distance at sea, but the *Edison* would cover it in less than an hour.

"So much for the easy shakedown cruise," Joe said, easing up beside Kurt and the captain.

Marks gave both men a grim look. "I heard the word 'attacked' on the call," he said. "That's a different kind of emergency than engine failure, a ship taking on water, or even a fire at sea. Half of this crew are fresh out of the academy and most of the others are new to the ship. I hate to ask this of you, since the two of you are only supposed to be observers here, but if we have to do anything out of the ordinary, I'd appreciate it if you'd take the lead."

Kurt nodded. If the captain hadn't asked, he would have suggested it. "We'll be ready to make ourselves useful."

3

By the time the *Edison* came in range of the *Heron*, night had fallen. Repeated radio calls and semaphore flashes had gone unanswered. Closing in on the ship, Kurt, Joe, and Captain Marks studied the freighter through night vision binoculars, each of them looking for signs of life or trouble.

"She's down at the bow," Joe said. "I can see scrapes and collision damage."

The freighter was still moving at a pace of ten knots, but the heading had varied considerably as the *Edison* approached.

"She's obviously still under power," the captain announced. "But she can't hold true at all. She's varying five degrees to port, seven or eight back to starboard. Have to believe there's no one at the helm."

Kurt studied the pilothouse, but couldn't see inside. "Can't see if she's under positive control or not, but there's no sign of any crew on the deck. No sign of any attackers either."

Joe lowered his binoculars. "Were you expecting pirates flying the Jolly Roger?"

"No," Kurt said, "since this isn't the 1600s. But I was expecting something other than a deserted ship and an empty sea. Is there anything on radar?"

Marks glanced back at the radar screen. It had been clear the whole way in and remained so. "Nothing but the freighter. If they were attacked, whoever did it is long gone. And to avoid our radar they would have to be using very small boats. Nothing larger than a ribbed inflatable."

Small boats remained a possibility, but the ship was eighty miles from the nearest spit of land, a long way out for such small craft to travel.

"The only way we're going to learn anything is to get on board," Kurt said.

The captain offered a dour look. "With the freighter meandering all over the place, it's not going to be possible to string up a line and shimmy across the gap. Nor would I want to try boarding her from a small boat."

Kurt agreed. "We'll have to drop in from above. You have an MH-65 Dolphin back on the helipad. I took the liberty of asking your flight crew to stand by."

"Have them shuttle you over," Marks said. "But be sure to keep me posted."

"Will do." Kurt handed the binoculars to the captain, then followed Joe back through the ship to the helipad at the stern. By the time they got there, the pilot and a crewman who would assist them had already prepped the helicopter for flight.

Under different circumstances, Joe might have flown the aircraft himself, but as he was to go onto the freighter with Kurt, he climbed into the back and took a seat.

Kurt sat next to him, strapping himself in as the helicopter began to power up.

In a few short moments, the roar of the helicopter's engine grew exponentially. They lifted off the deck, clearing the *Edison* to the stern, and then banking toward the freighter.

"Give us a slow circle," Kurt said. "I want to see if we missed anything."

The pilot did as ordered, taking the helicopter along one side of the freighter, around the bow, and then back down the other side. Despite the noise of the helicopter and the sweep of its searchlight, no one appeared on deck to greet them, wave them off, or take a potshot at them.

"All's quiet on the *Heron* front," Joe said.

"Looks that way," Kurt said. "Anything jump out at you? Besides the utter lack of activity."

"Nope," Joe said. "You?"

"Nothing, except she's kind of dark. No deck lights. No portholes glowing."

"It was still daylight when we got the distress call," Joe said. "Maybe no one's left to turn the night-lights on."

"A grim thought," Kurt said.

He hit the intercom switch. "We need to get on the deck."

The bulk freighter was equipped with four cranes that rose from the deck, designed to load and unload cargo from her four individual holds. Booms, wires, and cables sprouting from the cranes created a forest of obstacles that made a safe landing on the ship impossible.

"There's really nowhere for me to land," the pilot said.

"Just get us up over monkey island," Kurt replied. "We'll hop out."

Monkey island was slang for the very top deck on a ship. Usually, the roof above the pilothouse or bridge. On a freighter like this it was at the very top of the accommodations block.

As the helicopter approached from the stern, Kurt could see that there were a few obstructions in the vicinity, including a communications mast and the ship's funnel.

"Give yourself enough room to clear the mast and then do your best to keep us centered," Kurt said.

"The ship isn't maintaining a constant course," Joe warned the pilot, "so you'll have to fly it manually."

The MH-65 had an autopilot that could keep the helicopter in a perfect hover, but with the ship moving and wandering off its heading, that system wouldn't work.

All in all, Kurt would have preferred to have Joe at the controls, but the *Edison*'s young pilot did his job well and they were soon hovering directly above the rectangle that made up monkey island.

Joe was already hooked into his rappelling gear and ready to go out the door. He pushed out and dropped eighty feet in a matter of seconds. As Joe landed, Kurt hooked in and stepped to the door, turning around.

Even though the helicopter was rock steady, the ship below was rolling with the swells, which were coming in off the starboard bow. As Kurt glanced downward, the *Heron* rolled slowly away, its bow dipping into a trough between the swells. It lingered there for a moment and then rose up and back toward the helicopter as it climbed over the next wave.

The swells weren't large, but then neither was the freighter.

With Joe holding the rope down below, Kurt waited for the *Heron* to crest the wave before he pushed out from the helicopter. He allowed the rope to slide through his hands in a controlled fashion, timing his landing just as the deck began to drop away.

Released from the rope, he gave the all-clear signal to the helicopter. The crewman in the back of the aircraft reeled in the line and the helicopter pulled away.

"Nice landing," Joe said.

"Thanks," Kurt said. "Still no welcoming committee."

"And after we made such an impressive entrance," Joe replied.

"Come on," Kurt said. "Let's check out the wheelhouse and see if anyone's driving this thing."

Moving to the edge of monkey island they found a ladder down to the starboard bridge wing. Dropping down it, they found their first casualty. An older man, lying face down in the corner.

Kurt kneeled beside the crumpled figure. The man looked to be in his sixties and had the weathered face of an old sea dog. A week's worth of scruff on his cheeks was matted with sweat and salt.

"Who is he?" Joe asked.

"I think he may be the captain," Kurt said.

Rolling the man over, Kurt found that he'd fallen across a pump-action shotgun. He slid the weapon out from under him and clicked on the safety. By the weight he could tell that the magazine was probably empty. A quick inspection proved that to be true, while a whiff of the barrel revealed a strong odor of gunpowder. The weapon had been fired recently.

Kurt glanced around. He found only one spent casing, but the others could have been ejected overboard or rolled out through the scuppers as the ship rocked back and forth on the waves.

"Empty," he said, handing the weapon to Joe.

Joe studied the size and make of the shotgun. "Ten gauge," he said. "Long barrel. Something tells me he wasn't shooting at pigeons."

"Not unless the pigeons were the size of vultures," Kurt said. Few people used ten-gauge shotguns anymore, not unless they were hunting large birds like geese or wild turkeys.

Joe nodded. "The real question is, were the vultures firing back?"

It seemed like a distinct possibility, but looking the man over, Kurt found no sign of injury. No bullet holes, no knife wounds, nothing to suggest head trauma or blood loss. He touched the man's neck and found a rhythmic beat. "He's got a pulse. It's faint, but it's there."

"That's one member of the ship's complement," Joe said. "Based on the size of this freighter there should be another twenty or thirty aboard. We should probably start looking for them. Right after we assess how badly the ship is damaged."

Kurt agreed. He eased the captain into a more comfortable position and stood up. He noticed that the captain's eyes were moving underneath his eyelids, darting to and fro almost frantically as if he were caught in some terrible dream. "Whatever happened here, they didn't go down without a fight."

Joe handed Kurt the empty shotgun. "You think anyone stuck around for a rematch?"

"Only one way to find out."

They opened the weatherproof door and stepped onto the bridge. The space inside was dimly lit, with only a single emergency light adding any illumination to the glow of the lighted controls and navigation panels. There wasn't a single crewman in sight. The only thing moving was a dangling microphone that hung from an overhead transmitter. It was swaying like a pendulum as the freighter rolled over the waves.

"No one home," Kurt said.

They found charts on the floor, a coffee mug in a cup holder, and a handheld emergency radio lying on the deck.

As Kurt placed the dangling microphone back on the cradle, he noticed the face of the unit was dark. Several flicks of the power switch did nothing to revive it.

"Probably why they used this one," Joe said, picking up the radio. He toyed with the controls, but found it was as dead as the main radio.

While Joe gathered the charts off the floor, Kurt went to the main panel. It seemed like half the ship's systems were offline, though a few still had power. And obviously the engines were running.

He soon found the navigation unit that housed the ship's autopilot. Like everything else on the ship, it was old. He flicked several switches, hoping to set it to sea-keeping mode, which would stop the *Heron* from weaving to port or starboard every time it rode over one of the swells, but it was no use; the navigation screen was burned out like an old TV left on for a decade or two.

"Have you ever seen anything like this?" Kurt asked. "Some systems are online, some are off. Others have power but look like they've been fried from the inside out."

"Power surge of some kind," Joe suggested. "One that tripped most of the circuit breakers, but not all of them."

Logical, Kurt thought. "What about the handheld?"

"Who knows how long that thing has been waiting to be used," Joe said. "If it's half as old as the rest of this equipment, the battery might not hold much of a charge."

Also logical, but suspicious.

With no way to adjust the navigation system, Kurt found the engine controls and moved the throttle to idle. A reduction in vibration told him the engines were answering the helm. The *Heron* would now slow to a stop and wallow side-on, like a piece of driftwood. *Better a sitting ship than one wandering all over the sea.*

As the ship lost speed, it pitched forward, accentuating the nose-down posture. The slope was worse than Kurt expected. "She's taken on a lot of water."

"This might be why," Joe said. He'd found the indicator panel for the watertight doors. Within a stylized outline of the ship lay a dozen sets of colored flags. Each set represented the location of a watertight door down below.

Some were green, meaning the doors were shut, but a couple were red and others yellow. Red meant the doors were open when they should have been closed, yellow meant that status was unknown or the door was in transit. The plethora of yellow flags suggested the power failure had interrupted the operation of the doors and they'd either never finished closing or hadn't sealed properly.

"Cutting our speed should stop water from ramming into whatever breach they've torn in the bow," Joe said, "but with these doors open and the pumps off, this ship isn't going to stay afloat for long."

"Can you get the doors closed?"

Joe was already in the process of cycling the switches. He moved them from off to standby and then back to on. "No luck," he said. "The doors are either jammed or inoperative."

Kurt had expected that. "We can always do it manually."

"Not unless you brought your fins," Joe said. "Some of these locations are already underwater."

Kurt wasn't interested in swimming the corridors of an unfamiliar ship in the dark while it was taking on water. There were risks, and then there were risks. "What about the pumps?"

Joe had already tried activating them. "The circuit is out. But if we can get to engineering before it floods, I should be able to get them back on."

"How much time would that buy us?"

"It depends whether these doors are wide open or slightly ajar," Joe said. "Maybe an hour. Maybe three or four."

That would be enough time to get anyone they found over to the *Edison* and come back on board with dive gear and a proper salvage team.

Kurt glanced out to the bridge wing, where the captain lay dreaming. "He seems stable. Let's get down to engineering and get those pumps on before we lose this ship from underneath us. We can look for the rest of the crew on our way."

Switching on a pair of flashlights, Kurt and Joe cleared the rest of the bridge deck, found the ship's main stairs, and dropped down one level. They were now in the heart of the accommodations block, the vertical structure at the stern of most cargo ships and tankers that housed the living spaces, offices, storerooms, and everything else that the crew would use.

The compact nature of the accommodations block made it quick and easy to search. With the living spaces and operations rooms all combined into one seven-story apartment block, and the workspaces and engineering decks directly under them, there was no need to wander the length and breadth of the freighter.

Kurt and Joe made quick sweeps of each level, expecting to find others hiding, trapped, or in similar condition to the captain. But after pushing open doors and shining their lights into the dark recesses of the various compartments, they found no one at all.

The communications suite was unoccupied, the rec room was vacant, the cabins in officers' country were empty, as were the first block of compartments for the regular crew.

"If this freighter wasn't such a rust bucket, I'd wonder if someone had automated everything and done away with the crew," Joe said.

Kurt's face was stern. "Have a feeling the second part of your statement is going to prove true."

Descending another level, Joe sniffed at the air. "You smell that?"

Merchant ships tended to be filled with mechanical smells and industrial odors. In a freighter like this the engine room was directly below the accommodations block. Oils, solvents, and fuel were stored nearby, their volatile fumes often rising through vents and gaps in the deck. But Kurt and Joe were used to all of that. The odor Joe detected was different.

Kurt took a deep breath. There was a faint, acrid scent in the air, he could taste it as much as smell it, like a tire burning some distance away. "Electrical, maybe. I'm not sure."

They kept going, with the ship beginning to groan as it wallowed sideways onto the swells.

Reaching the galley and the officers' mess, they found a half-eaten tray of food on a table, but no one there to cook it or eat it. It was the first sign of life since they'd left the bridge.

Kurt aimed the flashlight at the far wall, moving it slowly in search of a dripping sound. Directly across from them an ice maker was dripping melted water.

"I'm starting to think this is a *Mary Celeste* situation," Joe said, referring to the famous merchant ship found adrift in the Atlantic in 1872, perfectly seaworthy and under sail, but missing her entire crew.

"Difference is this ship still has all its lifeboats," Kurt said. "The *Mary Celeste* was missing one."

"The crew may have jumped," Joe said.

The sound of something heavy moving across the floor interrupted him.

"Or maybe they didn't," Joe said.

"Hello?" Kurt called out. "We're here to help you!"

There was no answer.

"Maybe something fell over," Joe suggested.

A dull thud, like a hatchway closing, sounded from the deck below.

"Or not," Joe said. "I really need to stop guessing."

Kurt stepped forward holding the flashlight in one hand and the empty shotgun in the other. He strained to see into the deep shadows where the light was blocked by obstructions. Standing in the darkened compartment, on a slowly rocking ship with all the creaks and groans that accompanied it, was surreal enough. The idea that a crewman— or someone who'd attacked the crew—would remain belowdecks while the ship took on water and threatened to go down made it even stranger. "Something doesn't add up here," he said to Joe. "Let's be careful."

They finished clearing the galley and took the stairs down one more level. For the first time they could hear the water sloshing below them and smell the bilge and oil that was being swept through the ship as the lower decks flooded.

Kurt stepped off the stairs and into the new compartment. Metal panels painted a dull green and covered with switches and buttons sat in front of him.

"Engineering," Joe said.

Kurt shined his flashlight along the wall. Illuminating another set of panels marked with a high-voltage warning label. "And there are your breakers."

Joe saw it too. "On it," he said.

Circuit breakers on a ship were not like those on a house. Each breaker had its own dedicated panel, plus a set of green, red, and amber lights to indicate its status. Some panels sported a voltage or ammeter to let the operator know how much current the particular piece of equipment was drawing.

The circuit breakers on the *Heron* were set up in a wall like small lockers, three or four high. Since some circuits drew more power than others, and thus required a larger breaker housing, there was a jigsaw effect to the wall.

The boxes themselves were numbered, which wouldn't help Joe without a manual, but fortunately they were also marked with metal placards that named the system they were connected to. Unfortunately, the placards were as old as the ship and burnished with corrosion.

Joe stepped close to the nearest panel and rubbed the outside of his palm against the placard, holding the flashlight at an awkward angle in his other hand as he read off what he'd discovered. "Induction drive coolant," he said, reading the first one and moving on. "Air handler . . . Starboard lifeboat davit . . . Port davit . . . Cargo hold one . . ."

"This should help," Kurt said from a few feet away. He shoved a heavy switch downward until it locked into place and then pressed the green button beside it. Lights came on throughout the ship, including those that hadn't been shattered in engineering.

They revealed the crowded engineering section in much greater detail, and a shape rushing at Kurt from its recesses.

"Look out!" Joe shouted.

Kurt spun around to see a man in crewman's overalls charging at him with a fire axe held high overhead. His face was contorted wildly with rage or terror or both and a guttural scream escaped his throat as he lunged at Kurt, bringing the axe crashing down.

Kurt leaped backward, swinging the empty shotgun like a sword and parrying the attack. He deflected the head of the axe into the panel beside him, which erupted in a shower of sparks, plunging the compartment back into darkness.

While the crewman in the overalls pulled the axe free, a second crewman raced out of the dark and tackled Joe to the ground.

Flat on the ground, Joe jammed the flashlight upward, hitting the man in the face and temporarily blinding him. As his tackler arched his back, Joe threw him off, rolled away, and jumped to his feet.

Shining the flashlight around he spied two more men joining the fray. They rushed ahead in tandem. Joe jumped to the side and shoved the nearest man into his partner. He then pivoted in time to see his initial attacker coming for him once more. About to be surrounded Joe darted in the only direction available to him, sprinting a few feet before sliding under a table and popping up on the other side.

With the table between him and the three men, he used the flashlight as a weapon, shining it in their eyes and trying to keep them at bay.

Across the compartment, Kurt didn't have the same luxury. The crewman with the axe was lunging and swinging, cutting huge swaths in the air like a possessed lumberjack.

Kurt dodged one blow and deflected another, but this time the axe caught the shotgun in a manner that ripped it from Kurt's hand and sent it flying out into the darkness.

Better the long gun than my head, Kurt thought. But now he was unarmed.

After the briefest of pauses the crewman pressed the attack, swinging high. Kurt ducked beneath the deadly blade and then charged while the axe-wielding man was off balance. He slammed his shoulder into the crewman's ribs and tackled him to the ground. The impact with the deck jarred the axe from the man's hands. A mad scramble ensued as the crewman tried to reach his weapon and Kurt attempted to knock it out of reach.

Kurt won the race, lunging forward and shoving the axe across the floor, where it slid over the edge of the stairwell and dropped down one level to where the engines and generators resided.

With the deadly weapon now gone, Kurt hopped to his feet and turned to face the attacker on more even footing.

On the other side of the compartment, Joe was dealing with a numbers problem. Three of them and one of him. With the table between them he had a modicum of shielding, but his opponents quickly split up, with one man going to each side and the third rushing toward the table directly across from Joe. He slid under the table as Joe had, which left only one route of escape.

Joe rolled onto the table, swinging his legs up and over as the crewman grasped for them. Continuing his roll, Joe tumbled off the table and landed on his feet.

The pincer movement that had been meant to trap him had failed, but the attack didn't end. As the men came over the table after him, Joe raced along the compartment, headed astern, and slid to a stop in front of the weapon he needed.

He slammed his elbow through a thin glass door, pulled a dry chemical fire extinguisher from its holder, and turned to face the attacking trio.

The men were right in front of him. Their flushed faces and the rabid look in their eyes appeared far worse up close. Joe didn't hesitate. He squeezed the handle and blasted them from point-blank range.

The explosion of chemical powder propelled by frigid, pressurized nitrogen was enough to stop their attack in its tracks. The men were quickly covered in the powder, blinded, coughing, and retching as they backed up.

Joe wasn't exactly loving the air quality either, but at least he was standing on the right side of the nozzle. He pressed the attack, blasting them repeatedly and forcing them back down the corridor.

On the far side of the compartment, Kurt was staring down the man who'd attacked him, like a matador staring down an angry bull. The guy looked ready to charge, his chest heaving, his nostrils flared. He hesitated as if he might be done, then grabbed at his ribs where Kurt had tackled him and charged anyway.

This time Kurt was ready. He grabbed the upper part of the man's overalls in his hands and rolled onto his back, pulling the attacker toward him as he dropped and thrusting his legs upward. It was a classic judo roll, using the man's own aggression against him.

The stocky fellow careened through the air, arms flailing. He landed on his back, grunting in pain and swearing, as he crashed into the far bulkhead.

Kurt hoped this was the end of it, but the man got up yet again. He turned wearily to face Kurt.

"Get off my ship!" he shouted. His deep voice booming through the compartment.

Kurt had figured the man for part of the crew, but now he was certain. "We're here to help you," he insisted. "We picked up your distress call."

"You lie," the man shouted. "No radio! No distress calls!"

"Why would we be here if we weren't coming to help?"

The crewman squinted into the light of Kurt's flashlight. By now his partners had come back into the compartment, covered in powder and gagging as they tried to spit it out. One of them fell to his hands and knees. Another dropped beside him to help. The third man backed into the breaker panel, crouching and looking Joe's way and then Kurt's, like a cornered mouse.

"We just want to get you off the ship before it sinks," Kurt said. "You know it's flooding down below."

"Flooding," the crewman said. "Sinking . . . We told them it was sinking."

"Told who?" Kurt asked.

"They didn't listen. They just lie."

The conversation had become disjointed, as if the crewman was no longer talking to Kurt. He was looking down, shaking his head softly, his shoulders sagging. He leaned against the panel and slid down to the deck. There, to Kurt's utter astonishment, the man who'd tried to kill him with an axe began to sob.

The other men were in a similar state. Heads down, defeated, cowering like prisoners.

By now Joe had emerged with the fire extinguisher in his hands and the flashlight under his arm. He was as surprised as Kurt to see the outpouring of emotion.

Kurt turned back to the man he'd fought with. His overalls were a dingy white, grease-stained in places. He was the ship's cook. "We're not here to hurt you," he said. "We came to help."

The cook just stared at the floor. "No one helps," he whispered. "There's no one left to help."

Kurt crouched down, getting eye level with the man. "What happened on this ship? Where's the rest of your crew?"

The tears stopped and the cook looked up, a blank stare now spreading across his tear-streaked face. It seemed as if he were looking past Kurt. "Gone," he said coldly. "Some went overboard. The rest of them were taken."

"By whom?"

The man's face was a mask now, his eyes dilated and wide. "By the lights that came out of the sky."

4

The infirmary aboard the *Edison* was a well-equipped but compact space. It felt positively crowded with the five survivors from the *Heron* being tended to by the ship's doctor, two medical technicians, and a nurse in training. Especially with Kurt and Joe watching from one side and a now prickly Captain Marks standing on the other side with his arms folded and a scowl on his face.

The infirmary was run by Dr. Elena Pascal, a young doctor two years out of residency who'd given up a big-city hospital job for a spot with NUMA. Dr. Pascal had long dark hair and emerald-green eyes that were arresting when she looked right at someone, but were often hidden behind reading glasses that helped her see the fine print on medications, charts, and reports.

Short enough that she had to stand on her tiptoes to reach supplies on the top shelves, she was also a bundle of energy, talking and moving and doing three or four things at once.

After making sure the *Heron*'s captain was stable—and attempting unsuccessfully to rouse him back to consciousness—she turned to the patients who were awake. Questions went unanswered, as the men offered nothing but blank stares. They complied with requests, sat quietly, but would say nothing.

"What happened to these three?" she asked, referring to the men covered in white powder.

"Joe blasted them with a heavy dose of ammonium phosphate from a fire extinguisher," Kurt said.

She turned to Joe, looking shocked. "Is that how we rescue people these days?"

"In my defense," Joe said, smiling, "I was trying not to get bitten and turned into a living zombie."

"They're hardly zombies," she said, a hint of a smile on her face. "Probably just in shock."

Joe didn't bother explaining the attack again, they'd been through that already. Besides, with Dr. Pascal standing so close and looking directly at him, he'd lost his train of thought. "I, ummm . . ." was all he managed.

She turned to her med techs. "Take these three over to recovery, wash their eyes out, and get them started on breathing treatments. We need to clear their lungs."

Her two assistants stepped forward, leading the three crewmen out of the medical bay and down the corridor, escorted by a small number of the *Edison*'s crew, who would act as security guards.

"Is that really necessary?" Dr. Pascal asked.

"You tell me," Marks demanded. "What in blue blazes is going on here?"

"I wish I knew," Dr. Pascal replied seriously. "Aside from inhaling the powder from the fire extinguisher, I can't find anything wrong with those men. It might be shock, but their blood pressures and pulses are normal."

"What about these two?" the captain asked, referencing the unconscious skipper of the freighter and the now catatonic cook. "And Kurt and Joe for that matter?"

Dr. Pascal and her team had run a dozen tests at this point. They'd taken blood and tissue samples. They'd examined the *Heron*'s unconscious captain from head to toe, while trying every method possible to get information from the conscious but unresponsive cook.

Dr. Pascal looked over the latest test results. While twirling a pencil between her fingers, she flipped the page on the chart. The captain wanted answers. She had only guesses. "I can only offer a theory," she said. "But you're not going to like it."

"Try me."

She pulled the glasses off to speak. "The *Heron*'s survivors are displaying odd neurological behavior, which might be explainable by exposure to a toxin. The fact that all of them are suffering from widespread skin irritation, with the areas normally exposed to the elements—their faces, necks, arms, and hands—affected the most, suggests an airborne agent that settled on them and was partly absorbed or repelled by their clothing. But—and I can't stress this enough—we've checked their clothes and skin for a long list of dangerous chemicals and found nothing that should harm them. Still, it could be something unknown, even a mild nerve agent."

Kurt was concerned by that theoretical diagnosis. "Is there really such a thing as a mild nerve agent?"

"Plenty of them," she said. "But no sign of any such agents in their bloodstreams or on their clothes."

"What about their eyes?" Joe asked. "They're all bloodshot and jaundiced."

Dr. Pascal nodded. "Excellent observation, Mr. Zavala." She pointed to the cook, who was lying on a gurney, staring at the ceiling. "The dark red stain is the result of ruptured capillaries in both eyes. In addition, he has significant inflammation of the mucous membranes in the nose and throat. These symptoms also imply an exposure to something airborne. Something capable of producing paranoid delusions and mania."

"The kind that would make men jump off the ship?" Joe asked, thinking about the rest of the crew.

"That could be one manifestation."

"What about us?"

"Do you have an urge to jump off the ship?"

"Not after what happened to Oscar."

"Then you're probably fine," she said.

Joe laughed at her joke and Kurt noticed a hint of a smile on the no-nonsense doctor's face.

"The bottom line," she added, "is that neither of you have detectable levels of any known toxin in your blood. Nor do you show the same signs of inflammation that the *Heron*'s crewmen presented with."

"So we can go back and search the rest of the ship," Kurt said.

"With medical supervision," Dr. Pascal insisted. The smile returned, more of a mischievous grin this time. It seemed she wanted in on the adventure.

"Absolutely not," Captain Marks said, shutting the whole venture down. "Just because you didn't get exposed to whatever toxin affected those men on your first trip doesn't mean it isn't lurking over there, just waiting to be encountered. Fact is, we don't have the proper gear to safely send you in there—with or without medical supervision."

Joe found that eminently rational.

Dr. Pascal let her disappointment show.

Kurt wasn't ready to give up. "Captain, we need to look into this. We've got a freighter getting attacked in open waters, despite the fact that it was hauling nothing but cheap bulk commodities that aren't worth pirating. We've got a captain blasting away at the attackers with a ten-gauge Browning and a crew that chose to hide out in the dark on the lower levels of a sinking ship or jump overboard rather than face whatever he was shooting at. Not to mention the mystery toxin Dr. Pascal is talking about. Something bigger is going on here, and the answers to just what that is are over on that ship. If it sinks, we'll never figure out what we're dealing with."

Dr. Pascal jumped back in, appealing to the captain's sense of chivalry. "There may be other members of the crew still hiding on the *Heron*. Whatever affected them, whatever state they're in, it would be unethical to let them drown simply because they're too scared to come topside."

Captain Marks stood with both arms folded across his chest, looking at each in turn. A glimmer in his eye suggested that he appreciated the three musketeers' routine. But he wasn't about to budge. "Joe got the pumps on?"

"Last thing we did before we left engineering."

"And, aside from the malfunctioning doors, the ship is buttoned up?"

"As much as it could be," Joe said.

"Then we've done all we can," Marks said. "Time to turn it over to the Bahamian authorities. It's their ship and their crew. They want the honor of bringing her in and we can't stand in their way."

"Captain," Joe said. "Even with the pumps on, that ship won't survive long enough to be towed into Nassau."

"She's not going to be towed," Marks said. "They're bringing out the *Hercules* to do the job right."

"The *Hercules*?" Dr. Pascal asked.

Marks nodded. "It's their new floating dry dock. Self-powered and big enough to lift an ocean liner. It'll be here in a couple of hours. If the *Heron* is still afloat then, it's theirs to take."

Kurt stood down. The salvage expert in him knew that was the right call. It was certainly less dangerous than diving into its flooded corridors in an attempt to get the malfunctioning doors closed, and, considering the toxin scare, was probably safer than trying to man it with a skeleton crew when no one knew just what had driven the original crew mad.

Even then the curious part of his mind was not happy. His desire to get at the truth was overwhelming. Sitting there, he found himself thinking of ways he might change the captain's mind.

Marks probably guessed this because he spoke before anyone else could fill the silence. He addressed Joe first. "Zavala, I understand you're rated on the MH-65 Dolphin."

"I have two hundred hours on it."

"Good to hear," Marks said. "To keep you guys out of my hair, I'm going to send you up in it. No offense to Dr. Pascal, but we're going to ship these men back to Nassau, where more extensive examinations can be performed. You'll be the one to fly them there. Kurt will go along for the ride."

Kurt began to protest. "I don't think that's—"

Marks cut him off. "You located Oscar in the water long before any of my trainees. I'm sending you as a spotter, where you can put those sharp eyes to good use looking for the missing crewmen from the *Heron*."

Kurt saw the validity in what the captain was saying, even as he recognized it as a ploy to get him off the ship so he couldn't twist any arms.

"You want us to backtrack the *Heron*'s course," Joe confirmed.

"As far as you can without running out of fuel," Marks said. "That cook may be crazy, but I'd hate to think there are sailors floating around out there and no one was even looking for them."

Game, set, and match, Kurt thought. None of them could argue with that.

5

Kurt and Joe boarded the Dolphin just before dawn, with Joe running through his preflight check while Dr. Pascal supervised the loading of two of the *Heron*'s survivors, the captain and the cook, each of them on stretchers, secured with restraints.

Kurt noted that both men were now asleep. "Did the cook lose consciousness?"

"After I sedated him," Dr. Pascal noted. "I'm not taking any chances on them waking up and going berserk while we're airborne."

"Wise," Kurt said. "What about the others?"

"A Bahamian helicopter is on its way to pick them up. These two seemed in worse shape. I want to get brain scans on them ASAP."

With the patients secured, Dr. Pascal took a seat and began strapping herself in.

Joe looked back from the cockpit, smiling at this development. "You're coming with us?"

"I go where my patients go," she said. "Besides, I need to keep an eye on you two, make sure neither of you start acting crazy or delusional."

"Good luck differentiating that from Kurt's regular behavior," Joe said, turning back to the checklist in front of him and continuing the preflight.

"Don't listen to him," Kurt said. "I'm the calm one."

Joe shook his head, laughing as Kurt strapped himself in.

With first light breaking in the east, Joe began the ignition sequence. The Dolphin was officially classified as a light helicopter. As such it had plenty of power and responded to the controls with great agility. What it didn't have was extended range. Joe had calculated a flight path, taking into account how the current would push anyone or anything that had fallen off the *Heron*. It looked like an inverted check mark on the map. A seventy-mile leg retracing the *Heron*'s path back to where she was just prior to the radio call and a ten-mile section of switchbacks, allowing them to cover as much of the high-probability areas as possible. And then a swift about-face, following a slightly different course to the southwest on a direct line toward Nassau.

Two passes over open ocean with three sets of eyes looking for any sign of the *Heron*'s crew. That was as good as they could offer.

With clearance from the flight officer on the deck ahead of them, Joe advanced the throttle to takeoff power and the decibel level inside the cabin rose exponentially.

Lifting off the deck, Joe backed away from the *Edison*, which was now sitting idle. Clearing the ship, he accelerated and climbed in a wide circle, one that gave everyone on board a great view of the *Edison* and the *Heron* resting side by side, with the *Hercules* a mile off and approaching from the south.

Even at this distance the dry dock's size was obvious. She was longer than a battleship and nearly twice as wide, capable of swallowing the largest cruise ships whole. A great, monolithic rectangle floating on the calm morning sea.

With no time for sightseeing, Joe turned to the northeast, activating an infrared search pod, which had cameras in its nose to scan for any unusual heat signatures down below.

In the back of the Dolphin, Kurt prepared a set of high-powered binoculars, cleaning the lenses and getting ready to look for the crewmen the old-fashioned way.

"Do you have another pair of those?" Dr. Pascal asked. "I'd like to help."

A second pair of binoculars were produced and as Joe brought the helicopter into the search zone, both passengers began scanning the waters below. The next thirty minutes went by in silence as everyone concentrated on the difficult task of spotting a person floating in the dark cold sea.

The outward leg ended, and Joe flew the zigzag course that covered a ten-mile square. As he finished the last leg, a tone from the navigation computer let him know it was nearly time to head for shore.

"Anyone see anything?" Joe asked.

"Nope," Kurt said.

"Nada," Dr. Pascal added.

As they tracked to the south, Joe spoke with the leader of the Bahamian search team, who was vectoring a small fleet of airplanes, helicopters, and patrol boats into the area. Joe gave them wind and wave info over the radio and detailed which areas of the sea they'd already covered.

"Thank you, NUMA," the Bahamian commander said. "What's your fuel status?"

Joe was keenly aware of their fuel consumption and remaining supply, but glanced down at the indictors anyway. "Low enough that I wouldn't want to end up in traffic. But we can manage one or two more legs."

"You'll be fighting a headwind into New Providence," the commander said. "Advise you to head in early. We'll take it from here."

Joe looked back at Kurt. "I know the brush-off when I hear it."

"No point arguing with the man," Kurt said. "Let's head on out. But swing to the south as you go."

"Are you having a premonition?"

"Nothing so brilliant," Kurt said. "But from the wave pattern I can tell there's a major eddy in the current at the southern end of the search area. It's a long shot, but if someone got caught in it, they'd have been swept in the opposite direction to what we're assuming."

Joe banked the helicopter and made a long, smooth turn to the south. For a few minutes, as they tracked back over territory they'd already searched, Kurt rested his eyes.

"I hate to be the voice of despair," Joe said, "but if the crew of that freighter abandoned ship in a delusional panic, they probably didn't stop to grab life jackets before they went."

"And even though the water temperatures are elevated," Dr. Pascal added, "hypothermia would be setting in by now. The Bahamian operation is more likely to be a recovery effort than a rescue."

"Didn't realize I was traveling with the optimists club," Kurt said.

They continued southward in silence, heading out of the search zone and into unmarked territory.

"New water beneath us," Joe said, checking their progress on the navigation screen.

"All right," Kurt said to the crewmen in the back. "Eyes up. We give this section our full attention. Anyone spots anything—and I mean anything—lunch and drinks at the Westwind Club are on me when we land."

Showing she was game for a little competition, Dr. Pascal stretched, cracked her neck to ease the tension, and looked at Kurt. "You are on."

She raised the binoculars to her eyes, leaning into the task both literally and figuratively as she bent toward the open door.

Kurt blinked a few times and then did the same, scanning ahead and to the sides. Up, back, and over. Several minutes went by in silence, but it was Joe who shouted for joy. "Target, two o'clock; range, one mile."

Kurt gazed at the area. At first he saw nothing, but the cardinal sin of aerial searching was to move your eyes too quickly. You had to give things time to appear out of the troughs and catch the sun at just the right angle. "Are you sure?"

"I have it on the FLIR pod," Joe said. "Bright and hot."

Kurt glanced into the cockpit and caught a glimpse of what Joe was looking at. There was a clear target glowing white against the dark gray background of the sea.

He retrained his binoculars, spotting something that appeared much darker in natural light than infrared. It looked more like wreckage than a human in a life jacket, but it was something. And as they approached it, the object seemed to catch the light and shimmer, as if the surface was glossy or faceted in some manner.

"I've got it," Kurt said. "Bring us down to the deck."

Joe banked the helicopter and reduced the power. The helicopter slowed and descended as it changed direction.

As they closed in on the object, it appeared spherical or domed, like a giant egg bobbing on the surface.

"It's just floating junk," Dr. Pascal said.

Kurt didn't disagree, but they'd come this far, he wanted to see it up close. "Get up next to it."

Joe brought the helicopter right down on the deck and eased toward the mystery object. The closer they got, the larger it appeared. The round shape made Joe think it was a ship's bumper or a portable fuel tank. But the iridescent shimmer suggested otherwise.

Approaching the object at an altitude of ten feet, Joe swung wide, pivoting so Kurt could see the target directly from the side door. "What have we found?"

Kurt wasn't sure. He unstrapped his seat belt and grabbed for the shepherd's crook that was kept in the back of the helicopter to help with rescues.

Before he could use it to reach out to the object, the downwash from the rotor blades pushed it away. Worse yet, the sideways blast of wind lifted it up and flipped it over. It wasn't a sphere, but a curved shell sitting on the surface like an overturned soup bowl. The trapped air had been keeping it afloat, but as soon as it tipped over, water rushed in and swamped it.

The interior of the shell was a lighter color than the exterior, and the water looked minty green as it swept in and flooded the space. That green darkened as the shell began to sink.

Kurt tossed the shepherd's crook aside, pulled off his headset, and jumped into the water. He swam toward the sinking object, hoping to grasp it and keep it from sinking with the buoyancy of the MK-1 life preserver he wore.

Back in the helicopter, Dr. Pascal was in shock. "What is he doing?"

"Kurt's stubborn," Joe said. "Craves a sense of completion."

"Are you sure?" she asked. "Because this seems like the unstable behavior I was worried about."

"I told you with Kurt it's hard to tell the difference," Joe said.

Pivoting a little farther he could see that Kurt had reached the sinking object and saved it from its journey to Davy Jones's locker. As Joe watched, Kurt held the object with one hand while raising the other arm wide of his body and tapping himself on the head. He then made a throwing motion like an NFL quarterback.

"He's okay," Joe said. "Toss him the throw bag, but hold on to the rope. It's the red bag beside the—"

"I know what a throw bag is," she said. "I've taken all the rescue swimmer courses."

Joe laughed at her feistiness, but truthfully, he was impressed. Something about her earnestness and energy was very endearing.

As Joe kept the helicopter stable, Dr. Pascal grabbed what looked like a small red duffel bag from the aft section of the helicopter. Inside, looped up in an organized fashion, was a sturdy nylon rope. She secured one end to a hook by the helicopter's door and tossed the throw bag out to Kurt.

The weight of the looped rope collected up in the bag allowed it to carry like a solid object. It arced across the water, with the nylon line spooling out the back as it went. It landed only a foot from Kurt, who grabbed it easily.

"Haul him in," Joe said.

Dr. Pascal braced her feet and pulled on the rope, arm over arm. She dragged Kurt and the object ever closer to the hovering helicopter.

As they neared the helicopter, Joe knew he'd have to go down to get them. With great caution he descended the last ten feet, hovering just above the crest of the swells.

As each wave came by, Kurt and the section of debris rose up toward the open door and then dropped back down. After several waves, the pattern became easy to predict. As the next swell lifted him up, Kurt dropped low in the water, pushing the shell up.

Water spilled out of it, and the object became appreciably lighter.

Dr. Pascal grabbed it and pulled it in, surprised by how light it felt in her hands. She set it aside and then helped Kurt climb in.

Looking back, Joe saw Kurt lying flat on the deck, soaking wet. He waited for Dr. Pascal to finish pulling in the rope and the red bag. Then he twisted the throttle and pulled back on the cyclic, climbing away from the rolling waves and turning toward Nassau, ninety miles away.

"And that, boys and girls," he announced, "is a lesson in what not to do."

By now Kurt had pulled on a headset. "Very funny."

"I thought it was," Dr. Pascal said, joining in. "When I get a chance to teach critical decision-making, I'll be sure to use this as an example.

Rule number one: never risk your life to recover worthless pieces of floating junk."

Grabbing a towel to dry his face, Kurt just grinned at the commentary. He didn't mind. If there was one thing he didn't take too seriously, it was himself.

With his face dry and the Dolphin headed toward Nassau, he turned his attention to the piece of junk they'd recovered. It was nothing more than a shell, gray on the outside, beige on the inside. It was no thicker than a deck of playing cards, with a curved shape that resembled a dome or sphere and a jagged edge that suggested this was only a fragment, broken off from some larger structure.

"Looks like the hood of an old VW," Dr. Pascal said.

"Or part of a buoy that got run over by a passing ship," Joe said.

It certainly wasn't that impressive, Kurt thought. But devoid of water it felt almost weightless. That, along with the way the exterior seemed to reflect the light, indicated it might be made of carbon fiber or some other high-tech polymer—not the type of material used on old VWs or present-day navigation buoys. More important, there were a half dozen holes scattered near the jagged break. Small circular perforations, the size and shape of double-ought buckshot. Just the type one might use in a long-barreled, ten-gauge shotgun.

6

Rudi Gunn often arrived at the NUMA headquarters building with the sunrise. As the deputy director of an agency with operations around the globe, he valued the quiet time before the office began to buzz with activity. It allowed him time to catch up on the situations developing in far-flung time zones and to prepare for the day's meetings.

On this particular morning, he'd arrived even earlier, pulling into the garage below the NUMA building while it was still dark outside. He'd been well briefed via text and email as to what was going on down in the Bahamas and wanted to be in the office before the salvage operation began.

Sitting in the NUMA communications room with a strong cup of coffee, he spoke with Captain Marks over the radio while watching the *Hercules* approach the drifting freighter on a high-definition screen at the front of the room.

The *Hercules* dwarfed the freighter, but lifting a stricken ship out of the ocean was not a risk-free operation. Blocks had to be set up on the deck of the *Hercules* to cushion and support the keel of the freighter. The arrangement varied with the size and shape of the damaged ship's hull, but also with the load.

"What's the word on the *Heron*'s stability?" Rudi asked.

"A little on the high side," Marks insisted. "According to a manifest Joe found, the holds are empty, which makes her prone to rolling. But the water in the bow will help keep her from getting sideways. We think she has two, maybe three compartments flooded."

On-screen Rudi could see the *Hercules* lined up in front of the *Heron*. The massive rectangular ship was venting air from ballast tanks on both sides of its hull, which caused the dock to sink lower in the water. The two wings remained above the surface like seawalls at high tide, while the flat central section, known as the pontoon deck, was awash in seawater and slowly dropping out of sight. It would drop thirty-six feet below the surface before the dock moved forward beneath the damaged ship and began to rise up in far slower fashion.

"What's she doing running empty?" Rudi asked.

"According to the shipping line, she was deadheading back to Nassau to pick up a shipment of salts and crushed stone."

"Doesn't sound like a ship worth attacking," Rudi noted.

"If they were attacked," Marks said. "Our doctor thinks the crew may have been affected by a toxin that produced delusions and madness."

Rudi had already seen Dr. Pascal's report. He wasn't one to rush to judgment without enough data, but something stood out to him. "The damage to her bow isn't imaginary," he pointed out. "What'd she hit?"

"No idea," Marks said. "We have no reports of any collisions, and her AIS track doesn't cross the path of another ship until you go back three days."

A mystery, Rudi thought. Exactly the kind Kurt and Joe would sink their teeth into if not ordered to do otherwise. "Where are Austin and Zavala?"

"I sent them to Nassau with Dr. Pascal and two survivors from the *Heron*. Figured that would keep them out of trouble."

Rudi smiled. Marks had been around long enough to know Kurt and Joe's reputation. "We'll see," Rudi said. "Those two find trouble the way a prize bloodhound finds a scent."

Another look at the screen showed the *Hercules* completely submerged. The two wings looked like parallel walls with a moat in between them. "Who's in charge of the salvage operation?"

"A guy named Hastings. Senior commander in the Royal Bahamas Defence Force. Apparently, he was the inspiration behind building the *Hercules*. He's very happy to demonstrate what it can do."

"Hastings is a good man," Rudi said. "We've worked with him several times. He's as competent as they come. Stand by to render any assistance that's asked for and then get back to the training mission once the *Heron* is secured. This has been a good real-life experience for your crew. Something they'll remember."

Captain Marks acknowledged that. "My thoughts exactly. Do you want me to bring Austin and Zavala back from Nassau?"

"I would say yes," Rudi said. "But something tells me they'll be otherwise engaged."

7

PROVIDENCIA ISLAND
TWO HUNDRED MILES OFF THE COAST OF PANAMA

A man with thick red hair and a scruffy beard walked across the tarmac at a sprawling airport-style complex. He passed workers in orange vests, a pair of mobile cranes, and a six-wheeled tug pulling carts from an underground storage area. The words OSTROM AIRSHIP CORPORATION were plastered all over the men and equipment.

As he continued along a pedestrian path, the bearded man heard the sound of a helicopter lumbering through the air. He looked up to see a large Sikorsky fighting the trade winds and trying to climb. It was heading north, and soon crossed a ridge dotted with palm trees that were swaying in the wind.

Built into that ridge was the man's destination: a modern five-story structure made of glass and steel; its windows tinted the same Caribbean blue as the waters surrounding the island.

Radar masts whirled atop the building, while communications antennas and a pair of satellite dishes jutted out in various directions. He focused on a raised cupola that acted as a control tower, the people inside staring through binoculars or watching radar screens, all of them eager to catch sight of an approaching colossus: a great airship, over a thousand feet in length, which was coming to land on the island.

The bearded man had never seen an airship except in photographs. Even then they seemed to be ponderous, unwieldy machines. How they were going to land such a thing on the windswept island, he couldn't fathom. Thankfully, that wasn't his concern.

———

Inside the building, standing by the floor-to-ceiling windows, Martin Colon watched the bearded man approach. The visitor's name was Lobo, which meant "wolf" in Spanish. Lobo was an old colleague of Colon's. They'd worked together in the Cuban Intelligence Directorate, where Lobo had proven himself to be an efficient operative adept at the dark arts of assassination, coercion, and anything else requiring a strong dose of violence.

Colon had been at the other end of the spectrum, a thinker who put together complex operations, manipulating any adversary and using his own limited resources in just the right places and at just the right times.

Colon's ability to pull off the impossible saw him rise quickly through the ranks. He became a full colonel at a young age and was given what the Directorate called *privilegio especial*, a demarcation that meant his actions were not to be questioned except by the highest levels of the Central Committee.

With this privilege in place, Colon built an elite organization he named Los Picadors, after the cowboys on horseback who weaken and bloody the bulls in the ring by throwing spears into their sides.

In a bullfight, the job of a picador is to set up the matador to make the kill. The Picadors of Cuban Intelligence were charged with doing the same thing to the United States. They operated ruthlessly, assassinating Cuban exiles who spoke out against the regime, assisting drug smugglers who shipped illegal narcotics into Miami, and shipping weapons and ammunition to America's enemies anywhere around the world.

On the economic front, Colon's favorite targets were American technologies, and his preferred method of attack was to abduct those who had created or perfected them. He counted these efforts as a double blow, both weakening America and strengthening Cuba.

In the end, all the effort had accomplished very little. Despite the blood drawn by the Picadors, and the technologies transferred to Cuba and its allies, the paths of the two countries never wavered. The United States grew wealthier and more powerful year after year, while Cuba sank deeper into poverty and despair.

Despite his *privilegio especial*, Colon began to face questions from the men and women of the Central Committee. The Picadors found their freedom to operate being reined in, their funding being sharply reduced. An official report by the Central Committee suggested the more aggressive actions of the Picadors were risking American military retaliation. This warning seemed like clairvoyance when the Americans raided a farm in Arcos where the Picadors were conducting what some considered horrific experiments.

By then the group had already begun to disband, with Colon ushering his men into other positions where they might be able to help him in the future. Various members entered regular military posts, while others found their way to the political arena or into ranking positions in the folds of Cuba's state-run industries. Only Lobo had chosen to remain independent, deep-sixing the government altogether and using his skills and contacts to build a criminal enterprise, stealing, smuggling, and selling goods on the black market.

Ever the true believer, Colon had remained to the last, searching desperately for a way to harm America. Eventually he'd found what he was looking for, and then he'd taken it for himself, leaving the Directorate, leaving the government, and carefully constructing a plan that even the old men in Havana couldn't disrupt.

Down below, he saw Lobo take the stairs, his hair waving in the breeze like an animal's mane. Waiting for his old comrade to arrive, Colon hoped there was more of the Red Wolf left than just his wild coiffure.

———

Lobo entered the building, crossed the lobby to the receptionist's desk, and slid his phone under a scanner—displaying a code he'd been sent. His name appeared on the computer screen, along with the false details of his business on the island.

The receptionist smiled and handed him a visitor's badge, which hung on a lengthy red lanyard. "Señor Colon is waiting for you," she said. "First elevator. Direct to the fifth floor."

Lobo took the ID card, but carried it in his hand instead of slipping it over his head. In his old life, he'd nearly been killed by a man with piano wire. Ever since, he refused to put anything around his neck.

The elevator rode smoothly and quietly, bumping to a stop when it reached the fifth floor. The doors opened into a sprawling office with all the modern touches. Recessed lighting, glass-topped desks; sleek furniture covered in white and gray leather. Shelves holding a few bronze sculptures and a smattering of modern art. All of it sterile and colorless. The only feature with any character was a map on the far wall.

The sheer size of the map was impressive enough—it had to be ten feet high and twice that in width—but it was the construction that Lobo found interesting. It displayed the continents in flaky layers of gold and silver leaf, while the oceans were formed using chips of polished blue stone. The place-names were quirky as well, written on the map in some old-world script, as if they'd been copied from a chart once used by Ferdinand Magellan or Sir Francis Drake.

Ruining the charm of the map were a set of thin lines projected onto it from somewhere in the ceiling. The lines ran from cities all over the world to the small island, as if Providencia were ancient Rome and the rest of the earth its sprawling empire. Blinking dots on eight of the lines showed the location of Ostrom's airships, either on their way to the island or slowly tracking away from it.

Lobo turned his attention from the map to the man sitting behind a glass-topped desk in a handcrafted suit. "It's good to see you, Martin. You've done well for yourself. Who'd have thought the zealot of the Picadors would take to capitalism so easily."

Lobo was needling his old friend just to get a response. In truth, Colon was something of an enigma. There were rumors suggesting he'd left Cuba with millions in government money, and counter rumors insisting he still worked for the Directorate. No one knew the truth. Most likely Colon wanted it that way.

"The office is Stefano Solari's doing," Colon said, referencing the flamboyant majority owner and CEO of the airship company. "The suit is merely camouflage. I have to look like I belong in the club when I spend time with him."

"Sounds rough," Lobo said, trying not to laugh. "How ever do you manage?"

Colon shrugged. "And you? I understand you're a smuggler these days. Trafficking in stolen goods."

"Stolen is a such a harsh term," Lobo said. "Liberated is more accurate."

A grin cracked Colon's inscrutable face. "Well, much of what you've liberated has originated here, in my freight rooms."

Lobo wasn't sure what to make of this. No one who worked the black market ever really knew where their goods came from. The smart ones didn't ask. "This is news to me."

"Relax," Colon continued. "You're not stealing it. I've been making sure you get your cut of an operation I run. Piracy can be very lucrative. Especially if you do it the right way. And as you know, I like to see my old friends doing well."

Interesting, Lobo thought. Perhaps Colon wasn't the warrior monk everyone believed him to be. "Assuming that's true, you have my appreciation," he said. "But you didn't fly me out here just to tell me that. You must want something?"

"I want the Red Wolf back," Colon said, referring to Lobo's old moniker. "I need him to make a problem disappear."

Making problems vanish had once been Lobo's specialty. But that was in a former life. Back when there was a struggle to believe in. "I don't do that kind of work anymore."

"For me you will."

"What makes you so sure?"

"Because if you don't, the flow of merchandise will dry up, the authorities in Havana will raid your warehouse, and your boats and trucks will be impounded until you prove you haven't been carrying on illegal activities, which of course you can't possibly do."

Lobo felt a surge of energy in his core, the instant power from the fight-or-flight reflex—which in him leaned heavily toward fight. He held it back. "I don't know what you're after, but I have my own protection."

Colon nodded. "I know who protects you. He does it because I asked him to. How is our old friend Lorca these days? Enjoying the position I found for him?"

Lorca was another colleague of theirs from the Picadors. A little older and less ambitious. After leaving the Directorate, he'd found a cushy job in the Cuban Port Authority, a post that allowed him to make life easier for Lobo. *But if Colon was really the one who'd gotten Lorca the position . . .*

Lobo remained icily calm. "I can't say I'm interested in helping when you come at me like this, but go ahead, spell it out for me. If the job is reasonable, maybe I can find you someone to do it."

"There's a ship on the way to Nassau," Colon said. "A freighter named the *Heron*. I want to see it on the bottom of the ocean."

"So, sink it. You hardly need a specialist for that."

"We tried to," Colon explained. "But the captain got off a distress call and some Americans from an agency known as NUMA interfered. They boarded the ship, got the pumps working, and managed to keep the vessel from sinking long enough for the Bahamians to come along and secure it with a floating dry dock."

Lobo found himself wondering—with a sense of curiosity he truly wished he didn't possess—just what Colon had got himself into. "What's so important about this freighter that you need it to go down?"

Colon leaned back. "Let's just say there are materials on that ship that I don't want the Americans getting a good look at."

"Cargo?"

"Materials," Colon repeated.

That could be anything, Lobo thought. He knew better than to ask for more. "When does this ship reach port?"

"Tomorrow morning."

Lobo grit his teeth in frustration. "That's not a lot of time, Martin."

"Which is why I need you," Colon said.

Lobo sat back, trying to see through Colon's veiled words and guess at the reality behind the situation. It proved impossible, as it always had with Colon. The man was always three steps ahead of everyone. In matching wits with him, opponents often made what they thought to be masterstrokes, only to find out they'd been baited into it, doing exactly what Colon wanted them to do.

With no way to see through the smoke screen, Lobo had just one question: Why him? "I'm told you've hired a couple dozen men from our old units," he said. "And I know there are former soldiers working for you back in Cuba, living better on the money you provide than on anything they ever earned from the state. Why not use one of these groups?"

"Because our countrymen who work for me here are mechanics,

freight loaders, and security guards," Colon replied without missing a beat. "And the men in Cuba are in Cuba, not Nassau. You have contacts in Nassau. You can travel there freely without raising suspicion. And you're more qualified to get a job like this done."

Lobo moved some of the hijacked goods through the Bahamian port city. It was a bustling hub that Europeans and Americans could access far more easily than Havana. It made the margins on the smuggling operation much better.

"I don't use guns anymore," Lobo insisted. He'd shot too many people in his life at close range. He didn't need any more nightmares.

"Then find someone who does."

A sense of the inevitable settled in. Lobo knew he wasn't leaving this room without agreeing to take up Colon's assignment. "I may have a few contacts in Nassau," he admitted. "The kind of people who could be financially persuaded to take such a risk. But they're going to want a good price."

"Let them name their own," Colon said. "People usually undersell themselves, and once they do, they're committed. As for you, I'll make this worth your while in more ways than one."

"The only way that matters to me now is cash," Lobo replied.

Colon shook his head, as if he knew the Red Wolf better than himself. "Ever since the Picadors disbanded you've been alone. You of all people should know the lone wolf eventually gets slaughtered. You need brothers to protect you. You need a purpose to keep you going, or the women and the drink will consume you. I'll give you family and a purpose, and more wealth than you can ever spend. But you're going to have to earn it."

The Red Wolf sighed. He didn't want any part of what Colon was selling, but he found himself already on the hook. Colon had been taking care of him, ensuring his success and protecting him through Lorca. A debt had been built up. One that had to be paid.

"Just send me the details in an encrypted link," Lobo replied. "But I'm telling you now, if this dry dock is guarded by a hundred Bahamian marines, you're on your own."

"It won't be," Colon assured him. "And when you're done, we'll talk about the larger plan."

Lobo grimaced at the words. The mere mention of a larger plan meant Colon expected him for the duration of whatever complicated game he was running. Considering the opening move, Lobo knew it wouldn't be limited to piracy or destroying whatever "materials" had been left behind on the damaged freighter.

8

PARADISE ISLAND, THE BAHAMAS

The terrace at the Westwind Club boasted five-star dining, expensive cocktails, and a wave-shaped bar that faced the emerald waters off the coast of Paradise Island. At lunchtime on a sunny day the place was bustling with activity as tourists in beach attire mingled with waitstaff in Bermuda shorts and bright red polo shirts.

Leaving the tabletops for the regular guests, Kurt and Joe found a spot at the end of the bar, which allowed them to speak without having to turn their heads ninety degrees in the process.

As they were still officially on duty, Kurt would have to wait to fulfill his promise of ice-cold beer, but that wasn't stopping Joe from perusing the menu for every expensive item he could find. He'd already finished a conch salad and a plate of fried calamari, when he chose both the porcini-crusted salmon and lobster tails in black truffle sauce for his entrées.

"Where on earth do you put it all?" Kurt asked.

"I'm like a camel," Joe said, "but instead of water I store up good food. You should join me. It's back to powdered eggs and mystery stew once we reboard the ship."

"We're not reboarding the ship, if I have my way," Kurt said. "In fact, I've booked us rooms here."

Between bites, Joe nodded approvingly. "I take back all the bad things I've ever said about you. I assume you made sure I have a nice view."

"Of the dumpsters," Kurt joked, as if the five-star resort would even have such a room.

"I reinstate my previous complaints," Joe grumbled. "But out of curiosity, why exactly are we sticking around?"

"I want to see a friend about that piece of drifting plastic we found."

"You mean the floating barbecue cover?"

Kurt had to laugh. Every time the item came up in conversation Joe compared it to a different piece of worthless junk. The list had grown so long that Kurt had begun to admire Joe's creativity.

"I also want to be here when the *Hercules* brings that freighter into port," Kurt said. "One way or another I'm getting a second look at that ship."

Kurt glanced across the dining room. At the host station, near the front of the open-air restaurant, a pair of high-ranking Bahamian officials had appeared. They wore white uniforms with gold braids on the shoulders. Behind them stood an older man with a mustache. He wore tortoiseshell-framed glasses and civilian clothes. Next to him stood Dr. Pascal in her NUMA fatigues.

Joe followed his gaze. "I guess having the head honchos over for lunch and twisting their arms is one way to go about it. Do I even want to know what you're planning if that fails?"

"Probably not," Kurt said with a grin. "But if you see that waitress, order more lobster. It couldn't hurt."

Standing tall as the group came over to their section of the bar, Kurt offered a hand to the ranking member of the group.

"Good afternoon, Mr. Austin," the lead official said in a warm Caribbean tone. "I'm Senior Commander Hastings of the Royal Bahamas Defence Force. This is my aide, Lieutenant Phillips, and a representative from the Health and Wellness Ministry, Dr. Alfred Pinder. And of course, your own Dr. Pascal from the *Edison*."

Hands were shaken and a private table was procured, away from the rest of the clientele. As the Bahamian delegation took their seats, Kurt got right to business. "Thanks for meeting with us," he said. "I trust the *Hercules* secured the freighter without too much trouble."

Hastings beamed with pride. "Of course she did. The freighter is less than half the *Herc*'s maximum capacity."

"It looked truly impressive from the air," Joe added. "I wouldn't mind seeing it close up."

"Thank you, Mr. Zavala," Hastings said. "And let me extend the thanks of my government to both of you for your quick response to the *Heron*'s distress call and risking your lives in an attempt to help one of our ships."

"We did what any crew would do under the circumstances," Joe replied.

Hastings smiled at the humility. "While I suspect you did a bit more—and with greater alacrity—I'll accept your statement so we can get down to brass tacks, as they say."

Kurt agreed and then asked the first pertinent question. "When will the *Hercules* reach Nassau?"

"It won't," Hastings said. "We've ordered it to anchor offshore until we finish the investigation."

Kurt offered a suspicious look and Hastings deferred to the head of the island's health ministry. "Why don't I let the doctor explain."

Dr. Pinder cleared his throat and adjusted his glasses. "There has been some discussion," he said, "some loose talk really, about the symptoms experienced by the surviving crew members."

"Rumors," Kurt said.

"Yes," Dr. Pinder agreed, "rumors, stories . . . fables . . ." Finally, he hit on the word he was looking for. "Wild speculation," he finished emphatically, "as to what happened on that ship."

Kurt understood immediately. The Bahamian government wanted to keep a lid on the incident. "You're worried about the lights in the sky."

"The lights in the sky are nonsense," Dr. Pinder replied dismissively. "Too fantastical to believe. What we're concerned about are the things people have a right to fear. As you may know our group of islands suffered terrible economic consequences from the loss of tourism during the COVID pandemic. In truth we are still trying to recover. Until we know for sure what happened aboard the *Heron* we must maintain confidentiality. If rumors of a toxin or some type of sickness aboard that ship were to begin circulating . . . Well, let's just say, millions of dollars in business could be lost before we had a chance to disprove the speculation."

"I understand completely," Kurt said. "But the best way to make sure falsehoods don't spread is to get the truth out first."

Dr. Pinder nodded his agreement. "Which is why we're sending a team aboard the ship to conduct a thorough scientific investigation."

"A brilliant idea," Kurt said. "We'd like to be part of the investigation."

Dr. Pascal jumped in at this point. "Which is exactly what I proposed back at the hospital. It's eminently reasonable. And since Kurt and Joe were already aboard, they're familiar with the state of the ship. In addition, if there is a toxin or pathogen lurking there, they may already have been exposed, which makes them somewhat expendable."

Joe's eyebrows went up. "Expendable?"

"Bad choice of words," she said. "What I mean is, there's no sense risking additional personnel when we have two men that might already have come in contact with whatever created the state of confusion among the crew."

Dr. Pinder sighed and pulled off his glasses. "No one will be at risk," he said, turning slowly to the NUMA physician. "All the investigators will be wearing full hazmat gear. There is no need or reason for your people to be aboard."

"Turf war," Joe whispered to Kurt.

Kurt nodded. Instead of arguing with Dr. Pinder, he turned to Commander Hastings. No doubt the man with all the gold braid on his jacket had the final say.

"I defer to the commander," he said. "If you prefer it, Dr. Pascal, Joe and I can stay here and keep out of the way."

Dr. Pascal kicked Kurt under the table, a direct hit on his shin that took Kurt by surprise. He resisted the urge to react or rub his shin or even turn her way. After a slight wince, he kept speaking. "To be honest, we wouldn't mind a little rest and relaxation, along with a chance to enjoy a few sunsets and well-earned rounds of rum punch."

A wry grin appeared on the old commander's face. It told Kurt he saw the ploy a mile away. If he wanted Kurt and his team to keep the story under wraps—and he did—it was better to have them occupied and close by than enjoying an evening on their own with enough rum flowing to loosen anyone's lips. But just because he saw the ploy didn't mean it was ineffective.

Hastings turned to Dr. Pinder, overriding the health expert. "I think it best if we work together on this. NUMA has always proven to be a good partner. No reason they shouldn't be helpful in this case."

"But, Commander—"

"No," Hastings said, placing a hand firmly on the table. "I've considered the matter and rendered my decision. Arrange to take Mr. Austin, Dr. Pascal, and Mr. Zavala with you. The *Hercules* is on its way. It should be at anchor and ready to board in a couple of hours."

That gave them plenty of time to get in a quick nap, freshen up, and go see Kurt's friend in Nassau. "In that case," Kurt said, "why don't you join us for lunch?"

"A fantastic idea," Hastings said. "I insist on picking up the tab."

Kurt grinned at Joe, who spoke his thoughts aloud. "I hear the black truffle lobster is spectacular."

9

Every course of the meal was fantastic. And when it was over, Kurt needed the nap he'd been thinking about. Twenty minutes of blissful sleep followed by a hot shower had him feeling like a new man.

Returning to the lobby he met up with Joe and Dr. Pascal, who had decided to tag along with her NUMA colleagues rather than go with Dr. Pinder.

"We seem to have picked up a shadow," Kurt noted.

"I'm not complaining," Joe said.

"I can see that," Kurt replied. They made their way to the valet, where Kurt retrieved the car they'd picked up after their arrival.

With Joe in the passenger seat, Dr. Pascal had the back all to herself. She moved to the middle and leaned forward until she was all but situated between the two front seats. "Care to tell me where we're going?"

Kurt looked in the mirror. "If you'll share the reason you've latched on to us like a remora."

"The remora," she said, unperturbed. "A marvel of nature. I don't mind being compared to it. But for the record, I'm here for the same reason I volunteered to be the ship's doctor on the *Edison*. I like to go where the action is. This is a medical mystery. One that's likely to lead in directions no one can fathom at the moment."

Kurt accepted that and turned his attention back to the road.

"Besides," Dr. Pascal continued, "if I hadn't primed Hastings and Pinder with the idea that you two might be given to spreading rumors and loose talk, we'd all be sitting on the beach, depressed and bored out of our minds right now."

"I could find something to entertain me," Joe suggested.

"Not anything as exciting as this."

"Eh," he said, wavering. "You might be overestimating the fun quotient of where Kurt is taking us."

Of that Kurt had no doubt. "Did you get a chance to run more tests on the men from the *Heron*?"

"We did," she replied. "Unfortunately, we didn't learn much. The truth is, there's nothing physically wrong with those men."

"There has to be something wrong with them," Kurt said. "One man is in a coma and the others can't speak."

"Refuses to speak," she corrected. "The cook's vocal cords and lungs are healthy. When he's asked a question, we detect body movements and ocular reactions, but before he speaks, something in his brain shuts it down. We ran a CT scan to confirm it."

"What about fear?" Joe asked. "He was pretty terrified when we found him in the storeroom."

"Not a bad guess," she said. "But fear and anxiety light up specific parts of the brain on the scan. Primarily the amygdala and the hippo-campus. In the cook, these areas were completely subdued. The only part of his brain that showed an elevated response was the prefrontal cortex. Think of that like the final decision-maker in the brain. Other parts of the brain make suggestions, the prefrontal cortex makes the final decision. It's not an exact metaphor, but in the cook's case, the parts of his brain that wanted to respond to our questions were activating, only to be overridden by the prefrontal cortex, which shut down any form of response."

"What about the captain?"

"He remains in a deep subconscious state," she replied. "I would call it a coma, but he seems to be persistently dreaming."

"I could think of worse states to be in," Kurt said.

"Depends on what you're dreaming about," Joe said.

"Lights in the sky maybe."

"That wouldn't be my first choice."

Kurt figured Joe's first choice might involve Dr. Pascal, the beach, and a few glasses of rum punch. He glanced back at her again. "Why would the captain be affected differently than the cook?"

"That's part of the mystery," she said. "Normally two people exposed to the same toxin exhibit similar if not identical symptoms. But the captain's brain scan is much more active than the cook's and yet he's the one who's unconscious. The only real difference between the two of them is that the captain has a biomarker in his blood known as troponin."

"What does that mean?" Joe asked.

"It suggests that he suffered a heart attack."

"A heart attack?" Joe said. "But he survived."

"Not all heart attacks are fatal," she explained. "And in the captain's case, he had an ally to help him. He has a pacemaker in his chest, one that's equipped with an internal cardiac defibrillator. As near as I can tell it did its job, detecting the event and shocking him back to sinus rhythm."

"Would the heart attack put him in a coma?" Kurt asked.

"It's possible," she said, "but unlikely. It's almost as if whatever they were exposed to affected one man's brain and the other man's heart. Why, I couldn't tell you."

Kurt appreciated the information and Dr. Pascal's attempt to simplify it for them. He understood why she was so intrigued and grudgingly admitted to himself that she'd be good to have along.

"Okay, I've spilled my story," she said. "Now it's your turn. Where are we going?"

This time Kurt beat Joe to the punch. "To see a man," he said, "about a hibachi."

10

Kurt drove the length of Paradise Island and then up and over the Sidney Poitier Bridge, which took them across the channel and down into the heart of Nassau proper. Continuing past the tourist-filled areas and the well-maintained marinas filled with day charter fishing boats and cabin cruisers, they arrived at the more industrial section of Nassau's waterfront.

Here, they found supply outfits, a smattering of repair shops, and plentiful storage facilities, where small boats were pulled from the water on boat lifts. After passing a huge anchor that had been taken off a large ocean liner, they arrived at a warehouse-style building, painted black with bold red stripes. A temporary banner hung above the doors. It read: PERFORMANCE SAILING.

Pulling around back, they found a fabrication shop, where carbon fiber sailboat hulls were being put together and sealed with clear gel-coats that allowed the pattern of the material to be seen.

Kurt parked and stepped out of the car. One of the employees saw him and whistled to the boss, a stocky man in blue coveralls, who came out of the shadows, wiping his hands on a shop rag.

"Rolle," Kurt said, taking off his sunglasses.

The man offered Kurt a broad grin. "Austin," he said with a strong Bahamian accent. "It's good to see you, brother. Though I'm surprised they let you back on the island after all the chaos you caused the last time you were here."

After a fist bump and a bear hug, Kurt pointed to his partners. "I brought a pair of chaperones to keep me out of trouble. Rolle, meet Joe Zavala and Dr. Elena Pascal."

"Zavala," Rolle said, shaking Joe's hand. "I know you. You're the one who gets Kurt out of trouble and fixes all the stuff he breaks."

Joe laughed. "I do my best. I'll tell you this much, it's a position with plenty of job security."

Rolle chuckled and turned toward Elena. "Very nice to meet you."

"And you," Elena said.

"What can I help you with this time?" Rolle asked Kurt. "Or can I interest NUMA in a new sailboat, or three?"

"We prefer motors," Kurt said.

"And yet, I still like you."

Kurt laughed and opened the trunk of the rental car. "We all have our flaws," he said. "In your case, it's being a know-it-all. A trait I would like to take advantage of for a bit." He pulled the shell from the trunk. He'd had to jam it in there to make it fit, but in addition to being light in weight it was flexible and strong. "What do you make of this?"

Rolle rubbed his brow as he studied the half-dome shape. "Hmm," he said, touching the exterior of the shell. "It has an odd feel to it." He rapped on it with his fingers and then examined the jagged, broken edge. "Interesting. Let's look at it inside."

They left the sunny parking lot and stepped into the shaded section of Rolle's workshop. In one corner, a pair of men were splicing a mast together for a high-performance racing yacht. In another section of the workshop, several others were setting up a mold to create a one-piece hull for a thirty-foot powerboat.

"The future of boating," Rolle said. "Everything will be lighter, more fuel efficient, and stronger, to boot."

"Carbon fiber," Joe said, studying the work around them.

"Yes," Rolle said. "Five times stronger than steel. Twice the strength of high-grade titanium. Which means we can use far less of it. For instance—that hull over there, if it was made of steel, it would weigh eighteen hundred pounds, nearly a ton. Our hull weighs only three hundred and fifty. It makes the boat faster, more maneuverable, and allows a smaller motor that uses less fuel." He turned toward the area where the men were fabricating the high-tech mast. "Or if you prefer to be a true sailor, less wind."

By now they'd reached an empty worktable. Kurt placed the item in question on it. "I thought you might find this interesting."

"Where did it come from?" Rolle asked.

"Middle of the ocean," Kurt said.

Rolle was already looking the item over. He lifted it, tested the weight in his hands, and then flipped it upside down. The exterior had a depth to it, but looked matte black in the shade of the workshop. He shined a penlight at it, and a sheen of muted colors appeared. Running his fingers across the material, he could feel the texture.

His fingers reached the perforations. Little splinters broke off at the touch. "What happened here?"

"Not sure," Kurt said. "But my instincts tell me it got hit with a shotgun blast."

Rolle leaned closer. "Let's break a piece off and look at it more closely."

With Kurt's permission, Rolle used a crimping tool to cut a section from the edge. He studied it under a jeweler's loupe and then placed it in the mouth of a machine that closed with a solid click.

"Carbon fiber?" Kurt asked.

"I don't think so," Rolle said.

"But it's so light."

"That's the problem," Rolle told him. "It's not heavy enough. That shell weighs no more than eighteen ounces. If I made it here, it would be four or five pounds. And trust me, I cast some of the lightest carbon fiber around. This is something else. I'm not sure what, but don't worry, the machine will tell us."

"While the machine is thinking," Joe asked, "what do you make of the inner layer of material?"

A quick look at the edge of the shell revealed the construction of it to be in two layers. A thin outer layer that acted as a dark covering for the half-inch-thick inner layer, which was sandy beige, like a warm beach.

The jeweler's loupe came out again and Rolle looked at the edge. "Not sure. Insulation maybe."

The testing machine pinged, and Rolle tapped the computer hooked up to it to see what had been learned. A graph appeared revealing the chemical makeup of the dark outer layer. Several small spikes suggested impurities probably picked up from the water, but the primary result was a single element.

"Here's your answer," Rolle said. "All carbon. No fiber whatsoever."

Kurt cast a sideways glance at his friend.

"The outer shell is made out of graphene," Rolle explained. "Basically, pure layers of carbon molecules. It's thinner, lighter, and stronger than even my best carbon fiber mesh." Rolle wiped his brow. "This is pricey stuff."

"Guess it's not a hibachi, or the hood of an old VW," Joe said.

Rolle shook his head.

"Could this be part of a navigation buoy?" Dr. Pascal asked.

"Possibly," Rolle said. "But why build a buoy that you'd have to price like a Ferrari? Makes more sense to form them out of steel and cheap, heavy plastic."

"Who is using graphene these days?" Kurt asked.

"Formula One race teams," Rolle said. "Microelectronics companies use small amounts. But something this size . . . The only guys going to pay for large sheets like this are the aircraft builders. They have good reason to use it. Weight is their enemy even more than it's ours."

Kurt thought that sounded about right. "Aircraft builders, huh? What about drones?"

"Oh yes," Rolle told them. "Perfect for long-range drones. There are some prototypes flying already."

"Could this be part of one?" Kurt asked.

"It could be anything," Rolle said. "But it's not exactly aerodynamic. And I don't see the type of structural supports you'd expect."

That was a setback to Kurt's theory, but he wasn't ready to capitulate. "If it was a drone," he said, "or part of one, and it had powerful lights mounted on all sides, what would that look like from down below?"

"If they were bright enough," Rolle said, "you might not even see the body of the drone. Just the illumination."

"A glowing light in the sky?" Joe asked for confirmation.

Rolle nodded. "Yeah, man, but you'd need a lot of lights. And a lot of juice to amp them up to that level of brightness. And I don't see any sign of wiring or anywhere to mount even a single floodlight."

Dr. Pascal leaned over to Kurt. "You think the lights in the sky were real?" she whispered.

"The captain was shooting at something," he insisted.

"Lights in the sky," Rolle said, looking at Kurt suspiciously. "Shooting. What's all this?"

"Rumors and loose talk," Kurt told him. Before he could say much more, his phone began chirping an alarm from his pocket. Kurt pulled it out and checked the screen. They needed to head for the dock if they were going to get out and meet the *Hercules*.

"We have to go," Kurt said. "Okay if we leave that with you?"

"Cool by me," Rolle said. "I'll tinker around a bit and see what else I can figure out."

"Much appreciated," Kurt said. He shook Rolle's hand and clapped him on the shoulder. "And be sure to keep it under your hat."

"Yeah, I figured as soon as you showed it to me," Rolle said. "Don't worry. The boys and I have your back."

Kurt offered his thanks again and the three of them returned to the rental car. The dock was a twenty-minute drive. From there it was two miles out to where the *Hercules* would anchor. With a little luck they'd know a lot more within the hour.

11

On the western side of the island, Kurt, Joe, and Dr. Pascal stepped aboard a forty-foot runabout with Hastings, Dr. Pinder, and his team from the Bahamian health ministry. After a round of introductions, the group of seven left the harbor, heading west toward the floating dry dock anchored two miles away.

Approaching the *Hercules* in the small boat was an odd experience, more like approaching a walled city or a fortress than a floating vessel. The massive size of the dry dock was one thing, but it also had none of the regular visual clues one associated with a ship. Instead of a gracefully curving bow and a rounded stern or a tapering profile that grew wider from the water up to the main deck, the *Hercules* appeared as a massive rectangular block with a few small cranes perched on top.

It reminded Kurt of the brutalist architecture of concrete government buildings. And he wasn't the only one thinking that.

"Looks like a skyscraper laid down on its side," Dr. Pascal said.

"You're not too far off," Hastings said. "The *Hercules* is twelve hundred and sixty feet long and nearly three hundred feet wide. You could fit your Empire State Building in its confines. Except for the antenna."

While the *Hercules* appeared like a monolith when viewed from the side, it looked different when approached from the front or back. From those angles, the vessel took on the shape of a squared off *U*, with two vertical slab sides sometimes called wings, but which the builders of the *Hercules* had decided to label the port and starboard walls. In between these walls—making up the bottom of the *U*—was the pontoon deck, the wide flat surface upon which ships rested when lifted out of the water. Ballast tanks in both walls and the pontoon deck allowed the entire structure to submerge, move beneath a floating ship such as the *Heron*, and then slowly rise back up again, lifting the ship free of the water.

The runabout approached the *Hercules* from the port side, easing along the wall, which towered a hundred feet above them—high enough to block the afternoon sun and make the cranes mounted on top look small.

Continuing toward the bow they passed the front end and emerged from the shade into daylight. From here they could see the *Heron*, sitting up on blocks and held in place as if it were a model or a child's toy.

"This is one impressive vessel," Joe said.

The runabout motored to the edge of the pontoon deck, which rose several feet above the water and descended another twenty-six feet below it.

They idled alongside the edge of the platform, where a pair of orange-vested dockworkers waited for their arrival. As the runabout eased up against a pair of rubber bumpers, one of the crewmen hopped aboard. He looped a rope around the bow and stern cleats, pulled it taut, and tied it off. The runabout was now secured to the dry dock.

"Please be careful and watch your step," the crewman said, putting a block in place to help them step up onto the platform.

The team from the health ministry went first, followed by Dr. Pinder. Hastings and the NUMA crew followed.

With the full group gathered on the pontoon deck, Hastings took the lead, showing off his magnificent creation as they walked toward the captured freighter. While he pointed out this and that to the group, Kurt found his attention riveted to the *Heron*.

The ship was sitting in the center of the dock, bow facing them, and its sides equidistant between the two wings. Its keel rested not on the pontoon deck itself but on a row of thick timber blocks that helped support and distribute its weight. Up above, a lattice of cables had been strung from the walls of the dock to the top side of the ship for added stability.

Having grown up in a family that ran a salvage business, and then done a stint in the Navy, Kurt had spent time on plenty of dry docks, but he'd never lost the sense of awe that came with seeing a huge ship up and out of the water.

Looking at a great ship from the pier or from another boat was impressive enough. But standing below one, looking up at it from underneath, added a whole different dimension. It added another twenty to thirty feet of red-painted hull that usually hid out under the waterline. It revealed the oversized machinery that guided, propelled, and stabilized the great ships, but was never seen from the surface. Gazing at a rudder that was taller than a three-story house, or a propeller that boasted fifteen-foot blades and weighed thirty tons, had a way of making a person feel small and insignificant. As if the ship were a living thing, a giant of the seas, and the humans walking around on it were merely free riders, tolerated or ignored like tiny birds on the back of a fully grown elephant.

Even the *Heron*, a regional freighter, was impressive now that it sat high and dry on the blocks.

As they drew closer, the damage to the front of the vessel became painfully clear. The bulbous bow, which stuck out under the water to break the waves, was a mess of bent and mangled steel. Farther up and back, hull plates were dented and crushed inward. Several were missing. Despite its time on the blocks, seawater continued to drain from the fissures and plugs that the dry dock's crew had removed from the underside of the ship.

"High-speed collision," Kurt said, basing his supposition on the crushed nose and the long stretch of creases, abrasions, and other deformations that continued down the starboard side.

"She hit something smaller," Joe added, pointing out that the damage stopped halfway up the angled bow. "Ran it over pretty good."

Dr. Pascal nodded, appearing impressed with the deduction.

Dr. Pinder was not as moved. "We're more interested in what's on the inside."

They continued down the flank of the ship, navigating between the gray wall of the dock on their right and the barnacle-encrusted hull of the freighter on their left. Reaching an area roughly amidships, they came to a scaffold, which had been set up in the gap between the freighter and the port wall of the *Hercules*.

The scaffold held an open-walled elevator inside, like those in a mine or an old building. The elevator ran upward to a metal bridge that spanned the gap between the main deck of the *Heron* and an open hatch on the sidewall of the dry dock, beyond which lay the dock's control room.

Hastings assured everyone that both the elevator and the temporary scaffolding that had been erected to hold it was safe. He waved the group in and stepped in behind them, sliding the gate shut and grasping a controller that activated the elevator car.

The car began to climb with an uneven jerk, but continued smoothly after that to the top. It bumped to a stop at the bridge level, and Hastings slid the gate back.

"I'll be in the control room with the dry dock's manager," Hastings told them. "We'll keep an eye on you from there."

They went their separate ways, Hastings to the right, crossing the bridge and stepping into the control room through an open hatch, Pinder and his team to the left, walking along the metal bridge toward the *Heron*.

Dr. Pascal paused at the threshold, unnerved by the narrow metal walkway and the seventy-foot drop on either side.

"Just don't look down," Joe said.

"Too late for that."

She gripped the railing and forced herself to go forward, taking cautious steps until she was able to firmly set foot on the *Heron*'s main deck.

Kurt brought up the rear, following along until they reached a white tent that had been erected outside the accommodations block. Here they were issued hazmat suits with respirators, and an emergency air supply should they end up needing complete isolation from the shipboard air. Radios were passed out, though there weren't enough for everyone, so Kurt and one of the technicians went without.

With the gear double-checked, Pinder radioed Hastings. "We're suited up and ready. Clear us through."

Hastings was standing in the control room, looking through a picture window that sloped downward to allow a better view of the activity on the pontoon deck. To his left, the dock's manager sat in front of a console with a built-in computer keyboard and other controls. A pair of flat-screen monitors on top displayed the status of the dry dock's systems, including its ballast tanks. A series of icons showed all valves and vents closed, the pumps on standby, and the tanks ninety percent empty, which had the dock and its cargo sitting high in the water.

"We're riding a little high," Hastings noted.

"As the water drains from the *Heron* we're losing weight," the dock manager told him. "Four thousand tons so far. We'll rebalance once the investigation is done. But I wouldn't want to do it while people are on the platform."

Hastings nodded and reached for a table-mounted microphone. Bending it to his mouth he spoke to Dr. Pinder. "You're cleared to enter. Your radios are on an open channel."

Back out on the deck of the *Heron*, the investigation team entered the ship at the base of the accommodations block. They soon arrived at the main stairwell. Pinder stopped there and turned to Kurt and Joe. "I understand you men explored the accommodations block."

"That's right," Kurt said. "From the bridge down to one level above where we are now."

Pinder turned to his team members. "Go retrace their path. I need samples of the food in the galley, the water, and the other consumables. Also take swabs of the fabrics in the officers' quarters and collect regular air samples."

With these orders acknowledged, half the team moved off, leaving Kurt and Joe with the two doctors. "Since you're here," Pinder continued, "perhaps you could lead us to the areas of the ship that you hadn't examined."

"And then stay out of the way," Joe quipped.

Dr. Pinder smiled. "That would be perfect."

Pinder seemed to be enjoying this. Kurt didn't really blame him. The man had been forced to take on a trio of meddling outsiders, he might as well give them a hard time in return.

"Walk this way," Kurt said.

He led them to the next compartment and then through the crew's rec room. A locker room came next and then one of the ship's offices. At each stop, Dr. Pinder and Dr. Pascal took samples and placed them in marked containers.

Heading down a level, they arrived in engineering. Here, they found another body. This man was caught between a set of pipes and a metal bulkhead. He clutched a screwdriver in his hand.

"Did he get trapped while working on something?" Dr. Pascal asked.

It was impossible to tell for sure, but the screwdriver was held like a dagger and not a tool.

"I don't think so," Joe said. "I may be basing this on how the cook acted, but it looks more like he was hiding or preparing to fight something off."

Dr. Pinder reached down and pulled the man free. Once he'd been laid down on the deck, the testing began anew. Blood samples, skin samples, swaths run over his clothes looking for known chemicals. Much like with the cook, the only outward sign of injury were the red eyes and dried blood in his nose.

"We should swab his nasal passages," Dr. Pascal suggested.

Dr. Pinder concurred and they took more samples.

Tired of watching the man being picked over, Kurt did what he'd been ordered to do, he stayed out of the way by stepping aside and taking in the rest of engineering.

They were now one level below the main deck, just above the engine room itself. It was the type of space that was usually sweltering when the engines were running. Even now it was something of a hot box. Especially in the hazmat gear.

Thinking about the efforts that would be made to cool it, Kurt recalled the strange odor coming from the ventilation system and quickly found the open vents in the room.

"Someone should really check the air-handler and environmental units," he said. "If you wanted to gas people in a ship, that's the way to do it."

Joe moved to a panel where the environmental controls were set. "Based on what I'm seeing, exterior vents are open. They were sucking air in from the outside. Makes it unlikely they were gassed."

Made sense that the vents were open, it was a cool Caribbean night when the distress call had come in. Kurt ran his gloved fingers across one vent. A thin layer of gray dust appeared on the white plastic covering his fingertips. It reminded Kurt of creosote. Rubbing it between his fingers, it smeared.

"Please don't touch anything," Dr. Pascal said, stepping forward and wiping Kurt's fingers with a testing cloth. "Anything in here could be a toxic agent."

"That's why we're wearing these suits," Kurt said.

"Which can be easily punctured."

Kurt held his hands up as if to surrender, allowed Dr. Pascal to wipe them once more, and then stepped out of the way as she rejoined Pinder to continue their forensic investigation.

Properly chastised, Kurt stood still until Joe whistled for his attention. "Look at this."

Joe was standing in front of a whiteboard. A set of numbers and calculations had been scribbled on it, partially erased and then rewritten again. An accompanying diagram formed what looked like a triangle. A badly drawn object at one end resembled a boat.

"What are we looking at?" Kurt asked.

"These are bridle force calculations," Joe said. "You run them to determine the strain on a towing cable."

"Are you sure?"

"As sure as sugar." He pointed to another set of numbers. "See this set? It's a calculation of propeller race. When you tow a ship, your wake creates drag on the vessel behind you. Increasing your speed only serves to increase the drag and raises the strain on the cable exponentially. It's the reason barges are more often pushed than pulled."

"What does all this tell you?" Kurt asked.

"The *Heron* was towing something," Joe said. "And someone, maybe that poor man over there, was trying to figure out how much additional speed they could put on without snapping the line."

It was a good deduction, Kurt thought. But there was just one problem. "The *Heron* wasn't towing anything when we reached her. And we have no idea when these calculations were written down."

"I think we do," Joe said. He pointed to the red marker that had been used on the whiteboard and then over to the dead engineer. Red marks could be seen on the tips of his fingers and the butt of his palm.

"Looks like he held the marker pretty close to the end and used his palm to erase the first set of numbers instead of bothering to get a cloth."

"Sherlock Holmes has nothing on you," Kurt said proudly.

"This ship has two large winches near the stern," Joe mentioned. "I say we go check them out. If the load was too great, we'll find evidence of strain in the cable or the bridle."

Kurt nodded and got the attention of the doctors. When he spoke, it was in a quiet, apologetic tone. "As it turns out," he told them, "Joe and I feel like we're just getting in the way down here after all. So . . . if it's all the same with you, we're going to go back up on deck and wait for you there."

Dr. Pinder looked pleased, as if he'd won some prize. Dr. Pascal did not. She glared at Kurt suspiciously. When Kurt offered nothing through the clear plastic face mask of his suit, she focused her ire on Joe. "Why the change of mind?"

"It's awfully hot in these things," Joe ad-libbed. "And Kurt gets claustrophobic. We stay down here much longer and you're going to see a grown man cry."

The answers only made her more suspicious, but she played along. "I was a little worried about that," she said, before adding in a mocking tone, "Be brave, Kurt. I'll see you topside when we're done."

The two groups went in opposite directions, with the doctors descending another level to the engine room, while Kurt and Joe went up the main stairs toward the deck.

"She's onto us," Joe said.

"She'd have to have lost a hundred IQ points not to be," Kurt replied. "Claustrophobic?"

"It was all I could think of," Joe said. "Mostly because these suits are making me feel that way."

"That's okay," Kurt said. "She kept her thoughts to herself, which means either she likes you or she's going to use this against us later."

Joe hoped it was the first thing, but feared it was probably the second.

Reaching the main deck, they moved through the hatch and out underneath the tent. "Now, let's get these suits off and get ourselves to the stern."

12

As Kurt and Joe headed toward the stern of the freighter, a small boat with three occupants approached the *Hercules* from the shaded side.

The close approach wasn't reported because the man whose job it was to keep watch—a Bahamian named Grit—was already down on the lowest deck, opening a watertight hatch in the port wall.

As the hatch swung open, Grit looked over the new arrivals. A thin man with a red beard and thick ginger hair who was dressed in beige slacks and a black cashmere sweater, another man with stringy hair tied back in a ponytail wearing similarly bland clothing, and a third man sporting a pink sunburn, bright swim trunks, and a colorful short-sleeved shirt like every other tourist wandering the streets of Nassau.

Grit had been told by a mutual friend that the first man was a reporter from America who would pay a large sum for access to the dock and video of the damaged freighter. It sounded a little odd from the get-go, but Grit's friend had been given two thousand dollars just to arrange the meeting. With half the dry dock's crew put ashore amid swirling rumors of a toxin aboard the freighter, Grit was unhappy to have drawn a short straw in the process. He agreed to let the reporter come aboard for three thousand in cash.

Now that they were actually there, sitting in front of him, his nerves all but took over. "Come on," Grit said, urging the people in the small boat to climb aboard. "Be quick. I'm not interested in anyone seeing you."

With the boat held fast, the two men in slacks came aboard, while the sunburned fellow took the boat out away from the *Herc*.

"Which one of you is Lobo?" Grit asked.

The man in the cashmere sweater answered.

Grit focused on him. "Let me see the money."

An envelope stuffed with American dollars was produced. Three thousand had been promised. Grit looked through the stack quickly, fanning the bills and spotting twenties, fifties, and a few hundreds. He didn't bother to count it.

He tucked it away and closed the hatch. "Don't touch anything," he said. "Clear?"

They nodded.

"I can only show you the freighter from the lower deck. Anything higher and you risk being seen."

They nodded again and Grit turned down the hallway. "Follow me."

He'd gone a few steps, when the soft pop of a small-caliber weapon equipped with a suppressor went off behind him. Two bullets hit him in the back, and he dropped to the floor with both lungs punctured.

Hitting the floor, he found himself unable to scream for help, cry out in pain, or even ask why they'd shot him. He gasped for air like a fish out of water. He rolled onto his side to see the man with the ponytail standing with a small pistol in his hand. Lobo, the supposed reporter, stood next to him, eyeing Grit coldly and waiting for him to die.

After several long painful seconds, Lobo stepped forward, producing an expandable baton from a cargo pocket in his slacks. He flipped it open, but rather than striking Grit in the face, he used it to lift the flap on Grit's vest, exposing the envelope full of cash. His long-haired partner reached in and removed the cash-filled envelope.

From his position directly above Grit, Lobo stared coldly downward. In his opinion the man wasn't dying quite fast enough. He raised the baton and snapped it with lethal velocity, finishing Grit with a strike to the head.

With Grit dead, Lobo gave new orders. "Stash him out of the way and meet me at the main stairs. Let's make this quick."

13

Up in the control room, Senior Commander Hastings and the dock manager sat idle in front of the control panels while listening to the reports from Pinder and his crew.

As the discoveries inside were reported, the dock manager grew more nervous. "I'm not sure I like using the *Hercules* to quarantine a contaminated ship."

"It was the only option to keep that vessel afloat," Hastings said.

"Maybe we should have let it go down."

"Don't worry," Hastings replied firmly. "Dr. Pinder assures me there's no danger. Do you think he'd be inside the ship if there was?"

"I suppose not."

"This won't take long," Hastings added. "Once he's cleared the ship, we can bring a full work crew on, repair it, and put it back in the water."

"Sounds good," the dock manager said. He got up, stretched, and opened the door at the far end of the control room. He stood in shock at the sight of a man in a black sweater. He was still gawking when the man jammed a baton into his gut, doubling him over. He never saw the next blow, which struck him in the back of the head and laid him out cold.

Hastings spun in his chair at the sound, noticing the dock manager on the floor and a thin athletic-looking man standing over him. He didn't have time to protest the man's entrance or demand an explanation as the intruder lunged his way in, swinging the baton.

Ducking to avoid the worst of the blow, Hastings took a hit across the back of the shoulders. It sent him crashing into the bulkhead, but he quickly pushed himself off the wall, spun, and threw a punch.

The red-haired man sidestepped it with ease and struck Hastings in the back of the leg, dropping him to the ground.

Hastings looked up from the deck. The intruder eyed him without emotion, but never uttered a word; no threats, no warnings, no demands. There was no hint of emotion on his face, not even satisfaction that he was obviously winning the fight. Just detached malice. A predator waiting to make the next strike.

Hastings knew this was no random event. It had to be related to the freighter.

He lunged for the console, grabbing the microphone and squeezing the transmit switch, hoping to warn the others. He began to shout, but the nightstick came down on his arm, knocking it away from the microphone and breaking his wrist.

With a surge of adrenaline and pain, Hastings launched into offensive action, lunging and throwing all his weight into an overhand left that struck his attacker in the jaw. The punch was a quick and accurate counterstrike, it snapped the man's head to the side, but otherwise did not faze him.

He swung the baton once more, catching Hastings on the thigh.

The commander dropped to the ground, both legs and one arm injured. The smallest hint of satisfaction appeared on the attacker's face.

Realizing he had no chance against the intruder, Hastings lunged for the panel that would allow him to sound general quarters, an alarm that would alert everyone on board to the fact that they were in danger, even if they wouldn't know the nature of the threat.

The baton caught him across the face before he could press the alarm. He fell unconscious with a diagonal welt emerging as he rolled onto the deck.

Lobo stood over his defeated opponents like a gladiator in the Colosseum. He was mildly surprised when the door at the far end of the control room opened.

The commotion had drawn the attention of a crewman in the next compartment. The man looked in, started to ask a question, and then, assessing the situation correctly, turned to run.

"We have a runner," Lobo said calmly.

The long-haired man stepped up and snapped off a shot. It punched a hole in the man's torso, in the dead center of his back. The man dropped to his knees, glanced down at the pool of blood rapidly spreading through his shirt, and then fell face-first to the deck.

Lobo stood calmly. They'd killed eight men on their way to the control room, but there were others throughout the massive vessel. "Watch the door," he told the gunman. "I need to find the ballast controls."

14

On the main deck of the *Heron*, mercifully free of the stifling hazmat suits, Kurt and Joe had passed the accommodations block and arrived at the stern of the freighter.

Here they found a pair of large winches, one on each side of the centerline. Studying the first one, they focused on the cable, which had been wound tightly around the drum. The braided metal cable was a heavy line, two inches thick, and weighed seven pounds per foot.

"Heavy rope," Joe said, lifting the strand and sliding his hands along it until he found the end. Instead of a hook, buckle, or Flemish eye, which was a loop made from the strands of the metal rope, all they found was a loose end, complete with fraying and blackened strands of metal. "It's been cut."

Kurt could see that. The end was charred and some of the frayed bits showed signs of melting. "Hot cut," Kurt said. "Someone hit it with a blowtorch."

"That's one way to cast off whatever you're towing," Joe said. "Not the most reasonable or cost-effective method. More like something you'd do in an emergency."

Kurt nodded. "What's a dry bulk freighter doing towing something in the first place?"

"Good question," Joe said. "But the fact that whatever it was had to be cut loose so hastily makes me think the crew didn't want to be found with it."

"Or whoever attacked them took it away," Kurt countered.

"Also a possibility," Joe said.

Plenty of possibilities, Kurt thought, *no hard answers*. "We better let Hastings know about this. It'll keep us on his good side."

Joe plucked the radio off his belt and called the control room, but didn't get an answer. When a second call to Hastings was met with dead air, Joe reached out to see if anyone else was listening.

"Dr. Pascal, are you and Dr. Pinder reading me okay?"

"Barely," she told him, *"but we're down in the engine room. Not a lot of signals reaching us down here. Is something wrong?"*

Joe wasn't sure. Maybe the Bahamian commander was away from the desk. "No," he said. "Just some dead air. Thanks."

As Joe lowered the radio, he heard the sound of large metal valves springing open. A turbulent rush of air followed.

Both Kurt and Joe turned at the sound, quickly spotting a spray of mist above the starboard wall where the ballast tanks were venting trapped air.

"Must be adjusting our buoyancy," Joe said.

Kurt didn't like it. "Odd thing to do with the medical team still on the freighter," he said. He turned to the port wall and saw no sign of air escaping. "Odder still to do it one side at a time."

Without another word they both began to move forward, heading for the amidships bridge as they'd planned, but doing so with a quickened pace. After so many years on ships, Kurt could feel the slightest change in the deck's orientation in his feet and had a sense that the dock was beginning to list.

A quick look past the stern of the ship confirmed it for him. What should have been a perfectly flat horizon was slowly tilting to one side. The dry dock was taking on a list to starboard.

15

Kurt was jogging toward the midships station with Joe following along and continuing his attempts to raise the control room on the radio.

"Any response?" Kurt asked.

Joe shook his head. "Maybe they're trying to rebalance the dock because of all the water draining from the *Heron*?"

Kurt normally deferred to Joe on engineering matters but, having grown up around the salvage business, he knew enough about floating dry docks to know the current situation ran counter to every safety protocol in existence.

"They shouldn't have to rebalance the dock with the freighter at the center of the platform," he said. "Maybe bow to stern, but not side to side. They could easily destabilize the ship. Sitting up on the blocks like that, the *Heron*'s center of gravity is a good twenty feet higher than it is when it's out on the water."

Joe understood instantly. "If she topples over like a giant bowling pin, she'll tear into the starboard wall. The whole dock might come apart."

Various dry dock catastrophes flashed through Kurt's mind: a major incident in San Diego, where the gate failed; a Norwegian dock that rolled because of ice building up on the windward side; a Russian disaster in Murmansk, where the dry dock's pumps failed for unknown reasons. In that one, the dock sank in a matter of minutes and dumped fifty-three men into the icy waters. If they didn't stop the unbalancing, the *Hercules* disaster would top all of them.

As they reached the midships station, the *Heron* shifted on the blocks. It was the first move, and a subtle one, but it brought creaks from the timber and the hull and ominous groans from the mooring lines up above.

With no time to lose, Kurt rushed onto the cross bridge, which rattled beneath his feet. He'd only gone a few steps when the door to the control room swung open and a man with long hair appeared in the gap.

"Get down," Joe shouted.

Kurt saw the gun and processed the shouted warning at the same time. He dove face-first, hitting the metal deck of the bridge just as the gunman opened fire. Bullets whistled overhead, peppering the bulkhead of the *Heron*.

Looking up, Kurt saw the shooter lowering the weapon toward him. With nowhere else to go, he rolled to the side of the bridge and off the edge, grabbing one of the supports in the scaffolding's framework as he fell. With his hands locked tight, he swung his feet forward, ending up under the bridge as plinking sounds rang out and small holes appeared in the thin metal above him. Finding a spot to place his feet, he set himself in a more stable position.

Either the shooter assumed he'd fallen to his death or realized he was unlikely to hit Kurt firing blindly through the bridge deck, because the next battery of shots went high across the gap, aimed at Joe.

———

From his position on the freighter, Joe saw Kurt go off the edge and swing to temporary safety underneath the bridge. But the gunman was now focused on him, forcing Joe to scramble for cover without congratulating Kurt on his acrobatic move.

Tucked in behind a solid section of the ship's rail, Joe kept his head down as bullets ricocheted around him.

Risking a look, he popped up and dropped back down, having lingered just long enough to draw another round of gunfire from whoever had taken over the control room.

Safe behind the rail, he shouted to Kurt, "Are you okay?"

"Hanging in there," Kurt replied. "How about you?"

"Working on my tan," Joe said. "I guess we know why Hastings and the dock manager haven't replied."

"Unfortunately," Kurt said. "The bad news is, we need to get in that control room if we're going to stop the flooding."

"I knew you were going to say that," Joe replied. "What do you want me to do?"

"Find items you can throw and start peppering that doorway with them," Kurt told him.

"That's a very complex plan you've come up with," Joe said.

"And try not to get shot in the process."

Joe didn't have to ask Kurt what he was going to do, the quick peek over the ship's rail had revealed Kurt moving through the scaffolding like a kid on the monkey bars. He was making progress and out of sight. But when he reached the wall, he'd need to pop up and surprise the man with the gun. Which meant Joe needed to keep the shooter occupied and distracted.

Looking around for anything to use as a weapon, Joe spied a bundle of poles like those that had been used to build the scaffolding.

He pulled the bundle toward him, loosened a Velcro strap that bound them together, and slid one pole free.

It was eight feet long, iron, and probably about twenty pounds. Not bad, as makeshift weapons went. After testing the balance in his hand, Joe hefted the pole up onto his shoulder. Taking a deep breath, he stood and lunged for the door, releasing the missile as his weight went forward.

It traveled at a pretty good clip courtesy of Joe's strength. Unfortunately, it twisted as it flew, turning sideways in midair and clanging loudly against the bulkhead as it struck flat and broad.

The sound startled the shooter, and he backed out of sight for a moment. He emerged moments later, firing a new barrage.

Joe took cover once more. Loud pings and tiny dents appearing in the rail told him the gunman had found the mark, but the shells couldn't penetrate the quarter inch of steel. The shooter's suppressor was working against him now, reducing the muzzle velocity of his small-caliber weapon. That was some relief, Joe thought, but he still needed to keep the man from shooting at Kurt.

"Come on, Zavala," he said, wrenching a second pole free. "You played baseball and football for a decade. You can throw a better spiral than that."

While Joe's first thought was that he needed to make a better throw, his second thought, born from the engineer side of his brain, was that he needed a better projectile. Lifting a second pipe and twirling the length of iron in his hand, Joe found no significant difference in the weight on one side or the other. "What we really need are tail feathers."

Grabbing the Velcro strap, Joe measured out the length and then wrapped it around the tail end of the pipe. He left an eighteen-inch length of the strap dangling free, hoping the extra weight and drag would keep the lance pointed in the right direction.

To follow Kurt's second directive—the one against getting himself shot—Joe slid along behind the rail, remaining out of sight until he found a new position.

He popped up and stepped forward once more, this time running several steps before hurling the iron pole with true Olympian form.

Thanks to the weight and drag of the strap, this spear flew straight. It arced high, twirling like a spiral, and sailed into the control room through the open door. It nailed the long-haired man in the center of his chest, knocking him onto his backside and causing him to discharge a shot into the ceiling.

Down beneath the bridge, Kurt had crossed the gap using his hands and feet on the scaffolding. He'd arrived at the dry dock's port wall shortly after Joe's first spear clanged off the hull and plunged below.

Hanging on to the rungs, Kurt made the mistake of watching the pipe fall. The seventy-foot drop was far enough that it seemed to drop in slow motion. Right up until it hit the pontoon deck in jarring fashion and pogo-sticked up and to the side. The bounce was short lived, as the pipe fell back and began rolling to the low side of the deck.

Uninterested in following a similar path, Kurt set his boot on a foothold and waited, launching himself upward as Joe's second attack found its mark.

It was a move that rock climbers call a dyno and it propelled Kurt up high enough to grab the rail and swing his feet over the top.

He landed on the bridge directly in front of the open hatch, just as the gunman got to his own feet. Aggression was his friend at this point and Kurt rushed ahead, throwing a shoulder into the man before he could bring his weapon to bear.

Another errant shot discharged, this one into the deck underneath their feet. Before the gunman could fire a second time, Kurt knocked the man's hand to the side, slamming it against the bulkhead.

The man's fingers spread open with the impact. The pistol came out of his grasp and tumbled over the side, following the trajectory of Joe's pipe.

Kurt ignored it and threw a punch into the man's gut. He followed this with a headbutt to the face. The furious assault sent the man staggering backward, his nose broken and bleeding, his wind knocked out of him. Kurt went to press the attack, but his advantage vanished in a series of wild events.

Behind him, the *Heron* shifted once more, this time rolling a good ten feet. A hideous wrenching sound echoed through the port alley down below as the timber blocks were forced out of position and the freighter's steel hull dug into the metal decking beneath it.

The sudden and substantial movement was enough to destabilize the scaffolding and the bridge that sat upon it. Loose pipes fell as the whole structure swayed to one side. Rather than ride it down to the pontoon deck, Kurt launched himself forward, pushing off the bridge as it gave way.

He safety-rolled into the control room, popped up onto his feet, and found himself standing directly between the gunman with the broken nose and a smaller, narrow-framed man with an expandable truncheon in his hand.

Kurt's eyes shifted, going from one man to the other as he wondered who would attack first.

The thin man seemed amused by Kurt's arrival. He twirled the truncheon back and forth, as if deciding what to do. The mild look vanished suddenly, and he lunged for Kurt, swinging the baton at his head.

In the tight quarters of the control room, Kurt had no option but to step back, nearly tripping over the inert form of Commander Hastings in the process.

The move was just enough to avoid being clubbed, but as the baton hit the bulkhead instead of his temple, Kurt backed right into the man with the long hair and the broken nose.

Wiry but muscular arms wrapped around him, pinning Kurt's hands at his sides. The man leaned back, heaving Kurt up off the deck and carrying him toward the open door and the seventy-foot drop outside.

As they neared the hatch, Kurt threw his legs up, planted a foot on either side of the opening, and pushed hard.

Both he and his captor flew backward, slamming into the opposite wall. The strength of the grip loosened. Kurt dropped out of the man's grasp and threw an elbow into a vulnerable thigh, driving the hard bony point deep into the muscle.

The long-haired man howled in pain and fell to the deck, but the man with the club came at him, swinging the baton like it was a rapier.

Kurt dodged multiple slashes, moving back and to the side, but was rapidly running out of space in the narrow compartment.

Jumping back once more, he spotted Commander Hastings on the floor, bleeding and inert. A few feet from him lay a weapon Kurt could use. He dove to the floor, sliding under the control panel, and grabbing the length of pipe Joe had launched through the door.

The compartment was too narrow for Kurt to swing it, but he jabbed at the thin man, keeping him at bay and forcing him back.

Both men had weapons now, but the advantage in reach was Kurt's. He jabbed repeatedly, then flicked the end of the pipe upward, catching the man under the chin, snapping his head back and drawing plenty of blood.

The man pulled out of range, touching his chin and bringing his hand away soaked with blood. He seemed emotionless about the strike. His eyes focused dispassionately on Kurt.

Instead of attacking, he stepped back, moving to the far end of the compartment with his partner, who was now limping and bleeding. With the baton pointed at Kurt, the two of them backed to the door.

"Well done," he said, offering an odd compliment to Kurt. "I look forward to the next round. Assuming you survive, that is."

On that note, they backed out, slamming the door behind them. Kurt didn't bother to chase, he had far more pressing concerns.

He stepped toward the console, looking for the ballast controls so he could close the vents and turn on the pumps. He found only more bad news. The computer keyboard was smashed into useless bits of plastic. The flat-screen monitors had been battered and bludgeoned just as effectively and now displayed only colorful, tie-dyed patterns.

The truth was both simple and devastating: with the system in this condition, there was no way for Kurt to stop the flooding.

16

Joe had been thrown to the deck when the *Heron* shifted suddenly. Looking up, the first thing he noticed was that the port wall of the dry dock seemed lower and farther away and that the overhead stabilization cables were stretched to the max and singing with the tension. A glance toward the horizon told him the dry dock was now listing at nearly ten degrees.

This isn't going to end well, he thought.

Getting to his feet, he found the cross bridge was gone. He looked over the rail and down into the alley between the ship and the wall. The pipes that made up the scaffolding lay scattered on the pontoon deck like a heap of Pixy Stix. The elevator car was crushed and folded up on itself. It was impossible to be sure, but he didn't see Kurt lying among the wreckage.

That was better than the alternative, but it meant Kurt was over in the control room, fighting the big man—and any allies he might have brought—all by himself.

Joe stared across at the open hatchway. There was a sixty-foot gap between the edge of the *Heron* and the control room door. It might as well have been a mile; there was no way for Joe to cross it and help his friend.

As the seconds ticked by, and Kurt failed to reappear, Joe began to fear the worst. "Come on, buddy. Where are you?"

———

Kurt was in the control room, staring at the shattered console. With the monitors smashed he couldn't tell what the intruders had done. Worse yet, there was no way to fix it with the computers also destroyed.

There had to be manual overrides, but the *Hercules* was larger than an aircraft carrier. Kurt didn't have time to run around on a scavenger hunt looking for them.

He left the panel and dropped down beside Hastings, attempting to wake him. The dock was the commander's baby, he would know every inch of it.

Rolling Hastings over, Kurt saw a nasty welt on his face, similar to the one now rising on his own arm.

"Commander," Kurt said, shaking him gently. "Time to wake up."

Hastings began to stir, but his eyes remained closed.

Kurt grabbed a water bottle from a cup holder beside them. "Hate to do this, but . . ." He splashed some water on Hastings's face.

The senior commander shook a bit and opened his eyes. Recognition came slowly. "Austin . . ." he said before looking around at the ravaged control room. "How did you get here? What happened to the other guys?"

"They ran off," Kurt said. "But they've done their damage. The vents are open on the starboard side, but not over here. We're shipping water and starting to list. Can't get the valves closed or the pumps on because they smashed the control panel. Where can I find the manual overrides?"

As he grasped the situation, Hastings sat up with a jerk. "The *Heron*?"

"Holding on, but not for long. We need to right the ship before it topples."

"Yes, yes of course," Hastings said. "The manual controls are two decks below us. Compartment E-5. I'll show you."

He tried to stand but felt instantly dizzy, and Kurt had to help him into a chair.

"I'll go faster on my own," Kurt insisted.

Hastings nodded reluctantly. "You'd better."

With the commander situated, Kurt grabbed a handheld walkie-talkie and made his way aft. He radioed Joe as he went for the stairs. "Joe, this is Kurt. You out there?"

Joe came back almost immediately "About time you called. What happened in there?"

"Big fight," Kurt said.

"How'd you do?"

"It was a split decision," Kurt said. "But I've been promised a re-match at some point in the future. In the meantime, we have big problems. I can't stop the flooding from the control room. I'm heading for the pump room. But in case I can't get it done in time, you'd better get everyone off that ship."

"Great idea," Joe said. "How exactly am I supposed to do it? The elevator and the scaffolding are gone. There's no gangway or ramp."

"I don't know," Kurt said, "but you better think of something, or you'll all be going for the worst ride of your lives."

———

Thankful that Kurt was alive and kicking, Joe now focused on a survival dilemma of his own. The *Hercules* was continuing its slow roll, with the starboard side dropping and the *Heron* leaning and growing more unstable by the moment.

Staying on board the ship was out of the question. If the ship broke loose and fell into the starboard wall of the dry dock, it would be like remaining in a building that was falling during an earthquake. Either the fall would kill them, or the sudden stop at the end, or the debris landing on top of them—not to mention the flooding that would come afterward as the sea rushed onto the dock and into the capsized vessel.

Joe looked around. Ships were a lot of things. One thing they were not was easy to get off of in the absence of shore-based facilities. Without the bridge or the elevator, there was no way down to the pontoon deck or across to the relative safety of the control room and the port wall. Had they been at sea they could have jumped into the ocean and swam for safety. But in the current predicament that was just a multistory swan dive with a hard stop when they hit the metal deck.

He considered getting closer to the pontoon deck. It was conceivable they could head to the lowest deck of the freighter, throw open a hatch, and toss out a cargo net or a rope to shimmy down on, but that felt like running *into* a burning building rather than away from it. And that brought another problem into play: with the loss of ballast air, the *Hercules* was slowly sinking, but only on one side. Fifteen feet of seawater had already surged onto the pontoon deck, pooling on the lower, starboard side. If the *Hercules* suddenly righted itself, or if the *Heron* tumbled, the abrupt change would send a tidal wave surging toward the port side of the deck, and anyone caught in it would be thrown against the port wall and unlikely to survive.

Joe discarded that option. All of which left him grasping at straws, until an idea hit him that was so brilliant that he almost patted himself on the back. "Zavala," he told himself. "You are beyond genius."

With the alarms continuing and general quarters sounding over the dock's PA system, Joe brought the radio up close to his mouth. "Dr. Pascal, how do you read?"

After waiting for a response and getting none, he tried again.

"Elena, this is Joe. If you can hear this, get yourself and your team topside as soon as humanly possible. We need to get off this ship."

A static-filled reply came back. "We're already on our way," Elena told him. "What was all that shaking about? What on earth is going on up there?"

"Long story," Joe said. "It'll make more sense when you get back out on deck. Meet me near the stern, behind the accommodations block. We've got to get off this ship."

"What about the elevator and the bridge?"

"Gone and gone," Joe said. "We're improvising."

———

Down in the depths of the freighter, Dr. Pascal couldn't see Dr. Pinder's face through the hazmat suit, but she could tell he was struggling as they climbed the stairs.

Pain, exhaustion, and fear had combined to make the trip up from the engine room a figurative crawl. Every time a cable groaned, or the ship lurched, the doctor grabbed the rail and clutched it, not moving.

"I haven't spent much time on ships," he said, looking her way. "Never liked them much. This isn't going to change that."

She laughed and helped him up the next flight. They continued retracing their steps until they reconnected with the rest of the team and made their way out onto the deck.

Exiting out through the shredded tent into the chaos of multiple alarms made everyone even more uncomfortable. They unzipped their suits and lowered the hoods to take in the state of the ship.

"Oh my God," someone cried out.

"What's happening?"

"We're sinking," a third person insisted.

As this conversation gained steam and threatened to induce panic, Dr. Pascal moved to put a stop to it. "We're listing, not sinking," she told them. "But we are getting off the ship."

She led them toward the stern, peeling off her hazmat suit as she went. The sustained tilt made walking surprisingly difficult, while the continuous shudders and groans put everyone's nerves on edge. She only hoped getting off the ship would be a fast process.

Reaching the stern, she found Joe standing on the lower side of the ship. He was gazing at the churning water down below. It was flooding in from both sides and crashing together in the middle, a churning caldron of green water and white foam.

"We're not going down there, are we?"

"We are," Joe said. "In that."

He pointed up to where an orange lifeboat hung over the edge, pivoted outward on the arms of its davit.

"Everybody inside," he insisted. "As quick as you can."

She wasn't sure if it was madness or brilliance, but as another of the overhead cables snapped and the ship rocked another six feet, she realized there wasn't time to argue.

"Let's go," she shouted, leading the team members up onto the ladder and into the dangling lifeboat.

Joe urged them on, grinning madly and ushering them up the steps like a carnival barker trying to get the afternoon crowd into the big tent.

Some of them went willingly; others got nervous. Dr. Pinder froze looking into the gap down below.

The *Heron* was leaning closer to the wall, casting a shadow and creating an uncomfortable fun house effect that made it feel as if the wall were leaning toward them. "Couldn't we use the boat on the other side?"

Joe answered firmly but calmly. "The angle is too steep," he said. "We'd hit the side of the ship and tumble the rest of the way. Besides, there's no water on that side yet, so if you'll just move along . . ."

Pinder took another step, but froze again. "But we'll be crushed if the ship rolls."

"Which is why you need to hurry, Doctor."

Pinder moved ahead without further protest. Joe followed behind, climbing inside the lifeboat, strapping himself into the command seat, and reaching for a yellow T-shaped controller that operated the winch. He pressed the down button, but nothing happened.

"Tell me this thing doesn't need batteries," Joe muttered, shaking it.

Dr. Pascal leaned forward. "Down in the generator room I noticed the ship's main circuit breakers were tripped. I'm guessing the winch has no power."

Joe took a deep breath. "In that case, you'd better sit down."

"Everyone strap in," Dr. Pascal called out. She knew what was coming.

Joe disconnected the winch brake and pulled the gravity release bar.

The lifeboat dropped straight down, moving smoothly at first, but rapidly picking up speed as the cables unspooled. It hit the water, displaced most of it, and banged awkwardly against the decking beneath.

The seawater hit the wall and swept back in, slapping the lifeboat's hull and drawing a few shrieks from the startled passengers.

Joe was grinning from ear to ear. *What a rush*, he thought.

He started the engine and throttled forward, feeling extremely pleased with himself right up until a horrendous wrenching noise drowned out all other sounds and the *Heron* began toppling toward them.

He gunned the engine, which wasn't exactly saying much in a lifeboat, but they were only a hundred feet from safety.

Looking up, Joe saw the accommodations block plummeting their way. Then he saw the evening sky and the wispy clouds. They passed the stern end as the bulk of the ship hit the dry dock's starboard wall and gouged its way down.

The two structures ripped into each other, slowing the fall just enough for the lifeboat to escape into daylight before the stern crashed down behind them.

The *Heron* ended up on its side. Its fall forced the water from the starboard alley, sending out a ten-foot wave that hammered the fleeing lifeboat and shoved it off the edge of the pontoon deck into the sea.

Elation swept over the group, but as Joe turned the boat around, he wondered if that was going to be short-lived.

The massive freighter was lying on its side. The starboard wall of the dock was a shambles and the weight was now so unevenly distributed that the port wall—with the control room, the dry dock's crew, and Kurt inside—was rising off the bay.

Joe doubted the dry dock would capsize. More likely, it would bend in the middle and break. And then everyone would go down with the individual pieces.

Kurt was working on the pumps in compartment E-5 when the deck buckled beneath him and tossed him into the bulkhead wall. From the sound and the fury, he knew instantly that the *Heron* had finally broken loose.

Picking himself up, he pushed off a bulkhead that was leaning far more severely than it had been a moment before. He looked out the viewport and saw only the keel of the freighter. Down below it, he could see the deck plates bending and warping with the strain.

He'd found and already closed the starboard vents and turned on the pumps to force the water out, but that was not going to save the *Hercules* now. He had only one option.

He had to sink it.

Moving to another part of the compartment, he found the controls for the port wing. He threw open every vent and turned on all the pumps, setting them to cross-feed.

With the air escaping out the top of the tanks—and the water flooding in from the bottom—there was a chance he could make the dock settle, rather than rip itself in half.

The gauges on the panel told him it was working. Nine thousand gallons per second were flowing into the port side tanks. He could hear it. He could feel it beneath his feet. It was working.

Water flooded across from the pontoon deck, and the port side began to settle. But this was only half the battle. With the damage caused by the freighter's fall, the *Hercules* would flood once the water got too high.

He picked up the radio and called Joe. "Tell me you guys are not out on the pontoon deck."

"Safely away in a bright orange lifeboat," Joe replied. "All medical personnel accounted for. From the look of things, you might need me to come and pick you up."

"Circle around and look for swimmers," Kurt said. "I wouldn't be surprised if half the crew went overboard."

"Are you not joining them?"

"No," Kurt said, "we're about to create an artificial reef and the newest Bahamian diving attraction."

With Joe looking for any members of the crew who had gone overboard, Kurt found the intercom and buzzed the control room.

Hastings came on the line. "You did it."

"I did something," Kurt said. "We'll know if it's good or bad in a minute. Do we have power to the engines?"

"We do," Hastings said grimly. "Why?"

"We're sinking. Nurse us onto a sandbar and you can save the dry dock. And by save, I mean you can claim victory to the newspapers, as a man who wouldn't abandon his ship or let it go down."

Kurt heard the engines power up and felt the dock begin inching along. When Hastings came back on the line, he was decidedly more chipper. "I doubt this is going to work, but if it does? My best bottle of rum is yours for the taking."

"It'll work," Kurt said. They were only two miles offshore, in decidedly shallow waters. There had to be a sandbar around there somewhere.

17

Rudi Gunn stood in the foyer of the Mandarin Oriental Hotel watching through the doors as a torrential downpour soaked the city of Washington.

The gathering at the five-star hotel had been a political get-together involving a handful of U.S. senators, a dozen members of the executive branch, and a gaggle of foreign dignitaries, all of them discussing ways to protect the seas.

Rudi had spent the night glad-handing and engaging in small talk, while checking his phone for updates on the situation in the Bahamas and occasionally slipping away to glance at the televised news reports showing the dry dock, half submerged and stuck on a sandbar.

He knew that Kurt, Joe, and Elena were safe, and that the Bahamian government was appreciative of their help saving the dry dock and the crew, but these things had a way of turning. A disaster like this had to be blamed on someone.

Only when he saw a press conference by the senior commander of the Bahamas Defense Force indicating that terrorists had been responsible did Rudi begin to relax. No mention was made of NUMA. Not a word. A fact to which Rudi raised his glass.

With the get-together winding down and the situation in the Bahamas stable, Rudi decided to call it a night. Retrieving his overcoat from the coat-check room and pulling it on, Rudi stepped to the door. The rain was falling with a vengeance now, scouring the streets, flooding the gutters, rushing down the storm drains in narrow rivers.

As Rudi weighed how long he might want to wait it out, a figure came up beside him. "If it keeps raining like this, one of us will be asked to call in a boat."

Rudi turned to see Rear Admiral Marcus Wagner, recently promoted and put in charge of Naval Intelligence. "As long as we don't have to man the oars or run up the sails."

The two men shook hands.

"What brings you down here?" Rudi asked.

"I stopped by to check out the gathering."

Rudi raised an eyebrow. "This doesn't quite sound like the Navy's kind of party."

Wagner offered a look that said he was hurt. "We care about the seas," he insisted with great indignation. "Without the oceans, we're just . . . the Army."

Rudi laughed. Nothing like a good old interservice rivalry.

"Which way are you heading?" Wagner asked.

"Back to the office," Rudi said, pulling his collar tight. "I have some work to do now that the glad-handing is over."

"I have a car coming," Wagner said. "Why don't you ride with me?"

There was a tone in Wagner's voice that said he needed a chance to speak with Rudi alone and off the record. This was the kind of thing that happened at Washington get-togethers. It was half the reason Rudi didn't like going to them.

With a sigh, Rudi stepped forward, grabbed his umbrella, and pushed open the inner door. "You do what you want," Rudi said. "I'm walking."

Wagner offered Rudi a miserable look and then gazed out into the downpour. With a frustrated sigh, he buttoned his coat all the way to the top and pulled his hat on tight. Grabbing a spare umbrella from the doorman, he followed Rudi out into the rain.

The Mandarin Oriental sat on a circle at the end of Maryland Avenue. Rudi turned right, heading down the avenue as a minor flood washed down the street beside him.

The two men were several feet apart, a distance necessitated by the space required for the umbrellas.

"Why do you NUMA guys always do things the hard way?" Wagner asked. "We could be sharing a drink at the bar or riding along in nice, dry comfort."

"Comfort is overrated," Rudi said. "Makes people soft. More important, I needed to know how badly you wanted to talk. Pretty bad, it seems."

"And we both have to get drenched to satisfy your curiosity?"

"Come on, Marcus," Rudi said, chiding him. "If you can't take the weather, you might as well be in the Air Force."

Despite the irritation he felt, the Rear Admiral laughed. He realized Rudi had found them a space where they were extremely unlikely to be overheard. The downpour might as well have been the cone of silence. He got right to the point. "I understand some of your people were involved in the dry dock incident down in the Bahamas."

"Vicious rumor," Rudi said, "but if they were?"

"It's not the dry dock we're interested in," Wagner said. "It's the freighter."

Reaching the corner of Twelfth Street, Rudi turned north. The Smithsonian and the National Mall were a couple blocks away. So was the nearest Metro station.

"What about it?"

"We're very interested in what happened to it."

"We don't know what happened to it," Rudi replied. "Most of the crew was gone. Those that were still on board were incoherent."

"You mean crazy," Wagner said. "Talking about UFOs and such."

Rudi paused. A black town car swept by on the flooded road, drenching the sidewalk on the other side of the street. "Have you been reading my emails?"

"No," Wagner insisted.

"Then how could you know that?"

"Because this isn't the first ship to end up adrift on the ocean with a crew descending into madness."

This was news to Rudi. "You're not joking," he said.

"We believe it may be the result of a PSYOPS weapon."

"PSYOPS?" Rudi repeated.

"Psychological operations," Wagner said. "The latest front in warfare. And most likely soon to be the greatest."

"I'm listening," Rudi said.

"Killing your enemy is one thing," Wagner said. "If you have to do it, you do it. But unless we're talking about a particularly bad individual, or we're fighting Nazis, orcs, or zombies, it creates a lot of blowback. We already make an extensive effort to limit collateral damage and quite frankly an effort to go after the leaders of our adversaries rather than the rank and file where possible. But there's still a lot of carnage that wouldn't have to happen if you could get your enemy to surrender without firing a shot. That's what PSYOPS is all about. Getting him to throw down his arms and run away. Even when he has the advantage, even when he outnumbers you. Possibly even getting him to turn on his fellow soldiers and do your job for you. All through psychological manipulation."

"Tell me more," Rudi said.

Wagner shook his head. "I can't go there."

"Then why do you expect me to tell you what I know?"

"Because you're not sitting on compartmentalized information. I'm talking stuff beyond top secret at this point. Right now, that freighter is just a salvage job to you."

Rudi didn't put much stock in pride—it got in the way of results—but he was very protective of his teams. "Three of my people have risked their lives multiple times over this wayward freighter. I'd hardly call it a salvage job."

"So you admit there is more," Wagner said, arching his brow.

Rudi started walking again.

Wagner took long steps to catch up. "Come on, Rudi. Don't be like that. You got me, I got you. Now, let's cut out the games and talk honestly. The Navy helped you last year with information from our listening station at Naha. All I need is the same courtesy."

They crossed Independence Avenue and stopped at Jefferson Drive. The Smithsonian castle was to their right, the Museum of Natural History across the mall. Way down to their left, lit up against the backdrop of the dark night, was the Washington Monument. Its red warning lights casting an ominous glow on the underside of the clouds.

Similar warning lights were going off in Rudi's mind. "We don't know what happened on that ship," he said. "No one does. But considering that two of my men were on board at one point, I'd expect you to share any information you've got, especially if it might be relevant to their safety."

Wagner looked concerned. "Are your men all right?"

"You tell me."

"I wish I could."

"Do you have people investigating these sightings?" Rudi asked.

"Yes and no," Wagner replied. "It'd be more accurate to say, we did have such people."

So, they've lost someone, Rudi thought. He better understood Wagner's personal interest now. They'd all lost people in the field at one point or another. You got through it; you never got over it. Not if there was even a small chance you could have done something different to change the outcome.

Rudi stared at his old friend, making a decision that he suspected he'd come to regret at some point. "I'll share what we learn," he told him. "I'm going to assume you want it through private channels. I won't ask why."

Wagner nodded.

"In return," Rudi added, "I'm going to count on you to warn me if my people are in some lingering danger, even if the reason is classified."

Wagner didn't hesitate. "If I learn of anything that would affect them, you'll hear about it as soon as I do."

The rain continued to pour, providing a somber background and a shroud to cloak a deal struck in the dark.

There was nothing more to say. Rudi turned away, crossing Jefferson Drive and heading for the lighted escalators that would take him down to the Metro station underneath the mall.

Wagner looked around, as if just realizing where they were. "I thought you were walking?"

"To the Metro," Rudi replied. "The NUMA building is eight miles from here. Don't worry, your car with the Navy plates will be along soon. It only passed us three times already."

18

Kurt Austin was not a man given to deep philosophical musings, but as he lay down on the bed in his room at the Westwind Club it dawned on him that the most decadent luxury in the world was a good night's sleep, especially when there was nothing in the way of an alarm set for the next morning.

He'd had three hours of sleep and a short nap in the past twenty-four. He'd been physically and mentally taxed by the confrontation on the drifting freighter and during the dry dock attack. Worst of all, he'd been forced to sit through hours of questioning from various Bahamian officials, all of whom asked the same questions, only to seem utterly baffled when he gave them the exact same answers.

The fact was, no one knew who'd attacked the dry dock or why. Video showed a small boat approaching the dock shortly after the medical team arrived. One of the dry dock's crew, a man who was now dead, had allowed the intruders onto the dock and walked them inside.

The grainy images from the low-res security cameras were being processed in an attempt to provide the details of the men's faces but, as one official's off-the-cuff comment suggested, the men could have been almost anyone.

Not quite, Kurt thought. One of them knew how to handle a baton in a style that suggested he was ex-military or a former policeman. The other was thin and gangly with stringy hair that looked like it belonged on a seventies rock star. That combination of details told Kurt someone would put the finger on them sooner or later. Probably later, he guessed. Long after the men were off the island and back to wherever they came from.

In the meantime, both the *Heron*'s captain and cook remained catatonic. They'd been moved from the civilian hospital to a more secure, military facility, where they'd been placed under the direct care of Dr. Pinder with Dr. Pascal assisting.

Finally, Kurt had sent an important but cryptic message back to NUMA headquarters. It read simply: *Heron was towing something. Find out what it was and where it went.*

If Kurt was right, Rudi would fume privately at the vagueness of the message, then call Hiram Yaeger, who ran all of NUMA's computer systems, and order a search. With any luck, Kurt would have an answer when he woke up in the morning. In the meantime, all he had to do was close his eyes and drift off into a blissful state of sleep.

He turned on his side, repositioning the pillow in a futile attempt to get comfortable. The effort failed as his shoulder—tender and bruised from the baton strike—touched the mattress.

Kurt rolled the other way. That was better.

He closed his eyes, listening to the hum of the air conditioner and the creaking voices of tree frogs outside. He felt sleep coming on fast and was just about to doze off when his phone buzzed on the nightstand beside him.

Opening one eye, Kurt briefly considered smashing the phone to bits, but in a moment of extreme self-control reached out and grabbed it. "This better not be a telemarketer."

The screen showed a familiar name and Kurt answered. "Rolle, whatever the opposite of impeccable timing is, you have it. But since I'm still awake . . . What have you got for me?"

Rolle's smooth voice had more bounce in it than usual. "I've got good news for you, bruh. There's something weird about that piece of wreckage you dropped off with me earlier."

Kurt sat up. "Weird how?"

"Be easier to show you than to explain it over the phone. Maybe you and Joe should come down and take a look. I'll keep a light on for you."

Kurt was suddenly wide awake. There was no thought of delaying the visit till morning. "Are you at the shop?"

"Yeah."

"Hang tight. Joe and I will be there in fifteen minutes."

Kurt ended the call and then dialed Joe, who answered groggily, "Kurt?"

"You awake, amigo?"

"No," Joe grunted. "The real question is, why are you? And more important, why do you sound so happy about it?"

"Adrenaline," Kurt said. "Put your shoes on. We have somewhere to go."

Five minutes later, slugging coffee provided by the manager at the front desk, Kurt and Joe took the car from the valet and drove off down Ocean Front Drive. It was well after midnight and the streets were quiet once they got away from the big hotels.

As they crossed the bridge toward the lights of Nassau, Kurt looked Joe's way. "I'm surprised you didn't have company when I called."

Joe shrugged. "Even I'm too tired for the nightlife once in a while."

"I'm talking about Dr. Pascal," Kurt said. "Elena."

Joe smirked. "I think she'd be more interested in me if I was suffering from some rare medical condition."

"Does perpetual loneliness count?"

"Very funny," Joe said. "I haven't noticed any women breaking down your door lately."

Kurt laughed. "Honestly, unless they're sleep therapists, I don't have time for them right now."

Halfway across the bridge they picked up a follower as a car closed in behind them. Could have been anything, Kurt thought, but his sixth sense was on high alert. As he adjusted the rearview mirror, he tried to identify the car. From the lights, he concluded it was a Tesla.

The Tesla drifted back as they entered Nassau. Kurt took a left and drove along the Eastern Road. The Tesla followed, dropping back farther, but remaining in view.

Kurt slowed and pulled into the turn lane as they neared the marina. He waited deliberately rather than finishing the turn. The Tesla came up the road and drove past, continuing on without the slightest hesitation. It was a gray Model X. A blond woman was at the wheel. She kept her eyes on the road ahead, never even glancing Kurt's way.

Maybe it was nothing, he thought. Lack of sleep could make one paranoid too.

They entered the industrial section of the marina and parked behind Rolle's shop. The main building was dark, but the garage-style door was open and the lights in the workshop were on.

Heading inside, Kurt found Rolle with a cold beer in hand. He nodded toward the cooler. "Take one," he suggested. "You're gonna need it when I show you what I found."

With beers in hand, they followed Rolle over to the table where the familiar piece of wreckage lay. From the arrangement of tools and debris, Rolle picked up a small triangular fragment about the size of a pizza slice. "I broke this piece off myself so that I could test the purity of the graphene. That's when I got my first surprise. Take a look at the cross section."

He handed the fragment to Kurt, who studied it under the light. It looked like an extra-thin finger sandwich. With several layers of different colors.

Kurt was underwhelmed. "I'm not sure a beer is going to be strong enough. What are we looking at?"

Rolle sat down on a rolling stool and slid over to a laptop computer that sat nearby. Tapping the keyboard brought the screen to life. "Have a closer look."

A magnified image of the same sandwich-like construction appeared on the screen. Rolle used a pen tip to point out the different layers.

"Pure graphene," he said, pointing to the innermost layer. "One hundred percent pure, very expensive."

"You told us that already," Kurt reminded him.

Rolle laughed. "Have some patience, brother. It's just a recap." He aimed the makeshift pointer at the next layer, much thicker and gray in color, but slightly iridescent. "This is silicon, ninety-eight percent pure."

Kurt was still waiting to be wowed, but Joe, being an engineer, was more intrigued. "You're kidding."

"I never kid about materials," Rolle said. He tapped the pen against the third layer, which was more of a beige color. "And this is a sulfide electrolyte."

"Solid-state?" Joe asked.

"You got it. No liquid at all and no lithium anywhere to be found."

Kurt leaned away from the table and tipped the beer back. He knew when he was superfluous to a conversation. He let the two engineers geek out over the science without interrupting them. He figured they'd clue him back in when the time was right.

"What's the energy density?" Joe asked.

"Hard to say."

"Total charge?"

"Depends on the size of the complete structure," Rolle said. "What Kurt found is obviously only a portion of the device, but if the curvature went all the way around in a spherical shape it would be nearly eight feet across. That would create a tremendous amount of surface area and significant volume inside."

Joe nodded, looking impressed.

"Okay," Kurt said. "I didn't get up in the middle of the night for a reenactment of *Bill Nye the Science Guy.* You guys need to get to the point. What is this thing? What's so impressive about it?"

Joe deferred to the man who'd done the work.

"It's a giant battery," Rolle said. "A solid-state battery—which is the next step beyond lithium-ion. Mostly experimental at this point, but very promising."

"In what way?"

Joe jumped in. "Solid-state batteries can hold thirty times the energy of the most advanced lithium-ion system. And they recharge in a blink. We're looking at them for the next batch of submersibles and ROVs. Once they're perfected, you'll see them in cars, houses, maybe even aircraft. And the performance will change everything."

"Joe's on it," Rolle said. "Today's EVs lug around thousand-pound battery packs that take hours to charge. Switch over to a solid-state power pack and you get just as much juice from a fifty-pound box. Put two of them in the engine bay and you could drive a thousand miles on a single charge, then top up the battery in fifteen minutes."

Kurt glanced at the screen and then over at the curving shell the fragment had come from. "I knew it wasn't a hibachi," he said proudly.

"Oh, I bet you could cook on it," Rolle said. "Let me show you."

Stepping over to the workbench, Rolle connected jumper cables to opposite sides of the curving sphere. That done, he flicked a switch. The shell took on an instant glow, brightening slowly at first and then more rapidly. In a few seconds, the entire surface was ablaze.

Rolle dropped his sunglasses over his eyes. Kurt and Joe squinted and raised their hands to shade their eyes. It was like standing six inches from the brightest billboard in Times Square.

A brief glance in the opposite direction showed the whole workshop fully illuminated. Every nook and cranny lit up vividly.

Kurt was soon squinting even from the reflected light. "Okay," he said. "You can shut it off now. No need to give us a sunburn."

Rolle pulled one of the cables and the light vanished instantly. No glimmering filaments or slowly dimming emitters, just an instant return to the dull gray color.

Kurt stepped closer to the dormant sphere, blinking in hopes that it would help his night vision return. The curving shell was just sitting there, no moving parts. No wires. No sign of LEDs or lighting filaments. Nothing to indicate it could light up the night like it just had.

He touched the surface with his bare palm. "It's not even warm."

"Nope," Rolle said, standing up. "No wasted electricity turning to heat." He propped his shades back up on top of his head. "I don't know where this thing came from, but I gotta tell you it's next-level stuff. The kind of stuff that I don't even want to know about. You get what I mean?"

Kurt nodded without taking his eyes off the dormant sphere. "Where are the wires?"

"It doesn't need any," Rolle said.

Kurt wrinkled his brow.

"Graphene conducts electricity better than copper," Joe explained. "The graphene is the conductor."

"And the light? Where's that coming from?"

Rolle tapped on the shell. "The outer layer is made of gallium arsenide," he said. "It's like a screen made up of millions of tiny LEDs."

"Seeing this thing in the sky," Kurt said. "You might think the mother ship was landing."

"*You* might think that," Rolle said. "I'd be running for cover in the other direction."

"It's too bad that you didn't run for cover," a far too familiar voice said from the opening to the garage. "It would have been better for all of you."

Kurt turned to see the saboteurs he'd fought on the dry dock. The thin man had a blood-soaked bandage on his chin where Kurt had hit him with the long pole. The long-haired man had tape over his nose.

Neither of the men held a nightstick this time. They'd come with guns drawn and three additional comrades to make sure the odds weren't anywhere close to even.

19

The men with the guns stepped into the workshop and one of them found a switch to lower the main garage door. It came down smoothly and hit the floor with a slight bump.

"So much for round two," Kurt said, looking at the man with the bloody chin. "Some other time maybe."

"There won't be another time," the man replied.

"Didn't think so," Kurt said. With a shove of his foot, Kurt sent Rolle's rolling chair across the garage floor at the men. At nearly the same instant, Rolle flicked the switch on the charger and the shell came blazing to life.

The gunmen shut their eyes against the glare and then, realizing they'd been blinded, began firing wildly around the workshop.

Kurt and Joe dove in opposite directions as Rolle ducked for cover behind the heavy workbench. The gunfire soon converged on the luminescent panel as the men attempted to shoot out the light. Yet even as they drilled it full of holes, the blinding light continued to pour forth, dimmed only fractionally by each bullet like a television with a few malfunctioning pixels.

A few yards away, Kurt found a crescent wrench and hurled it at the nearest man. It flew end over end, like a tomahawk, knocking the attacker to the ground.

With the man rolling on the ground concussed, Kurt rushed to grab his weapon. He was driven back by cross fire from the bearded gunman and ended up sliding across the floor into a spot of cover.

On the other side of the workshop, Joe was looking for a weapon to call his own. He found a partially assembled mast lying on its side. He looped a length of rope around it and pulled it backward, bending it like a sapling in the wind. As one of the gunmen came into view, Joe released the rope. The forty-foot length of carbon fiber snapped forward, catching the gunman in the chest and knocking him across the garage.

Joe moved before the gunfire came his way, but lingered long enough to see the man rolling over on his side, clutching his chest.

Two down, three to go.

In the midst of all this, Rolle was hiding behind the workbench. He wasn't the most agile of men, and he really had nowhere to run, but he knew something no one else did: the workbench had wheels.

Releasing the tiny brakes on the feet, he turned the bench into a mobile shield and began moving toward the front of the building. He'd gone halfway when the extension cord pulled out of the wall and the glowing shell lost power. The room went instantly dark.

Fortunately for Rolle, the human eye could not adjust so quickly. He picked up the pace, shoving his barricade along unseen until he ran into Kurt.

"Sorry for turning out the lights," he said. "But something tells me the party's over."

Kurt could see the bearded man and his remaining associates squinting and blinking. Their night vision was fried. But it would come back.

Joe came bounding over. "What's the word?"

"We've lost this round," Kurt said. "We need to get out." He looked at Rolle. "Can we get to the front of the shop from here?"

"That's where I was headed."

"Go," Kurt said. "I'll try to cover you."

As Joe and Rolle moved to the front door, Kurt kept watch on the attackers. The bearded man was directing traffic. One man was sent left, the other to the right. Meanwhile the guy Kurt had hit with the crescent wrench was rejoining the fight. Kurt doubted he'd be much good in his condition, but he still had a gun.

"There!" the bearded man shouted, spying Joe and Rolle as they opened the door to the front of the building. "Stop them!"

Gunshots rang out and peppered the far wall as Joe and Rolle squirmed through the door with their heads down. To offer some form of cover fire, Kurt whipped a chisel at one of the gunmen and then shoved the workbench toward the bearded man.

As the bearded man jumped out of the way, Kurt raced for the door, which Joe or Rolle had thankfully propped open with a push broom.

He slid through it on his hip and then scampered out of the doorway on his hands and knees, moving as fast as he possibly could while yanking the broom free.

The door closed firm and Joe shoved a chair beneath the handle.

"This way," Rolle urged.

"Should have parked out front," Joe said. "We'll never get to the rental car now."

Kurt turned to Rolle. "Where's your ride?"

"Sorry, bruh, I bike everywhere these days."

Rolle did not exactly look like a bicyclist. "Really? It doesn't show."

"Not my fault," Rolle said defensively. "Too much good food here."

"No choice but to run," Kurt said. There was a dark alley between the workshop and the next industrial building. "Come on."

They cut across the front of Rolle's shop and rushed down the adjacent alley, heading for an opening at the far end. Before they could get halfway, headlights appeared ahead of them as a car came charging their way.

They stopped in their tracks and turned back, but a second later a pickup truck came barreling into the alley behind them. Kurt looked for a door or a way out. No doors, windows, or fire escapes presented themselves. They were trapped.

The three men pressed themselves against the wall as the first car reached them and skidded to a stop. Kurt noticed it was the gray Tesla Model X with its falcon-wing doors open high and wide. The blond woman was at the wheel. She shouted at them from the driver's seat. "Don't just stand there. Get in!"

This wasn't the time to argue. Kurt ushered Rolle ahead and all but hurled Joe into the car. He dove in after them, landing awkwardly as the woman threw the car into reverse and began backing down the alley.

The truck was still charging their way, but the Tesla sprinted backward, picking up speed rapidly as its electric motors hummed. As they reached the end of the alley, the woman flipped the steering wheel around and stomped on the brakes. The car spun, slid, and resumed its momentum with the nose pointed in the opposite direction.

If he wasn't in the process of being thrown about the cabin, Kurt would have applauded the high-precision turn.

He looked back at the truck just in time to see someone stand up in the back of the truck bed and open fire over the top of the cab.

"Incoming!"

The woman slammed on the brakes and swerved onto a crossing road. When she'd finished negotiating the turn, she stepped on the accelerator and the electric motors in the wheels kicked in with such force that Kurt had to work to keep from getting whiplash.

The truck skidded into the turn behind them and went partially off the road, managing to get back onto it while spraying a cloud of dust and gravel out behind its spinning wheels. Whether the gunman in the back had been thrown out or had miraculously managed to hang on, the pickup was no match for the Tesla. And with the speedometer in the Model X hitting one hundred and ten, the truck was rapidly left behind.

With the danger receding, Kurt turned to the driver. "Thanks for the rescue," he said. "That was a fantastic piece of driving. Care to tell us who you are or why you've been following us?"

"Commander Jodi Wells," the woman said. "Naval Intelligence. I've been following you because I need your help. And because if we're going to get to the bottom of what those men are after, you're going to need mine."

20

After a few false turns to ensure they were no longer being followed, Commander Wells drove them to a small bungalow sitting on a half acre of manicured grass on the far side of the island.

The place wasn't much to look at. It had slab walls, a flat roof, and faded paint, but there were no other buildings within a thousand feet and the lawn behind the house sloped down to a rocky cliff that dropped fifteen feet to the sea.

Kurt recognized the advantages of the location. With the open turf on three sides and the cliff and the ocean protecting the fourth, the house couldn't be approached without an aggressor being detected by what he could only assume would be a suite of hidden cameras and motion sensors.

The setup was anything but temporary. It meant Wells had been working in the Bahamas for an extended period, a theory supported by the tawny shade of her sun-kissed skin, too deep and even to be a tourist's tan.

After pulling into a garage, shutting the door, and disarming the alarm system, Commander Wells let them into the house. They sat at a kitchen table, discussing what happened at the shop, while Commander Wells checked a series of camera feeds to make sure the house was secure.

"Welcome to my humble abode," she said, returning to the kitchen.

"I've stayed in worse," Kurt joked.

Joe smiled and offered a compliment. "Nice work behind the wheel. You could make good money as a getaway driver when you finish up with the Navy."

"I'll keep that in mind," she replied. "The way things are going I might need a new career before too long."

"Why is that?"

"I'm looking into something that no one else wants to investigate," she said. "Something you two may have stumbled across and then inadvertently delivered to Mr. Rolle here."

"The lighted shell," Kurt said.

She nodded. "If I'm right, that shell is part of a drone aircraft. One example of a type that have attacked numerous ships over the past couple years."

"Attack them how?" Joe asked.

"With what we call a psychic weapon."

Rolle had been watching the exchange with a concerned look on his face. "Psychic?" he asked. "As in, call us at 1-800-something-something and we'll tell you all about your future?"

"Not that kind of psychic," Commander Wells replied. "Psychic as in affecting the mind. Using various electromagnetic frequencies to alter brain waves and induce states of extreme emotion like fear, anger, or excitement."

"Mind control?" Kurt said.

"That term is a little strong," Commander Wells replied. "But close enough for government work."

Kurt's mind flashed to men on the *Heron*. They were living in fear, like rats down in a tunnel afraid to come out.

Before more could be said, Rolle held up a hand. "Listen, brothers—and new sister—I'm a civilian and I'd really like to keep it that way. In other words, whatever this is, I don't want to know any more about it. Better if I go call my cousin on the police force and tell him my shop was broken into. While I do that, you three can discuss this privately." He turned to Kurt. "You think it's safe to send the boys in blue over there now?"

Kurt figured the intruders were long gone at this point, but he deferred to Commander Wells. She'd had them turn their phones off earlier.

"Should be," she said. "But use the landline in the living room. And don't say anything you don't want the U.S. government to know about. The line is recorded."

Rolle slid back from the table and stood. "Thanks for the heads-up."

As he left the room, Kurt studied Commander Wells. She was wearing civilian clothes—khaki pants and a black top—but she was squared away. The bungalow was neat as a pin. Everything in its place. As soon as they'd come inside, she pulled her blond hair back into a ponytail. He figured her for mid-thirties. She was attractive, athletic, and fit, but there was a weight on her shoulders that went beyond a Navy officer with a mission. "You were talking about mind control."

"Officially it's termed RCM," she said. "Ranged cognitive manipulation. Think of it as a method of influencing people from a distance, getting them to do things they wouldn't otherwise do. In our case, the interest is in finding a way to stop a battle before it starts. It's far more humane to make your adversaries throw down their weapons than to obliterate them with missiles and bombs."

"Humane in war," Kurt said. "But what about in peace? It sounds like a way for someone to control everyone—whether they want to be controlled or not."

"That's an obvious and understandable concern," she admitted, "but our intended application—and what we believed to be the limits of the technology—was to affect short-term emotions, turning bravery into fear or anger and resentment into a sense of calmness. There's no method of long-term control when using emotions; good or bad they only last so long. And getting people to do specific things . . . Forget it, that was nothing more than a pipe dream. Or so we thought. But someone seems to have perfected a weapon that can make people do things they would never otherwise do."

"Like jumping off a perfectly seaworthy ship without a life jacket," Joe said.

She nodded. "Or stopping your ship in the middle of the ocean, giving up your cargo without a fight, and then being unable to remember doing any of it when you reach port weeks later."

"Has that happened?" Kurt asked.

"More times than anyone is willing to believe," she insisted. "My research has turned up fifty-nine acts of piracy matching this pattern over the last two years. In almost all cases, high-value cargoes vanished mysteriously while the officers of the vessel remained oblivious to the disappearance. In some cases, members of the crew went missing as well."

This was the first Kurt had heard of it. "How is this not front-page news?"

"Because no one wants it to be," she said. "The shipping firms are more interested in maintaining their reputations than getting at the truth. In most cases, they've paid out of pocket to avoid bad publicity. In a few cases, they've accused their baffled crews of being complicit."

Joe chimed in. "No cargo line wants the public to think its ships and crews are unreliable."

"Exactly," Commander Wells said. "So, the official records end up pointing to storms or simply of mishandling the cargo. And when they do indicate criminal behavior, the shippers blame the point of origin, suggesting the theft occurred dockside before the cargo was ever loaded. But when you get a look at the original interviews, it's obvious that the crewmen were suffering from memory loss and cognitive impairment, and that the final reports were doctored to cover it up."

Kurt had dealt with enough shipping companies to know how the game worked. For years they didn't even report container losses publicly, even though thousands of the giant metal boxes fell into the sea every year.

"Thing is," she continued, "one bad crew is believable. Several bad crews might suggest a syndicate. But fifty-nine different crews? Across eight different shipping lines? None of whom have any connection to each other? Impossible. There has to be an outside actor. Actual pirates doing the piracy."

In principle Kurt had to agree. "Why is the Navy so interested? Piracy hasn't been their concern since the mid-1800s."

Commander Wells didn't hesitate. "Because we think there's a connection to the piracy and the swarms of drones that have been harassing our ships over the past couple of years. You've probably heard about the incidents off California where drones shadowed and surrounded a pair of our guided missile destroyers on a training mission. There's been plenty of similar incidents that never became public. Drones have been spotted following our ballistic missile submarines while they were operating on the surface in and out of their home ports. Others have harassed larger ships, including the USS *Kearsarge*, which was tracked and hounded for several nights by automobile-sized glowing orbs. And earlier this year one of our largest support ships, the *Rappahannock*, was buzzed repeatedly by similar glowing spheres."

Kurt understood the concern. He'd seen some of the reports. "Don't we have defenses against this kind of thing?"

"Of course," she said. "All our major surface ships carry the DRAKE system, which is a high-intensity jammer designed to block the signals being used to control the drones. And, because it's considered a high-priority target, the *Kearsarge* had a team of 'Ghostbusters' on board,

Marines who handle an even more advanced anti-drone system. Neither weapon had any effect."

"Should have crossed the beams," Joe said, referencing the ultimate use of the particle accelerators in the *Ghostbusters* movie.

Commander Wells cracked a smile. "That only works against the Stay Puft Marshmallow Man."

Kurt laughed, impressed that she knew the climax of such a classic movie. "Any damage to the ships?"

"No," she said. "But some of the crew experienced migraine headaches and nausea, while the ship itself had some radar and communication issues."

"So, nothing like what happened on the *Heron*."

"No," Commander Wells admitted, "but with each attack, the drones have been getting closer. We think they're testing our defenses, probing for a weakness."

"Any idea who's behind it?" Joe asked.

"The usual suspects are in play," she said. "Russia, North Korea, Iran. We know the Iranians have a big drone program, and they've never been afraid to go after U.S. ships, but oddly enough there have been no attacks in the Persian Gulf."

"I notice you didn't include China," Kurt said.

"There's a reason for that," she explained. "Four days ago, we picked up an open-channel transmission from a Chinese spy trawler suggesting the ship was in distress and had been attacked by 'lanterns in the sky.' Lanterns. Lights. Drones. That trawler ended up dead in the water, drifting aimlessly, until the *Heron* came along and took it under tow."

"Something tells me that wasn't an accidental encounter," Kurt said.

"The *Heron* was on its way down from Charleston on a course that would take it within twenty miles of the drifting ship. My partner, Gerald Walker, flew out to meet it. He made a deal with the *Heron*'s captain. The ship changed course, confirmed the trawler was a dere-lict, and took it under tow."

"Until they were attacked by 'lanterns' from the sky," Joe pointed out. "And somebody cut the trawler loose and sent it to the bottom."

"Are you sure it went down?" she asked.

"We found hastily cut cables at the stern. They'd been deployed and then sliced through with a blowtorch rather than reeled in and properly stowed."

"I'm not surprised," she said, "but are you sure it sank?"

She was very keen on this point.

"There was nothing on radar within fifty miles by the time we reached the *Heron*," Kurt said. "Unless that trawler grew wings, the only place it could have gone was down."

She looked away. Kurt could see the gears in her mind turning. He asked the next obvious question. "What was so important about that Chinese ship?"

"The data it was carrying," she said. "The typical Chinese spy boat is loaded with the most advanced radar and sonar systems, plus other intelligence-gathering equipment. We believe they saw, heard, or recorded something that might identify the drone operator or perhaps their origin."

Kurt thought that sounded reasonable. "We didn't find any Chinese equipment on the *Heron*. Nor any Chinese crewmen for that matter."

She knew this. "According to Walker's initial report, the crew of the trawler were dead at their stations when he arrived."

"Dead?"

"Yes. Strapped into their seats or fallen where they stood. He didn't get a chance to determine the cause because the captain of the *Heron* refused to allow the bodies to be brought aboard his ship. But let's be clear, anything that can affect the brain at one power level can kill if that level is raised high enough."

Joe exhaled rather loudly. "Are you saying someone fried their brains?" A weapon that could kill crewmen inside a ship without punching a hole in the exterior was the type of threat he didn't want to face.

"I'm not saying anything," she replied, "just sharing my report. But I assume you've heard of Havana Syndrome?"

"Sure," Joe said. "Embassy personnel in Cuba getting sick for no reason, hearing strange noises and humming sounds, supposedly caused by some sort of directed-energy weapon. Didn't the CIA call that a hoax? Putting it down to bad tequila and mass hysteria?"

"They tried to," Commander Wells said. "But they were either wrong or being deliberately misleading. Fact is, Havana Syndrome affected hundreds of people at various locations, not all of them in Cuba. Many of the incidents resulted in physical symptoms that looked like radiation burns or exposure to caustic chemicals. And while the CIA didn't buy off on it, Naval Intelligence felt differently."

"Why is that?"

"Because the Navy's advanced weaponry division was working on a similar weapon," she said. "At least they were until one of the scientists, a guy named Wyatt Campbell, disappeared and resurfaced in Havana."

"That does sound ominous."

"It gets worse," she said. "We tracked Campbell from Havana to a place called Arcos, a small town in the middle of tobacco country where the Cubans were doing experiments. I led a recon mission to see if he was present, find out what he was up to, and bring him back if possible. It turned out to be a trap. The Cubans knew we were coming, but instead of taking us out they let us in, so they could test their weapon on hostile outsiders."

"Welcome to my parlor," Kurt said, citing from the old fable "The Spider and the Fly." "At least you managed to get out."

"Barely," she replied. "Our advance team got trapped in there, and the Cubans used whatever they were working on to turn one of my men into a killing machine willing to gun down his own people."

This was one step above what had happened on the *Heron*, but too close to deny the obvious similarities. "How?"

"We don't know."

"How did you get away?" Joe asked.

"I shot him at fifty yards, after I saw him unload half a clip into one of my guys," she said coldly. "But by then the lab was in flames and trouble was on the way. We left there with no intel, one injured and three dead. Our escape was cut off and we had to hoof it across Cuba in the other direction to get out. Three days on the run."

The room went silent. The gravity of the admission obviously weighed on Commander Wells. "Now you see why Lieutenant Walker and I haven't given this up."

Kurt nodded. "I hate to tell you this, but we didn't find any sign of your friend Walker either."

A brief flash of emotion crossed her face. "I didn't expect you'd find him. Whoever cut that trawler loose would have had to go through him to do it. Which means Walker's gone, and our only hope of finding whoever killed him, and whatever the Chinese stumbled upon, is to find that trawler. Wherever it hit bottom."

"Finding it shouldn't be too hard," Joe suggested. "But what are the chances that the data survived?"

Commander Wells was confident. "The Chinese hard drives are robust. They're built something like the black boxes on commercial aircraft. The water won't affect them in the short term. And unless there was a massive explosion, they should be in one piece."

Kurt sat back for a moment, considering what she was requesting. He accepted her assessment of the Chinese systems. Of the three of them, she should know. And he imagined they could find the ship and retrieve the hard drives without too much trouble. But a big question remained.

"Let me get this straight," he said. "You're an intelligence officer working for the largest and most powerful seagoing organization in the world. But when you learned about the drifting trawler, you and your partner bribed the captain of a freighter to drag it to Nassau instead of sending a Navy tug to bring it back to the States."

"Did you miss the part where I said it was a Chinese vessel in international waters?"

"Didn't miss that at all," Kurt said. "But now that it's sitting on the bottom, nothing could be easier than calling in a Navy team. Last I checked, the Navy wasn't short on divers, submarines, or salvage gear."

This time she paused before speaking. "I know it sounds odd, but I'm deliberately leaving the brass out of the loop."

"Why?"

"Because every time I've gone through official channels, word got out. I've had two missions blown, one informant killed, and another who just disappeared. The Cuban mission I told you about was a setup from the word go. Unfortunately, there's no other reasonable explanation. Someone at Naval Intelligence has been compromised."

Joe let out a long whistle and sat back. "Oh boy."

Kurt held silent, watching her. It was a serious accusation. There was nothing to suggest she was taking it lightly. If true, it certainly gave her reason to operate on her own. Whether that would matter at the end of the day was another story.

"Look," she continued, "if you're worried about getting rolled up in something, you don't have to be. I'm not completely off the reservation. I just don't have a handler. The brass think I'm tilting at windmills like Don Quixote, but they haven't tried to rein me in, just in case I'm actually on to something. Which I am."

Kurt didn't need to think about it for long. After what he'd seen on the lower decks of the *Heron*, he was certain they were dealing with an actual weapon, not some form of mass hysteria. And if the level of cognitive manipulation it allowed was anywhere close to what Commander Wells was suggesting, then the people using it had to be stopped.

"No one should have the power to take over a person's mind," he said. "I wouldn't want our government to have it, and I damn sure wouldn't want any of our enemies to have it either."

"So you'll help?"

Kurt nodded, but wouldn't speak for Joe.

He needn't have hesitated. Joe could hear a list of victims crying out for justice. Starting with the eight Bahamian workers who'd been killed on the dry dock and the fifteen men who'd gone missing off the *Heron*, sixteen if they included Walker. Not to mention all the merchant sailors missing from the other ships and the men and women who'd been harmed in the Havana Syndrome attacks.

Truth was, Joe took most parts of life lightly but hated anything that smacked of abandonment or injustice. Simply put, this wasn't the type of thing he could just walk away from. "I'm in."

"Thank you," Commander Wells said. "Thank you both."

"There is one condition," Kurt said. "You need to hand over the data you've collected so our people can run it. Guessing you haven't had much access to Navy analysts if you're operating on the down-low. Maybe there's something you missed."

"I can do that," she said eagerly. "What about the trawler?"

Kurt grinned, proud of himself. "As fate would have it, I've already got someone looking for its final resting place. When they tell me where it is, we'll dive on it together."

"Deal." The agreement had been reached. No handshake or signed document was necessary.

As they finished up, Rolle reentered the room. "Bad news," he said. "Those guys took the thingamajig you brought in and burned my shop down. The fire company is over there right now, putting out the embers."

Kurt winced. "Sorry."

"Don't be, I'm sending you the bill," Rolle replied. "Wait till you see the new shop I build, once all that U.S. government cash rolls in."

"I'm sure we'll get you back into business," Kurt said. "In the meantime, it sounds like you might need some work. And . . . as it turns out, we need a boat large enough to tow a submersible and a captain who knows the waters around here."

Rolle seemed pleased by the request. As a joke he asked what they'd be fishing for, then thought better of it. "Never mind. I don't want to know."

21

WESTERN CUBA

Martin Colon sat in the back of a rugged-looking SUV as his driver navigated a street that had last been paved several decades ago. Most of the concrete had been worn away by the rains, or covered by the ever-encroaching dirt, but here and there stubborn chunks remained, sticking out like fossils or icebergs or land mines. They reminded Colon of himself. The last bastions of what once was. Unwilling to be washed away.

The former colonel was back in Cuba for the first time in almost a year. A sense of nostalgia flowed through him as they drove past broken-down homes and farmers using cattle to plow their fields.

There was a purity in how the Cubans worked the land, a type of dignity they retained by doing it their way and not needing the West. And there was peace and quiet here, the likes of which he never found in Rio or Miami or even on bustling Providencia. For a brief moment, Colon wondered if he was making a mistake trying to change things.

Then they passed a group of homeless mothers sitting in rags while waiting for handouts beside a crumbling municipal building. The poverty grew worse every year. Malnutrition was rampant in many places. Alcoholism as well. It left fifty-year-old men looking like they were ninety. It left children with hollow eyes.

Last year, for the first time in decades, there had been real protests in cities and towns across the island. A wave of desperation was building, the kind that could not be held in check by the secret police or the slogans of the past. Not for long.

On the far side of the municipal building was an equally dilapidated structure. A faded red cross suggested it had once been a hospital. It reminded Colon of the place where his wife had died for lack of a simple drug easily available in America, but impossible to find in Cuba because of the embargo and the poverty.

It was her loss that had embittered him, but her death was not the first time his family had suffered at the hands of America. Colon's great-uncle had marched with Castro from the mountains to Havana, only to die in a hail of bullets fired by Cuban expatriates at the Bay of Pigs. Colon's father had been in Grenada as a military contractor when the shrapnel from an American mortar round had shattered his spine. He'd died slowly over the next year and a half, with Colon watching him slip away, day by day.

As the abandoned hospital fell behind them, Colon recalled a superior in the Directorate who'd asked him rhetorically if an operation was worth pursuing when it risked starting a war with the United States. Colon rejected the question. As far as he was concerned, his family had been at war with America for sixty years.

"Why did you bring me here?" a voice asked from beside him. "This place depresses me."

Colon turned toward Lobo, battered and bruised from his combat in the Bahamas, but looking more lupine than ever. A bit of fat had been burned off. A bit of tooth had begun to show. Good. A wolf should have teeth.

"Is it any worse than Havana?" Colon asked.

"Worse than my part of Havana," Lobo insisted. "Where are we going anyway?"

Colon offered a single word. "Home."

The SUV continued until it reached a farmhouse on a sprawling piece of hilly land. Around the back stood a pair of long barns that had once been used to hang tobacco. A dozen vehicles were parked under the shelter of the first barn, a mix of cars, four-wheel-drive vehicles, and SUVs.

Colon had the driver pull into the shade. He stepped out of the SUV and crossed to the other barn with Lobo following.

A trio of well-armed men stood waiting beside a steel door. Another man was up on the roof with binoculars and a long gun. Lobo recognized them for what they were, former military men, now working for Colon.

The guards moved out of Colon's way without uttering a word. The door was opened for him. Stepping inside revealed a different world.

Much like with the facility at Arcos, they had kept the barn's exterior rustic so as not to draw attention to it, while the interior held a modern production and testing center. The floor was concrete, the walls made from panels of high-strength plastic, their smooth surfaces reflecting the glow from overhead lights.

Behind a glass wall, men in yellow hazmat suits worked in a small but pristine room. They were operating machinery stolen from the American computer chip manufacturers and using the equipment to produce a weapon that would bring the West to its knees.

As Lobo watched, a small amount of liquid poured from a high-tech foundry into a tempered glass tray. As it cooled, the liquid took on a mirrored, copper color, at which point it was gently advanced into a large machine, which used a process called photolithography to turn the tray of silicon into a repeating pattern of microscopic computer chips.

When separated from one another, these chips would number in the millions, each one smaller than a grain of pollen. If jostled or dropped, they would float on the air just as easily as the invisible dander that turned so many eyes red in the spring. If tossed upward in a handful, they would spread out like a cloud and drift like smoke.

Colon and his men called this product "dust." In one corner of the lab, tiny amounts of the refined dust were being tested and processed and then sifted carefully into test tubes.

Lobo stared, baffled by what he saw. "Is this what was on that freighter?"

"Enough of it to give us away," Colon admitted.

"What is this stuff?"

"The future of Cuba."

The dust was like a skeleton key that could be used to unlock the human mind. Once it was inhaled, injected, or swallowed, it rapidly entered the bloodstream and soon found its way to the brain. Its size and shape allowed it to penetrate what was known as the blood-brain barrier and once it had passed this formidable wall, it lodged in the gray matter beyond.

Embedded in place, the dust remained harmless until it was activated by a low-frequency signal, which each tiny chip would receive and retransmit in harmony with the others. With only a few thousand grains in place, less than one-tenth of a gram of material, this harmonic transmission could overwhelm and wreak havoc on the bioelectric system that humans called the mind.

Through years of brutal experiments—the kind that historians would label evil if they ever found out about them—Colon and his scientists had learned how to activate the dust to manipulate emotions, and later on, how to prepare a subject's mind to accept outside suggestions as if they were coming from within.

At a certain frequency many of those infected with the dust became entranced in a way that was similar to hypnosis. In this state a man could be made to do almost anything. Colon had watched men let out bloodcurdling screams because they believed they were on fire, when in fact they weren't. He'd watched a man shoot himself with a gun that was offered as a way to end the pain. He'd seen others place their hands over a blowtorch and never flinch because they were told there was no heat.

Much like hypnosis, different people responded differently, some required more indoctrination, others less. Some could never quite be controlled and instead pitched into madness at the conflicting thoughts in their brains.

For those who could be taken to deeper levels of submission, complex orders could be given, posthypnotic suggestions could be placed. These subjects would act completely normal until the sounding of a specific tone, or the utterance of specific words designed to trigger their program. They became the ultimate moles: men and women who didn't even know they'd been compromised.

With the technology in his pocket, Colon had left the Directorate, gone to ground, and emerged inside the Ostrom Airship Corporation. He'd used the dust in small doses against those who stood in his way. He'd used it in larger amounts for the far-flung piracy scheme. Now, at long last, he was ready to deploy his masterstroke. And for this he would use every ounce that could possibly be manufactured.

"Come with me," Colon said, tearing Lobo away from the men in the clean room. "Your old friends want to see you in person."

Leaving the production space, they traveled the length of the barn and entered a guarded room at the far end. Several men waited for them inside, all that remained of the true believers of the Picadors.

22

olon and Lobo entered the back room. There were no computer screens or glass-top desks here, nothing resembling the stylish furniture from the office in Providencia. Just a plain floor, brick walls, and a long wooden threshing table that was a relic of farming practices from the previous century. The Picadors sat around it, dressed like men of the country.

This is how Colon wanted it.

He could have flown them to Providencia or Rio, where Ostrom offices were at his disposal, they could've met in Havana at a more prestigious location, but considering what was at stake, he felt it was necessary for the men to meet in this simple room. To remind themselves of who they were.

"It's good to see you all again," he began before pointing to Lobo. "Most of you know the Red Wolf. I'm happy to say he's back with us now."

With a nod, Lobo moved off to one side. He sat in a chair beside the wall, crossing his legs and watching the proceedings with a sense of detached curiosity. His assessment of Colon during their meeting in

Providencia had been correct. He was definitely after something more than stolen cargo. It seemed they were all about to find out just how much more he wanted.

With the door barred behind him, Colon moved to the head of the table, ready to receive an update from the others. On his right, first and closest, sat Anton Perez.

Perez was the oldest of the group at nearly seventy. He'd made it to colonel in the Intelligence Directorate much like Colon, but had run afoul of the higher-ups soon after. His career had been foundering until Colon tapped him and brought him into the Picadors.

Perez had always been grateful for that second act and for the fact that Colon had treated him as a mentor of sorts, even though technically Perez answered to him.

"It's good to see you, my old friend," Perez announced. "And the Wolf is welcome at my table at any time of the night or day."

Colon allowed a beat for Lobo to respond with a note of gratitude and then said, "How are you feeling these days? I'd heard you were suffering from the herculean effort to keep the helium flowing."

Perez had gone from the Picadors to a position in the Ministry of Production, which oversaw the management of Cuba's raw materials. Early on, Perez had achieved some mild success by increasing the production of nickel and copper. Shortly afterward, his people located substantial reserves of natural gas below a small range of hills in the center of the country.

This discovery had been fortunate for Cuba, and even more fortunate for Colon. By a quirk of fate, the gas contained a high concentration of helium, the production and refinement of which had allowed Colon to link up with Ostrom Airship Corporation and its enigmatic CEO, Stefano Solari.

While most people thought of helium as a worthless gas used to make party balloons float or raise a person's voice, in the twenty-first century it had become a valuable and increasingly rare commodity.

Helium was necessary for the manufacture of silicon chips, fiber-optic cables, and computer screens, all of which had to be made while bathed in pure helium or they would end up containing air bubbles that ruined the end product. Helium was also used in medical and scientific equipment, to cool the superconducting magnets in MRIs and other high-powered devices, and was stored under pressure in a billion airbag safety devices in the world's ever-expanding fleet of cars.

Because of this increased use—and the fact that all the helium ever released into the atmosphere eventually escaped into space—the cost of helium had risen by two thousand percent in just the past decade. It was expected to rise continuously—much like the gas itself—into the foreseeable future. All of which was good news for Cuba and very bad news for the Ostrom Airship Corporation.

When Solari initially launched his business, refined helium sold for less than thirty cents a cubic foot. More recently, the spot price had touched four dollars for the same amount. It still didn't sound like all that much, until one realized that each ship in the Ostrom fleet required over ten million cubic feet of the stuff just to get off the ground. And while most of the gas was conserved in the lifting cells for a number of years, it still meant spending forty million dollars per airship on gas alone. Which came to nearly half a billion dollars for Solari's planned armada of seventeen vessels.

At this price, Solari would go bankrupt trying to fill the airships he'd already built, let alone finishing the rest of the fleet. But, sensing an opportunity, Colon had urged Perez to contact Solari and strike a deal. Ostrom would get cheap helium from Cuba—and lots of it—in return for a stake in the corporation that would remain hidden, a stop along the trade route that would add some prestige to the island nation, and the permanent placement of Martin Colon as director of security and the VP of freight handling—a pair of unglamorous jobs that Solari could have cared less about anyway.

Once inside, Colon had built up a network of people loyal to himself, bringing in Cubans who'd once worked for him in the military or the Intelligence Directorate. These men and women became an organization within the organization, a hidden group who answered exclusively to Colon.

With that nest built, Colon had "borrowed" the drone and battery technology from one of Solari's high-tech initiatives. Melding the drones with the dust, he'd launched his complex piracy operation, but that was merely a way to field-test his creation and generate cash needed for bribes and research. And all of it was merely preparation for the world-changing event he would announce this evening.

Colon was an avowed atheist, but if he'd believed in any god, he would have given thanks for Perez and the helium reserve he'd found.

"Don't worry about me," Perez insisted. "Chest pains from too much wine and good food. I'm fine now and well enough to wrestle a bear."

"And the helium?"

Perez didn't hesitate. "We had trouble with some protesters, and we faced a three-week shutdown when the collection system was damaged. But the protesters have been dealt with and the refinery is back in operation. The delayed shipment left port earlier this week aboard a Honduran freighter. It should reach Brazil in time for Solari to launch his newest monstrosity."

Colon was glad to hear it. That monstrosity was the key to his plan. "Good news on both fronts."

A nod of appreciation came from Perez, but Colon sensed he was anxious for more. They'd been selling the helium cheap for quite some time now. He wanted to know why.

That answer would be forthcoming. First Colon needed to hear from the others. He turned to the man at the end of the table: Victor Ruiz.

Ruiz was younger than Perez, but old enough to have a Russian-sounding first name, which had been in vogue in Cuba during the Cold War.

Sporting thick black hair and a trim physique, Ruiz had a photogenic look. At Colon's suggestion, he'd left the Directorate and gone into politics, using his skills and handsome face to make a good impression. This, along with bribes and payoffs funded by Colon's piracy operation, had allowed him quick entry into the National Assembly. From there he'd made an even quicker jump to the Council of State, the group of twenty-one men who truly ran the country. Ruiz was the youngest among them and often considered the most brash.

"What is the status within the party?" Colon asked.

"Several of the old men have been treated with the dust," Ruiz confirmed. "As of now they're ready to confess and take the fall should anything go wrong with your plan. Though you still haven't told me what they'll be confessing to."

"I will explain momentarily," Colon insisted. "And don't worry, it's highly unlikely they'll need to say anything at all."

The final surviving member of the Picadors sat to Colon's left. Lorca—who went by only his last name. He was broad shouldered and stout, built like bulldog or perhaps one of the tugboats his people operated.

After leaving the Directorate, Lorca had taken a ranking position in the Cuban Port Authority, where Colon had him watching over Lobo and the rest of the smuggling operation.

Lorca was not an aggressive type, but he was sturdy and reliable. He made sure the smuggling effort went on unimpeded by law enforcement and unmolested by other criminal groups. He did his job perfectly, applying grease when needed and a hammer when it was called for. He'd even delivered to Colon a captured narco submarine that had been repurposed for his piratical needs.

The vessel was designed to carry a substantial amount of cargo in a bulbous outer housing. It looked like a pregnant guppy and moved like molasses, but it had an efficient power train and a lengthy ocean-going range. It was perfect for the job of sidling up to a drifting ship, taking cargo aboard unseen, and then vanishing.

"Status update on the *Gulper*," Colon requested.

They called the submarine the *Gulper*, after a strange deep-sea eel that could unhinge its jaw and swallow much larger prey.

"After what happened with the Chinese, I had it swing wide, avoiding Andros, where the Americans have a listening post," Lorca explained. "Because of that it's thirty-six hours behind schedule. My understanding is the cargo is in excellent shape. It should bring top dollar."

Colon no longer cared about cargo or the piracy operation or the money. The usefulness of that front was falling away—but there was something aboard that sub that he wanted. "A passenger was taken on during the last stage of the *Heron* operation. What's this man's condition?"

Lorca grunted as if this were an uncomfortable topic. It was his sailors who worked the sub. They hadn't liked being stuck with a hostage for the long journey back. "I'm told he's alive and subdued. Still under the effects of the dust. But if you ask me, he should have been tossed into the sea."

"I want him brought in," Colon said. "Unharmed."

"Martin," Lorca implored. "The captive is an American Intelligence agent. Whatever you're planning—whatever we're about to do here—taking an American hostage is a dangerous idea."

"You'll feel differently once I explain," Colon promised. "Especially as he won't be the last."

Lorca exhaled loudly, but he nodded in acceptance.

With that settled, Colon turned to the one member of the group who wasn't officially a Picador. Thin and gangly, and somewhere in his late thirties, Yago Ortiz was the opposite of the tough older men at the table. If they were the brawn, then he was the brain.

A neuroscientist by training, Yago had been schooled in both Cuba and Russia, working with the FSB and even doing a short stint at a psychiatric hospital in Vladivostok, where convicted political prisoners were subjected to experiments and forms of correction also known as mental torture.

Upon his return to Cuba, Yago had been brought into the Directorate. After working on the directed-energy weapons that caused the well-known Havana Syndrome, he'd ended up in Colon's employ, switching his focus to the more subtle ideas that became the dust and taking a lead role in the experiments at Arcos.

It was Yago's expertise that made it possible for Colon to kill the foreign scientists and take full control of the weapon without worrying that the work would stall.

"The production report," Colon demanded of Yago. "Where are we?"

The scientist cleared his throat. "We have twenty-six thousand pounds of dust stored and ready to use," he announced. "Considering the dispersal patterns, this is enough to cover a small city if released from an altitude of five thousand feet."

The men around the table went from alert to alarmed. The number sounded astronomical. Especially when a tenth of a gram was all they needed to incapacitate a man.

"Thirteen tons?" Ruiz said. "How is this possible? By your own admission this facility creates only a few pounds of material each week."

"That's correct," Colon said. "But I realized this facility could never produce enough dust for a strategic move. To remedy that, I built a larger, more automated facility on Providencia."

Colon was already the leader, but the men around the table

recognized a consolidation of power when they saw it. With the facility on Providencia out of their reach and under his singular control, Colon could not be questioned. He no longer needed them. If he ever really had.

"This was not agreed upon," Ruiz snapped.

"Because it was not necessary for me to seek your approval," Colon replied coldly.

Colon was an expert in the wielding of power. He seldom raised his voice. Preferring to arrange the board in a way that others had no other option but to follow his commands.

Ruiz fumed, but went silent. Perez looked on curiously. Lorca grew nervous. "Is that what we're doing?" he asked. "Attacking a city?"

"If so, it should be Miami," Ruiz suggested, changing his tone suddenly. "To punish the plantation owners and exiles who left our country and keep it in ruins."

Ruiz was such a politician. He even followed the number one rule: No speech in Cuba was worth making if one didn't include a stab at the plantation owners and exiles.

No," Colon told him. "Revenge is for fools and the shortsighted. The pleasure you get is gone in a day. We'll be using the dust for something bigger and more permanent: the complete reversal of the balance between our nation and the United States. With one great stroke we'll force them to end the economic embargo, pay us billions in reparations, and return the land at Guantánamo Bay to our rightful control. All while ensuring that no American force ever sets foot on our soil again."

An eerie silence fell over the room. Achieving just one of those goals would be an impressive victory, but to attain all four at the same time was something far beyond dreaming. It was fantasy.

It fell to Perez to speak up. "Martin," he began softly, "we all commend you for what you've done here. Bringing together those of us who would still fight. Getting us out from under the corruption of the old men in Havana, so we could act unimpeded. Tricking not only our government but also the Iranians, North Koreans, and Americans into thinking the research had been destroyed. Each step of your scheme has been brilliant, planned and executed with your trademark precision. But with all due respect, how on earth do you propose to accomplish these fantastic dreams?"

"By dusting the base at Guantánamo," Colon replied, "and causing the Americans stationed there to attack each other and fight to the death."

This statement caused concern, but it also hit a unique nerve. Knowing what the dust could do placed the idea in the realm of the possible.

"Go on," Perez said.

"As each of you know, Guantánamo Bay has been an American possession since 1903," Colon continued. "Ever since the imperialists forced the colonial government to give up control of the land in perpetuity. While we consider this an illegal agreement that should not be honored, we've never had enough military or diplomatic power to change it. There are, however, two methods spelled out within the treaty by which the Americans would be obliged to legally surrender their claim. The first is by mutual agreement between their government and ours. Something that even your children's children will never live to see."

Nods from around the table told him they agreed with that timeline.

"The second is more direct," Colon said. "It's known as abandonment. In the case of abandonment, all American rights to the land cease to exist. It's my intention to make the Americans abandon Guantánamo, by covering it with a blanket of the dust. Once their personnel have been compromised, we'll broadcast a powerful activation signal from three directions. The Americans on the base will attack each other in an escalating wave of violence, fighting with every weapon they have until very few are left alive."

"And what happens when the Americans strike back?" Perez asked.

"First they must decide who to strike," Colon replied. "Their servicemen will be killing each other. We'll merely be standing by, watching from outside the gates, as we always have. Eventually—when enough carnage has occurred—we'll broadcast a new signal that urges the few survivors to flee—the fight reflex changed to flight. Of course, we'll assist this departure, providing ferries across the bay and opening travel corridors around the base. It's the 'humanitarian' thing to do. And then, with the base all but empty, our men will move in, clear out the holdovers, and raise the Cuban flag over what will now legally qualify as abandoned property."

Lorca responded this time. His fear growing with every nervous heartbeat. It wasn't the power of the dust he doubted, but Colon's paper-thin reasoning about what would happen afterward.

"Whether they can prove it or not," he said, "the Americans will wake up the next morning and assume we are complicit. We might hold the base for twenty-four hours before Tomahawk missiles rain down on us like a plague from the heavens. You risk us all."

"I'm well aware of what the American military can do," Colon said. "They've spilled my family's blood for three generations. I promise you, in this case they'll be prevented from acting."

"By what?"

Colon lowered the boom. "By our possession of an American ballistic missile submarine and all the city-killing warheads it carries. A vessel that I will secure and control personally."

Ruiz had heard enough. He stood angrily. His face red. "Are you insane?" he shouted. "You're inviting not just missile strikes, but a full-fledged American invasion and the distinct possibility of Armageddon for our island. They will burn us to a cinder for this."

"Not unless they wish to be burned in response," Colon replied. His words were icily calm. "Have you never wondered why they treat us so harshly, but avoid North Korea and speak endlessly about striking a deal with Iran? The reason for this is simple, those countries possess nuclear weapons and that evens the score for them. Once a nation enters that club no one can threaten or abuse them the way we've been threatened and abused for half a century."

Colon looked around the table. The logic of his appeal seemed to be working.

"Trust me," he continued. "With this submarine in our hands, there will be no invasion, no Tomahawk missile strikes, nothing to hint at Armageddon. The Americans understand better than anyone what their missiles can do. Once we prove to them that the submarine is in our possession, they will negotiate in private. The embargo will be removed under the threat of our transferring the submarine to Russia or China. Reparations will be paid in exchange for return of the missiles, one per year, until the payments are complete—with three missiles to be maintained by our nation as a deterrent against any future American aggression. This will take place over a period of decades and by the time it's complete, our country will be remade."

Explained this way it almost sounded reasonable. At least Perez seemed to think so. He sat back in his chair looking smug, like a gambler who'd bet everything and was pleased with the card he'd drawn.

Lorca danced with his fears for a moment, but could only nod. He was a follower at heart.

Yago bit at the cuticle of one finger, reeling from the magnitude of what was being discussed and focusing on his own part in the tale.

He considered objecting—not for moral reasons, but out of fear—but what would be the point? He had no vote, nor anything approaching power. He wasn't a true member of the Picadors. Just their technician. Beyond that, it was too late now anyway. The dust was already made and stored, the process automated and industrialized.

The fact was, they no longer needed him. He held silent and hoped Colon wouldn't suddenly look at him as expendable.

Only Ruiz remained at odds with the idea. He'd gained much since leaving the Directorate. He had power, prestige, influence. He was a celebrity of sorts, being groomed to be a popular leader. The old men liked being seen with a young virile newcomer. And those beneath him looked up to him worshipfully.

His easy life and his future political ambitions would go up in smoke if things went sideways. Which meant he could see the downside to this plan much more clearly than the up. He glared across the table at Colon. "And what if you fail?"

Colon understood the question. Only fools didn't plan for the possibility of failure. "If *we* fail, then the old men on the council who you've infected will take the fall. They'll confess to the conspiracy and shoulder the blame. After a trial, the party will have them executed for endangering Cuba."

None of them believed that would be the end of it if Colon failed, but every Picador must risk being thrown from his horse or trampled by the bull.

"But *when* we succeed," Colon continued, looking directly at Ruiz, "you will claim the credit and become the unquestioned favorite for the position of first secretary. In due time, you will run Cuba."

Left unsaid was the fact that Colon would run Ruiz, much the same way as he manipulated Solari.

Ruiz brightened. The upside of the equation suddenly became more obvious. And while he didn't exactly jump for joy at the revelation, the idea soaked into him, affecting him slowly like an intoxicating beverage. As Colon had rightly predicted, Ruiz would not risk everything for Cuba, but he was willing to risk Cuba for himself.

"I require a vote," Colon said. "It must be unanimous."

"I'm for it," Perez announced without delay. "It's time to act decisively."

"I'm for it also," Lorca added less convincingly. "It is written that we must risk much to gain much. So be it."

Ruiz hesitated, but only for effect. He was hooked and Colon knew it. "I concur," Ruiz said boldly, as if he were the decision-maker. "Proceed with your plan."

Colon would have done so anyway, but this way he didn't have to kill his partners to do it. He offered them his thanks.

With the vote taken and the path set, the Picadors began to disband for what might be the last time. One by one they said their goodbyes and went out the door.

When they were gone, only Yago, the neuroscientist, remained. He came up to Colon, fidgeting and nervous, pale as a ghost.

He leaned in close. "I certainly have no say in the matter," he whispered. "But to take over an American submarine requires getting the dust inside. We would have to catch one running on the surface, hatches open and vents pumping fresh air into the hull. This is a very rare occurrence. It happens only within a few miles of their coastline, near their most heavily armed bases, under sight of helicopters and fighter jets. I don't see how we could get within miles of one. Let alone get the dust inside."

Colon grinned and spoke confidently. "Leave that to me."

23

NUMA HEADQUARTERS
WASHINGTON, D.C.

Rudi Gunn entered the high-tech wing of NUMA headquarters in search of Hiram Yaeger. He found him in front of a computer screen in a darkened room, doing some coding on a new program.

Yaeger was NUMA's resident computer genius and the head of the Information Services division. He was also a pioneer in the field of voice-activated systems and other advanced interfaces. To find him tapping away at a keyboard in front of a boxy, squared-shaped monitor in a beige plastic case was like stepping back in time.

"Rebelling against the metaverse?" Rudi asked.

"Not at all," Yaeger said. "Max," he called out, speaking to the supercomputer he'd designed and updated over the years, "restore normal lighting."

As the lights came up, the computer monitor, the wall decorations, and the stacks of equipment around them disappeared. They were standing in a hologram chamber. The only items that were made of solid molecules were the desk, chair, and keyboard. Even a picture of Yaeger's wife in a fancy frame vanished from its spot on the desk.

"I can create whatever reality I want in here," Yaeger said. "That was a replica of my first office at NUMA, right down to the push-button phone and the dial-up internet station. But with a word I can change this into a lovely forest . . ."

As Yaeger spoke, the room turned green, with trees soaring all around them. The sound of birds chirping and the slight rush of a breeze through the leaves up above was so real it was disorienting.

"Or say I want to go for a walk and gaze at the Smithsonian . . ."

The room changed again. Suddenly they were standing in the center of the Washington Mall, not far from where Rudi had entered the Metro station. Only, it was clear and sunny in the holographic chamber.

"Or," Rudi suggested, "you could go for a walk in an actual forest or wander over to the real Smithsonian on your lunch break."

"Sure," Yaeger said. "But who has the time?"

That, Rudi thought, was a problem for another day. He pulled up a chair, making sure it was real before he sat down. "Did you get Kurt's message from last night?"

"About the *Heron* towing something?"

Rudi nodded. "Anything?"

"We processed a number of satellite images from the area. Nothing sharp enough to get a definitive identification, but the freighter had something tucked in behind her for about twelve hours."

"Could it be a Chinese spy ship disguised as a trawler?"

"It wasn't displaying a banner announcing that to the world," Yaeger said. "But the size and shape fit the profile."

"Kurt thinks it went down. Sunk deliberately during or after the drone attack."

"From the timing of the images, I'd have to agree. It shows up on the satellite feeds until about half an hour before the *Edison* arrives. At which point it's nowhere to be found."

"Can you give me a location?"

"An approximate one," Yaeger said.

"How tight?"

"Based on the wind and the currents, I've narrowed it down to a cone of about nine square miles to search."

"A cone?"

"The farther you get away from the last confirmed spot the wider the set of factors determining its ultimate resting place becomes," Yaeger explained. "It's not a large area, though. I was just about to send Kurt the data."

"Send it to me first," Rudi replied, standing. "I need to think this through one more time before we go all ahead flank speed."

"Will do," Yaeger said. "Anything else?"

"Kurt and Joe ran into an officer from Naval Intelligence down there. She's hunting the same thing we are. She uploaded a fair amount of data on the drone sightings. I need you to run the data and look for a pattern. Anything that would suggest who might be behind the attacks and how they're accomplished."

"Why is she sending it to us?"

"Let's just say, she has her reasons."

Yaeger didn't need more than that. "Max and I will get to work on it. I'll let you know if we find anything."

"When you find something," Rudi corrected.

"Your confidence is inspiring."

Rudi turned to go. "Just one way of creating my own reality."

24

Hiram Yaeger brought Max online and uploaded the data he'd received from Kurt. Commander Wells had documented fifty-nine attacks or incidents around the world. Dates, times, and local weather patterns were factored in. Shipping lines, crew rosters, cargo manifests, and other pertinent items were entered for analysis.

"Got all that?" Yaeger asked aloud.

"It was a simple process," Max replied. "Barely worth engaging my main processor for."

Yaeger chuckled. Max had her own AI system and had developed her own personality over the years. Forced to describe it, Yaeger would have said she was very proud of herself. And why shouldn't she be? Max was among the five most powerful computer systems in the world. Coupled with Yaeger's unique method of programming and the well-developed AI system that was hers and hers alone, Max was officially more valuable than any five of NUMA's most advanced ships put together.

"Well," Yaeger said. "You might want to limber up for this next part or you might sprain an algorithm or something. I need you to cross-reference the data for patterns and correlations. To do that, you'll need to tap into every public and private database we have access to and—"

"Correlation detected," Max announced, cutting him off.

"You might have let me finish explaining first," Yaeger said. "But go ahead with your initial finding."

"All attacks occurred at sea," Max replied.

Yaeger wasn't sure if this was a joke or not. Max did have a sense of humor, but it was also a fact he hadn't told her to ignore. "As these are oceangoing freighters," Yaeger said, "that's not a big surprise."

Max began listing additional findings. "All attacks happened in international waters. All incidents happened during periods of average or better visibility. With the exception of the *Heron* incident, all attacks occurred at least two hundred miles from any landmass."

That was slightly more useful, but also something that could have been gleaned from a quick glance at the map. "Maybe I gave you too broad of an instruction."

Max continued, unwilling to be interrupted. "All attacks happened during good weather conditions," she announced. "Sea states of three or better. Winds less than fifteen knots. Roughly two-thirds of the attacks happened at dusk or later. In no case was there a significant storm or cyclone within five hundred miles of the location."

"Any link between the shipping lines, cargoes, or crews?"

Max took a few seconds. That was a lot of data to cross-reference. "No statistically significant connection between personnel or corporate entities. No discernable pattern to ports of departure, ports of arrival, or pirated cargo."

"Really?" Yaeger asked. "Kurt described the stolen cargoes as high value."

"Kurt is mistaken," she said assuredly. "Some of the cargoes were high-value. Others would be of little value on the black market. In four cases, the attacks did not result in missing cargoes. Only missing crew."

That sounded odd to Yaeger. "Really?"

"I'm not programmed to deceive."

"Let's be thankful for small blessings," Yaeger replied before switching subjects. "I want to focus on possible sources of attack. Drones can only fly so far. Since we already know that the attacks happened far from any landmass, we should look at shipping. Compare data regarding the positions of both naval and civilian vessels within drone range of the targeted ships."

"What range?"

"Let's go out to a hundred miles."

"Accessing data from around the world," Max said. "Please stand by."

Time began to pass without any quick answers. "This is not like you," Yaeger said. "What's taking so long?"

"I'm accessing data from nineteen different systems around the world," Max explained. "Marine traffic reporting systems, published and unpublished military position reports, known and suspected submarine movements based on sonar readings reported from our own buoy system, and the U.S. Navy shared-information network. Some of these systems are streaming the data on low bandwidth channels."

"In other words, it's them, not you."

"Precisely."

Another few seconds passed. "Dataset complete," Max said.

"Let's have it."

"Dataset is negative," she concluded. "There's no discernable link between the drone activity and the movement of known surface or submerged vessels."

No wonder the Navy brass thought Commander Wells was tilting at windmills. He decided to ask a catchall and have Max put her AI system to work. "At this point I need you to search for anything you can find that might lead us in the right direction and let me know what it is. However absurd."

Yaeger sat quietly, wondering if he should turn the hologram back on as Max went back to computing. After several minutes Max announced a positive finding. "One statistically significant correlation detected."

"And that is?"

"Eighty-six percent of the attacks happened within two hundred miles of a travel corridor being used by the Ostrom Airship Corporation. In forty-one percent of the attacks, an Ostrom craft can be confirmed within ninety miles of the targeted vessel prior to the start of the incident."

"Ostrom Airship," Yaeger said, racking his brain. "The one that transports high-value cargo across the oceans?"

"Precisely," Max said. "Ostrom is named after a hot humid wind coming from the south. Take a look."

Max turned the hologram back on and ran an advertisement for Ostrom Airship that had been used during a fundraising session. It showed a sleek yellow and blue craft the size of an ocean liner cruising above a city. The next shot cut to a video of passengers inside looking down on the skyscrapers. A follow-on vignette showed the craft landing and then disgorging freight by the ton, including a small fleet of gleaming cars and trucks, just to show how much it could carry.

As these scenes played, commentary in the background described the capabilities of the airship. It was being touted as both a luxury transport equal to any five-star ocean liner and a swift and powerful freighter, capable of ending supply chain bottlenecks, as it could haul two thousand tons of cargo—more than what fourteen fully loaded 747s could carry—across the Pacific in just three days. Making the journey in one-tenth the time it would take an oceangoing freighter.

"For high-value cargoes that need to be delivered just in time," the announcer explained, "there is simply no better option than the Mark One airship from Ostrom Airship Corporation."

The advertisement ended and the room returned to normal.

Yaeger had heard of Ostrom and their high-tech versions of the old German zeppelins. He considered the engineering interesting, but hadn't paid much attention to the company. What he did know was that they started with a couple billion dollars in venture capital, burned through that pretty quickly, and then got a huge second round of funding, which he assumed they were going through now. The economics of an airship line were tough to pull off, even with modern aircraft and government subsidies.

"Show me the route map," Yaeger said.

A world map appeared with routes crisscrossing five continents and both the Atlantic and Pacific. Many of them converging on Providencia Island in the Caribbean, about two hundred miles north of Panama, where Ostrom operated a freight hub, like the famous FedEx hub in Memphis.

As Yaeger understood it, the airships traveled to Providencia from all over world, landed to off-load their cargoes and take on other shipments for travel to distant shores. The hub was supposed to be the key to profitability that had not yet materialized. It was also served by a number of ships and propeller-driven cargo aircraft, enhancing the delivery and transport routes.

"Show me the locations of the known and suspected drone attacks," Yaeger said.

A smattering of orange dots appeared on the map. The travel corridors straddled the blinking marks with significant accuracy. Even without the statistical calculations Yaeger could see the connection.

Still, correlation did not prove causation.

"Why would a company worth billions of dollars be involved with what are, by comparison, penny-ante piracy jobs?"

Max sighed audibly. "As humans run the corporation, the answer to that query lies somewhere in the realm of human psychology and decision-making. Subjects that continue to baffle me and defy any form of logical understanding."

"It was a rhetorical question," Yaeger explained. "But your response is no different than mine, most days. Thanks for your help. I think we may be getting somewhere."

25

Paul Trout stood six foot eight, a height that made it easy to see over crowds and difficult to squeeze into compact cars. He'd spent his formative years near Cape Cod before studying ocean sciences at the Scripps Institution of Oceanography. Which is also where he met the woman of his dreams, a tall and athletic spitfire named Gamay Morgan, who became his lab partner, his best friend, and then his wife.

Together Paul and Gamay had joined NUMA and since then had been a crucial part of its scientific investigations. Not once during that time had either of them been asked to handle an administrative task, like budgeting or logistics or purchasing. Now, sitting in the comfortable oversized chairs in Rudi Gunn's office, the two of them listened to details of their new assignment with skeptical ears and furrowed brows.

"We've been transferred?" Paul asked.

"To purchasing," Rudi said.

"As in shopping for supplies and arranging deliveries?"

"There's going to be more to it than that," Rudi replied with a hint of conspiracy in his eyes.

Noting the twinkle, Paul held back, but Gamay didn't see it and let him have it with both barrels.

"Rudi, we're scientists," she reminded him—both of them had PhDs. "We belong in the field doing hands-on work, not behind a desk pushing paper around."

Gamay was the more vocal one of the two, less able to hide her emotions. Paul put that down to an upbringing where she was forced to keep up with the boys in her neighborhood, playing sports and dealing with the constant waves of competition and jockeying for position among a group of young men filled with testosterone.

Paul, on the other hand, had rarely ever been challenged, probably because of his height and size. And as a result, he grew up with the reputation of a gentle giant. Paul considered the description to be accurate. He couldn't remember the last time he'd truly raised his voice.

From across the desk, Rudi focused on Gamay. He seemed to be enjoying this. "Someone has to shuffle the paper around," he said, moving a stack of files from one side of his desk to the other. "Besides, it's a promotion. Paul is going to be elevated to the newly created position of executive director of Alternative Vehicles Procurement and you've been promoted to assistant director."

Her eyes narrowed on Rudi, a withering stare that Paul had endured too many times to count. "I'm not sure I like being the assistant."

Rudi shrugged. "In that case, you can be the boss. And Paul can be your assistant."

Gamay sat back as if that was more acceptable, but she now saw that Rudi was toying with them.

With Paul looking on and suppressing a grin, Gamay folded her arms across her chest and continued to glare at Rudi. "Okay, what's the real story here? Aside from the fact that I've never heard of either position, what do Paul or I know about procurement? Or alternative vehicles for that matter. We still drive a Humvee."

Rudi's stern face cracked, and a broad grin appeared. "All of that is noted, but I need you to learn enough to fake it in the next twenty-four hours, because I'm sending you to Rio on a business trip."

Paul found himself suddenly more interested. "Rio? As in de Janeiro?"

"Is there any other Rio worth mentioning?"

Gamay laughed. "Hold on, Paul. Something tells me we're not going to be on the Copacabana sunning ourselves and admiring the women in Tangas and the men in their Speedos."

"I'll pass on the Speedos," Paul said. "And in all honesty, I might burst into flames if I sat on a beach for any length of time."

As a New Englander, Paul loved the fog and gloom. While out in San Diego he'd preferred it when the marine layer hung around all day rather than burning off.

"You are looking more pale than usual," Rudi said.

"Been up in Newfoundland doing some research," Paul replied. "Nothing but overcast for three straight weeks. Just glorious."

"Well, you'll need to pack your best sunblock," Rudi said. "You'll be meeting with a man named Stefano Solari. He runs the Ostrom Airship Corporation. He's probably going to want to show you around during daylight hours."

Paul's eyes lit up when he heard the name. "Meeting Solari would be incredible. The man is a genius."

"You've heard of him?" Rudi asked.

"Of course. He's like Richard Branson and Elon Musk all rolled into one. With a solid helping of South American flair added for good measure."

"You might not know this," Gamay said to Rudi, "but Paul has been obsessed with blimps since he was a teenager."

Paul cleared his throat loudly. "Excuse me, but a blimp is a structureless, nonrigid vessel that inevitably ends up shaped like a bulging sausage and is best used to waddle around in the sky above sporting events. Airships are rigidly structured machines the size of ocean liners. They mesh artistic design with the limits of engineering to produce a vessel as elegant as any classic seafaring ship. The wrongly maligned *Hindenburg* and venerable *Graf Zeppelin* traveled the world for years without incident, while the average propeller-driven airplane of the time lasted less than four months before being involved in a fatal crash."

"You've hit a nerve," Gamay advised.

"And found the right man for the job," Rudi added. "Which is good, because your assignment is to go meet with Solari and enter negotiations to buy one of their airships for NUMA."

Paul and Gamay were temporarily struck silent. Rudi let them off the hook.

"It's the only way we could get you a meeting and arrange for you to poke around their production facilities."

"In search of what?" Gamay asked.

"Drones," Rudi said. "And not your run-of-the-mill drones either."

He slid a pair of folders toward them. Each contained a breakdown of everything that had been learned so far. Up front was an artist's rendering of a full-sized drone based on the fragment that had been found in the sea. It looked like a brilliantly lit donut with a single, massive propeller fan in the opening at the center. The estimated size was that of a compact car.

As they studied the reports, Rudi went on to explain what Kurt and Joe had been through since the distress call from the *Heron* and why they were acting so surreptitiously.

"This is a little out of the norm for us," he explained. "But if we can get enough information, we can crystallize the threat for the Navy and turn the matter back over to them."

"Are you suggesting Solari is behind these attacks?" Paul asked, looking crestfallen.

"Could be," Rudi said. "Although, I must admit, a motive escapes us at the moment. Bottom line: no one knows what the connection is and I'm counting on you two to figure it out."

While Paul wasn't exactly excited by the idea of playing spy, he was thrilled to get a look at the Ostrom facilities close up. In some ways this was a chance to play out a childhood fantasy. Who knows, he might even get to ride in one of the great airships.

He wondered if Gamay was sharing his enthusiasm and looked her way. Despite giving Rudi the third degree, she was energized by the challenge. It was like she was back on the field with all the boys who thought they could run faster or throw the ball harder. Just another chance to prove herself.

"And if these guys get suspicious?" Gamay asked.

"You're going down there on an official invite," Rudi said. "That should keep you out of danger."

"Might as well make the best of it," Paul said. "I'll pack my sunblock, my tuxedo, and favorite bow ties."

"Might want to bring something more lethal," Gamay replied. "I have a feeling sunburn isn't the only thing we'll have to worry about."

26

RIO DE JANEIRO, BRAZIL

Paul and Gamay flew into Rio on a Gulfstream G650 painted in the NUMA color scheme. The American-made private jet had the largest cabin and the most room of any private aircraft in the world, something Paul certainly appreciated. Even then, he had to lower his head to avoid bumping it on the ceiling when standing up.

The long journey had given both him and Gamay plenty of time to research Ostrom Airship and the company's enigmatic CEO and majority owner. Stefano Solari was a handsome man with a full head of wavy, graying hair. He tended to wear expensive sport jackets, off-the-rack blue jeans, and crisp designer shirts, usually with two buttons open and fairly often in the bright yellow or verdant green found on the Brazilian flag.

Like so many modern CEOs he was part businessman, part salesman, and part celebrity. He'd dated several Brazilian fashion models and at least one Hollywood actress and had once been a constant presence on social media and Brazilian TV. Though from what Gamay had found, that presence had been scaled back to almost nothing over the past few years.

"Typical outgoing, optimistic captain of industry," she concluded.

It was a character Solari must have played well. Ostrom Airship Corporation had drawn several billion dollars of investment from around the world and had launched the first international airship service in nearly a hundred years.

"Did you know," Paul asked, "that Solari was born into a wealthy family, but shunned the money and joined the Brazilian air force at seventeen instead? And that he put himself through engineering school while serving?"

"I read that this morning," Gamay replied without looking up.

Undaunted Paul began again. "Did you know that the original airship design he came up with has been nominated for a Queen Elizabeth Prize for Engineering for all the advancements that he incorporated?"

She continued to study the documents in front of her. "I read that while we were waiting for the plane."

Paul narrowed his gaze as if trying to think of a fact that might surprise her. "Did you know that after a decade in the aviation industry, Solari decided to strike out on his own and quickly made himself into an international tycoon building composite fuselage sections for other manufacturers? And that he arrived on the world's list of billionaires by the time he was forty?"

This time Gamay looked up, cutting her eyes at him. "Are you going to fanboy over Solari the whole time we're down there?"

Paul grinned and shook his head. "Not if I get it all out now."

She took that with a grain of salt and asked a question of her own. "Did you know that Solari slipped off the list of billionaires three years ago when Ostrom Airship almost went bankrupt?"

Paul cocked his head. "I did not. What happened?"

She was looking over a piece in *Forbes* magazine. "Production delays with the first airship, a fire in the maintenance hangar, and an accounting scandal all in one year. With nearly seven hundred and fifty million dollars in loans due and no more room on his line of credit, the vultures were circling."

"What happened?"

"He went to New York to beg and plead for an extension. After a weekend of fevered discussions, he left with an extension on the debt payments and an additional billion dollars in funding."

"That's a neat trick," Paul said. "I can't even get the electric company to waive the late fee when you forget to make the payment."

Gamay offered a sideways glance. "I thought you were in charge of the electric bill?"

"I am now."

She looked back to her reading, a coy smile on her face. "Then my plan worked."

"To a T."

The Gulfstream G650 landed at Rio's Tom Jobim International Airport on Governador Island, which was separated from the rest of the city by a narrow strip of water. After a short taxi, the aircraft parked in an out-of-the-way corner and the door opened to a hot and hazy morning.

Gamay found the exit first, pulling on a pair of sunglasses and feeling the humidity on her skin as she stood at the top of the stairs. The more famous sights of Rio were blocked by the airport terminals, but she could see across the bay to Ilha da Prata, the artificial island where Solari had set up shop to build his massive machines.

From where Gamay stood, the production facility looked like several football stadiums had been constructed side by side and joined together. Most of the building was painted white, but broad yellow and blue stripes swirled across the upper half and the Ostrom name and logo were emblazoned in a font so large that each one used over a thousand gallons of paint.

Paul joined her on the stairs, and they made their way to the bottom as a strange-looking vehicle drove up to the parked aircraft.

They'd been told a car would meet them, but this contraption was not the limousine with tinted windows they'd been expecting. It looked more like an open-topped bus, but sporting an arrow-shaped front, a boattail stern, and large, oddly protruding wheels.

The man at the controls was none other than Solari himself, tanned and grinning, dressed much as he'd been described, though without the sport coat. He pulled in beside the NUMA jet, parked the bus, and lowered a ramp of his own.

Bounding down the ramp like a triumphant warrior, he called out to Paul and Gamay. "Hello to my esteemed visitors," he said in accented English. "Welcome to Rio. City of Dreams."

Neither Paul nor Gamay knew what to say.

"Thank you," Gamay mustered. "We weren't expecting to see you until this afternoon."

"Of course," Solari replied. "That was, in fact, the plan. But I was so excited to take your visit, I simply had to come pick you up myself."

He stepped toward Gamay with his arms held wide, inviting her into a hug, but she had already stuck out a hand. After a moment of awkwardness, he gave in and shook her hand with both of his. The grip was firm and confident without the common attempt made by many to crush their opposite's fingers in an odd display of strength.

"We're glad to be here as well," Gamay said.

Paul shook Solari's hand next. "And we're looking forward to discussing how an airship might fit into NUMA's needs," he added, sounding as official as possible, before pointing at the strange-looking vehicle. "But first I have to ask: What exactly is this thing?"

"Aqua Bus," Solari said proudly. "Amphibious transportation for the masses. Very good for cities with crowded streets but wide-open rivers and bays. You could take this to New Jersey and drive across the Hudson without using a bridge or tunnel and then head right down Fifth Avenue without missing a beat."

"We do have ferries for some of that," Paul noted.

"Yes, of course," Solari said. "But ferries require cruise terminals, and piers, and parking, not to mention endless hours loading and unloading, sitting there idle with engines burning diesel and fouling the air. The Aqua Bus is battery-powered, fits most city streets, and needs only a standard boat ramp to get in and out of the water."

He grinned infectiously. "I tell you, these are going to be very handy in the future, once climate change really kicks in. Flooded streets because of a high tide, no problem. Central Park becomes Central Lake, no problem. If I was mayor of Miami, or Amsterdam, or Bangkok, I'd order a thousand of them today. Just to beat the rush."

Paul laughed and nodded. Gamay could only smile. The effervescent CEO was everything he'd been described as, part huckster, part genius. "Well," she said, "NUMA might be interested in picking up a few of these as well."

"Once you see it in action, you're going to . . . How do you say it . . . fall head over heels?"

"Something like that," Gamay replied.

He led them toward the Aqua Bus. "Anyway, come aboard."

"Are you taking us to the hotel in this?"

"The hotel can wait," Solari said. "I'm taking you over to Ilha da Prata. We're doing some final work on the *Condor*, the newest and most luxurious of my airships. She's going up for a test flight this afternoon. I want you to join me on board."

That was music to Paul's ears. Christmas, Easter, and a twenty-first birthday all rolled into one. He lifted their suitcases from the tarmac with instant enthusiasm. "We'd love to join you."

Gamay didn't contradict him, but she would have preferred he not jump at the chance so obviously.

They climbed aboard the Aqua Bus and stored their luggage before taking seats up front. Solari sat in the driver's seat, while a man they hadn't noticed before sat in the back row. From his conservative clothes, mirrored sunglasses, and the complete lack of interaction with anyone or anything, Paul figured him for a close protection agent or body-guard.

Putting the bus in gear with the click of a button, Solari maneuvered it using virtual controls on a large touch screen in front of him, manipulating the image of a steering wheel and adjusting a throttle by hand.

The Aqua Bus picked up speed in a silky-smooth manner, not lurching or swaying like the average city bus.

Paul stood and found he didn't even have to hold on. "Smooth."

"I manipulate the throttle," Solari said, "but the computer does the actual accelerating. It's designed to pick up speed very slowly at first and then slightly faster with each passing instant. Instead of jerking free from inertia we ease away from it casually. A far more sophisticated way to make an exit, don't you agree?"

Paul nodded. Gamay was too taken by the scene to respond. Especially as the Aqua Bus continued toward the edge of the airport and down a ramp that led into the bay. As the arrow-like nose entered the water, the bus began to float. Momentum carried it from the ramp, the wheels folded in, and a water jet housed in a tunnel where the transaxle would have been on a regular bus began to thrum. Before long, the Aqua Bus was crossing the bay at a relatively sprightly ten knots.

As they cruised the still waters, the massive buildings housing the production facility loomed ever larger.

"I had to build them out here on pontoons and a small spit of reclaimed land," Solari explained. "I wanted the people of Rio to see our buildings and be proud of what we're doing, but I didn't want to knock anyone's house down to put up the factory or to build on the wetlands north of here, as some suggested. So, we made our own island. It has many advantages, of course. Not the least of which is, large parts can be brought in by ship. And then there's security. After the fire a few years back, I wanted to be somewhere that was more inaccessible."

"Was the fire not an accident?" Gamay asked.

"Not unless you call sabotage an accident," Solari said. "Someone was trying to stop me from launching the first ship."

"Did you ever find out who?"

He shook his head. "Don't worry, though. I've brought in our new security team. Since then, we've never had another problem."

Paul and Gamay exchanged a look. Solari's voice suddenly carried an ominous tone. Completely opposite to his earlier, jaunty manner.

They arrived beside the production facility and angled toward the far end, approaching a building labeled FAB-1. A set of doors large enough to allow the airship in and out were closed, but a smaller portal was open, and the Aqua Bus cruised through it.

Arriving inside the giant structure was an experience that struck many people silent. Paul and Gamay were no exception. The roof soared three hundred feet above them, held in place by thin, curving ribs, but defying gravity due to a thousand rectangular gas cells filled with helium. The same technology that allowed the huge airships to rise made it possible to build them beneath a ceiling that was lighter than air.

As Paul and Gamay gawked at the ceiling, their eyes adjusted to the lower level of light. Suddenly they realized that the central part of the building was occupied by the gleaming shape of Solari's newest airship, the *Condor*.

From this angle they could see only its wide and smiling face. But even so, the craft was so large, and the front rounded in such a manner, that it was hard to understand the perspective until Solari eased the Aqua Bus to one side and the incredible length of the *Condor* began to come into view. It seemed to stretch on forever, the exterior illuminated by a combination of skylights in the ceiling and rows of floodlights along the hangar walls.

Though Paul had spent years studying the airships of the bygone era, he was overwhelmed by the moment. "It's incredible," he said reverently.

They continued down the starboard side, moving beneath its curved overhanging hull. Instead of a tube shape like the old zeppelins, the *Condor* was designed with a wider and flatter shape. It had a V-shaped underside, made of aluminum and capable of flotation. In fact, the craft was sitting on the water now.

A section of forward-canted windows and a slight bulge under the chin revealed the bridge of the airship, with two levels of open-air balconies along the side, and several rows of windows looked disproportionally tiny, even though they were floor-to-ceiling glass.

Despite her previous eye-rolling, Gamay was dumbstruck as well. When she finally spoke, all she could manage was a whisper. "I feel like I'm looking at a ship designed to explore the stars."

"I leave that to other billionaires," Solari said, laughing at his own joke.

As they continued along the side, a smattering of workmen could be seen here and there: nothing more than tiny figures in bright vests, some of them suspended on roped platforms from the ceiling of the hangar, like window washers on the side of a skyscraper.

Passing the first quarter of the ship, they came to the cavernous air intakes, one on either side and each as large as the entrance to a highway tunnel.

"Is that where the engines are?" Paul asked.

"No," Solari said. "The power plant is deep within. We use huge, electrically controlled impeller fans. They're centered amidships and down low for stability. A series of ducts run through the ship in all directions. During normal flight we direct the exhaust air out the stern for propulsion, but any time we need to we can divert thrust into vertical exhaust vents for additional lift or through numerous vents and exhaust ports along the sides. Something like your bow and stern thrusters, but much more precise. I'm not boasting when I tell you the *Condor* has fifty-two different exhaust ports and a computer-controlled stabilization system that keeps it in perfect trim despite updrafts, downdrafts, and crosswinds."

"Surely you have issues with wind," Gamay said. "Even skyscrapers bend in strong gusts."

Solari shrugged the idea off. "We don't plan to operate in hurricanes, of course. And with a top speed of nearly one hundred and fifty knots, we can outrun and avoid any storm in the world, but with her nose into the wind the *Condor* is rock steady."

"What about takeoff and landing?"

"Whenever we conduct operations near the ground—takeoffs, landings, low-level scenic passes, for example—we launch a small fleet of drones that spread out around the craft in an orbit of several hundred feet. These sense the changes in wind and transmit that information to the ship instantly, allowing the airship's propulsion and stability system to react by opening and closing appropriate vents, before the actual gust of wind hits the ship. The *Condor* anticipates rather than reacts. A much more effective way to maintain its stability."

Paul was impressed by the technology, but Solari mentioning drones brought him back to the reason for their trip. A look from Gamay told him she was on the same page.

"You launch the drones from the airship?"

"Yes," Solari said eagerly. "We have a spacious hangar bay in the stern."

"How many drones do you carry?"

"Several dozen, of different types," Solari replied. "The navigation drones I just mentioned. Also, a set of scout drones we send out to take video of things our passengers might want to see along the way. Pods of whales breaching, herds of animals on the Serengeti, things like that. It's an incredible feeling to drift over the savanna like a silent cloud while you watch a hundred elephants wander beneath you or a family of giraffes racing like sailboats across the grasslands."

"It does sound incredible," Gamay admitted.

"Then there are the shuttle drones," Solari replied. "Large enough to pick up supplies and even passengers from down on terra firma. No reason to land the ship every time someone wants to come aboard. Or when you run out of coffee or whipped cream. Which never happens on my watch."

It made sense, Paul thought. Plenty of supplies were delivered to ships at anchor by smaller vessels. Why should an airship operate any differently? More important, it made him wonder if Rudi had been wrong when he suggested that a drone couldn't lift a cargo container from a pirated ship. "That's just the type of capability NUMA would be interested in," he said, jumping back into the role of purchasing director. "Can you include the drones and the launch bay on the tour?"

"Of course," Solari said proudly. "There's not an inch of the *Condor* that I won't show you." He held his arms wide to indicate the vastness of the airship, then added slyly, "but I think you'll need more than an afternoon to explore it all."

Once again Solari laughed at his own joke. Paul laughed along with him.

"Maybe we could just hit the highlights," Gamay suggested.

The Aqua Bus was finally nearing the midpoint of the airship, where a set of lengthy pontoons extended from the underside of the craft and into the water. The pontoons acted as a combination outrigger and landing gear, which allowed the *Condor* to sit stably on the bay.

Solari guided Aqua Bus between the extended pontoon and the hull of the craft like he was easing into a slip in some marina. He bumped against a lowered platform with only the slightest thump.

A pair of Ostrom crewmen secured the bus to the dock. Behind them stood a welcoming committee. A dark-haired man in a black suit, a stocky engineer wearing a hard hat, and a man in short sleeves with rectangular glasses on his face.

Solari seemed less than pleased to have encountered them. He turned to Paul and Gamay. "These are some of my employees," he said. He directed their attention to the man in black. "Martin Colon, our vice president of cargo operations and head of security. Luis Torres, one of our finest engineers. And . . ." For a moment Solari drew a blank. He knew he'd seen the man before, but wasn't sure where.

"Yago Ortiz," Colon reminded him.

"Of course, now I remember, he's a consultant who works with Señor Colon."

Hands were shook, pleasantries exchanged.

Solari turned his attention back to Colon. "Surprised to see you here, Martin. To what do I owe the pleasure?"

"Do you think I would miss the launch of our newest ship?" Colon asked.

"You've missed the last three," Solari said.

"This one is different," Colon replied. "The *Condor* is the largest and the fastest, and we have nearly a thousand tons of freight going on board along with some important passengers. Unfortunately," he added, "I've been given some bad news."

He turned to Torres. "I'm sorry, Señor Solari, but we cannot approve a test flight today. Our preflight inspection revealed a crack in the number three impeller disk. It has to be replaced. If we're to operate it in this condition it could break apart under stress."

"I'm well aware of what could happen," Solari snapped. "I designed the system. Where are we on a replacement? Even if we skip today's flight, we're scheduled to begin the goodwill tour tomorrow."

Torres glanced at Colon and then looked back at Solari. "The foreman says he can get the broken impeller out and the new one seated tonight. But it won't be operational right away. You'll have to take off with three-quarters power."

Solari did the calculations in his head. "Three-quarters should be plenty. We're only taking a half load of passengers and the show cargo. What are we hauling this time?"

"Robotics for a factory being built in California."

Solari seemed less than impressed. He loved the idea of a world-class ocean liner plowing the skies. He would have preferred they keep the freight-hauling news to industry gatherings.

He sighed. "Even in the beginning of aviation it was like this. Passengers got the headlines, but the airlines made all their money by carrying the mail."

True or not, Gamay was more concerned about the sudden change of plans. She found it all too convenient, a neat way to promise them access and then keep them off the airship all the same. "Looks like we won't get a chance to fly with you after all," she said, sounding dejected. "We could still use a tour."

"Nonsense," the flamboyant executive insisted. "You'll join me on the goodwill tour as my personal guests. We're traveling from here to Providencia before heading across Central America and over to San Diego. I can drop you there if you like, or you can switch airships in Providencia and journey with me all the way to Paris. But only if you like five-star dining, spa treatments, and endless spectacular views."

That sounded almost too good to be true. It also struck down the idea that Solari didn't want them aboard. Something didn't add up.

"We'd be delighted to join you," Paul said. "At least to Providencia, although my wife may insist on more time to study your design, especially if it means getting to see the Eiffel Tower and the Champs-Élysées once again."

"Then it's settled," Solari said. "We'll dine tonight at La Mirage and board the *Condor* at dawn."

27

Denied boarding until the next day, the Trouts left the platform with Solari, busying themselves with a tour of the ground-based facilities. Colon waited for them to go out of view before retreating into the *Condor* with Yago and the hard-hatted engineer.

They strode down a corridor, passed through an airtight door, and entered the mechanical spaces of the huge airship, soon arriving at a compartment near the stern. This area was usually occupied by Colon's freight handlers, but at the moment it was still being prepared. A rank-and-file employee who was finishing some electrical work looked up as they entered.

"Leave us," Colon ordered.

The man took one look at Colon, put down his tools, and left the compartment. It was commonly known that Colon and his gray-shirts were not to be trifled with. There were spaces on the ship only they were allowed to enter, and at least half the regular Ostrom employees thought they might be drug smugglers or criminals of some other kind. They certainly kept everyone away from the cargo bays and the freight houses.

As the electrician left, Colon turned to Torres. He wasn't a member of the gray-shirts, but he was another ex-Cuban on Colon's payroll and was heavily involved with everything that had happened, especially in the use of the drones.

"What are those agents from NUMA doing here?" Colon snapped.

The engineer looked helpless. "Solari invited them down," he said. "I only heard about it this morning. I figured you wouldn't want that, so I came up with the idea of the cracked impeller disk. How was I to know Solari would ask them to join us on the full flight?"

Colon didn't care about excuses, he wanted the problem solved. "Go make sure that impeller looks damaged," he ordered. "I don't want Solari sending someone else to inspect it."

The engineer left and Colon turned to Yago. "I need the Americans gone. Get Solari to uninvite them."

"That may be a more difficult than it sounds," the scientist said.

"I'm not asking you to talk him into it," Colon snapped. "Make him do it. Hit him with another treatment."

"I know what you're asking," Yago replied. "And I'm telling you, I wouldn't recommend it."

Colon paused. Yago had always shown unabashed loyalty, but ever since the gathering at the farmhouse he'd become skittish. "Your reluctance concerns me."

"It's not reluctance," Yago insisted. "We can only use the treatment so many times before the subject begins to experience deterioration. Back at Arcos we saw people go mad. Remember? We had to shoot them because they couldn't be stabilized."

Colon wondered if the scientist was playing this up. "Those men were hardly the picture of sanity when we pulled them out of prison."

"To some extent it doesn't matter," Yago said. "The more times we dust someone and clean them up, the more damage is done to the brain's basic operating system. Why do you think I keep that tranquilizer gun with me when we're treating people?"

Yago had a specially made double-barreled tranquilizer gun that resembled a side-by-side shotgun. In Colon's opinion it was mostly for show, but it had been used once or twice.

"How close is Solari to cracking?"

"Impossible to tell, but he's already been treated more often than any subject in our experiments. His behavior has become erratic. We've had to sedate him several times to keep him out of the public eye. Thankfully his flamboyant reputation predates our arrival, but I wouldn't activate him again unless you're ready to be done with him."

"So, he's carrying the dust, but hasn't been activated?"

Yago nodded. "Consider him on standby. He'll be his normal weird self until you use the frequency generator. After that, he might need sedation."

It would have been simpler if they could have kept Solari in a compromised condition. But once the dust was activated, it changed the brain waves from alpha to slower theta and gamma ranges. That gave the subjects a dulling affect, as if they'd become intoxicated or drugged. They could be directed to do things, to say, believe, and feel things that weren't real. But to those who knew them, it was obvious something was wrong. For that reason, they'd had to dust Solari to get their way and then clean him up in between sessions so he could go out in public and act normal.

Colon couldn't risk Solari going mad on the day he launched the *Condor*. But neither could he have two members of NUMA—who were obviously lying about their reasons for being there—poking around the ship. Not this ship. Not on this flight.

"We could dust the Americans," Yago suggested. "Aside from each other, there's no one on board who knows them well enough to notice a difference."

Colon wasn't interested in that risk. "They'll have to report in. They might even have to video call back to Washington. And they still have to meet with Solari tonight."

"I wouldn't allow that to happen either," Yago suggested. "Who knows what he'll say if they start questioning him?"

On this they agreed. Colon would have preferred deception, but the situation called for a more brutal solution.

"Rio is a dangerous place," he mused. "No one thinks that more than the Americans. We need them to have an accident. Something that can't be traced back to us. A mugging, a shooting, an automobile crash. Any one of those things would do the trick."

Yago stared. "I hope you're not asking me to do it?"

Colon almost laughed. He could barely imagine the scientist using his tranquilizer gun. "Relax. I have others better suited for this kind of work."

28

After finishing their tour of Solari's facility, Paul and Gamay were shuttled back to the airport in a regular boat and picked up by a dark green SUV that took them to the five-star Grand Copa Hotel.

Despite being given a large suite on the top floor with a balcony overlooking the beach, Gamay felt claustrophobic. She desperately wanted to discuss their meeting with Solari, but it was Solari's people who'd set up the accommodations. That meant the room couldn't be considered secure. Listening devices, cameras, and Wi-Fi scanners might be present. She even considered the idea that someone could be in the room next door with a glass or a stethoscope to the wall.

Paul went to the balcony, gazing down at the beach and the boulevard. "I wonder if the Girl from Ipanema is down there."

Gamay sighed. "They're all from Ipanema, Paul. That's where we're staying."

He grinned at her smart-aleck answer, but had one of his own. "Some of them may have driven in from the country."

He had her there. Turning, she glanced at the clock. It was one thirty. They wouldn't meet for dinner until seven. The idea of waiting around for hours staring at the walls was too much for her. "I think we should go for a walk."

"To the beach?"

"And have you burst into flames?" she said. "No, thank you. Let's go up to Sugarloaf Mountain and ride the cable car. Or go see the statue of *Christ the Redeemer.* Might as well act like tourists while we have the chance."

Paul understood her plan without having to ask. He groaned for a moment in the fashion of an annoyed husband, went to the closet, and changed into khakis and a golf shirt, which was about as casual as he got. "Not a fan of cable cars," he said. "But I can deal with a statue and solid ground beneath my feet."

"You may change your mind when we get up there," Gamay said. "More important, how are you ever going to handle being on an airship?"

"That's different. You can be afraid of the water and still go on a cruise. Airplanes and helicopters don't bother me. Except when Joe's the pilot," he added. "Then I'm concerned for different reasons."

Gamay laughed and silently agreed. She changed into shorts and a sleeveless top, while Paul called the concierge to arrange for a car.

A few minutes later they met a driver named Eduardo in the lobby. He led them outside to a black sedan with ample legroom and drove them away from the beach and up toward the looming hills. Eventually, they turned onto a climbing, twisty road known as the Estrada das Paineiras. It took them upward through the urban rainforest that surrounded Rio. Instead of cliffside overlooks, the view was mostly green jungle foliage with warm sunlight filtering through. Something Paul was just fine with.

Reaching the base area around the statue complex, the driver parked and assured them he would wait for their return.

Paul and Gamay thanked him and left the car behind, stepping into a reception area filled with tourists from different countries. They bought tickets, moved through the queue, and gained a sense of anonymity with so many people and different languages being spoken around them.

A security screening came next and then the option to take an escalator up or climb a long flight of what looked like several hundred stairs.

To Paul's chagrin, Gamay chose the stairs.

Despite his disdain, the stairs had several advantages. They were less crowded and allowed an easy look back to see if anyone was following or shadowing them. Gamay stopped halfway up, watching the people on the escalator funnel past, and then eyeing the few other travelers on the stairway.

After a few minutes of rest, and letting other tourists go past, they continued on, arriving at the top of the walk, near the base of the magnificent art deco statue.

Looking up at the statue was awe-inspiring. From a distance it appeared to be made of gray concrete. Up close, Gamay could see that the surface was covered with thousands of triangular tiles. It gave the statue a texture and depth, while the clean lines of the design drew the eye upward to the outstretched arms, which seemed to beckon to the world.

Gamay had wanted to come here in order to find space where they could safely talk, but for a moment she found herself admiring the incredible sculpture. Turning to look down on Rio and the Copacabana Beach was just as inspiring.

"Worth the climb," Paul admitted.

Gamay had to agree. "I guess these are the kind of views Solari is promising from his blimp."

"Airship," Paul corrected.

"Right," she replied. "Now, tell me what you make of him."

"He's a salesman," Paul said. "And he has a certain jaunty, anything-goes manner. But he doesn't strike me as the head of a piracy operation. Certainly not a cutthroat one that leaves men catatonic or sends them jumping suicidally into the ocean without life jackets."

"My thoughts exactly," Gamay said. "But the exuberant salesman could be a front. He managed to walk into Wall Street and defang the wolves who were ready to pick his bones clean. It would take nerves of steel to negotiate an agreement like that. Or something else."

Paul nodded. He saw where Gamay was going with this. The same psyops methods that could make sailors jump off their ships could be used to make a Wall Street banker think it's in their best interest to rip up a large outstanding debt and then borrow even more money. "It's a leap," Paul said. "But not a huge one."

"Did you notice how his mood changed when Señor Colon and the others showed up?"

"They brought him bad news," Paul reminded. "No one likes to hear that their billion-dollar toy is broken before they get to play with it."

"True," she admitted. "But his face fell before they spoke a word. It was almost like seeing them, he expected bad news."

"Some people are like that," Paul said. "Your cousin Jerry, for instance. Still, we should have Rudi run a profile on Colon and the other guy, Yago."

"Couldn't hurt," Gamay said.

They walked as they spoke, watching as a few puffy clouds drifted across the sky and out over the beach, temporarily offering shade to the crowds down below.

"If Solari is behind the attacks," Gamay asked, "would he really tell us about the drones?"

"I wouldn't expect it," Paul said. "He even bragged about how capable they were."

"And would he invite us for a three-day ride on his ship? Offering to show us every square inch of the vessel?"

Paul shook his head. "We weren't even pressing him for it. To paraphrase an old country music song, it makes me wonder if we're looking for trouble in all the wrong places."

"Love," she said.

"What?"

"The song says looking for love in all the wrong places."

"Love, trouble," Paul said, "pretty much the same thing."

"You're such a romantic," she replied. "Truth is, inviting us on his ship could cut both ways. Could be some sort of trap. Maybe we should decline his invitation."

Paul didn't want to pass up the opportunity to see the ship. Both for personal and professional reasons. He also doubted they would be in danger. "I can't see him trying to harm us while we're in his company. It would bring too much attention his way."

Gamay found the point mildly comforting, but she remained wary. "I'll remind you of that when you're having an uncontrollable urge to leap off the ship without a parachute."

Paul laughed. "There's nothing in the world that could make me do that. I'm not even getting near the edge, so if they tell you I fell off the airship, you'll know I've been pushed."

Gamay didn't want to think about such a thing, even as part of a joke. She changed the subject. "Let's get a bite to eat. I hear there's a great little café on the other side of the statue."

———

While Paul and Gamay acted like tourists, their driver waited in the parking lot. For a short time he sat in his car, taking care of a few bills and conducting some business on his phone. Then, tired of sitting, he stepped out of the car into the sunshine, took off his jacket, and rolled up his sleeves. The day was simply too nice to waste looking at a screen.

Leaning against the hood of his car, he struck up a conversation with some other drivers. As so often happened in Brazil, the conversation soon turned to football, and it wasn't long before a hearty discussion of Brazil's various teams was underway. A subject on which there was no shortage of firm and differing opinions.

The discussion ended when the other drivers left to pick up their fares. For a moment, Eduardo was left alone. At least until a nondescript man walked up to him with an unlit cigarette between his fingers. The man was fumbling through his pockets as if in search of a lighter.

He abandoned the effort as he drew close. "Do you have a match?"

"Claro, claro," Eduardo said. "Of course. A good driver always carries a lighter."

He dug into his breast pocket to recover the nickel-plated lighter he kept with him. He handed it to the man, who appeared to light the end of the cigarette without touching the flame to the paper. As the lighter snapped shut, the man exhaled, breathing out through the cigarette and forcing a puff of air that was oddly dark for cigarette smoke.

Eduardo breathed it in without thinking.

The man returned the lighter and stepped backward. He waved at the smoke with his hand as if he was sorry for the incident.

"That's strong," Eduardo said. "What brand are you smoking?"

The man looked at the cigarette in his fingers as if examining it for the first time. "Foreign," he said. "Turkish, I think. Want one?"

"Definitely not," Eduardo replied. "Smells like exhaust."

The man laughed and nodded. "Thanks again," he said, then added strangely, "You, sir, are more than a driver."

It was an odd comment and Eduardo had no idea what the man meant by it, but he assumed it was a compliment. He put the lighter back in his pocket and—other than the fact that he preferred milder tobacco—thought nothing more of the incident. But as clouds drifted by and the sun came out from behind the clouds, he found the light to be more intense than before. He noticed a myriad of reflections off the windows and chrome around him.

He slid on a pair of sunglasses and then climbed back inside his car, starting the engine and adjusting the air-conditioning to its coolest setting. As the cool air swept over him, he began to feel a bit better.

He looked up the hill at the crowds of tourists coming and going, but saw no sign of the tall Americans. He hoped they'd be back soon because he was ready to call it a day and go home.

29

Paul and Gamay returned to the parking lot without stopping for any souvenirs. They found Eduardo and climbed in the back of the sedan as soon as he released the locks.

Paul thought nothing of it, but Gamay was surprised that Eduardo hadn't jumped out to open the door for them. Not because it was necessary, but because he had done so at the hotel and then again when dropping them off below the statue.

Still, it was getting hot, and Rio was always humid. She sat in the back and pulled her seat belt on, thankful for the cool air blowing from the vents. "Thank you for waiting," she said. "I guess it's back to the hotel for us now."

"*Claro*," he said. "Sure thing."

As they eased from the parking lot, Gamay reached over and put her hand on Paul's. He turned to look at her and she smiled. For a moment they were just a couple of vacationers.

Up front Eduardo drove without saying a word. As they turned onto the Estrada das Paineiras, they passed two motorcycles aligned on the side of the road like policemen ready to chase anyone foolish enough to speed down the twisting, turning road. Gamay heard them revving their engines and pulling out behind the sedan.

She turned to look. The motorcycles had fallen in behind them, just a few car lengths back. She and Paul had been on too many assignments where they'd been attacked for her to completely dismiss the men on their bikes, but so far they'd done nothing aggressive.

She squeezed Paul's hand to get his attention. He nodded. He'd seen them.

Eduardo had seen the motorcycles too. He seemed more concerned. Motorbikes were often used in criminal acts around Rio because they could escape through the traffic, driving between lanes and off-road, if necessary.

He kept one eye on the road and one eye on the mirror, only to be startled by the ringing of his phone. Like many drivers, he drove with a Bluetooth speaker in his ear so he could conduct conversations hands-free.

"This is Edo," he said, using the shortened version of his name.

"You, sir, are more than a driver," the voice on the other end of the line said.

The odd statement struck a chord in Eduardo. His mind flashed back to the man with the Turkish cigarette. Before he could answer he felt and heard a ringing in his ears. High-pitched, almost inaudible. He imagined it was the kind of thing dogs could hear.

"You, sir, are more than a driver."

Of course he was.

"You're a man with a mission. It's very important that you complete it. You remember this? You understand?"

The odd tone continued in the background, but Eduardo heard it less and less. He was focused on the sound of the man's voice.

"Get your passengers to the bottom of the hill," the voice instructed. *"You must hurry. There's no time to lose."*

Without thinking about it, Eduardo pressed down on the

accelerator. The sedan picked up speed on the descending straight-away. It didn't become a problem until they neared the next turn. Realizing he was going too fast, he hit the brakes firmly and the car nose-dived and wallowed through the turn.

"*Faster,*" the voice said. "*Look behind you. Don't you see? Those men will kill you if they catch you. They'll kill you all.*"

Eduardo glanced in the mirror as a bead of sweat ran down the side of his face. The motorcycles were gaining on them. Headlights blazing as they caught up. He glanced up ahead and stomped on the gas, launching the sedan into the next straight.

"Hey," the American woman said. "Take it easy."

"*Don't listen,*" the voice in his ear said. "*Faster. Hurry. Your life depends on it.*"

Eduardo took the car through the next turn, tires screeching as the rubber tried valiantly to hold the road.

"*That's it. Don't let them catch you. Faster.*"

In the back of the car, Paul and Gamay had been whiplashed from side to side as the car swerved through the turns.

"Something's wrong," Paul said.

"You think?" Gamay replied.

"They're trying to kill us," Eduardo announced.

He sounded panicked beyond all reason.

"They're just tourists on bikes," Gamay shouted.

"No," Eduardo cried. "They have guns."

The car screeched into another turn, this time sliding hard enough to bang into the guardrail. It slid along it and then caromed back onto the road.

As the car straightened up Gamay twisted around. The motorcycles were still following, but not all that closely. She wouldn't call it a chase. "Slow down," she shouted.

Her words had no effect and Eduardo kept the pedal down, passing a slower car in front of them and narrowly missing an oncoming bus in the process.

Gamay undid her seat belt and lunged into the gap between the front seats. She managed to knock the gear selector into neutral and then reached for the wheel, hoping to guide the car into the high side of the road.

Eduardo slugged her with a backhand, knocking her into the passenger's seat. Before she could right herself, he'd put the car back in drive and stepped on the accelerator.

"Paul!" Gamay shouted.

Paul had already undone his seat belt. He lunged forward, wrapping his long arms around Eduardo and pulling him back against the seat rest. Eduardo fought and squirmed, but Paul had all the leverage.

With one arm around Eduardo's neck, Paul used the other to karate chop his hands off the steering wheel, which Gamay lunged for and grabbed, just in time to negotiate another turn.

Gamay might have had the wheel, but the driver still had access to the pedals. He stomped on the gas and the car sped up once more. Paul tried pulling him back over the top of the seat, but he was belted in.

In desperation, he reached down beside the seat and found the controls. Pulling the knob toward him, Paul released the driver's seat. It slid back and banged against the stops. With Eduardo's feet off the pedals, the car began to slow, but not nearly enough.

"Brakes!" Paul shouted.

Gamay dove down into the footwell. She slammed the brake pedal with both hands. The tires locked up and the car skidded toward the edge of the road, onto the shoulder, and then out into the forest beside the road, down a subtle slope. After crashing through a number of bushes, it plowed into a grove of bamboo, snapping off stalks and coming to a stop.

Paul held Eduardo as Gamay extricated herself from underneath the steering wheel.

"They were going to kill us," the driver said, sobbing now. "They told me."

"Who told you?" Gamay shouted.

Paul kept the man in a headlock even as he cried. In this position, Paul's own ear was very close to Eduardo's. It allowed Paul to hear the tiny voice speaking to him over the earpiece.

"Sleep now," it said. *"Do not wake."*

To Paul's surprise, the driver stopped fighting and his body went limp. When Paul released him, he slumped to the side.

"What'd you do?" Gamay asked.

"Nothing," Paul said. He pulled the speaker from the driver's ear, but the line had been cut.

Gamay found the key and turned the engine off. Sitting up, she looked out the window and back up to the road. Other cars had pulled to the side and several people were working their way through the trampled foliage to offer help. Behind the rescuers, the two motorcycles stopped briefly. They propped up their visors, looked directly at her, then shut them again and took off down the road.

She wasn't sure if the bikers had anything to do with the incident or not. But she was certain they were on the right trail. She turned to Paul. "Seems we're looking for trouble in exactly the right place."

30

The wreckage of the Chinese spy trawler emerged from the gloom along the ocean bottom, filling the view through the curved plexiglass window of the NUMA submersible.

"There she is," Joe said. "Right where Yaeger said she'd be."

They'd been searching for no more than an hour. An infinitesimally small amount of time when looking for a sunken wreck.

"If his computers get any better at pinpointing wrecks, we're going to be out of a job," Kurt joked.

Like many sunken ships, the trawler sat nearly upright on the seafloor. A phenomenon caused by weighting of the ships—most of the heavy equipment and ballast was in the lower half of the hull.

"Will you look at that," Joe said, pointing to a jagged, diagonal wound near the midpoint of the trawler. Torn and bent hull plating lined the edges, some of it bent inward, while other sections were twisted out.

As Kurt and Joe stared, Commander Wells appeared behind and between them, looking over their shoulders like a kid in the back seat of a car. "Puncture wound," she said. "In and then back out. Guess we know what the *Heron* rammed into."

Joe pointed out a bend in the hull caused by the force of the impact. "It must have hit at high speed. Let's hope whatever the Chinese recorded wasn't damaged or destroyed in the collision."

"The Chinese use redundant systems," Commander Wells said. "Pretty robust. Unless the computers were stored right behind that bulkhead, they should be in one piece."

Kurt had a feeling she'd done this before. "Only one way to find out." He turned to Joe. "Put the sub in station-keeping mode. I'll let Rolle know we're going for a swim."

To avoid showing their hand, Kurt and Joe had left the *Edison* back at port, sneaking off with the ship's submersible and rendezvousing with Rolle, who was piloting the largest vessel in his catalog, a ninety-foot sailboat designed for around-the-world travel.

The craft was twice the size of the average blue-water sailboat, and with all her sails up and rigged, powerful enough to tow the submersible without any trouble at all.

With Rolle alerted to their find, Kurt left the copilot's seat and stood up, careful not to hit his head on the low ceiling. The plan was for him and Commander Wells to make the dive. They were at a depth of three hundred feet, which meant every twenty minutes would require an hour of decompression. Fortunately, the submersible's dive locker doubled as a decompression chamber, but someone still had to be up front to drive the sub.

"This isn't going to be an easy dive," Joe said. "Sure you don't want me to go with you?"

"With all due respect to your diving skills," Commander Wells said, "I'm the only one who knows anything about Chinese spy ships and the only one who can read a lick of Mandarin. If I'm right, we will have to deal with several layers of security, including explosive charges that will need to be disarmed. Snip the wrong wire and boom."

"On second thought," Joe said, "enjoy your swim."

Kurt smiled at the exchange and then stepped into the dive locker, where he pulled on a harness, tanks, and a helmet and waited for Commander Wells to do the same. The NUMA gear was a little different than the standard U.S. Navy kit she was used to, but she quickly had everything in place.

When she gave him the thumbs-up, Kurt sealed the door and opened the valve, allowing water to begin filling the locker. As it crept up past their chests, Kurt sealed his helmet and checked the comm system. "You reading me okay?"

"Like you're right next to me," she replied.

The more time he spent with Commander Wells, the more Kurt thought she would fit in at NUMA. "How many deep-water dives have you made?"

"Fifty or more," she said. "I lost count a few years back."

That was reassuring. "How many wrecks have you explored?"

"Two, counting this one."

That was less inspiring.

"I assume you're talking actual wrecks," she said. "Not the tourist kind you dive on and take pictures of with all the colorful fish swimming behind you."

"I am," Kurt said. "What other wreck have you explored?"

"The Navy had me take a look at a freighter that went down off the coast of Okinawa. Turned out someone had already cut into it from the outside and detonated an explosive device in the cargo hold. Apparently, the ship was carrying powerful computers that had gone missing."

"Sounds exciting," Kurt said, fairly certain he knew the ship she was speaking of. "Find anything?"

"Only that the computers were gone, and someone had scrawled 'NUMA was here' on the bulkhead wall."

She turned toward him, grinning inside her helmet. Kurt doubted she'd been there, but the story proved that she'd done her research on him. "I can neither confirm nor deny what you're referring to."

"I would expect nothing more," she replied.

The water rose, soon covering them. The internal lights dimmed and the locker went dark.

Unlike Hollywood diving gear—which is designed to show the actors' faces—NUMA's full-face helmets did not have lights illuminating the inside of them. This was for the obvious reason that such lights blinded the swimmer by ruining their night vision and reflected off the inside of the faceplate. This meant all expressions became invisible. But Kurt had a sense that Commander Wells was still smiling.

A green indicator on the wall lit up, telling them interior and exterior pressure had equalized. Kurt pressed a button allowing the circular hatch on the floor to release and fall open.

"I'll lead you in," he said, growing serious again. "Follow my instructions until we find what you're looking for. Then I'll be glad to take a back seat and watch you work."

For all the banter, she was a professional. "Roger that," was all she replied.

Kurt went out first, dropping through the open hatchway and into the warm Bahamian waters. Below him lay a seemingly endless expanse of barren white sand. They were at the northern edge of the Bahama Banks, a massive sloping hill of calcium carbonate and limestone. Little vegetation grew here, making it something of an underwater desert. As Kurt scanned the surrounding area, he saw no kelp or seagrass, not even tube worms, which were sometimes common in the area. Just an endless plane of sand and the odd sight of the Chinese trawler sitting upright in the middle of it.

Assuming it remained where it was, the trawler would soon be colonized by sea life including sponges, seaweed, and different types of coral. That would attract small fish looking for places to hide, and the small fish would attract predators looking for the elusive prey. Ten years on, the Chinese trawler would be a little oasis teeming with life in the middle of an underwater desert.

As Kurt considered this, Commander Wells emerged from the submersible and began orienting herself to the surroundings. "How's the current?"

"Slight drift to the north," Kurt said. "Shouldn't be a problem."

She gave him a thumbs-up, and he kicked away, moving toward the sunken trawler illuminated by the submersible's lights.

Up close, the damage to the trawler's side was even more remarkable. Red paint from the bow of the freighter had left a scar on the hull that looked like a swath of blood, while the puncture itself was at least eight feet from top to bottom and perhaps ten feet wide. The hull plating was not only bent and buckled, but twisted and stretched like some exhibit of modern art.

Easing up to the buckled plates, Kurt looked inside. The *Heron* had struck the trawler between decks, leaving a bent and mangled floor across the open space behind the impact. Both levels appeared accessible.

"Might as well go in here," he said. "Much easier than using a deck hatch."

"Right behind you," Commander Wells replied.

Kurt switched on his lights. Two on the helmet. Three more on the dive harness behind him, and one built into the right arm of his wetsuit. The idea was that lighting from multiple points and directions allowed for fewer shadows and a clearer view of whatever the diver was looking at. "Which level do you want to explore first? Sporting goods or loungewear?"

Commander Wells eased into the gap beside Kurt, treading water to stay in place. "Lower deck looks like it's all machinery," she said. "What we're looking for will be on the mid-deck. Let's start there."

Kurt kicked once and rose upward until he was looking into the mid-deck. "Stay a few yards behind me," he said. "And remember, even with our streamlined equipment it's easy to get hung up. Move slowly and try to visualize the larger frame of your body including the harness and the tanks. If you get caught on something, back up slowly or wait for me to pull you free. Twisting and turning will only make it worse."

"Understood," she said.

Kurt went in. As luck would have it, the freighter had struck the hidden command room of the trawler. The near wall was demolished, with pipes, electrical cables, and insulation hanging down. To their left was a closed hatchway that led forward. To the right a second watertight door stood ajar.

"Forward or aft?" Kurt asked.

"Aft," she said.

Kurt turned to the right. Putting his hands on the door, he forced it open. The door was heavy and not counterbalanced. Nor was it hanging on its hinges all that well after the impact. It creaked and groaned as he pushed it wide.

Looking into the next compartment, he saw the nerve center of the intelligence-gathering operation. On the far side lay a bank of computer systems and screens, fronted by swivel chairs that were bolted to the deck. Two chairs were occupied by drowned members of the People's Liberation Army Navy. They remained at their posts, courtesy of lap and shoulder belts.

One was facing the computer in front of him, hands floating at his side. The other was turned away, face down, a set of headphones still in place over his ears.

Despite Kurt's admonition to stay behind him, Commander Wells eased up next to him.

"Sonar or radio intercept," she said. "The other guy might be a radar jockey."

Kurt moved to the side. "You might as well take the lead."

While Kurt wedged a piece of debris against the door to keep it from accidentally closing on them, Commander Wells swam into the compartment. She paused in the middle, turning from point to point, and then drifting over to the first station, where she released the belts holding the dead man to the chair.

Freed from his harness, the dead man turned slowly toward her, black hair wafting in the water, eyes open and staring blankly. With a modicum of respect, she eased him out of the way.

"This man was on the radar station," she said. "By the looks of it, they're running a type 938. It's similar to their standard air-defense radar. We used to see these guys off the coast near Norfolk all the time. They spend a lot of time tracking our fighter aircraft in and out of Chambers Field."

"Is it a good system?" Kurt asked. "And by that, I mean is it good enough to pick up drones?"

"Might be," she said.

As she opened a small tool set, Kurt swam over to the dead sailor, who wore an ID tag with a name and photo on it. He removed the tag and then placed the dead man on the far side of the room, securing the body so it wouldn't float around the compartment.

By the time he turned around, Commander Wells had the computer panel opened.

"Any booby traps?" Kurt asked.

"Almost certainly," she said. "But nothing that should explode. The Chinese use a two-layered system hoping to prevent us from doing what we're about to do. One layer of security is a high-powered electromagnet that's designed to permanently erase the data from the hard drives. Disconnect the power to that and it can't do its job."

Reaching inside the panel with a pair of cutters, she snipped a couple of wires.

"The second layer is a thermal charge," she said. "Either thermite or magnetite, which burns at four thousand degrees"—she looked back at him—"or a type of rocket propellant called APR, which is aluminum powder mixed with ammonium perchlorate. That stuff burns even hotter. The idea behind that is, broken things can be put back together, but melted things become goo."

Kurt laughed. "Is that the technical term?"

"Very technical," she replied.

Kurt remained well behind her, floating in a spot where his lights added to her own. He could see her working on the panel using a small screwdriver and the wire cutters. The required cuts and snips were delicate. Fortunately, the Bahamian waters were relatively warm, and her hands had yet to lose their touch and dexterity.

After a few minutes, she put the tools back into their small case, reached into the panel, and pulled out a gray cylinder covered with orange stripes.

"Thermal charge," she said, handing it to Kurt. "Take this home and you'll be the envy of everyone next Fourth of July."

Kurt took the charge from her and then watched as she removed the hard drive from the radar unit. A few minutes later she performed a similar procedure on the sonar units. With both hard drives secured in the pouch at her side, she pulled away from the panel.

"Easy as . . ." She was about to say "pie," but she froze at the sight of something she hadn't expected.

A third booby trap—one that she hadn't been briefed on and that was triggered by removing both hard drives. It consisted of a block of explosives in a metal casing, connected to a digital timer. She could see it ticking down but found no method to shut it off.

"Go," she shouted to Kurt. "Get out. Quickly!"

Her voice was garbled over the comm system, but her actions were obvious. She was kicking furiously and heading for the hatch. She went too high. Her head made it through, but her tanks banged against the upper part of the bulkhead.

Kurt kicked toward her, pulled her down, and then shoved her through the hatch. He followed right behind her, performing a flip turn the second he'd cleared the door so he could remove the wedge of debris. That done, he leaned hard on the door, hoping to close it.

The door banged shut and Kurt spun the handle. The wheel caught after a quarter turn. It was shut, but by no means secure.

"As good as it's going to get," he said, turning and pushing off the bulkhead in an attempt to catch up with Commander Wells.

The goal was the opening they'd swum into. Commander Wells had just about reached it when the explosion went off behind them.

The charge rocked the ship and blasted through the watertight door, which flew sideways as a shock wave burst through it.

Kurt was thrown forward like a man caught in a crashing wave. He pulled his arms and legs in to keep them from breaking as he crashed against the far bulkhead. He felt the impact as a heavy thud against the upper part of his back as his tanks hit the wall and his helmet banged off something. He was woozy for a moment, his inner ear convinced he was still tumbling, his eyes certain that the room around him was moving.

Commander Wells was shoved forward as well, but the shock wave forced her out through the opening in an awkward twisting motion. As she was pushed through the gap, she banged her head against the warped hull plating, hitting it hard enough to dent her helmet. Her leg scraped another section, leaving a gash in her suit and a trail of blood wafting out behind her.

She vanished into the open sea as the trawler rocked one way from the outward blast of the shock wave and then back the other way as the temporary bubble collapsed and the water surged back in.

Looking around, Kurt tried to get his bearings. The visibility inside the trawler dropped to less than a foot as huge clouds of sediment were sucked into the hull. Kurt swam toward the exit, but ended up tangled in some insulation.

Carefully pulling himself free, he held still, waiting for the visibility to improve as the sand settled out.

After checking to make sure he wasn't losing any air, he called out to Commander Wells on the radio. "Jodi, do you read me? Commander Wells, what's your status?"

Waiting for a reply, he took long slow breaths to make sure he wasn't hyperventilating—which could easily cause disorientation at this depth. To his surprise, the flock of silver bubbles venting from his helmet moved sideways instead of upward. They pooled on the bulkhead wall, holding their shape like large drops of quicksilver, instead of drifting overhead.

The disoriented feeling returned. He moved a few feet and exhaled again. The flow of exhaust air followed the same sideways track. It wasn't Kurt's balance that was off. The geometry of the ship had changed. The wall was now the ceiling. The floor and the ceiling were now the walls.

Kurt swam toward what should have been the gaping hole in the hull, only to find that the opening was now blocked by the sand dunes of the Bahama Banks. The shock wave had pushed the trawler over on its side.

31

For the duration of the dive, Joe kept watch on the trawler, while stealing occasional glances at the chronometer, which marked the time at depth for the two divers. Because of the depth and the pressure, they only had a short time to accomplish what they wanted to do.

As he listened in on their chatter, Joe found himself wanting them to talk less and work more. Then he heard the panic in Jodi's voice. And then just grunting and effort as the two of them swam for safety.

The blast shook the trawler just as their lights appeared in the opening. It sent a bulbous shock wave through the breach in the side, which surged outward, expanding like a bell. It whipped up the sediment and hit into the submersible, banging against the hull like an angry fist.

The sub was forced back as if it had been shoved by a giant hand. It wasn't a bad impact, all things considered. More noise than fury at this range. But Joe knew that wasn't the case for the divers in the water.

After a brief check for damage on the systems panel, Joe retrained the submersible's powerful lights on the trawler. As the sediment thinned, he saw one of the divers drifting away. More critically, he noticed that the trawler was leaning over on its side, rolling toward him.

Joe pushed the throttle into its full forward position and the submersible began to accelerate. He angled the dive planes and brought the nose down, hoping to get under the edge of the trawler and keep it upright, like jamming a proverbial foot in a closing door. But it was already too late.

The trawler rolled onto the sand. What remained of its superstructure crashed down just in front of the submersible. Joe put the engines into reverse, pulling back to avoid getting tangled up in the mess.

The trawler may have been a spy ship, but it was still disguised to look like a fishing boat, and carried several outstretched booms complete with lines and nets to keep up the façade.

As Joe pulled back, one of the booms scraped across the top of the submersible, grinding across the hull and then sliding off to one side.

"Close one," he said to himself before pressing the transmit switch on the subsurface radio. "Kurt. Jodi. Do either of you read?"

Joe moved the submersible back even farther, pivoting and allowing the lights to cut through the dark, cloudy water.

The sediment was thinning now, most of it settling, some of it wafting away on the mild current. Joe looked one way and then the other, but saw no sign of either diver. He repeated his radio call, but to no avail.

At this point, he figured whoever had been thrown clear had to be unconscious. That meant they'd be drifting with the current.

Pivoting to the north, he moved past the downed trawler and shut off his lights. He quickly spied a dim glow in the distance. It had to be the lights on someone's dive harness.

Locking in on the target, Joe pushed the throttle forward. Bringing the lights back up, he noticed that the diver was ascending slowly, perhaps due to a lost weight belt or air leaking into the buoyancy compensator from a damaged valve.

He reset the dive planes and shallowed his depth a bit, getting close enough to confirm that he was chasing Commander Wells.

"Jodi, do you read me? You're drifting higher. Adjust your buoyancy."

While it might have seemed like a harmless thing—or even a safety measure for a diver to have positive buoyancy that would take them up to the surface in the event something went wrong—it would have been a disaster in this case.

At three hundred feet, Kurt and Commander Wells had been diving under so much pressure that their blood was now filled with compressed gases, which would bubble up like a hastily opened soda can if they ascended without decompression time.

Joe glanced at the depth meter. "Two hundred and fifty feet," he said to himself, doing some quick calculations.

She hadn't gone too high yet, but the farther she rose, the faster she'd climb. Neoprene wetsuits were normally buoyant, a fact that was erased at great depth when the suits were squeezed by the pressure. As Commander Wells drifted upward, the neoprene would expand, and she would gain more positive buoyancy and begin to rise ever faster. If he didn't stop her quickly, the situation would spiral out of control.

Joe decided overkill was the best option. He put the sub into its emergency ascent mode, quickly rising above the drifting diver.

Seeing her up close, Joe realized how much trouble she was actually in. She was floating face up and rolling slightly to one side. Her arms were stretched outward and bent in a crooked position. She was obviously unconscious.

At the same time, she was bleeding from a gash in her leg. Joe hadn't yet seen any sharks around, but these were warm waters. The finned beasts couldn't be that far away.

Slewing the submersible around so he could keep an eye on her, Joe considered his options. None of them were good. He could grab her with the mechanical arm, but touch was not the gripping claw's strong suit. He might lose her if he didn't use enough pressure and could easily break one of her bones if he used too much. Nor would she be an easy catch. The arm was designed to pick stationary items off the seafloor, not grasp a limp and rotating human figure. Every attempt and miss would cost him time, allowing her to continue rising higher and letting decompression work its lethal damage.

He couldn't risk that.

He switched the exterior cameras on and aimed them downward, pointing them beneath the sub. Adjusting his course, he moved in over the top of her and flooded the ballast tanks. The sub stopped rising and began to sink.

Watching the screen, he saw her floating into view. "A little to the right," he told himself, nudging the thruster control. "Back it up," he added. "Just a bit more . . ."

Her limp form filled the screen as she floated up past the cameras. A dull thud registered as she hit the underside of the submersible.

The depth read 217. He'd stopped her ascent, but she couldn't stay there.

Joe vented more air from the tanks. A little at a time, until the submersible was sinking at a rate of five feet per second, pushing the unconscious scuba diver deeper along with it.

When he got below 250, he set the controls to neutral buoyancy and tried to contact her using the comm system. She didn't reply. She was still unconscious.

Somehow, he had to get her into the air lock and the decompression chamber. And he needed to do it soon so he could go look for Kurt.

There was only one option.

"Now for my next trick," Joe said to his imaginary audience.

Using the thrusters, he pushed the submersible up and ahead just a few feet. Stabilizing again, he heard the commander's tanks clunking against the underside once more.

"Just a little farther," he said to himself.

He bumped the thrusters once more. Up and forward, and then down.

This time he heard nothing.

Checking the air lock camera, he saw Commander Wells drifting into the flooded chamber and rising toward the top.

"What a catch," Joe told himself. "They should play that on ESPN."

With Commander Wells safely in the dive locker, Joe reached over to the internal controls, closing the door and beginning the depressurization process.

The high-intensity air forced the water out of the compartment, but kept the pressure at 9.8 atmospheres, equal to the water pressure outside. Normally the automated system would begin a long, slow depressurization schedule, but Joe paused it because he would need to open the air lock again to let Kurt inside.

Assuming, of course, that he could find him.

32

While Joe rescued Commander Wells, Kurt remained where he'd been for the past ten minutes, trapped inside the now overturned fishing trawler. His ears were still ringing from the percussive shock of the explosion and his ribs were aching from where he'd been slammed against the bulkhead. It was the same side that had taken the strike from the baton during the fight on the *Hercules*.

"I'm going to have to start rolling the other direction," he said to himself.

After digging in the sand for a moment, thinking he could tunnel out, Kurt cut the attempt short. It was a futile effort. Each scoop of sand he removed was replaced by more sediment sliding into place. Worse yet, the exertion had raised his heart rate and respiration.

Calming himself and slowing his breathing, Kurt let himself drift in the zero-g environment. It was almost a meditative state.

After a minute he was back to breathing slowly and thinking clearly. He noticed a salty taste in his mouth, but it wasn't water leaking in, it was blood from a ruptured capillary in his nose.

"All right, Austin," he told himself. "Time to get out of this trap."

As he made his plan, Kurt spoke loud enough for the microphone in his helmet to pick up his voice. He couldn't hear anyone responding, but that didn't mean they weren't receiving his transmission. It was possible that his speaker could be out or his receiver malfunctioning.

"Trawler is over on its port side," he said. "If you guys can hear me, I'm going to go forward and see if I can find an exit to the main deck."

He moved to the forward hatch, loosening the wheel and pulling on the door. Fortunately, when the door opened, it fell toward him and stayed that way.

"Entering what looks like the main passageway."

Swimming through a narrow passageway on a ship that was lying sideways was a fairly claustrophobic experience. And because the corridor was now wider than it was tall, Kurt found he had plenty of space to his left and right, but almost no room above or below him. As he moved along, his tanks scraped against the ceiling several times.

"A fair amount of debris in here," he reported.

The rollover had dumped equipment and loose items onto the port wall, which was now beneath him as the floor. At one point he had to push some of it out of the way and ease over the top. On the other side, he found another dead sailor. The man's face was scratched badly, one eyeball missing and the other bloodied and bruised. There was blood and tissue under the man's fingertips, suggesting he'd done the damage himself.

Even though China and the U.S. were at odds these days, Kurt felt a sense of compassion for the man. *What the hell could those drones be doing, that they could make someone claw their own eyes out?*

As he stared at the man, it brought to mind the missing and catatonic crewmen from the *Heron* and the other ships all over the world. A deep fire began to burn inside him. Cool and calculating rather than emotional, Kurt found himself wanting to punish whoever was behind the attacks.

He realized part of that feeling was natural, while another part of it was the result of being in the depths and breathing in the trimix. It was very easy for thoughts and emotions to run rampant in these conditions.

He removed the man's ID badge, secured it with the one he'd taken from the radar operator, and swam past.

"Coming up on the forward bulkhead door," he announced.

He pulled on it repeatedly. Even put his feet on the wall for leverage. It wouldn't budge. It was either secured by a locking system that could only be released on the far side or was jammed and inoperable due to the impact of the collision or even the recent explosion.

"So much for plan A," Kurt announced. "If you guys are keeping track, it's trawler of doom, one. Austin, zero."

He turned slowly in the corridor, finding an opening to another compartment. Swimming inside, he discovered a porthole with the glass missing. Despite offering a tantalizing glimpse of freedom, the dinner plate–sized opening was useless as a way of escape, so Kurt went back to the corridor.

As he entered the passageway, an alarm went off on his dive computer. Kurt glanced at the device, which was strapped to his forearm. A yellow warning light was flashing. His gas supply had dropped below ten minutes.

Kurt's slightly woozy mind struggled to figure out how that had happened. Either one of the tanks was leaking, or he'd used a lot more than he thought. Either way, he slowed his breathing further and now moved along at a snail's pace.

Two more compartments on starboard were similarly useless in trying to escape, while the compartments to port were face down in the seabed.

After a long, slow circuit, Kurt found himself back where he'd started. He briefly considered the possibility of searching aft, but that meant going through the room where the explosion had taken place, which was now an impassable jumble of tangled metal, bent pipes, and loose debris.

"Trawler of doom, two," he announced. "Austin still zero. If you guys are out there, now would be a good time to show up and help me out."

He waited.

"Anyone?" he said, then added, "Bueller . . . Anyone . . ."

Kurt laughed at the line from *Ferris Bueller's Day Off.* A great movie, but a sure sign he was beginning to get loopy.

He looked around, remaining calm, despite what seemed like a hopeless future. He knew Joe would never abandon him, not unless he had absolutely no choice. But waiting for his best friend to cut a hole in the ship and set him free was too passive for him.

Cut a hole in the ship.

The words reverberated in his mind and a broad grin stretched across his stubbled face. "Of course," he said to himself. "Why didn't I think of it before?"

33

With Commander Wells in the decompression chamber, Joe went in search of Kurt. He had no real idea where to start. He realized that Kurt would have drifted in the same direction as Commander Wells, and at the same general speed, if he'd been ejected from the trawler. But he hadn't seen any sign of Kurt during her rescue, which meant the only rational thing to do was to search downstream and then work his way back.

He drove the submersible in a sidewinder pattern. Back and forth along the direction of the current, wider with each turn, looking in all directions, dousing the lights and then bringing them back up again, while switching the cameras into motion-activated mode.

After a few short minutes he'd found nothing. A quick calculation told him Kurt couldn't have drifted any farther in the elapsed time. He decided to backtrack along the bottom. Commander Wells had been floating slowly upward, but that didn't mean Kurt would be in the same condition. If he was unconscious and properly weighted, he'd remain at depth. Rolling and scraping along the sand, which would slow his progress.

Moving along the bottom in the same side-to-side pattern, Joe shut off the exterior lights. If Kurt's suit was still illuminated, he would be more likely to see it in the dark.

"Come on, amigo," he said. "You're out there somewhere. Just give me a sign."

A moment later, Joe saw a light. Not drifting free or sliding along the bottom, but pointing straight up through the water like a beacon. He nudged the thrusters and moved toward it.

To his surprise, the light was coming from inside the trawler. Shining out through a porthole. It had to be Kurt.

Joe tried to reach him on the comm. "Kurt, this is Joe. How do you read?"

Hearing nothing back, Joe decided to try another method of communication.

Moving the submersible in close to the trawler, he extended the robotic arm and banged on the hull several times.

The light coming through the porthole dimmed and Joe saw Kurt's helmet pressed up against the opening.

The opening went dark a second later, followed by a strobe-like flashing in Morse code, which Joe translated aloud.

"Napping?"

Joe laughed and then flashed a message back. *Jodi was. In deco now.*

———

Trapped inside the trawler, Kurt processed the message, wondering how Joe had managed to get an unconscious diver into the air lock and then deciding he'd have plenty of time to ask later.

He flashed his next message and noticed his fingers getting numb as he tried to tap the message out. *4 min. To cut. Stand by.*

Joe began flashing a response, but Kurt had already looked away. It was time to act. He'd spent the last few minutes pulling the false wall and insulation away from the outer hull plating around the port-hole. And using his knife, he'd carved a small cone-shaped hole in the end of the thermal charge that Commander Wells had pulled from the computer panel.

With that done, he'd fashioned a crude device from the wreckage around him, which would allow him to hold the charge up against the wall.

Pulling an emergency flare from his pouch, he prepared to use it as a lighter. Under normal circumstances, holding a flare to a can of rocket fuel would be the epitome of bad ideas, but it was all he had left. *If this doesn't work*, Kurt thought, *at least I go out with a bang*.

He lit the flare and waited a second. With the magnesium flare burning steadily, he touched the flame against the open end of the thermal charge. A couple seconds went by with nothing, then a puff of smoke that swirled through the water. Then, all at once, the thermal charge erupted in a blinding jet of incandescent white flame.

Kurt dropped the flare, swam upward, and held the charge against the bulkhead. The four-thousand-degree flame made quick work of the half-inch steel plate, burning through it, releasing crimson globs of molten steel that fell through the water toward Kurt like blobs of cooling lava.

Kurt dodged them the best he could, but his focus was on the bulk-head up above. He drew the makeshift torch along the bulkhead until he'd made a two-foot horizontal cut. A ninety-degree change in direction started a crosscut.

This incision was a little messy, as the water had become turbulent and cloudy from the smoke. Kurt went back to where the line had dis-connected and then moved on. Soon he was carving a line through the steel back up to where he'd started.

He hoped to cut a square when all was said and done, but his art skills weren't the best under normal circumstances. His last line was anything but straight. As he tried to correct it, a large blob of melted steel broke loose. It cooled to a solid as it dropped through the water, but remained several hundred degrees. Kurt slid to the side, but it caught the edge of his wetsuit as it fell past him, melting the neoprene to his skin.

The pain was intense, but dulled quickly by the chill of the water. Kurt grunted and kept the blowtorch up against the metal. The flame was fading, stuttering, and sparking. It went out as suddenly as it had started.

With the magnetite exhausted, the work was done. One way or another.

Kurt discarded the makeshift torch and swam up to the bulkhead above him. The cut wasn't pretty, but the lines had crossed each other. He put his gloved hand through the porthole and pulled.

Once, twice. Nothing.

The torch had skipped over small sections here and there. Just enough to keep the squarish section locked in place.

The light on his dive computer was now flashing red. Less than one minute of mixture left. The air in the helmet was already getting stale and hot. Knowing he would soon start to black out, Kurt put both feet against the bulkhead and pulled with all his might.

The square flexed but refused to break loose.

Kurt could feel his vision beginning to tunnel. He saw Joe flashing the light in Morse code.

The reduction in oxygen made it hard for Kurt to process.

Mo . . . Mo . . . And then finally: *Move!*

Kurt realized the submersible was charging at him. He pushed off the bulkhead and swam back just as the submersible's nose rammed into the square he'd cut. The plating broke loose, folding in and hanging on for a second until the last finger of metal gave way and it dropped to the floor.

Kurt swam upward. "NUMA was here," he called out while heading for the submersible.

Light spilled from the air lock as Joe opened it. Kurt kicked toward it, but found his muscles weakening. It felt as if he were swimming in molasses, everything slow and heavy. He focused on the ladder, reached for it, and began to pull himself up. As he emerged into the air and lost the natural buoyancy of the water, he suddenly weighed more than his oxygen-starved muscles could support. It became impossible to move.

He was about to slip back into the depths when a pair of arms grabbed ahold of him, hauling him off the ladder and onto the deck. By now Kurt's helmet was fogged up, but as it was pulled off, he took in a deep breath of life-giving air and the welcoming sight of Commander Wells kneeling over him.

She had a bruise on her forehead and was bleeding from her leg. But she was awake and alive and had probably saved Kurt's life as well.

"That's twice I've had to rescue you," she said. "Isn't this supposed to be the other way around?"

After several deep breaths he sat up next to her. "You're a mess," he said. "A beautiful mess. Thank you."

She pointed to his bloody nose and the melted neoprene on the side of his skin. "You're quite a wreck yourself."

He reached over and hit the switch to close the hatch. Even that move proved to be painful. "Just tell me it wasn't for nothing."

She pointed to a container on the far side of the air lock. It was the pouch from her harness. "The hard drives are secure. Now we just need to find out what's on them."

34

WASHINGTON COUNTRY CLUB
ARLINGTON, VIRGINIA

Rudi Gunn stood on the tee box at the seventeenth hole of the Champions Course at the Washington Country Club with an old-fashioned wooden driver in his hand. He initiated his backswing, drove his legs, and struck the ball with near perfect timing. The persimmon clubhead launched his shot effortlessly down the fairway, a center-cut drive with a slight fade designed to hold the ball up against the sloping grass, which ran down to a trickling creek.

Marcus Wagner stood behind him with a cigar clenched in his mouth and a crooked grin on his face. His own shot had been just as well placed, but twenty yards shorter. Removing the cigar, he offered Rudi a compliment of sorts.

"Nice shot," he told his playing partner. "But tell me, what ancient shipwreck did you find that club on? Looks like something Ben Hogan might have used . . . in his younger years."

"I like the old clubs," Rudi said. "You have better feel and more control. Considering your issues with control, you might want to invest in a set."

The grin went away. The cigar went back in the Rear Admiral's mouth. With the clubs returned to their golf bags, the two men piled into separate carts. They drove side by side down the fairway.

Pulling close, Wagner leaned toward Rudi. "I don't have issues with control," he shouted. "Just the lack thereof."

Rudi kept his eyes on the fairway. "How much control are you exerting over Commander Jodi Wells these days?"

Wagner kept his speed up. "Did she make contact with your people?"

"In a manner of speaking," Rudi said. "Would have been easier if you told us she was down there."

"She hasn't exactly kept us apprised on her location," Wagner said. "Or much else for that matter."

"So I heard," Rudi said. "What I want to know is how she knew about NUMA's involvement?"

Wagner was smiling now. "You think I told her?"

"Did you?"

He laughed. "If I could reach her, I wouldn't have needed your help. Fact is, Austin and Zavala have been running around Nassau like a herd of thundering elephants. As capable as they are, those two leave a trail of wreckage everywhere they go."

Rudi couldn't really dispute that. "Still, you were hoping they'd hook up. Why?"

Wagner slowed his cart, but continued to drive, chewing on the cigar as much as smoking it. They reached the bottom of the hill and moved through a narrow part of the fairway that was wooded on both sides. There was no one else around. He pulled to a stop a few yards from his ball. "Look, Rudi, I don't like this cloak-and-dagger stuff any more than you do. But it's necessary."

"Again I ask: Why?"

"Because my unit isn't secure right now."

Rudi was shocked at Wagner's frankness. "You're compromised? How badly?"

Wagner shrugged. "Classified data and information have been stolen. At least two operations have been blown. Including a mission that I sent her on."

"Go on."

"I told you we were looking into these drone attacks," Wagner said. "But it didn't start there, it started with incidents in Havana, Seoul, and Moscow. Embassy and military personnel getting sick for no reason. Most of them reporting some level of auditory hallucinations."

"Havana Syndrome," Rudi said. "I've heard of it."

"What you don't know is that Commander Wells and her team were tasked with tracking down leads. Including a missing American scientist who'd been working for the Navy and looking at ways to remotely disrupt brain waves and other parts of the central nervous system. We picked up good intel suggesting experiments were being conducted at a spot east of Havana, near a town called Arcos. Satellite passes told us an old mill had been converted into a test site. Too much traffic in and out. A large radio tower built out back. Dead cattle all over the property. We sent her in with a combat team to get a look and bring the American scientist back. As I'm guessing she told your guys, it went badly."

"I've heard her side," Rudi admitted. "Now tell me what I don't know."

"The whole thing turned out to be a setup," Wagner explained. "Three guys got killed, two badly wounded. Two more were trapped and left behind. Commander Wells got her wounded out and then went back in to get the others. She took a bullet and suffered second-degree burns in the process. She spent a month in the infirmary. I went to see her every day. And the day she was discharged, she vanished along with another naval intelligence operative named Walker. They've been on a private safari ever since."

"And you're letting them run?"

"Sometimes you have to trust your people first."

Rudi understood that. "According to Kurt, Walker is missing. Apparently, he was on the *Heron*."

Wagner swore under his breath. "All the more reason I need your help. Otherwise, she's alone."

Rudi understood the fire in Wagner's voice. But there was just one catch. "Unless I'm wrong, you're one of the people she doesn't trust."

"She's just being smart," Wagner said. "Too many things have gone wrong to take any chances. Very few people knew about the mission to Cuba. I was obviously one of them. She has to consider the possibility that I could be the leak."

"Are you?"

"Sure," Wagner said, smirking. "It's been my master plan all along. Fight my way out of a tough neighborhood near Albany, graduate near the top of my class at the Naval Academy, and then spend the next thirty years rising through the ranks, all so I could sell out to some random drone pirate when I got to the top of my profession. And then—just to make things interesting—I figured I'd reach out to an old friend at the one agency in Washington known for unwavering tenacity at solving various mysteries and ask them to investigate . . . me, apparently."

Rudi laughed. He didn't think Wagner was a problem, it was more a way of pushing his old friend's buttons. "You were always known for your long-term goals."

"Not that long."

"Okay," Rudi said, "but if not you, then who?"

Wagner shook his head. "We've tried every trick in the book to figure that out. No dice. Whoever compromised the mission has gone to ground and they're not coming up again until they have no other choice. In other words, whenever we get close to the final answer."

"Which is why you're happy enough letting Commander Wells run her private operation," Rudi said. "As long as she gets our help."

"She's going to see this through whether you help her or not," Wagner said. "I'd like her to have a fighting chance."

Rudi understood that. He had a few people cut from similar cloth. He pulled to a stop. "In that case you need to tell me everything. Starting with the Chinese spy trawler. What do you know about it?"

Wagner didn't bother with the song and dance. He just answered. "It was patrolling the waters off the Georgia coast, spying on our submarines as they came in and out of Kings Bay. The Chinese want sonar profiles of all our boats, in hopes they can track us one day. We make sure the boomers run past them while making an inordinate amount of noise so they won't have any idea how quiet they really are."

"What does it have to do with the drones?"

Wagner shrugged. "Never got that memo."

Rudi had the data from the hard drives now. He wasn't sure how much to share with Wagner at this point. He gave him a broad overview. "The Chinese picked up suspicious radar signals that turned out to be a drone attack on a Moroccan-flagged freighter. After closing in on the stricken ship, they detected a small, electrically powered submarine departing the area and heading south into the Caribbean. It turned to follow and shortly thereafter got pasted with the same treatment as the men on the *Heron*. Only, based on Kurt's report, the Chinese got it worse than anyone. Most of them dead at their duty stations. One of them ripped his own eyes out. Which suggests this weapon you've been worried about can be tuned up and down for effect."

The look on Wagner's face said this was new and unwanted information. "What's the make on the submarine?"

"Unknown."

"What's it used for?"

"We're going with the idea that the drones hit the ships and incapacitate the crew. Then the submarine shows up and takes the cargo."

"Sounds reasonable," Wagner said. "Where was it headed?"

"That's the million-dollar question," Rudi replied. "South, but to where?"

"Some of the missing cargoes have been smuggled through Havana."

Rudi nodded. He knew this. "I can't help but notice that Cuba keeps popping up in the narrative."

"Cuba's the Wild West. Beyond our reach and beyond the international system of laws for the most part. The goods are being smuggled through Havana because it's the easiest place to move them without having to worry about American interference or international scrutiny. But the Cubans are not behind this."

"How can you be so sure?"

"Because if they had this technology, they'd be doing a lot more than stealing cargo and making random sailors jump off their ships."

It was hard to argue with that assessment, Rudi thought, but the trail led where it led.

Setting the brake, he stepped out of his cart and grabbed a seven-iron from his bag.

He walked over to the nearest ball, lined up the shot, and swung hard and clean, launching the ball in a towering arc. It flew up the hill, carried the front of the green, and dropped softly onto the dance floor just out of sight. From the sound alone, Rudi was pretty sure it had checked up and stopped within ten feet of the pin.

Wagner was impressed. Except for one thing. "You realize you just hit my ball."

Rudi knew that. "Isn't that what you're asking me to do?" Rudi said. "To finish the game for you?"

Wagner nodded slowly. "It eliminates any chance of a leak."

To make sure that was the case, Rudi imposed his own news

blackout. "I'm going to cut you out of the loop after this. No more surprise appearances at Beltway fundraisers or golf at five in the morning."

Wagner understood. "Do whatever you have to," he said. "And don't worry about me. I'm going to visit another old friend who's finishing up his last deployment. That'll keep me out of your hair for a while."

Rudi thought that was probably for the best. "My people are at risk now, right along with yours."

"I'm sorry about that," Wagner said. "But something major is happening here. Something bigger than piracy, sabotage, and tricky little mind games. Which means we're all facing some kind of risk. We just don't know what it is yet."

On that, the two of them agreed.

35

SOMEWHERE OVER THE CARIBBEAN

The modified NUMA C-130 was heading west from Florida, on a mission to drop sonobuoys as part of a study related to whale migrations in the Gulf Stream. The weather was fine, it was a perfect day for flying. The pilots were well settled into their routine, almost bored, when the communications officer who was linked to NUMA HQ came forward.

"Change in orders, guys," he said. "New flight path. And a narrow window to drop the buoys." He handed them a printed sheet.

The captain looked at it and scratched his head. "They say why?"

"Nope," the comms officer said. "Just set the buoys to listen for a new frequency and drop in this pattern."

"That's a pretty tight spread," the copilot said. "Less than a mile between them."

"Yep. And they want all forty of them dropped ASAP."

"This can't be right," the captain said, handing the printout back. "Double-check with them."

"I have," the comms officer said. "Twice. This is what they want. And they want it done now."

The copilot let out a soft whistle and began plotting a new course. "So much for the whale watching."

The captain shrugged. "Never a dull moment." He switched off the autopilot and took control of the plane, banking to the south and putting on some speed.

———

Eighty miles away, directly south of Key West, a NUMA research vessel was receiving a similar order.

"They want us to do what?" the executive officer said.

The navigation officer drew an X on the chart. "Head at flank speed to these coordinates." He drew a line from there to the southwest. "Begin dropping hydrophones and sonobouys along this course until we hit Cuban territorial waters. Then launch our AUVs and have them extend the line to within five miles of the coast."

The XO was baffled. "For God's sake, why?"

"No reason given," the navigation officer said. "But if you ask me, this is setting a picket line. They're looking for something, and it's not a fish or a whale."

The executive officer nodded. He'd commanded a frigate in the Navy before joining NUMA. He knew what they were looking for.

"Flank speed," he ordered. "Get those sensors ready. Whatever HQ is looking for we don't want to miss it by being late."

The helmsman began the turn, a grin lighting up his face from all the excitement. What none of them knew was that similar orders were being given to every asset NUMA had in the Caribbean.

36

PRINCESS MARGARET HOSPITAL
NASSAU, BAHAMAS

Dr. Pascal stood at the nurses' station on the fourth floor of Princess Margaret Hospital in Nassau. She and Dr. Pinder had been caring for the *Heron*'s surviving crew members and were now discussing their situation with Commander Hastings and several other Bahamian government officials.

After the disaster with the *Hercules*, the public wanted answers and, therefore, so did the politicians.

"We don't have any answers to give you," she told the assembled dignitaries.

All eyes went to Pinder. He was their man.

"I'm afraid Dr. Pascal has spoken with great accuracy," he said. "The crewmen discovered belowdecks have returned to a nearly normal state. But one that includes memory lapses, sleep issues, and what I would consider a subdued affect. While awake, they still appear as if they're under the influence of some drug."

"But there's nothing in their blood," Dr. Pascal added.

"What about the captain?" Hastings asked. "All along his condition has been different. Is he still in a coma?"

Dr. Pinder explained what had become a very nuanced diagnosis. "We don't consider his condition to be the equivalent of a coma or a vegetative state. There's too much brain activity. At the moment we're describing it as unconsciousness with continuous rapid eye movement suggestive of a dreaming state."

"If he's dreaming, we should wake him up," one of the government men said. "What about using stimulants or adrenaline injections? Surely there's something that can jolt him out of this."

Dr. Pinder tried to hide his frustration. "These things have been tried on many unconscious patients. They simply don't work."

"Actually, there may be a way," Dr. Pascal said.

As they focused on her, she wrestled with an internal dilemma. Sleep was one of the main ways the human body protected and healed itself. In fact, badly injured patients were often put into medically induced comas to allow their bodies to heal through the initial stages of significant injuries. To wake an injured man could be unethical and counterproductive, but as far as they could tell the captain wasn't technically injured in any way. And as one set of tests suggested that his brain activity was slowly diminishing, she worried that he might be sinking further and further into the dreamworld.

"And that way is . . ." one of the government officials prodded.

"Ambien," she said.

"Ambien?" the other minister said. "Isn't that a sleeping pill?"

"It's normally used for that purpose," Dr. Pascal said. "Because it can slow down the effect of overactive neurons. But it has been used successfully to bring people out of vegetative states and back up to what we call minimal consciousness, where they can respond to questions. Success is often limited by the type of injury that put the patient into the coma in the first place, but we haven't detected any sign of injury to the captain's brain. Just a wave of activity that seems to override any outside stimuli."

She looked at Hastings and tried to explain it in military terms.

"Think of it like a radar-jamming technique. Instead of blocking the signal, you overload the signal so that the radar system sees thousands of returns instead of just one. The captain's brain is experiencing something similar, so much activity that it can't be sorted out or organized."

"And your sleeping pill will reduce this storm of activity and allow us to speak to him?" Hastings asked.

"Possibly," Dr. Pascal replied. "No guarantees."

"Is it dangerous?"

"Possibly," she repeated.

Hastings looked around. The ministers hemmed and hawed, not wanting to go on record. That left it up to him. Hastings made the decision on the spot. "Wake him up . . . If you can."

———

Captain Handley was in a private room in the ICU with two guards out front and another down the hall. Drs. Pinder and Pascal entered the room first with the government entourage following close behind.

With the door shut and proper entries made into the chart, Dr. Pascal prepared a syringe. The injection was given, and a stopwatch started. "Now we wait."

Ten minutes went by before there was any sign of the medicine taking effect. The first indication was a subtle reduction in heart rate and blood pressure, and then a flattening of the erratic brain wave patterns being printed out on the EEG.

"It's working," one of the government officials whispered.

Dr. Pascal remained silent. The tiny effects were promising, but they didn't prove anything.

Another minute went by. And then two more. For a brief second the EEG flatlined. But as it rebounded, the captain woke up with a jerk.

He bolted upright on the gurney. The sudden move taking everyone by surprise. His hands went up as if swatting at something and he began flailing around uncontrollably.

"Get off my ship!" he shouted.

Dr. Pinder leaned closer, trying to calm him, but the captain threw him backward with a one-handed shove. Pinder crashed to the floor and Hastings moved in to help.

"Stop!" Dr. Pascal shouted. "Let him be. He's working out the last memories. They've been playing on a loop in his mind for days."

It was a guess, but a reasonable one.

Hastings stepped back as the captain continued shouting. His voice was high and hoarse, his movements jerky. With awkwardness that suggested his muscles hadn't woken up yet, he climbed from the bed, ripping the skullcap filled with electrodes from his head.

Stumbling but staying upright, he grabbed the IV pole. But instead of using it for support, he turned it sideways and began swinging it back and forth in a wide arc, saline solution streaming around the room.

The guards burst in after hearing the commotion. Hastings stood them down with a hand gesture and Dr. Pascal tried to get the captain to focus on her.

"You're not on the ship anymore," she said. "Look around. You're safe now. You're in Nassau. At Princess Margaret Hospital."

He looked past her as if she weren't there. "The ship is under attack."

"I can promise you that the ship is no longer in any danger," she replied. There was some truth to that, assuming one discounted rust and saltwater corrosion from the list of dangers.

Sweat poured down his face. His brow furrowed as he tried to focus on her. Each time he went to speak he winced as if he were feeling intense pain. "I . . . I . . ."

One of the few instruments still attached to him was a heart rate monitor taped to his chest. It began chirping an alarm. The numbers on the telemetry unit pegged his heart rate at one fifty and then one eighty and still rising.

"Captain, you need to calm down," she said.

He looked at the beeping machine and clutched at the wire on his chest. Looking up, he tried to say something, but once again the words caught in his throat.

"Captain?" Dr. Pascal said.

His body stiffened and his eyes rolled back in his head.

"Captain!"

He toppled over like a falling tree, slamming to the floor as the alarm on the wall changed its tone and the heart rate indicator went to zero.

"He's coding!" Dr. Pinder shouted.

Dr. Pascal had already figured that out. But why? He had a pacemaker with an internal defibrillator in his chest. It had saved him from the heart attack on the ship, it should have kept his heart rate down and shocked it back to normal rhythm.

"Get the crash cart," she called out.

Pinder had already grabbed the cart from its spot by the wall. Dr. Pascal dropped down beside the patient, removing the heart monitor and the other leads. A shrill whine told her the paddles were charging.

"Clear!"

She pulled back as Pinder applied the shock.

The captain's body spasmed and fell back. The smell of burned skin wafted around the room.

Dr. Pascal leaned in, searching for a pulse. There was none to be found. She looked up at Dr. Pinder and shook her head.

He raised the power output and charged the system once more. "Clear," he said more calmly this time.

She pulled back and the second shock was applied. The captain's body contracted once more, but his heart remained in cardiac arrest.

"Maybe this was a mistake," one of the ministers suggested.

"You can sue me later," Dr. Pascal said. "Now get out of the way."

She began compressions while wondering if her idea to wake him would end up causing the man's death. "Come on, Captain," she urged. "Come on back to us."

"Clear," Dr. Pinder said once more.

Dr. Pascal had lost her focus for a second and was checking the captain's eyes as Dr. Pinder applied the shock again. Part of the current went through the captain's body and into hers. She saw a flash and heard a snap as the electricity jumped from his skull into her hand.

The charge knocked her backward and her body tingled from head to toe. She grabbed her arm, which felt as if it had been set on fire and numbed at the same time. Grunting a string of bad words that she hoped the others couldn't quite make out, she rolled over and turned back to her patient.

The pain and distress vanished. The captain was sitting up, panting like he'd just run a marathon, but not fighting or screaming or turning blue. He looked around from one person to the next and then finally spoke a few husky words. "I'd pay a week's wages for a nice cup of water."

Dr. Pascal could hardly believe what she was seeing. Not only was the captain alive, but his behavior was suddenly normal. No more clenching and seizing as he tried to get words out. His eyes were no longer darting around the room in a panic. Something had changed. Instantly and drastically. It was too sudden, rapid, and complete to be an effect of the Ambien. It had to be the defibrillator.

The electric shock had done more than reset his heart rhythm, it had rebooted his malfunctioning mind.

37

THE CARIBBEAN SEA

Kurt, Joe, and Commander Wells were gathered on the foredeck of Rolle's sailboat as it tracked south across sparkling waters underneath a cloudless sky. But instead of enjoying the sun and wind, they were huddled in the shadow of the main sail gazing at a computer screen.

The screen was divided into two sections. One side displayed an image of Dr. Pascal, while the other side showed a silvery object with a pair of long, curving wires attached to it. Corrosion of some type was evident along the wires like a buildup of limescale.

"What exactly are we looking at?" Kurt asked, returning his focus to Dr. Pascal.

"This is a biventricular pacemaker," Dr. Pascal explained. "Equipped with an internal defibrillator. The metallic square is a pulse generator. The long wires you see are leads that go into the heart and deliver the electrical impulse that causes the heart to contract. We removed it from the *Heron*'s captain late last night and replaced it with a new one."

"And that's important why?"

"Remember when I told you he'd had a heart attack?" she said.

"This thing saved him, but it did so at a cost. Drawing all this plaque out of his bloodstream instead of allowing it to go to his brain."

Kurt figured she was building toward something and chose not to interrupt with a bunch of questions. "Go on."

Dr. Pascal directed their attention back to the pacemaker. "The pulse generator is made of titanium, a noncorrosive and nonreactive metal. The leads are made of platinum coated with silicon for insulation. Neither material should be suffering any corrosion or sedimentary buildup, but the leads are almost completely encased."

"I assume it's not high cholesterol," Joe said.

"You assume correctly," Dr. Pascal replied. "Let me give you a closer look."

The image on the screen changed to a photograph that had been taken through a microscope. It showed a long cylinder covered in elongated ovals.

"The cylinder is a section of the platinum wire at a magnification of two hundred and fifty," Dr. Pascal explained. "The ovals, which look vaguely like a colony of bacteria, are the plaque buildup you saw in the other photo. But now take an even closer look."

Another image appeared, this time at a thousand times magnification. Now they could see the individual ovals. They were more crystalline in shape than they had appeared farther out, translucent, and appearing to contain microscopic coils inside.

Kurt and Joe came to the same conclusion at the same time. "They're machines."

"Electromagnetic receptors," Dr. Pascal said. "Half the size of an average grain of pollen."

"What do they do?" Commander Wells asked.

"When stimulated with the right frequency they emit a local current in a harmonic manner," Dr. Pascal said. "Working together they create a low-wave pulse in their immediate vicinity. For the captain of the *Heron*, this meant trouble with his pacemaker and the heart attack. For the other members of the ship—the deck crew especially—it meant an overriding electrical wave coursing through their minds at a frequency tuned to match human brain waves. This made them violent, psychotic, and in some cases suicidal. Eventually—when enough damage was done—they turned catatonic. Think of it as the mind shutting down because it knows its program is crashing and needs to be rebooted."

"How did they get in his system?" Kurt asked.

"There are several possibilities," she said. "Injection, inhalation, even surface contact. Based on what we learned earlier, I'd guess they were airborne, sprayed out in a fog of sorts. Once the crew breathed them in, they would enter the bloodstream using the lungs and the mucous membranes in the nose and throat. From there they circulate until they reach the blood-brain barrier, which they seem particularly well designed to penetrate."

Joe asked the next question. "But why did they go to the captain's heart and everyone else's brain?"

"They're attracted to electrical activity," Dr. Pascal said. "Most of them would normally be drawn to the brain. And scans show the captain has several deposits of them in his gray matter. But the pacemaker and its electrical current attracted enough of them to his heart to keep him from becoming incapacitated. That's why he was able to grab the shotgun you found and fight back, while the rest of the crew was collapsing or jumping overboard."

Commander Wells asked, "If this was an airborne fog, why were the crewmen inside the ship affected?"

"The particles are so small they would be sucked in through the ventilation system and dispersed throughout the ship. While some percentage of them would be filtered out or end up adhering to the various surfaces, there would still be plenty left over to affect the interior compartments. Though probably to a lesser degree."

Dr. Pascal paused for a moment and adjusted her glasses before addressing Commander Wells directly. "You weren't with us yet," she said, a small amount of territorial pride in her voice, "but Kurt actually found a layer of grime on the exhaust vent in the *Heron*'s engineering compartment. If the ship hadn't sunk, we might have been able to test the residue for confirmation, but I wouldn't be surprised if that layer of grime was filled with these particles."

"Sorry I missed it," Commander Wells said.

"Glad I wore my hazmat suit," Kurt said.

Joe glanced at Kurt. "Receiving a lower dose of these particles might explain why the crewmen belowdecks were still conscious and active but delusional."

Kurt thought that sounded reasonable. "Let me get this straight," he said. "The crew breathe this stuff in, it goes to their brains and makes them crazy. The more you absorb, the crazier you get. Is that it?"

"Close," Dr. Pascal said. "But my exam suggests that the particles remain inert until an external signal activates the coils inside. It's only then that the harmonic pulse overrides the person's own natural brain waves. Something like hypnosis."

Joe wrinkled his brow. "I always thought hypnosis was kind of a scam, with actors planted in the audience and such."

"Not at all," Dr. Pascal said. "I've used hypnosis to perform surgery on patients who were allergic to anesthetic. When I was a resident, we used it on soldiers with terrible PTSD and some patients with untreatable depression."

"That's incredible," Joe said. "I had no idea."

"Truth is," Dr. Pascal continued, "with normal hypnosis, about fifteen percent of people become what hypnotists call 'highs,' or highly hypnotizable persons. These people can be made to do almost anything. Most people are 'mediums,' who respond moderately to hypnosis but not to the extent that you could perform surgery on them. The last fifteen percent are considered 'lows,' meaning they're nearly impossible to get into a hypnotic state, usually because they're stubborn and don't believe in the process to begin with. But with a person's brain waves altered by these tiny microchips, almost everyone will be a 'high.' That is, they'll be easy to hypnotize, capable of being directed to do things they would otherwise never do."

"Like shoot the other members of your fire team," Commander Wells said darkly.

"Or jump off a ship without a life jacket," Joe added.

On-screen, Dr. Pascal nodded. "Both the captain and the surviving crewmen recall hearing a voice giving them orders. These voices could be a by-product of the brain wave disruption, a form of auditory hallucination. Or they could be something more. The captain insists he heard someone commanding him to cut the trawler loose, and that even as he was fighting the idea, he felt almost compelled to obey. We know that trawler ended up being cut free. It suggests another member of the crew may have heard that same command and given in to it."

"What are the chances of two separate people suffering the same auditory hallucination?" Kurt asked.

"It's almost impossible," Dr. Pascal replied, "which tells me the command was being broadcast somehow. Perhaps from the drones."

"Is there any way to tell if someone is acting under this hypnotic influence?" Kurt asked.

"Most likely they'd seem out of it," Dr. Pascal said. "As if they were mildly intoxicated or drugged or really tired."

That was something, Kurt thought.

"But there is another danger I can't rule out," Dr. Pascal said. "Posthypnotic suggestion. It would allow a person to return to their real life and normal behavior, only to be activated by a code word or a series of tones. In those shows Joe talked about, the hypnotist usually sends someone back to their seat after planting the suggestion that they'll bark like a dog or cluck like a chicken when they hear a certain word. And then of course, several minutes later, he utters that word, and they jump up and start barking. If you've ever seen one of those shows, the hypnotist has to remove the suggestion before he lets the person leave or it will linger. With the power of these brain wave–altering microchips, a far more complex suggestion could be placed. And that person would appear perfectly normal until they were activated."

"You're talking full *Manchurian Candidate* stuff here," Kurt said.

"Or *Winter Soldier* stuff," Joe added. "If you're into superhero movies. Or anything that happened after the sixties."

"I like old movies," Kurt said. "Classics."

As Kurt and Joe laughed, Commander Wells exhaled with a sense of frustration. "Mass hypnosis," she began. "It's the fever dream of every PSYOPS supporter I've ever met. I've heard them promise to end riots without the help of a single policeman or win wars without firing a shot. Could you imagine if the Russians had something like this when they went into Ukraine? Or what the Chinese would do with this if they had it in their arsenal?"

"You could turn an army against its people," Dr. Pascal added from the screen. "Turn soldiers against their units."

"Why even bother to invade?" Joe said. "Just get to the leaders and give them a dose of this stuff. They'll do whatever you tell them."

Kurt was not oblivious to the far-reaching dangers of the weapon. But the fact was, it hadn't been used in such a way. At least not yet. He figured there was a reason for that. "There has to be some good news," he said. "How'd you get the captain back to normal?"

"We tried to wake him up last night," she said. "As a result, he experienced an arrythmia and went into cardiac arrest. We shocked him to get his heart beating again. The surge of electrical current overloaded the coils inside the particles. Burning them out, like a million little fuses."

"Interesting," Kurt said. "So, there's a countermeasure."

"If you want to try electroshock therapy, yes."

"What's the captain's prognosis?" Commander Wells asked.

"Short-term, he's fine," Dr. Pascal said. "Dealing with some confusion and balance issues. Long-term, who knows? Some damage may have been caused that can't be undone."

A natural pause hit the conversation and the air went quiet. Commander Wells broke the silence with a sigh. She looked concerned, but also as if a weight had been lifted off her shoulders. She'd been bucking the system and looking for proof that she wasn't on a wild-goose chase for two solid years. Now, thanks to Dr. Pascal, she had some.

She looked into the camera and put her hands together in a gesture of appreciation. "Thank you," she said. "That's the first solid evidence we've had."

"You're welcome," Dr. Pascal replied. "Take care of my guys out there. Make sure they know I'm not happy at being left behind."

"I'll do my best," Commander Wells said.

Kurt laughed. He had a feeling the women would have bonded, given the chance. "Anything else before we sign off?"

"Just be careful," Dr. Pascal said. "And if you come up on a fog bank, steer clear."

Kurt nodded and signed off. Looking back, he saw Rolle standing at the helm and gesturing at something up ahead.

Kurt looked past the main sail. Thankfully, there was no fog up ahead, only the impressive sight of a humpback whale splashing back down into the water after a powerful breach. He considered it a good omen.

Joe stood up and stretched his legs. "I'll go take over for Rolle. He's been at the wheel all morning."

Joe moved off, resolute and ready as always. Kurt was feeling good as well. They finally had some information about the threat—and more information was always better than less. To his surprise Commander Wells seemed downcast. Her body language suggesting apprehension and a sense of foreboding.

"You okay?"

She looked up at him, her blue eyes catching the sun. "I'm fine," she said. "Just not looking forward to going back to Cuba. A lot of bad things happened there."

"Well," Kurt said with a grin, "you don't have to worry about that now. We passed Cuba in the middle of the night. We're heading for another island."

Her eyes widened and her face brightened. "What?"

"Rudi took a chance," Kurt said. "After he got the information from the Chinese trawler and identified the sonar signature of the mystery submarine, he realized it was small and quiet, but also slow and not impossible to track. He ordered every ship and plane at NUMA's disposal to start dropping sonobuoys along the sub's possible path. Just to see if we could pick up its trail."

"And?"

"Havana was the obvious destination," Kurt explained. "But the sub bypassed it, never getting within twenty miles of the coast. It rounded Cape San Antonio and turned south. It's about a hundred miles in front of us, but based on the latest picket line of sonar pods, it hasn't changed course a single degree."

"Where's it heading?"

"A small island off Panama called Providencia."

Kurt looked up at the sail and the sun. Rolle's boat was running smooth and fast. "We're doing seventeen knots, the sub is doing four and a half. With a little luck, we'll arrive before it does."

"And then?"

"We see who shows up to collect the spoils."

38

RIO DE JANEIRO, BRAZIL

Boarding the *Condor* reminded Paul of embarking on a great ocean liner in the bygone days of travel. He and Gamay entered the fabrication building and traveled up a long gangway, assisted by a moving sidewalk beneath their feet.

At the top of the gangway, they entered a luxuriously appointed hall with a thirty-foot ceiling and a magnificent swirling stairway that rose to the next deck. Art deco fixtures lined the walls, while a large chandelier cast a warm glow across the space.

The great hall spanned the lower deck of the airship, sporting sharply raked windows that allowed the passengers to look out and down on both the near and far walls.

At the center of the room, a tuxedoed man sat in front of a gleaming grand piano, smoothly coaxing music from the ivory keys. Like everything else on the *Condor*, the piano had been specially designed to save weight. It was made from a special wood putty filled with air bubbles and laid over a hollow aluminum core. Instead of weighing seven hundred pounds, the piano weighed only ninety.

The sleek furniture was designed in similar fashion and the obsession with reducing weight went even to the crew. Strict standards of height and weight had been enforced, and in general, smaller crew members had been selected. Directly ahead of them, a receiving line of uniformed officers greeted every guest, not one man or woman any taller than Gamay.

Wearing the uniform of a commodore, Solari greeted the Trouts himself. He took them on a tour of the main lobby and then down a corridor to their quarters. "I've given to you the Presidential Suite," he told them. "Only the best for my friends from America."

At the touch of a button, pocket doors slid back to allow them into their room. It was of modern design, with a king-size bed and a luxurious bathroom.

A steward placed their bags in the closet as Paul and Gamay were drawn to the full-length windows on the far side of the compartment. Like those in the salon, they were tilted down with the angle of the airship's hull, affording a view of the world below. For now, all they revealed was the interior of the massive hangar and the calm waters below.

Craning his neck to see the far end, Paul noticed a growing aura of light as the massive doors began to slide open. Down below, a pair of tugboats eased into position, one to offer a gentle push from behind, while the other pulled the airship softly ahead.

Gamay turned to Solari. "How much would a cabin like this cost on a transatlantic run? If, for example, someone wanted to plan a second honeymoon or something."

"Forty thousand per night," Solari said. "U.S. dollars."

A bemused look appeared on Paul's face. "Guess we'll have to enjoy it while we can."

Solari laughed and handed them two thick ID cards. "These will give you run of the house. While the luxury appointments are all very nice, I suspect it's the mechanical spaces and capabilities of the craft that are more interesting to NUMA. Once we've launched, I'll arrange for one of my crew to take you wherever you'd like."

Gamay took the cards and thanked Solari.

"I shall see you at the reception on the Astra Salon in thirty minutes," Solari added. "Trust me, there's no better spot from which to enjoy our departure."

The Astra Salon did not disappoint. Situated nine levels above the main deck at the very front of the airship, it was an arrowhead-shaped balcony, open to the air around them and equipped with retractable wind deflectors and chest-high rails made of clear acrylic.

A few dozen passengers were gathered here, sipping champagne delivered by cocktail waitresses in uniform. Gamay spotted several Brazilian dignitaries, a few celebrities whose names she couldn't quite place, and dozens of others who would count themselves among the world's rich, if not the famous.

As this run was technically a goodwill tour, the *Condor* was only half full, though Solari insisted they were carrying a thousand tons of time-sensitive cargo.

Sipping champagne and admiring the view, Gamay took the opportunity to ask a few questions. "Five thousand tons sounds like a lot of freight, but it's small potatoes compared to your average seagoing ship."

"We carry things that sell at a premium," Solari explained. "And we deliver in days instead of weeks. Remember the supply-chain bottlenecks? When the ports were clogged and the ships were stuck waiting to dock, our fleet made two hundred and nineteen journeys across the Pacific in a nine-month period, helping put an end to all that. And since we work off a hub-and-spoke system, instead of point to point like container ships, our economies of scale improve every time we launch a new vessel—like this one."

Paul was impressed. "What's your fuel burn?"

"Zero," Solari said. "This is a fully electric vehicle. You haven't seen it yet, but I'll take you to the top deck of the ship and show you the solar farm. It's made out of solar film. Twenty thousand square feet of it. Completely flush with the hull. It even curves around the side, so we can absorb solar radiation when the sun is low."

"How much power do you generate?"

"On a sunny day, enough to power a small city. More than enough for our engines and onboard use."

"What about on cloudy days?" Gamay asked.

Solari grinned. "There are no cloudy days where we're going."

"But there are long nights."

"We use a solid-state battery system," Solari replied. "Lighter and more powerful than any lithium-ion system. One day of solar radiation can store enough electricity for thirty-six hours of full-powered flight. If we ever need to conserve power, we can turn a few lights off or operate on one engine."

Paul felt himself entering a state of bliss. He wanted to see the engines and the solar farm and the batteries. He couldn't wait to explore the ship from nose to tail.

Gamay was listening more critically. Solid-state batteries were the type used in the drone wreckage Kurt had found.

"When do we lift off?" Paul asked. "I can't wait to see how this thing flies."

"Why, Mr. Trout, haven't you noticed? We're already off the ground."

Paul glanced across the balcony. They'd eased from the fabrication building and into the bay, but they'd also began to rise. There'd been no surge to tell him they were going, no whine of the engines or howl of propellers. It was as if the background were moving instead of the *Condor.*

Soleri urged them toward the railing. Gamay took the bait and leaned into it, looking out and then down. Paul kept several feet of space between him and the clear railing. He could see fine from where he was.

"This is amazing," Gamay said. "We're already a hundred feet off the ground. I never felt us moving."

"For the most part, you won't," Solari insisted. "Another advantage of airship travel, there's very little of what you'd call turbulence."

Similar expressions of amazement and glee were being uttered by others around them.

The *Condor* rose and turned, flying back past the fabrication building and out across Rio. As it picked up speed, a series of mesh wind gates lowered to deflect some of the air around the salon. The result left enough of a breeze to keep the space fresh and airy, but prevented any gusts strong enough to whip up the decorations or ruin anyone's hair. Eventually, once the airship accelerated to cruising speed, the mesh gates would retract and clear acrylic windows would slide in place, meeting up with the chest-high railing, completely shielding the Astra Salon from the elements, but for now it was like riding on the deck of a cruise ship.

With Paul remaining safely away from the railing, Gamay marveled at the sights and sounds from below. They moved south, easing across Ipanema Beach at an altitude of five hundred feet. The engines were so quiet and so far from the Astra Salon that they couldn't be heard. Instead, she picked up the sound of gulls calling and waves crashing down on the beach below.

Down below, the giant shadow of the craft moved silently across the sand and sea. The crowds of people watched it pass, putting whatever they were doing on hold and staring upward until the stately ship had gone by.

Soon they approached Sugarloaf Mountain and the *Christ the Redeemer* statue she and Paul had visited the day before. They eased past the statue, a half mile out, but roughly even with the height of the observation deck. Gamay could see hundreds of people waving. She waved back. Moments later she heard a great cheer go up, and the *Condor* sounded some type of air horn to acknowledge them.

With the review completed, the *Condor* turned east, heading out over the Atlantic and then bending its course to the northwest on a path that would take it across Brazil and Venezuela. By morning they would be cruising over the blue waters of the Caribbean.

Gamay rejoined Paul. "This is incredible," she said. "Easily worth forty thousand a night, if I do say so myself."

Solari grinned. "Let me build one for NUMA and this can be your office."

"I could get used to that," she said.

Paul shook his head. Ironically, he wanted no part of it.

Solari looked hurt. "I thought you'd be enjoying this, Mr. Trout?"

"I am," he said. "I just have a small fear of heights."

"But you're seven feet tall," Solari pointed out.

"Not the first time I've heard that," Paul replied. "What can I tell you?"

As Solari and Paul spoke, Gamay noticed Colon and Mr. Torres coming toward them. She recognized them as the pair who'd put the kibosh on the shakedown flight the day before.

As they arrived, Solari's emotions seemed to nosedive, much as they'd done the day before.

"Sorry to interrupt," Colon announced. "But business calls." He looked directly at Solari. "We need you to speak with some of the investors."

"Understood," Solari said, his voice suddenly a monotone.

Gamay glanced at Paul. There was definitely something odd going on.

Colon turned to them. "I understand you're looking to explore the ship. Be careful. There are some areas where work is continuing. Particularly in the stern."

"No shame in that," Paul said. "Many a vessel has left on its maiden voyage with a work crew putting the final touches on the design." Paul found himself remembering the *Titanic* as one of the more well-known ships that had set sail in such a condition. He kept that part to himself.

"Be that as it may," Torres said, "I can't have them being interfered with and we certainly want to make sure we avoid any type of accident to passengers or crew on our maiden voyage."

39

With Torres, Colon, and Solari off to address their investors, Paul and Gamay had a post-departure snack in the main dining hall, whispering among themselves.

"What do you think about that?" Paul asked.

"Odd," she said. "That's the second time Solari has suddenly changed his personality upon their arrival."

"I was talking about the warning to avoid the stern engineering spaces."

"I wouldn't make that your first stop," she said.

"*My* first stop," Paul said. "I thought we were doing this together?"

"I have an appointment with something called the Angelus Spa," she told him. "I'm not sure what it entails, but I'm willing to risk it."

"Good luck finding clues with cucumber slices over your eyes," Paul said.

As Gamay laughed, a pair of the airship's crewmen came up to them. A young man with curly hair wearing an engineer's overalls, and a woman dressed in the uniform of a spa attendant. These were their separate guides.

"Meet you back at our cabin," Paul said. "And don't be jealous when I have a better time than you."

"Literally not possible," Gamay insisted.

———

Fifteen minutes later, Gamay was in her bathing suit, stepping into a pool of saline water that was heated to a temperature of eighty-six degrees, such that her skin could barely detect the presence of the liquid once she'd immersed herself.

"How's the water?" the spa attendant asked.

"Goldilocks zone," Gamay said. "Not too hot nor too cold."

"Perfect. Now pull the goggles on and lie face down in the water."

Gamay had been given a set of curved goggles. They fit snugly to her face and allowed a nearly one-hundred-and-eighty-degree view with very little distortion.

With the goggles affixed she lay down in the water, breathing through a snorkel, as she'd done a thousand times in her life. The dark pool was relaxing. A sort of sensory deprivation tank, she assumed. Then it started to move. Descending on hydraulic arms.

She wasn't sure how far they'd moved, when the motion ceased.

"Everything okay?" she asked. "I'm not being lowered into a shark tank or anything, right?"

"Of course not," the spa attendant said. "Please just try to relax, this is an immersive experience."

People telling her to relax had a way of making Gamay tense up, but she fought against it this time and took slow deep breaths while floating and staring downward into the darkness. And then the darkness began receding. The pool or pod she was in was essentially an acrylic tub, its walls changing from smoked and opaque to clear. As the shading vanished, she realized she was now floating in the water, but extended out and below the hull.

Directly underneath her lay the trees of a rainforest, the shadow of the great airship racing across the tops. To the right she watched thin filaments of mist passing like smoke trails. While from the left came a flight of large birds. They swung close and then veered away, revealing their colorful feathers, only to pick up speed as they dove and then raced back up toward the airship, soon joining it in a bit of formation flying. The pattern of their movements reminded her of dolphins playing in the bow wave of a ship.

For the moment Gamay was in awe. Suspended weightless in the water, she felt as if she herself were flying.

"Ms. Trout," the attendant said quietly. "Please remember to breathe. This experience is best if you exhale slowly."

Gamay realized she'd been holding her breath. She followed the instructions, breathing calmly and looking around in every direction. It was peaceful and also somewhat disorienting. Like a dream, only real and visceral.

She stared and stared and soon lost track of time. She found herself thinking it was one of the most amazing experiences of her life and one that Paul wouldn't have lasted ten seconds in once the acrylic turned clear.

———

As it turned out, Paul was looking through a clear acrylic barrier of his own. But instead of mist and trees and birds he was staring into the vast intake tunnels that brought the air to the gleaming ceramic impeller blades that powered the airship. The huge disks were spinning slowly, compressing the air and forcing it out through exhaust nozzles at the stern. The effort propelled the *Condor* along at a leisurely forty knots.

Like everything else about the *Condor*, the engines operated smoothly and quietly. Standing in the engine room, Paul heard nothing that resembled the buzz of high-speed propellers, the howling of jet engines, or the endless thumping of overhead rotors. Just a smooth and steady rush, like water through a large pipe.

The chief engineer walked him through the control systems, boasting that the *Condor* and its sister ships could reach a top speed of one hundred and fifty knots, and then explained that it was rarely necessary to do so, because they took advantage of wind patterns that spanned the globe, traveling with a tailwind almost everywhere they went.

From the engine room Paul went forward to the control deck, which sat in the lower section of the airship's nose. It was wide and spacious and more like the bridge of an oceangoing vessel than the cramped cockpit of an airliner.

He met Captain Miguel Bascombe, a man in his early sixties, who sported gray hair beneath a captain's hat, lengthy sideburns and, of all things, a handlebar mustache.

Bascombe stood behind a pair of crewmen, who kept watch through the forward-leaning windows, while also keeping an eye on huge computer screens that displayed the outside view through a number of cameras.

"Our primary concern at this altitude is avoiding bird strikes and downdrafts," Captain Bascombe said. "When we first began traveling this route, the birds scattered like . . . Well, like crows . . . But now they've gotten used to our big, quiet ships. They join us and fly formation on either side, at times soaring over the top and dropping in behind us to ride our wake."

"What do you do if one tries to take you head-on?" Paul asked.

"Not much we can do," Bascombe admitted. "But we're pushing so much air that even the most determined harpies get washed out of the way before impact."

Paul laughed. "Same thing used to happen when I drove our Hummer on the interstate."

The captain pointed to a pair of flight officers standing just ahead of the lookouts. The pilot was to his left, the systems engineer to his right. The controls were all computer based, what pilots called a glass cockpit made up of touch screens and keyboards.

The pilot stood motionless, his hand resting on a single protruding lever with a handgrip and a triangular point sticking out in front of it like a directional arrow.

"We call that lever the All-Con, for 'all control,'" Bascombe said. "We use it for manual control, when landing and taking off or performing maneuvers close to the ground. It can be pushed forward, pulled back, moved to either side, and even raised and lowered to change altitude. It can even be twisted side to side in a yawing motion to utilize the side thrusters and breezeway tunnels, to straighten us out if we're operating in a crosswind—which we are loath to do for obvious reasons."

Paul understood. The side of the ship was like a hundred sails unfurled. Operating in a significant crosswind would mean moving sideways like a crab no matter how hard they fought against it.

"So one man can fly this ship with just that lever?" Paul asked.

The captain nodded. "Would you like to try it?"

"Are you kidding?"

"Not at all."

Paul moved into position, put his hand on the All-Con, and took a deep breath. For a brief second, he felt like a kid again, recalling the time his father had let him drive the family car around an empty parking lot at age twelve. The thrill was the same. Once he was comfortable, the captain switched off the autopilot.

"Make an adjustment in our heading," the captain said. "Port or starboard, your choice."

With his hand on the All-Con, Paul turned the nose to the left. The helm answered slowly, but he could soon feel the deck tilting under his feet.

The captain wrinkled his nose, the handlebar mustache tilting back and forth. "That's not a turn," he said. "Put some oomph into it. Bring her around. Remind these coddled passengers that they're on a ship, for goodness' sake."

Paul turned the control more firmly and the airship began to swing to the left with far more vigor. Shockingly fast, in Paul's opinion, for a vessel the size of a skyscraper.

As the turn progressed, he noticed the horizon becoming filled with more trees and less sky. He'd unintentionally pushed the nose down as he rolled the ship into the turn. It wasn't exactly a swan dive, but after hours of incredibly stable flight it felt worse than it was. The fact that they were only five hundred feet above the green carpet of the rainforest made it even more unnerving.

"Bring her back up," the captain advised, his hands clasped behind his back.

Paul pulled back on the All-Con to stabilize the descent and the huge ship pitched up like a Coast Guard cutter climbing a wave. With the sky now filling the windscreen, he knew he'd gone too far. He eased it forward and allowed it to settle.

"Well done for a first timer," the captain said, taking the control back from his nervous visitor. "Probably not enough to spill any drinks, but with a little luck, some of the pool water is sloshing over the edge."

Paul stepped back sheepishly. He thanked the captain, took one more look out the forward windows, and then left the bridge with his escort. "What's next?"

"Lifting chambers," the tour guide said.

Instead of taking the main deck passageway, they went up a ladder and took an engineering corridor that led to the interior of the forward lifting compartment, a vast space reminiscent of the interior of a domed stadium. Up above were seemingly endless bundles of inflated cylinders strapped together in batches of seven. Each tube was fifty feet long and eight feet in diameter. They were made of some light-weight material and filled to maximum volume with helium.

Rows of the bundles stretched out above him and on both sides. Walking through the chamber was like a walk among the clouds. At the tail end of the walk, a figure waited.

"Señor Solari," the engineer said.

"I'll take it from here."

Solari seemed back to his old self. "Mr. Trout," he said. "How are you enjoying your tour?"

"Incredible so far," Paul said.

"Have we overcome your fear of flying?"

"It's not a fear of flying," Paul said. "More like a fear of falling or crashing."

"Don't worry," Solari insisted. "We have a thousand safety features in place that didn't even exist a century ago. We use helium instead of hydrogen. As I'm sure you know, helium doesn't burn. Our ship is made of the strongest and lightest materials. Our satellite weather tracking is second to none. We even have multiple redundant power plants in case one goes out."

"One of them is already out," Paul reminded him. "What happens if the other impellers crack or fail?"

"Even if we were adrift," Solari said, "we can use the tails to control our orientation, release helium to get closer to the ground and, once there, employ what I call our Captain Ahab contingency."

"Captain Ahab contingency," Paul repeated. "What, pray tell, is that?"

"We carry rocket-propelled anchors both fore and aft, a dozen of them. They can be fired into the ground like harpoons to stabilize the ship, just like a seagoing vessel's anchors," Solari said. "And if something does go terribly wrong, this ship can land on the water, or shuttle passengers to the ground in aerial lifeboats."

"You have lifeboats?"

Solari nodded. "We carry plenty of inflatable lifeboats of the usual kind," he began. "And a number of large, multi-person drones that can ferry passengers and crew back and forth from the ground. They can be used for escape should something go drastically wrong. The newest ones carry six passengers, and a ten-passenger version is on the drawing board. In fact, at the rate the technology is developing, I foresee a day when they're large enough and plentiful enough that we never have to land the ship, just move in over the loading area and hover while the drones go back and forth."

Paul found the idea intriguing and figured this might be his only chance to get a look at the drones they were carrying. "Now, that's something I'd love to see."

"Then come with me," Solari said.

They continued along the catwalk, passing through several dividing bulkheads and entering the aft lifting chamber. Along the way, they crossed other catwalks arranged horizontally, branching out to the sides of the hull. Ladders led upward and downward, connecting different levels of the catwalk system. Paul imagined it must all look like a 3D grid of city streets. But it was hard to see in person, because in every direction the bundles of inflated gas cells blocked the view. As they moved on through, it dawned on Paul that a person could get lost in there for days.

Nearing the stern, they passed a larger, more substantial structure. It ran up through the hull to support the main vertical stabilizer, which stuck out through the top of the airship, five stories overhead. The beams were oval shaped and made of carbon fiber, much like the masts of Rolle's sailboats.

Behind this support structure, they reached another bulkhead door. A placard on it read AFT FLIGHT DECK. AUTHORIZED PERSONNEL ONLY

Unknown to Solari or Paul, this was an area the regular crew had learned to avoid. It was controlled by Colon's fright teams, the gray-shirts, and watched over by his security goons. Rumor had it that more than one person had strayed into the Aft Flight Deck and never returned.

As they approached the door a member of the security team stopped them. He stood with an air of arrogance, but got nervous once he realized who was approaching. "Señor Solari," he said. "Very unusual to see you back here. How can I help you?"

"I'm taking this man on a tour," Solari said. "We're here to see the flight deck and the drones."

"I'm sorry," the man said. "It's very busy in there. A lot of work being done. Perhaps later would be better."

"Nonsense," Solari exclaimed. "This is the perfect time." He pushed forward and the man stepped aside.

Paul followed Solari through the door and into the aft-most compartment of the airship, a large open space with a high ceiling and a flat deck. It reminded Paul of the hangar decks he'd seen on aircraft carriers, though significantly smaller. Here and there, he saw men working on various machines. To the left a small fleet of the navigation drones sat on charging stations. To their right a pair of deckhands were preparing a refrigerator-sized drone for a flight, while directly ahead of them was a view that surpassed even that from the cockpit.

At the tail end of the compartment a pair of forty-foot-wide doors had been opened and lowered, revealing an incredible letter-box view of the world behind them. It framed clouds building up in the distance, floating above the carpet of dark green below, their upper reaches a brilliant and blinding white in the midday sun.

As Paul stared, a small drone was brought in for a landing. It came around from the port side, trailed the airship for a moment, and then eased inward, crossing the threshold and touching down on this side of a yellow warning line that no person was supposed to step over.

Its propellers shut down almost instantly. As they went silent, Paul noticed that the rest of the flight deck had gone silent too. The gray-shirts and the mechanics were staring at the intruders. But it wasn't the return of the navigation drone or the appearance of the CEO in a blue-collar workspace that had brought things to a screeching halt.

Near the center of the compartment, an elevator platform was in the process of rising, filling an opening in the middle of the deck. To Paul's utter surprise, one of the donut-shaped drones was sitting on it. Several men rode up along with the machine. Paul recognized Torres and Colon among them.

Unfortunately, Colon recognized him as well.

Paul stepped back. "We should probably be going."

"Stop," Colon shouted.

Paul didn't obey the command, but backed straight into the gray-shirt who'd come up behind him. The man shoved him forward. Meanwhile, the security guard who'd briefly blocked their entry stepped in and sealed the door.

"What's going on here?" Solari demanded.

"You shouldn't be back here," Colon said.

The deckhands looked on in shock, unsure what to do.

"It's my company," Solari said. "My ship. I can go anywhere I damned well please. Now, whatever you're doing here, it stops this instant."

Colon shook his head like a disappointed parent. "We've been through this before," he insisted. "I handle the freight rooms. What goes on here is my business."

"Not unless I approve it," Solari insisted.

"Of course," Colon said dismissively. "But you always approve. I make sure of it."

With that he pulled a small device from his pocket and pressed a switch.

Paul flinched as if they were about to get shot or stunned, but nothing happened. At least nothing he could see or hear. A few feet away Solari reacted differently. He stiffened and went silent.

"Sit down, Señor Solari." Colon spoke the words loudly, as if they were command words for a trained animal. "Count to a thousand before you speak again."

Solari looked straight ahead. A million-mile stare that suggested he wasn't seeing anything at all. Then he walked to a nearby workbench and sat on the chair beside it.

He continued to stare off into the distance, and seemed, in Paul's eyes, to be doing exactly as ordered.

Paul didn't want any piece of that. He spun away from the man who'd blocked him and rushed for the door. The security guard tried to block his path, but Paul bowled him over and sent him crashing to the deck.

Reaching the door, Paul grabbed the handle and yanked on it. The door was locked, the handle wouldn't budge. He stepped back, ready to throw his body into the lightweight aluminum panel and batter it down, but before he could deliver the blow, he was set upon by two of Colon's men.

One of the mechanics grabbed his arm and tried to bend it back, while a second tackled him around the waist. The three of them went down together. With a wrestling move learned in his younger years, Paul twisted and threw one of the men off. The second guy was pushed aside as well. Paul might not have been the most agile of men, but he was large and strong.

Free for only a second, Paul got up just in time to spot a third crewman swinging a wrench at him. It caught his stomach and doubled him over. As Paul crumpled, two more gray-shirts arrived. He was quickly outnumbered five to one and subdued.

With the fight over, Paul saw Colon approach him.

"I tried to make this easy on you," Colon said. "All you had to do was enjoy your trip, drink your champagne, and go home quietly. Now I'll have to show you what it really means to fly."

Colon turned to the men who'd subdued Paul. "Throw him out. We'll tell the world he got too close and slipped."

The men lifted Paul and began manhandling him toward the opening. Paul fought against them. Twisting and turning, kicking and punching. His size was an advantage, as was an intense determination not to let them drag him across that yellow line.

Pulling from both sides toward the middle, he slammed two of the men together. One lost his grip, the other held on until Paul slung him down. With those two gone, Paul elbowed the third. But other crewmen soon joined in, and there were now too many for him to defeat.

One of the men kneed him in the back of the legs and dropped him to the ground. Another put him in a choke hold and dragged him ahead. Paul saw the yellow warning line only inches away. There was only three feet of decking after that. As they slid him forward, he found himself panicking and then growing angry, angry enough that rather than fight he decided he'd take as many of them with him as possible. At least that was the idea, until another thought occurred to him. A way to use Colon's fears against him.

"We know you're behind the drone attacks," Paul shouted. "If I vanish, a hundred FBI agents will meet this ship when it lands in San Diego. And if you go anywhere else, Interpol will do the same. It's over. You might as well not add murder to your list of crimes."

Colon leaned in to Paul. "You're shockingly naïve if you think murder isn't already on my list. And trust me, by the time we reach San Diego, neither the FBI or the CIA or even the American military will be able to affect any of my plans."

That meant the curtain was about to be pulled back. Whatever Colon was planning, it would happen in the next couple of days. Assuming he didn't get thrown to his death, Paul had to find some way to report that information.

Report, he thought. *Yes, of course.*

"I have to report back nightly," he shouted. "If I don't check in with my superiors, this ship will be surrounded by American military aircraft before dawn."

Colon paused, trying to calculate the chances that Paul was bluffing. Ultimately, he decided he couldn't risk it. He turned to Yago. "Take him below . . . And treat him appropriately."

Paul didn't like the sound of that either—even if it was better than getting tossed from the airship without a parachute. He pulled free one more time, but before he could land a punch, he was clubbed in the back of the head with the wrench.

Paul saw stars and darkness. Felt himself falling. By the time he hit the deck, he was out cold.

40

PANAMA CANAL ZONE

The nuclear submarine USS *Maryland* (SSBN-738) sailed under the Bridge of the Americas, which spanned the entrance to the Panama Canal Zone on the Pacific side. Long, low, and painted midnight black, the submarine looked cunning and lethal as it eased through the shallows.

Though there were nearly fifty ships lined up waiting their turn to enter and transit the canal, a continuing agreement between the United States and Panama provided that certain military vessels would be given priority no matter what time they arrived. Nuclear ballistic missile submarines like the *Maryland* were always given top priority.

The sub moved past the container ships, bulk freighters, and tankers that had been waiting for the better part of the day and then slid in front of a cruise ship packed with gawking onlookers just before reaching the Miraflores Locks.

Standing atop the *Maryland*'s sail, Rear Admiral Wagner took in the sights. The *Maryland*'s commanding officer, Captain Robert Lyle, stood beside him.

"Nice day to make the passage," Lyle said. "Last time I came through here it was raining and cold."

Wagner scanned the blue sky and saw only a few cotton-ball clouds off in the distance. The morning sun was warm and pleasant. "Well, Bob, I don't think you'll have that problem today."

"You neither, sir." Lyle and Wagner were old friends, but they still held different ranks. Even thirty years at sea and being a full captain didn't give Lyle the right to call Wagner by his first name. At least not on duty. It didn't prevent him from ribbing his superior officer, however. "I do think it's funny how you jumped on board my retirement cruise, just so you could get the Order of the Ditch to put up on your wall."

The Order of the Ditch was an unofficial Navy certificate, garnered by passing through the Panama Canal. Similar to the Shellback Certificate given for crossing the equator and the Blue Nose Certificate for crossing north of the Arctic Circle.

"I had no choice," Wagner replied. "You don't get much chance to transit the canal while riding a desk back in Washington, which brings me to the real reason I'm here. Have you thought about my offer to join Naval Intelligence? We're dealing with a whole new world of subsurface threats. There's a need for someone with your background in the building."

Lyle smiled politely, but shook his head. "I've spent the last twenty years under the surface, where there's no sign of fresh air or sunlight. Unless you can put my desk on the sand at Turtle Bay, I'm not your man."

Wagner laughed. He'd come aboard the *Maryland* after she surfaced off the coast of Panama. Since then, he'd squared his stuff away and gone on the obligatory inspection tour of the ship.

Ballistic missile submarines were spacious compared to the attack subs, but it was still a cramped vessel, devoid of sunlight and filled with odd smells—some of which came from the machinery, including the CO_2 scrubbers, and some of which came from the crew. Wagner wasn't looking forward to a week in such conditions as they crossed the Caribbean on the way to Kings Bay, so he certainly understood Lyle's desire for fresh air after two decades without.

They came to a full stop just short of the locks, waiting as a small boat with two pilots came toward them. The pilots would man the sail along with Wagner and Lyle, while the sub went into the Miraflores Locks to be lifted upward fifty-four feet in two stages. From there it was on to the Pedro Miguel Lock, which would lift the submarine the last thirty-one feet and release it into Gatun Lake. At that point the pilots would leave the boat and the *Maryland* would navigate slowly across the lake for the better part of the day, reaching the Gatun Locks in the afternoon, where a second set of pilots would come aboard to ease them into the Atlantic.

The *Maryland* didn't really need the pilots. Despite its size, which was impressive for a submarine, it was far smaller than the tankers and cruise ships that had been designed to use every available inch of the canal. While they would squeeze into each lock, leaving less than a foot of space on either side, the *Maryland* would have fifty feet of clearance both port and starboard, and at least a hundred feet of space in front of the bow and stern.

"What's the operations plan once we get through Pedro Miguel?"

"We have five hours at minimum speed as we pass through the Culebra Cut and cross Gatun Lake," Lyle replied. "Then we have the Gatun Locks on the other side."

"Easy glide," Wagner said. "Why don't you bring some of your men topside and let them enjoy this? Give 'em a reward for all that time deep and dark. I'll haul my old admiral butt downstairs and make room for them up here. It was a long flight down anyway. I wouldn't mind a nap."

"You're going to miss the passage," Lyle said.

"Need my beauty sleep," Wagner said. "Besides, I came to see you. This, I can see from a cruise ship."

Lyle nodded, informed the XO to clear the ladder because the Rear Admiral was coming below, then snapped a salute to his old friend before he climbed down.

Wagner dropped down the ladder with surprising grace for a man who hadn't been at sea for years. It helped that they were in flat waters, but he was mildly proud of himself. He passed the XO, left the conn, and made his way through the boat to his quarters.

Entering the small but relatively spacious compartment, he put his cap on a hat rack, pulled off his windbreaker and hung it up, then took off his shoes and loosened his tie. Lying down on the bed, he'd just let his head touch the pillow when his watch started to beep.

The chirping was soft, like an electronic cricket, but it opened Wagner's eyes wide. After five seconds listening to the alarm repeat, he sat up and reached over to his bag, pulling out an MP3 player and its attached set of earbuds.

He put the earbuds in snugly and then turned the player on. Using the touch screen, he scrolled down through a list of songs and recorded podcasts, eventually stopping on a file labeled QUIJANO.

Staring at the name, Wagner was dimly aware that it was familiar, but also a mystery to him. He had no idea whether it was a song or a podcast or some other recording, only that he had to listen to it.

The chirping of the watch became louder and louder and soon became oppressive. It vanished as Wagner pressed play and began to listen to the recording. First came the series of tones. Then a deep, slightly accented voice. It was always the same. But he listened through because he had to.

"Get the orders to the captain first. Then to the chief engineer. The mission must go forward . . . The mission must not fail . . ."

41

OSTROM AIRSHIP *CONDOR*

Gamay lay on the bed wearing yoga pants and a comfy top. She'd been in the spa for half the day and felt as if her body were made of rubber. Lying on her side, she watched through the window as the rainforest moved past down below. It was a dreamy experience, and she was starting to doze off when the electronic key hit the lock.

She turned to see Paul in the doorway. He came through awkwardly, clipping his head on the frame, which was half an inch lower than his full height.

"Ouch," she said for him, though he barely reacted. "How was your tour?"

He looked at her oddly, cocking his head. "Tour."

"The engineering spaces around the ship," she said. "The stuff you've been dying to see since Rudi told us we were coming down here."

"I enjoyed it," he said flatly. "It was very informative."

She got off the bed and stood up. "What happened to my fanboy? You seem bored."

"I have something for you," he said.

She grinned. "From the jewelry store?"

He didn't reply and she began to worry. Only now did she realize he'd left the door open behind him. Something her fastidious, squared-away husband never did. "Paul?"

He stared.

"Paul?" She'd just finished reading Dr. Pascal's report on the microscopic chips that could affect the brain. "Are you okay?"

"I have something for you," he repeated.

From Paul's perspective it was like a dream. As if things were happening, but not by choosing them and making them happen. He saw Gamay standing there. He found it hard to decipher the emotion on her face. He knew she needed his help, but why?

He was supposed to give her something. He had it in his hand. He looked down, opening his palm. The syringe was still capped. But she needed it. He had to give it to her.

"Paul?" She called his name, but it sounded as if she were miles away.

He pulled the cap off the needle and stepped forward. He grabbed her with his right hand and held the syringe with his left.

She shouted and twisted, but he held her. She needed the injection. It was important. He had to give it to her.

"What are you doing?" she shouted.

He held the needle up. He'd been told it didn't matter where he jabbed her, but Gamay was afraid of needles, he didn't want to scare her.

"No," she shouted, seeing the needle. "No!"

"I have to give this to you," he replied.

He was holding her by the arm, squeezing her too tight. He could see the pain on her face and the fear.

"Paul, please!"

He tried to change his mind, but the noise inside his brain flared each time he resisted. He had to give it to her.

She squirmed and twisted, kicking him in the shin. He felt nothing and gripped her even tighter. Reaching toward her, Paul opened his palm. "I have to give this to you." He didn't jab her with it, he didn't inject her.

Gamay stared up at him, trembling. She knew the worst had happened. But her husband was still in there. He was fighting it. She understood this was a reprieve that might vanish if she didn't act.

She grabbed the hypodermic, shoved him onto the bed, and ran. Flying out the door she bolted to the left and down the companionway. She spied a couple of crewmen at the far end, looking at her oddly. She hit the brakes, sliding in her socks. To her right was a door. It read: CREW ONLY. She pushed it open and ran inside. It led to ladder that took her up to the central catwalk.

She looked left and then right and decided to run toward the stern, dashing through the engineering spaces and into the lifting compartment.

She stopped and listened. She could hear footsteps below and someone coming up another ladder. She took off once more, nearly silent in her stocking feet. She was long gone when the crewman reached her level. Gone and hidden away, but how long, she wondered, could she stay that way?

———

Mrs. Trout escaped," one of the gray-shirts informed Colon. "She's hiding somewhere in the hull."

Colon was annoyed. "Does she have any electronics with her?"

"We don't think so," the man said. "Her phone, computer, and tablet were all found in the suite. She's not even wearing shoes."

"What about her husband?"

"He's still in the room. He's just standing there."

At least that part had gone according to plan, Colon thought. "He's been ordered to stay there. Grab their computers and lock him in just to make sure. We'll have to hack their passwords and send a false report later."

"What about the woman?"

Colon thought about that for a moment. By hiding in the lifting compartment, the woman had basically trapped herself in an area where she could cause little trouble. "Post guards at every exit and start a deck-by-deck search," he ordered. "If we don't find her, at least we keep her bottled up in there where she can't get to a phone, or a radio, or start interacting with the other passengers or the regular crew. Once we get to Providencia, this crew switches over to the *Eagle* for the journey to Paris, while my personal team comes on board. We can expand the search for her once we have more manpower."

42

PROVIDENCIA ISLAND

Providencia Island was one of the few unblemished specks of land left in the world. At least that's how Kurt remembered it from a diving trip several years back.

He'd been put up in a large multiroom house that had been painted in shades of turquoise, pink, and orange. It had no air-conditioning, phone service, or internet, but did come with an ample supply of rum and an endless variety of lizards running up and down the walls at all hours of the day and night.

Some rooms had come with beds, others just hammocks. Kurt had ridden around the island in a souped-up golf cart, sharing the road with a few mopeds and scooters. The food was great, the people were warm and friendly, and there was only one main road that encircled the island, which meant you couldn't really get lost because if you kept on going, you'd end up back where you had started. There were no big hotels, few cars, and only the once-a-day puddle jumper arriving at the airstrip and its grass-shack terminal.

As Rolle guided the sailboat into the harbor, it didn't seem like much had changed. The channel was marked with buoys and the short concrete dock had a pair of small freighters and a couple of fishing boats tied up to it. The only thing out of place was a large cargo vessel siting in the anchorage with a helicopter lumbering toward it.

Looking around, Kurt didn't see any warehouses crowding the water's edge, or any inlets of sheltered spots that might offer a place to dock a submarine unseen. The freighter was the most likely mooring point. Either on the far side, where no one would see it, or through a port underneath.

While checking in with the harbormaster, Kurt asked about the freighter. It must have been a sore subject because the harbormaster jumped at the chance to complain.

"Been there since Ostrom showed up," the man said gruffly.

"Ostrom," Kurt repeated, recognizing the name. "They own the ship?"

The harbormaster nodded. "Made us dredge the channel, make it deeper and wider. Then they just parked it there. Now those helicopters fly back and forth at all hours of the night, while their big trucks break up our roads and the cost of diesel hits twenty dollars a gallon."

"Twenty dollars a gallon?" Commander Wells said. Even in this day and age that sounded outrageous.

Standing nearby, Rolle whistled. "Prices keep going like that, everyone's gonna need sailboats."

"You'll be rich before you know it," Kurt said.

"Good thing you have sails," the harbormaster added. "Sometimes them Ostrom boys take all the fuel. None left for anyone else until the next tanker shows up."

"What do they need all that diesel for?" Kurt asked.

"Construction," the man said. He pointed off to the south. "They're still building their SkyPort on the other side of the island. Every once in a while, they unload a bunch of steel or concrete and haul it up the mountain. I guess the lighter materials get flown in and out on those helicopters."

Kurt wasn't surprised by what he was hearing. At this point they were certain Ostrom was involved, but what exactly Ostrom was up to and why they were doing it remained a mystery.

Rudi had suggested reaching out to the officials on the island to see what they might know, but Kurt had shut that down. The odd politics on Providencia meant there would be little to learn through traditional channels. The island was officially a territory of Colombia, geographically nearest to Nicaragua and Panama, and controlled at this point by Brazil's Ostrom, which was by far the largest employer and investor on the island. With a setup like that, there was no telling which official might be in whose pocket.

Signing the customs forms, Kurt thanked the harbormaster for the info. Glancing back at the freighter, he triangulated a spot between the ship and an outcropping of rocks nearby from which it would be easy to watch the far side of the vessel.

The rocks were known as Morgan's Gold because they sparkled in the afternoon sun, and because the pirate Henry Morgan, who'd once made this island his home base, was rumored to have sunk a chest of gold somewhere in the vicinity.

"Any chance we can anchor off Morgan's Gold? I'd like to see the sunset without that ship in the way."

"I could let you tie up over there," the harbormaster said. "For a small fee."

Kurt handed over enough money to cover a few gallons of over-priced diesel and then reboarded the sailboat with Rolle and Commander Wells. Joe was still on board, pulling together some diving gear.

"What's the plan?" Commander Wells asked.

Kurt smiled at her. "I figure we tie the boat up, ice down a few beers, and then kick back and watch the sunset. Maybe work in a short nap."

"I know it seems like we're on vacation here," she replied, "but shouldn't we be checking out that freighter or scouting out Ostrom's SkyPort? Or both?"

"Sure," Kurt said. "But we might as well wait for the submarine to get here. That way we can see what it's hauling and get an idea of where they're taking the spoils."

Her gaze narrowed. "You said the submarine was a hundred miles ahead of us. I know this sailboat is fast and that Rolle found every gust of wind in the Caribbean, but there's no way we made up that kind of distance."

"We didn't," Kurt said, sitting and putting his feet up. "But look around you. This water is clear as glass. Between the reef surrounding the island and the substantial distance between this place and any large source of pollution, Providencia boasts the cleanest waters in the Caribbean. No one's sailing their secret submarine up the channel in broad daylight. Even if it could remain submerged—which it most probably can't—anyone onshore would see it coming."

"Hmm," she said, grinning. "I can't decide if your confidence is endearing or annoying."

"Annoying," Joe said. "Please tell him it's annoying."

Kurt said nothing as the others laughed at his expense. "High tide is two hours after dark. I'm guessing we'll see it then."

43

With the sailboat anchored off Morgan's Gold, they were parked directly across from the Ostrom freighter, giving them a perfect view of the vessel. That cut both ways. If anyone was watching from the freighter, Kurt wanted them to get a good look and decide they had nothing to worry about.

He decided it was best if they looked like a group of friends here to have a good time. He filled a cooler with ice and made sure everyone had a cold beer in their hand. At the same time, Rolle fired up a built-in grill and threw on a spread of freshly caught fish and frozen shrimp.

Up near the open space on the foredeck, Commander Wells and Joe lay down to soak up the sun. To enhance the distraction, she'd pulled on a coral one-piece bathing suit and donned an oversized white hat that one of Rolle's girlfriends had left behind. Beside her, Joe took his shirt off, arranged a pair of fold-up chaise longue chairs, and dialed up some music on the sailboat's built-in sound system.

With the music just loud enough to be heard by someone on the freighter and the smoke from the grill drifting on the breeze, Kurt figured the façade was complete. He made his way to where Joe and Commander Wells were stretched out in the sun.

"Good work," he said. "Nothing like a little bit of eye candy to distract any lookouts."

"I find that comment insulting," Commander Wells said. "But thank you."

"Me too," Joe replied. "Why can't you just appreciate me for my mind?"

Kurt laughed. For a brief second it did feel like they were all on vacation: a moment with the tension lifted. He hated to ruin it.

"Did you set up the spotting scope?" This to Commander Wells.

She nodded. "It's in the port window of the main cabin. I hooked it to the computer, set it to record, and left it on a wide focus so we can see the full stern of the freighter. You're sure the submarine won't dock near the bow?"

"To get near the bow, the sub would have to weave its way around a pair of algae-encrusted anchor chains. No way they're going to try that."

"Sounds reasonable," she said. She lay back on the chair, tilting the brim of the hat to keep the sun out of her eyes. "Let me know when you see something coming."

Kurt shook his head.

"You know," Joe said, "it's possible the sub doesn't come in through the channel and instead sits offshore waiting for these guys to send a boat out to greet it."

It was a good point, but Kurt didn't think that changed much. "We'll be able to see a tender heading out just as easily as the sub coming in. Either way, it's the same routine. While they dock, we dive. While they unload, we take advantage of the heightened activity to sneak on board."

"The gear is ready and waiting at the stern," Joe said. "Who's going?"

"Commander Wells and myself. You and Rolle keep watch."

Joe rubbed some oil on his shoulders and arms. "Sounds good. Try not to get yourselves blown up like you did the last time."

The sun fell slowly, brightening Morgan's Gold as it dropped toward the sea. While the others relaxed, Kurt took the time to read over the latest report from the Trouts and some intel from Rudi. The main focus was shifting to a man named Martin Colon. He'd once been part of Cuban Intelligence and was now working for Ostrom, though his path into the airship line was highly suspicious. He also had connections to a certain redheaded man named Lobo, who'd been identified as the leader of the attack at the dry dock.

It stood to reason, Kurt thought. The Ostrom organization was simply too large and complex for everyone to be part of the piracy campaign. It had to be a subset of the organization, like Colon's freight unit—or even a niche group within that unit.

Kurt studied Colon's picture and bio, then put the computer away and enjoyed the sunset, until the blazing orange globe dropped into the sea at the far edge of the world.

Dusk didn't last long, and it was soon dark and quiet. By nine o'clock, Kurt, Joe, and Commander Wells were crowded into the forward cabin, watching the computer screen connected to the scope. Rolle remained up on deck keeping watch, to make sure nothing approached the sailboat.

At nine seventeen they spied activity on the freighter. Deck lights came on at the stern, men began shuffling around. At nine twenty-two a tender was lowered into the water and began motoring out into the channel.

Joe asked the obvious. "Should we follow?"

Kurt shook his head. "Let's wait till they come back."

Come back they did, but not loaded down with cargo. The tender was as empty as it had been on the way out.

"False alarm," Commander Wells suggested.

"Pilot boat," Kurt corrected. "There's something following in its wake."

The tender eased down the channel acting as a point of reference for whoever was driving the submarine. It also made for a well-lit distraction in case anyone was watching from shore, its noisy engine rumbling in the dark, its illuminated deck drawing the eye, while its slowly spreading wake would cover for the water displaced by the moving submarine as it passed by.

With the naked eye, Kurt could see no more than a shadow trailing behind the tender, but Commander Wells had set the scope to night mode, and on a computer screen to her left the shape of a bulbous conning tower about ten feet long and six feet tall could be seen. A net cutter jutted angrily upward from the bow, while a vertical rudder about seventy feet aft revealed the stern of the ship. The sub rode low in the water, using the depth that had been created in the channel for the freighter that never moved.

"Time to go," Kurt said.

He and Commander Wells were already in their wetsuits. They moved up to the deck and slid over the transom. Their gear was waiting for them in the water. Fins, helmets, and, this time, closed-circuit rebreathers that wouldn't leave a trail of air bubbles to give them away as they swam toward the freighter.

They pulled the gear on, dropped below the surface, and swam beneath the sailboat and toward the freighter. It was about three hundred yards to the freighter and for the moment they had the tide with them. There was no need to hurry. Up ahead, the submarine had to slow and maneuver to align itself to dock in the dark.

"How's the leg?" Kurt asked, testing the comm system and referring to her injury from the last dive.

"Numb," she said. "And your arm?"

"Hurts when I brush my hair. So I haven't bothered."

"That explains a lot," she said, smiling to herself.

As they continued the swim, they began to hear metal clanking against metal from somewhere up ahead. The sound of a whirling propeller surging and then stopping came next, a sign that the sub was maneuvering into position.

In the dark, they were forced to estimate their speed and direction. Kurt counted his kicks and checked the magnetic compass on his arm. He modified his direction from time to time, just to make sure the needle wasn't stuck and to get a feel for the current.

To some extent it was like flying in the clouds, it required a lot of thinking and very little seeing. He figured they were about halfway there when a dim area of light appeared up ahead. It grew brighter and wider as they swam toward it and was soon reflecting off the sand below.

"What are they doing?" Commander Wells asked.

Kurt wasn't sure. He could see fish darting into the lighted area and then a larger shape, bulbous and heavy. The submarine.

Kurt increased his pace and went a little deeper. Now he could see that the light was coming from inside the freighter, and the submarine had dropped down into the more deeply dredged area beneath the ship so it could come up underneath, where the bottom plates of the freighter had been removed.

"They've set the ship up with a docking bay," he said. "Looks like they pulled out the engines to do it. No wonder that freighter never moves."

Kurt slowed as he approached, waiting for the submarine to get into position. He could see nothing to suggest the underside had any sort of retractable doors and concluded that it remained open at all times.

The sub came to a stop, one last backward spin of the propellers breaking its momentum and churning up some sediment. It was now directly under the freighter, blocking most of the light. The rushing sound of air echoed through the water as the sub blew its tanks. It began to rise, moving up until most of its bulk was hidden inside the freighter and it was essentially surfaced.

"This is our chance," Kurt said, kicking hard.

He swam down toward the bottom, putting as much sediment and water as possible between them and anyone who might have been watching. When he was directly under the freighter he swam upward, slowing as he neared the barnacle-covered hull.

Commander Wells arrived beside him. Entering the area beneath the docking bay, they eased into a shaded corner and surfaced, watching as a large ramp was maneuvered into place opposite a cargo hatch on the side of the submarine.

Ramp in place, the cargo hatch was pried open from the outside. A rush of air hissed out, and a pair of men from the dockside moved in with dollies and hand trucks. Soon crates of material were being hauled out and wheeled away.

"There's your piracy ring in action," Kurt said.

A man from the freighter stood by with a clipboard. "Looks like he's checking off a grocery list," Commander Wells said. "Not exactly the swashbuckling image conjured up by the Blackbeards and William Kidds of this world."

Kurt had to agree with that. The unloading was efficient and organized, as methodical and boring as the daily activity in any dockside warehouse. About the only thing that set it apart from a union job was the lack of hard hats and OSHA posters on the wall. The workers even wore gray Ostrom overalls.

Just when Kurt was wondering if the submarine might be autonomous or controlled remotely, a second hatch opened. Two men climbed out. They looked scruffy and ragged with full beards and wild eyes. One of them blinked in the light as if it hurt his eyes, the other swore loudly but happily, obviously thrilled to be out of the small sub.

The foreman made a face. "Damn, you guys really smell."

"Two weeks without a shower," the first man said. "What do you expect?"

The foreman didn't answer that. "Where's your passenger?"

"Inside the forward hold," the second man said. "We tied him up. Just in case he got wild."

The foreman didn't look happy. "He'd better be in good shape," he warned. "Colon wants him up at the SkyPort ASAP."

"He's fine," the submariners insisted.

"Then get him out here."

With an annoyed look, the two men climbed back down into the hull and returned moments later, dragging a third man. This passenger had a lot of stubble, but not a full beard. He seemed disoriented and confused as the sub's crewmen dragged him out into the light. The foreman pulled out a knife and cut a set of ropes off the man's wrists.

Kurt studied the man, wondering who he was and realizing that his beard was about half that of the submariners. That suggested a week between his capture and the current moment. It meant he'd come from the *Heron*.

Commander Wells didn't need to wonder. She recognized him instantly. "Oh my God," she said. "That's Walker."

44

Commander Wells watched as the foreman and another Ostrom employee marched Walker across the ramp and toward a pressure bulkhead that led to the interior of the freighter. Attempting to keep him in view, she pushed out from their sheltered spot, kicking recklessly with her fins and stirring up the water.

Kurt grabbed her harness and pulled her back into the shadows and then down under the water.

"What are you doing?" she demanded. She was smart enough not to struggle, but still angry.

"You can't just swim out there and say hello," he said coldly. "You'll get us both killed."

"You're right," she said, coming to her senses. "I'm sorry. I just can't believe he's alive. How? Why?"

Kurt didn't have the answer to that, but he could guess where they were taking him. "We need to go visit the SkyPort."

"You don't want to search this ship once they're done unloading?"

Kurt shook his head. "This is just a drop-off point, whatever we'd find here would probably pale in comparison to what's up there. Now, let's back out of here cautiously without attracting too much attention."

It was a good idea, but a little too late. Commander Wells's sudden movements had attracted attention. The lights came on around them, illuminating the water in a swirl of yellow and green. Someone up above shouted as they spotted the divers, and seconds later, the muffled reports of guns being discharged sounded. As Kurt and Commander Wells dove deeper, trails of bubbles appeared around them as rifle bullets drove deep into the water.

Kurt kicked hard and swam sideways, dragging his startled companion under the submarine with him. They hugged the bottom of the hull, safe from the bullets for the moment.

"Now what?" Commander Wells asked.

"Back toward the stern," Kurt said, "and then straight down to the bottom. They can't shoot us as long as we stay directly under the sub."

He began to move. She followed him.

"What if they send divers with spearguns after us?"

Even though the freighter's crew probably had dive gear on board, Kurt doubted they were standing by to jump in the water and fight off intruders. "You've read too many adventure novels. Trust me," he said, "the gunfire is the only real danger."

With the trails of bullets still cutting through the water in diagonal lines, it seemed as if Kurt was correct. Then someone tossed a grenade into the water.

The flash lit up the sandy bottom in an instant of brilliance, followed by an expanding shock wave and rush of cavitation. Fortunately for Kurt and Commander Wells, it had been thrown into the water back where they'd been a few moments before. The distance was enough to keep them safe, but the concussion wave slammed into them hard none the less.

"And after Joe went through the trouble of warning us not to get blown up again," Kurt said. "Whatever you do, don't tell him about this."

"What's worse," she asked, "Joe making fun of you for getting blown up, or actually getting obliterated?"

"It's kind of a toss-up," he admitted.

Up ahead, an apple-sized object plunged into the water, dropping toward the seabed.

"Back! Back!" Kurt shouted.

The second grenade went off with an identical flash, but was farther away. The impact was less painful than the first one.

Kurt felt as if he were a World War II submarine being peppered by depth charges. His ears were ringing, his ribs hurt, and a small crack had appeared in his faceplate. Beads of water were already forcing their way inside. He was glad they weren't at any sort of depth, or the faceplate would have caved in.

"This feels like we're trapped," Commander Wells said.

She was right, Kurt thought, they were trapped. They couldn't swim to the side because they'd be easy targets for the men with guns up on the freighter's internal dock, and they couldn't swim down to the bottom to escape because the grenades sank so fast. "At this rate," he admitted, "we may end up facing those divers with the spearguns yet."

Up inside the freighter the situation was chaotic. The foreman and the crew was running about and shouting, appearing more panicked and unnerved than the two divers who were under attack.

"Where did they come from?" the foreman shouted. "Who are they?"

No one knew the answers.

A couple men with guns prowled either side of the dock, shooting down into the water at any shadow larger than a fish. The grenades had echoed through the docking chamber, launching towers of water upward and drenching several of the men. The sediment they stirred up made it difficult to see.

"What the hell is going on here?" the submarine driver shouted as he came back up through the tower hatch. He spied a man with a belt full of grenades preparing to throw another one into the water.

"We have intruders," the foreman shouted. "Divers. Who knows how many? They could be U.S. Navy SEALs."

The submarine commander looked around. He was an ex–Cuban commando. He saw no sign of danger. "Where are they?"

The foreman turned to a screen on the wall. It was attached to a camera used to help guide the sub into place. The image was degraded by all the swirling sand, but the camera showed two distinct shapes.

"Directly under the submarine," the foreman said. "Right behind the main cargo hatch." He turned to his men. "Two grenades this time. Hold them for four seconds and then toss them so they detonate near the surface."

The men didn't seem excited about that idea. The sub driver was positively furious.

"Are you insane?" he snapped. "You'll crack the hull. Put those away. I'll take care of them."

"How?" the foreman asked.

The man didn't bother to explain, he just climbed back into the submarine and slammed the hatch tight.

———

Stuck against the bottom of the sub, Kurt weighed the odds of several different plans. Each one was basically a roll of the dice. "I'm going to get their attention," he said. "While they're shooting at me, you go deep and swim hard back to the sailboat. That way at least one of us gets out and gets word to NUMA about Ostrom."

"That's the dumbest idea I've ever heard," Commander Wells said.

"You have a better one?"

Kurt could see her looking around, studying things. "I think we should—"

A deafening roar blotted out whatever else she said. Kurt heard it and felt it throughout his body. But it wasn't an explosion, nor was it a propeller turning over. It was water and air rushing together.

Even as he recognized the sound, he was powerless to react. His legs were drawn up and pinned against a grate on the underside of the submarine. Though his arms were free, he couldn't move an inch.

Commander Wells was affected differently. She was pulled away from him as if she'd been lassoed and dragged backward. She ended up pinned against a similar grate, ten feet forward of his position.

"What's happening?" she grunted.

Kurt knew the answer and it wasn't good.

45

The water flowing into the grates was crushing Kurt's legs up against them, the force so powerful that fighting against it was simply impossible. He could bend and twist his upper body like a man doing sit-ups, but he couldn't move his legs at all.

"What's happening?" Commander Wells asked again.

Kurt heard her more clearly this time, as the water flow into the grates had become linear and less turbulent. "The sub is venting its tanks. Air out the top, water in through the bottom."

Commander Wells had been in the Navy long enough to have a basic understanding of submarines. "Crash dive," she said dejectedly.

Kurt wasn't sure the old narco sub had crash dive capability, but it was definitely taking on water to increase depth. He could already feel the hull settling and see the bottom, which appeared to be moving up toward them.

He strained and twisted, but there was no way to free his legs from the water rushing in. The problem was the weight of the water, over eight pounds per gallon. With a hundred gallons flowing past his body every few seconds, it was like being pinned by an eight-hundred-pound gorilla. Making it even more difficult was the fact that his back was to the submarine. No matter how he twisted and turned he couldn't get to a position where he could affectively use his arms.

Commander Wells was in even worse condition. She'd been pulled onto the forward grate, but was face up against the bottom of the sub. Her legs and stomach were being crushed against the barred opening, her ankles turned awkwardly outward.

Kurt looked around for anything resembling a handhold, his only hope being to pull himself free. He spied a welded metal skid, designed to protect the sub in case it scraped bottom.

Wrapping both hands around it, he pulled himself forward. A few inches at first and then a few more.

"We're sinking," Commander Wells said.

Kurt looked down. They were drifting slowly toward the dredged-out bottom, sixty feet below. Refocusing on the task at hand, he pulled hard. With each inch gained, less water tried to force him into the grate. The pressure reduced. The pain lessened.

Even though his arms had begun to cramp, he didn't dare relax. He grunted and curled his arms once more, thankful for all the rowing he'd done over the years. With one more bout of exertion, he pulled free. Drawing his legs off the grate and up into a yoga-like pose so his legs wouldn't be sucked back onto the grate.

"I'm free," he shouted.

"Get away, go," she told him.

"And go face Joe's 'I told you so' all by myself?" He pushed forward to where she was, grabbed her arm, and pulled. The first pull moved her a bit. The second moved her farther. The suction was lessening now as well, since the tanks were nearing their full capacity.

Kurt was thankful for small favors. He yanked hard one more time and pulled Commander Wells free. "Go," he shouted. "Out and under."

They kicked hard, scuffling through the sand like a couple of rays as the submarine came down behind them. The impact forced some of the water sideways, propelling them on.

They were clear. Bruised, exhausted, but clear.

They swam hard, spurred on by adrenaline. Neither one said another word until they reached the far side of the sailboat and surfaced.

Rolle and Joe were waiting. Having heard the grenades, they'd known something went wrong.

"What happened?" Joe asked, helping Commander Wells get her helmet off.

"We got blown up again," she admitted.

"You people need to listen to me," Joe said.

Rolle helped Kurt up and took his helmet as he removed it. "You cracked your faceplate. Glad this is NUMA stuff. You're hard on the gear, man."

"Technically, someone else cracked it for me," Kurt said. "But you have a point."

"Was it worth it?" Joe asked.

"Yes, no, and maybe," Kurt said. "Couldn't tell what they pulled off the sub, but we did see who." He pointed to Commander Wells. "They have her friend Walker. They must have taken him off the *Heron*."

"And brought him all the way back here? Why?"

"They must know who he is," Commander Wells said. "They must know he's Naval Intelligence. We have to get to him before they torture him for info."

It was a reasonable assumption, but Kurt had a feeling there was more to it.

"What do you want to do?" Rolle asked.

"Won't take them long to guess where we came from," Kurt said, peeling off the now-tattered wetsuit. "You get out of here and head north. Contact Rudi, tell him about Walker, and let him know Ostrom is definitely behind this. And don't stop for anything until you link up with one of the NUMA ships Rudi used to drop the sonobuoys. I don't want these guys jumping you."

Rolle had a shotgun out and loaded already, he wasn't overly concerned about getting jumped, but he understood Kurt's concern. "Okay, I'll go north," he said. "What about you three?"

"We're going ashore to investigate the SkyPort," Kurt said. "First we need to break into the dry cleaner's and make a withdrawal."

As usual, no one really knew what Kurt was planning. But this time, they just nodded and went along with it, never doubting for a second that he had something up his sleeve.

46

The Ostrom SkyPort was a sprawling complex half a mile inland from the southern tip of the island. Unlike a regular airport, it didn't require a long, narrow runway, but rather a large, nearly square footprint. The airships could land vertically if they needed to, but like boats and airplanes, they had more control if they were moving forward. For that reason, the landing pads at the SkyPort were circular in shape, allowing the airships to approach from any direction, which kept them pointed into the wind no matter which way it was blowing.

As they rode up the hill in a "borrowed" Jeep, Kurt, Joe, and Commander Wells could see a glow across the sky, caused by all the lights at the complex.

"Burning the midnight oil," Joe pointed out.

Cresting the hill gave them a brief glance down into the SkyPort. It was a busy place. Ground crews could be seen arranging equipment, while various vehicles both small and large were driving around and getting into position.

Kurt was dismayed. "I was hoping there'd be no one here but the cleaning crew."

"There's an airship coming in," Commander Wells said, pointing out to the south.

Kurt and Joe looked that way. Out in the distance they saw an illuminated shape in the sky. Mostly white, with a bit of color coming from blue and yellow stripes. The big airship was illuminated from the outside and from within. Because of its size and the lack of perspective, it was difficult to tell how far away it was, or how fast it was moving. It seemed almost stationary, hanging in the sky like a second moon.

"The place might be busier than you wanted," Joe said. "But we're less likely to be noticed if everyone's got their eyes on that thing."

"Not just that one," Commander Wells said excitedly. "There's another one coming in from the west."

The narrow road allowed only a quick glance to his right, but that was enough. Kurt turned and saw the second airship, farther off and a bit higher, but headed toward them just like the first one. "Must be rush hour around here," he said. "Let's make good use of it."

They continued down the hill, pulling off the newly built road and onto a dirt path that had been cut diagonally to allow power cables and waterlines to be run. Switching off the headlights, Kurt drove using only the glow from the SkyPort, stopping as they arrived at a fence.

Turning the engine off, Kurt climbed out and closed the door softly. Joe and Commander Wells did the same. Moving through the dark they came up to the fence, each of them wearing a set of gray Ostrom coveralls.

"Good idea to steal these uniforms," Commander Wells said. She had a fourth one tucked into her backpack for Gerald Walker. If they could find him. "What made you think of it?"

"There's only one dry cleaner on the island," Kurt said. "Someone has to do the laundry for Ostrom's five hundred local employees."

"Why gray?" Joe asked. "There were some nice blue mechanics duds in there. You know I look good in blue."

"Sorry to offend your fashion sense," Kurt joked. "But when I looked over Paul and Gamay's last report, they flagged a guy named Colon as a possible suspect. He runs the freight division. His people wear gray."

"Colon?" Commander Wells asked.

"You know him?"

She seemed to be searching her memory and then shook her head. "Who is he?"

"VP of freight handling and a former member of Cuban Intelligence," Kurt said. "Turns out the redheaded guy with the baton was once part of the same group. His name is Lobo, by the way."

"More links to Cuba," Commander Wells said. "My gut tells me they have something to do with this, even if Colon and Lobo are privateers now."

Kurt felt the same. There were too many connections for it to be a coincidence, but what Cuba gained from stealing small amounts of cargo, from ships around the world, he couldn't imagine. He figured there was only one way to find out.

They reached the fence, checked it over for electrification or motion sensors, and then started to climb.

———

The *Condor* approached the island slowly, coming in at an altitude of five thousand feet and affording a view from the bridge that was spectacular and awe-inspiring. Though he'd been on dozens of flights in the various Ostrom airships, Martin Colon never missed a chance to be on the bridge when the ship approached its destination.

He stood beside the captain, gazing through the floor-to-ceiling windshield. The teardrop-shaped island of Providencia lay ahead and below them. The southern point was mostly dark and ringed with thin lines of white where the waves crashing on the beaches caught the glow of the moonlight. Just in from the southern beach, he spotted a dashed line of yellow lights that led directly to the landing complex of the SkyPort, which was now lit up in all its possible glory.

Standing there, arms crossed, Colon felt like some kind of god descending to earth on a heavenly chariot. It dawned on him that if Solari had just given the Wall Street bankers this experience, they might have loaned Ostrom another billion without Colon having to dust them and force their hands.

"Altitude forty-five hundred," the pilot called out. "Air speed thirty, ground speed twenty-six. We're lucky tonight. Not much wind to speak of."

Captain Bascombe nodded at the report. "Steady on, take us to three thousand and hold."

"Hold, sir?"

The captain pointed off to the left. "We've got traffic. *Eagle* is inbound from the west. It's my understanding they're cleared to land first." He looked at Colon, from whom the order had come.

"They have a large cargo to pick up," Colon said. "I want them on the ground loading it as soon as possible, not waiting for us to touch down and secure the *Condor*. Besides," he added, "Solari wants the passengers to get a look at the operation. They'll get a great look as *Eagle* touches down."

The *Condor* descended to three thousand feet and then began a wide turn, circling the southern tip of the island and giving everyone on the port side a perfect view of the *Eagle's* approach. It crossed beneath them, slow, graceful, and quiet, like a whale gliding beneath a ship.

It turned as it approached the island, lining up with the band of yellow lights and then tracking into the wind toward the complex. As it eased across the perimeter fence it seemed almost to be crawling. A sideways slide to the left put it over the number one landing pad, and there it stopped, hovering and holding station. The process was so much more meticulous and less kinetic than the sometimes-violent landing of a jet aircraft.

Vectoring its thrust through an array of forward and side vents, the *Eagle* held its position against a mild breeze. With the airship stopped, cables dropped from a series of ports along the sides and in the bow and stern.

As the ropes hit the landing pad, members of the ground crew raced to thread them through pulleys and connect the ends to a series of winches. When all nineteen were attached firmly they activated the winches, which drew the airship slowly, methodically to the ground. The crew of the *Eagle* assisted the process by venting helium from a number of lifting cells, while a set of large fans in the landing pad spun slowly, creating a mild downdraft by pulling air through the pad and expelling it out the sides.

The *Eagle* touched down softly and was quickly tied to the ramp by the Lilliputians on the ground, like an aeronautical version of Gulliver.

Watching the other airship land had indeed been a treat for the passengers on the *Condor*, but Colon had other reasons for allowing it. The *Condor* would switch crews and take on some military-grade cargo once it landed, but the *Eagle* had a far larger job. His ground teams would need to load two hundred pressurized tanks, containing twenty-six thousand pounds of the mind-altering dust, and connect them to a series of lines and vents especially engineered to disperse the dust in a fine spray. It would be a slow process, but one that was required if the dust was to cover the American base at Guantánamo Bay. He estimated it would take half the night to accomplish and, as he wanted the *Eagle* to cross Guantánamo before dawn, every minute counted.

"We're cleared for landing," the pilot said.

"Take us in," Bascombe ordered.

The *Condor* would follow the same path the *Eagle* had taken, diverting to the second landing pad and touching down fifteen minutes after its sister ship. By the time it was tied down, Colon had left the bridge and was heading for the gangway.

47

Kurt, Joe, and Commander Wells watched the two airships land with a genuine sense of awe.

"Not every day you see something larger than the Empire State Building drift down out of the sky and land as soft as a feather," Joe said.

With two airships on the ground, the SkyPort complex became a combination of Grand Central Station and Shibuya Crossing in Tokyo. All at once, hundreds of people and dozens of vehicles sprang into action, converging on the airships from different parts of the facility.

First up, a series of mobile gantries swung into place around the ships. Some held gangways, which were attached so that passengers and crew could exit. Others lifted maintenance personnel into positions where they could open inspection ports or climb onto ladders that were permanently attached to the sides of the ship.

As the maintenance crews checked vital components and individual systems, a small fleet of trucks rolled up to various cargo hatches and other openings, restocking provisions, removing trash, and servicing lavatories.

Watching from a short distance away, Kurt was bumped twice as men and women from the ground crews hustled by. It dawned on him that the three of them might look like tourists in New York City, staring up at the skyscrapers, while the regular New Yorkers rushed around with heads down and phones to their ears. "We need to look busy."

"Easier to ride then walk," Joe said, pointing to a small tug that no one seemed to be using.

They climbed aboard the tug and found the key dangling from the ignition. For those who worked on the ramp at the airports of the world, the rule was to always leave the key with the cart. You never knew who might have to move it at a moment's notice.

Joe took the driver's seat, started the tug, and waited as the others got settled. "Where to?"

"Colon was riding on the *Condor*," Kurt said. "Let's start there."

Joe drove off, navigating a narrow track and avoiding other vehicles.

"Let's hope Paul and Gamay don't wave and shout our names if we happen to run into them."

They eased past the tail of the *Condor*, passing an exit ramp that led to an area filled with idling vans. A few people were walking down the ramp, but there was nothing resembling a mass exodus. As far as Kurt could tell, it was only members of the crew.

"Don't see a lot of people getting off," Commander Wells said. "This must not be a regular stop."

"Freight stop in the middle of the night," Kurt said. "The passengers are either having drinks or sleeping. And unless you're into industrial design, there's not exactly much to see here anyway."

"How are we going to find Colon or Walker in this place?" she asked, growing frustrated. "It's huge."

It was a fair question. Ideally, they'd have come to the complex, found it quiet and dark, and had the opportunity to search for Commander Wells's old partner in relative silence. The arrival of the airships, the overwhelming size of the facility, and the vast number of people zipping about made that an impossibility.

"What about up there?" Joe asked, pointing to the office building on the hill.

Kurt turned to look. The modern-looking structure was only half lit up at this hour, but even then, it felt too public and upscale for their needs.

"Dress code will be suits and ties up there," Kurt said. "We'll look out of place if we start poking around. Look for a freight house. The kind of place where business can be done out of sight."

"Does underground qualify as out of sight?" Joe pointed to a line of tugs emerging from an underground storage area between the landing pads. The tugs were moving slowly, climbing up a curving ramp and easing onto the main pathway. They towed carts loaded down with large stainless steel containers.

"Looks as promising as anything," Kurt said. "Find us an entry ramp."

Continuing around the bend, Joe discovered a new path and curved onto it. Soon enough he'd pulled in behind other tugs heading back into the underground complex like a conga line of unevenly spaced ants.

They moved slowly and methodically, disappearing into the tunnel without anyone batting an eye.

———

Martin Colon walked down the gangway toward a waiting Mercedes van. Solari and Yago were with him, Solari plodding along methodically, Yago as jumpy as a college student on Adderall.

With the van door closed, Colon spoke to the driver. "Take us to the castle."

A nod from the driver was the only response. The van moved off in silence. At one point, Yago seemed ready to blurt something out, but Colon silenced him with a glance. "Wait until we're inside."

The scientist held his tongue, checked Solari's pulse, and turned a new shade of green. Solari's heart rate and blood pressure were all over the place. His eyes were dilatated like a pair of train tunnels. He was decompensating and if they didn't deal with it quickly, he would collapse or have a seizure.

The van pulled up to the illuminated blue office building and into a private garage. Colon got out. Yago helped Solari exit.

Colon, Solari, and Yago stepped toward a private elevator inside the garage. Two men stood beside the door, waiting: Lobo and Walker.

"Hail, hail," Lobo said. "The gang's all here."

Colon took a good look at Walker. He seemed healthy, but smelled atrocious. "What's his condition?"

"He doesn't talk or eat or complain," Lobo said. "Throw him in a shower and he's the perfect roommate."

Colon directed Yago to examine Walker. A quick check of pulse, respiration, and blood pressure revealed the truth. "He's as stable as Solari is unstable."

"Good," Colon said. "Get him down to the simulation room and get him acclimated. I want him ready to go in a few hours."

"You might want to do that yourself," Yago said. "If I don't get Solari's brain waves back to normal, he's going to have a seizure resulting in partial, or possibly complete loss of mental function."

Colon didn't appreciate the scientist's tone, but he needed Solari to hang on for just a bit longer. "Get him over to medical and do what you can. I'll deal with this one."

He pulled out a key card, held it against a reader, and pressed a button, summoning the elevator. The five of them entered and the doors closed.

When they opened again, the men were five stories below the

complex. The finished hallway was sparse and sterile. The lighting muted but sufficient.

Yago left the elevator with Solari in tow and turned to the right. Colon and Lobo took Walker to the left.

As soon as they were out of earshot, Lobo spoke up. "We had a problem at the freighter tonight."

"What kind of problem?" Colon asked.

"A pair of divers snuck in after your submarine docked."

"Who were they?"

"Impossible to tell, but I'm guessing from NUMA."

Colon was stunned. He'd been led to believe the NUMA operatives were heading to Havana. "What makes you think it wasn't a couple of locals or overzealous adventure travelers?"

"Their equipment for one," Lobo insisted. "Top of the line re-breathers. Full face helmets. Obvious communications gear. Not the stuff packed by locals or adventure divers on holiday. Beyond that, there was a sailboat that came in a couple hours before the submarine. It weighed anchor right after the incident. It's out of Nassau. Owned by Performance Sailing. That's the shop where they had the drone wreckage."

Colon's jaw tightened. NUMA seemed to be closing in. There were two members of the organization on the *Condor* and now a team roaming around the island. He had no doubt who he was dealing with. After the near debacle with the dry dock, he'd done some research on his adversaries. The agents—which he certainly considered them to be—were two men by the names of Kurt Austin and Joe Zavala. Their official bios were rather plain, but his contacts in the intelligence world suggested that was just a cover. The men had a long list of accomplishments that bordered on the incredible, along with a penchant for interfering in things that were none of their business.

He explained this to Lobo.

"If they're the same men who were on the dry dock, you can be certain they won't stop until they've found their way down here."

Colon considered that along with the overall situation. The Sky-Port was crowded and busy, an easy place to hide in plain view. That wouldn't hold if Austin and Zavala came down to the production level. "We need to turn their curiosity against them."

"How?"

"If they've already been to the freighter, this will be their next stop. Instead of trying to keep them out, I think we should invite them in. Get rid of the guards, leave the doors unlocked, but keep your eyes wide open."

Joe drove the tug slowly, keeping in contact with the convoy ahead of him, but making sure not to tailgate anyone. The route took them through a vast underground warehouse, stacked with loaded pallets and cargo containers of all shapes and sizes. At the far end, they came to a pair of tunnels. The tugs ahead of them were entering the right-hand tunnel.

"Shall we?" Joe whispered.

"Can't see turning around now," Kurt said.

Joe gave the tug a little more gas, coaxing some speed out of the ungainly machine and closing the gap between their vehicle and the one just ahead. Reaching the entrance, they passed a pair of men with guns, who stood by the gate watching as the convoy went by.

Joe kept his eyes forward. Kurt looked at the men and offered a bored half wave. The men didn't react in the slightest, focused only on lowering the gate after the last tug had gone through.

The tunnel led north, away from the landing pads and up toward the blue office building. Narrow, dimly lit, and poorly ventilated, it had accumulated plenty of grime and a strong odor of exhaust.

"Just our luck," Joe said. "Every vehicle in Solari's fleet is electric, except these things."

"I've been breathing island air too long," Commander Wells said, coughing lightly. "This is killing me."

Kurt kept his breathing as shallow as possible and focused on the path ahead. He could see that the tunnel was widening. A short distance ahead, it ended in a curved loading zone cut from the living rock, where flatbeds loaded with additional stainless steel canisters waited.

The tugs out front pulled to a stop, hooked up to the flatbeds, and moved off again.

Joe held his position until the last of them were gone and then parked as far away as he could.

"What do you make of those?" Kurt asked, motioning toward the stainless steel tanks.

"Could be helium," Joe suggested. "These ships use an awful lot of it."

It was a possibility, Kurt thought, though he'd have expected Ostrom to keep its helium in a large central storage tank that could be accessed with hoses dropped directly from the airships, not in cannisters that had to be driven in and loaded one by one.

"Where to now?" Commander Wells asked.

There was only one real option, the freight elevators cut into the wall.

"Grab the keys," Kurt said. "And the tool kit."

Joe lifted the tool kit and placed it on the hood of the tug. They'd hidden several weapons inside. A Colt .45 pistol of Kurt's, a 9mm Beretta for Commander Wells, and a 9mm Glock for Joe, which he took out and slid deep into the pocket of his overalls.

Heading over to the elevator, Kurt pressed the call button. Before long the doors opened to reveal a freight elevator the size of a one-car garage. They stepped inside. There were several levels below and only one above.

"Deepest darkest secrets are going to be hidden down below," Kurt suggested. He pressed the lowest button, a placard beside it said PRO-DUCTION LEVEL.

The elevator jerked into action and began descending.

"We're literally getting to the bottom of things," Joe said to a smattering of laughter.

"Why do I feel like we're descending into the ninth circle of hell?" Commander Wells asked.

"Because that's where the traitors are," Kurt replied.

48

Reaching the production level, Kurt watched cautiously as the doors opened. The halls were empty. Whether it was the hour, or all the work going on up above, there seemed to be few people down below.

"This is our chance to find out what's going on," he said. "Walk like we own the place. But do it quickly."

Moving down the hall, they passed a couple of locked rooms and then came to a clean room separated from the rest of the facility by an air lock. Sterile suits hung on hooks. Boxes of sterile shoe coverings, latex gloves, and double-layered KN95 masks occupied a shelf in front of a double-layered air lock door.

On the other side of the glass, a row of centrifuges rested on the floor like so many hot tubs. The next section was occupied by complex-looking machines that Commander Wells recognized. "Photo-lithography units," she said. "Used to etch the circuits on the tiny microchips."

"Like the ones Dr. Pascal found in Captain Handley's brain," Joe said.

Trays of what looked like sand or pumice lay on the far side. Kurt eyed the trays suspiciously. "Something tells me that's the finished product."

A row of cylindrical steel tanks stood untouched by the wall, while several others were hooked to the lithography machines by a system of hoses and valves. The tanks were identical to the ones being towed toward the landing pads. It left no doubt what was being loaded onto the airships.

"Dr. Pascal said it took less than a tenth of an ounce to completely compromise a human brain," Joe reminded them. "If they're loading hundreds of canisters of this stuff onto those airships, they must be planning something huge."

Kurt agreed. "And something imminent. We need to figure out what the target is. Let's move on."

They left the lab, passing a pair of men in blue overalls in the hallway. For a brief second Kurt wondered if they'd worn the wrong color to the dance, but the men ignored them and continued on.

The next rooms were merely storerooms for raw materials used on the production line, but at the end of the hall they came to a double door. It had a coded lock, but the LED was glowing green. Kurt gave it an easy push. The door was open.

"That's either good luck or bad," Joe said.

Easing through, they found themselves in a curving, descending turn that took them back underneath the lab into a completely darkened hallway with a door at the far end.

Kurt opened it a crack and squinted to see inside. To his surprise, he saw men in U.S. Navy uniforms sitting at consoles of familiar-looking equipment. They were running through procedures. Calling out headings, speeds, and other data. At the center, an executive officer stood on a platform, giving orders to the men around him.

It was the control room of a warship. But not just any warship. It was designed to look and feel like the combat information center at the heart of a nuclear submarine.

49

Easing the door a bit wider, Kurt noticed the crew was rather scruffy looking for a U.S. Navy outfit, and the men were older in most respects than a typical U.S. Navy crew. Certainly, they weren't fit and trim kids in their twenties. They all wore earpieces on their right sides—through which he assumed they were receiving instructions. Most surprisingly none of them reacted to the arrival of three outsiders, even as they slipped into the simulation room. One man walked right toward them and then veered off to sit at a weapons station.

"They don't see us?" Commander Wells whispered.

"They're entranced," Kurt said. "Like the crew of the *Heron*."

"Should we do something to snap them out of it?" Joe asked.

Kurt shook hie head, remembering the violent actions of the men in the cargo hold on the *Heron*. Like those men, these had been given a different reality. Waking them up from it might be a bad idea. "Let's hold off on that."

As they watched, a man wearing captain's bars entered the simulated control room. At his side was Gerald Walker, dressed in a lieutenant's uniform that didn't quite fit.

Kurt felt Commander Wells stir at the appearance of her old partner. He put a hand on her arm. "Don't move."

She held back as Walker found his way to the sonar station and took a seat. The captain moved to the center of the compartment and conferred with the executive officer, who barked out new orders, including a change of depth and heading. The imaginary ship began to change course and dive, the floor underneath them tilting as it went.

"Pretty good simulation," Joe said. "But who are these people?"

Kurt had been pondering that since they'd walked in. Walker's arrival settled it for him. "The missing sailors from the drone attacks."

"What are they doing here?" Commander Wells asked.

"Training for a mission."

"I don't understand."

"This is Colon's endgame," Kurt explained. "No wonder the list of stolen goods never made any sense. He was never after the cargo. He was after the crews."

As Kurt finished speaking, the piped-in sounds designed to resemble the hushed environment of a submarine's CIC vanished. The floor leveled and the lights came on.

The "crew" stopped what they were doing and stood at their posts, not exactly at attention, but unmoving and staring off into the distance.

"*I must commend you,*" a deep voice said over the simulation's loudspeaker. "*You're quite perceptive. But your curiosity has led you astray.*"

50

Kurt looked up. With more light in the room, he could see a wide pane of glass in the wall above the simulation chamber. It reminded him of the gallery in an operating room; a place for someone to watch and evaluate the training while staying out of sight. Shadows could be seen behind the glass, but no definitive shapes.

"I appreciate the compliment," Kurt said, looking up at the glass. "It'd be nice to know who was giving it."

"*I think you know who I am,*" the voice replied.

"Martin Colon," Kurt guessed. "Former member of Cuban Intelligence, freight handler extraordinaire, and a pirate of the air and sea."

"*Such a vivid description,*" the voice said, laughing. "*I'll take it.*"

"You're also a coward," Kurt added, "who uses others to do his bidding."

"*And you're nothing but a prized bull, caught in the center of the ring. Marked for death.*"

"Haven't seen too many bullfights," Kurt admitted, "but even I know, sometimes the bull wins."

The speakers rasped Colon's reply. *"I can assure you that won't be the case tonight."*

As Colon's words echoed around them, doors opened at either end of the compartment. A squad of armed men entered. Three from one side, two more from the other end, and another pair appearing in the doorway that Kurt, Joe, and Commander Wells had used to enter the simulator room. Finally, the redheaded man from the docks arrived, Lobo.

True to form, the others carried firearms—submachine guns that were either MP5s or knockoffs—while Lobo held only a small staff with a silver tip, a longer, more powerful weapon than the extendable baton he'd used before. Kurt had no doubt it could break bones on contact.

"Throw down your guns," Lobo ordered. "We know you're carrying."

Kurt was surprised to hear the warning. In all honesty, he was surprised they hadn't been shot to pieces already. But when he looked at the men with the submachine guns, he realized they were holding their weapons at the ready, barrels pointed down and away, not at the intruders . . . or the crew.

Of course, Kurt thought, the crew. Colon had spent the last year collecting these men, indoctrinating them, training them. They were valuable to him. Assets that he didn't want to lose. Realizing this Kurt considered the awful truth. The only way to stop Colon might be to gun down his crew of innocent, hypnotized civilians.

Still hoping another option might present itself, Kurt slid a hand into the pocket of his overalls, wrapping his fingers around the grip of the Colt. A few feet away Joe had done the same thing. Commander Wells was more directly behind Kurt, and he couldn't risk turning all the way around to check on her, but he expected she'd be ready if the shooting began.

Turning back to the window up above, Kurt hoped to distract Colon. "The level of control you have over these men is impressive. Far more precise than what we saw on the *Heron*."

"The men on the *Heron* were dusted once. And quite heavily," Colon said. "That level of influence tends to make them unstable. And we only had time for rudimentary coercion. These men have been here for months. They've been treated and indoctrinated repetitively. And with the lightest of touches."

"Making them believe they're a U.S. Navy crew," Kurt said.

"Most of them were at one time or another," Colon replied. "These men worked on submarines and nuclear-powered surface ships before they entered the merchant marine."

"Maybe I should tell them you're a threat," Kurt said. "Get them to act out their sworn duty to defend the United States."

"Go ahead," Colon said confidently. "You'll merely be wasting your breath. They obey the first voice they're exposed to, post activation. It imprints on the cerebral cortex and becomes the voice of reason in their minds. You can shout until you're blue in the face and they will stand as they are, but if I speak one word they'll rip you to shreds with their bare hands."

Kurt didn't doubt it. "What you have in mind is obvious at this point," he said. "And I'll spare the vain attempt to suggest you won't succeed, because I'm sure you have it all planned out, but what exactly do you plan on doing with a nuclear submarine once you have it?"

"Any number of things," Colon replied cryptically. "None of which I'll be sharing with you."

"And when our Navy hunts the submarine down and sinks it?"

Colon's hollow laugh sounded over the PA system. "American submarines are notoriously hard to detect," he said. "By the time your Navy realizes what they've lost, the submarine will be hidden somewhere deep and dark. At any rate, your military will be busy dealing with more obvious threats and issues."

Kurt wondered what that meant and then decided he'd have to worry about it later, if there was a later.

"Joe," he whispered.

"I know what you're thinking," Joe replied grimly. "Just say when."

Kurt was gripping the weapon in his hand more tightly than normal. He relaxed a bit, allowing his body language to suggest surrender, and then dove to the side, firing at Lobo and his men as he flew through the air.

Lobo stepped out of the way as if he were expecting the attack, but Kurt hit two of the three men around him.

A split second after Kurt's first shot, Joe spun and opened fire at the men on the far end of the room, scattering them like crows, while Commander Wells dropped behind a console and fired at the men blocking the door they'd used to enter.

With Colon's gunmen diving for cover, Kurt turned and aimed at the viewing gallery, unleashing a hail of bullets into the glass up above. It shattered and fell like crushed ice, but Kurt saw no one behind it. Colon had obviously taken cover. Which left shooting the crew as the only option to stop the madness.

Kurt saw Colon's men rushing in. He fired at one and then took another shot at Lobo, who spun out of the way once more.

With an instant to change tactics, Kurt turned toward the captain of the replacement crew. Before he could pull the trigger, he felt something strike him in the thigh. It wasn't a bullet, or the bone-crunching pain of Lobo's staff. It was something deeper and more diffuse.

Kurt stumbled forward, dizzy and unbalanced. He fell against a console and the Colt discharged into the floor. Fighting to keep himself upright, Kurt dropped the pistol and grasped the edge of the control panel. He felt his breath coming in spurts.

Turning to the injury, he saw a feathered dart stuck in his leg. It was the kind of dart used to tranquilize a wild animal. Whatever drug it carried, the effect was near instant. Kurt's head swam. He pawed at the dart in a vain attempt to pull it free, but his fingers were numb, and despite repeated attempts he couldn't get them to close on the narrow cylinder.

He slid down to the floor, dimly aware that the fighting had ended. Joe and Commander Wells had been hit with similar darts. She was crawling and crumpling face-first into the deck, while Joe was toppling over like an uprooted tree. He slammed to the deck without the slightest attempt to break his own fall.

Looking up, Kurt spied a man leaning out through the gallery window with a double-barreled weapon in his hand. He had dark hair, pushed forward and gelled, and he wore squared-off glasses. He gazed at Kurt the way one might look upon a wounded bird.

Kurt fought desperately, attempting to tap into some superhuman reserve of strength, while hoping to overcome the effects of the tranquilizer. He forced himself up on arms that felt like rubber. He raised his head, which felt like it might be made of stone. He briefly reached his feet, only to see Lobo approaching with the staff.

Instead of bashing Kurt with the stick, the Red Wolf grinned at him, lowering the weapon and pointing the silver tip at the center of Kurt's chest. With a subtle tap he poked Kurt in the sternum. It might as well have been a knockout punch. Kurt lost his balance, fell over backward, and blacked out before he even hit the deck.

51

Gamay Trout knew the *Condor* was on the ground. Where, she wasn't exactly sure. She assumed it was Providencia, but had no way of knowing if they'd changed course and gone somewhere else. They could be in Cuba or Panama or Caracas. Considering how long she'd been hiding, they might have gone back to Rio.

It didn't really matter, she thought. Off the ship was better than on the ship, no matter where they were.

She eased out of her hiding place, stepped onto the catwalk, and crept along it. With each step she did her best to emulate the feline creatures for whom the path was named. She stepped softly, crept low, and moved silently, stopping and listening every few steps.

She heard a few voices down below. Glancing over the railing, she saw nothing but gas cells, but when she reached the ladder that ran vertically, she was able to see two men down below just standing there.

More guards. She'd spied them each time she'd tried to escape from the lifting bay. But previously it had been one man at each ladder and one man at each door. Now there were two.

She wondered if it was a changing of the guard, but as she waited and watched, the men just stood there, talking at times, standing quiet at others. Neither of them appeared ready to leave.

"Hey, you!" a voice shouted. "Stay right there."

She'd lingered too long in the open and had been spotted. Two men came running along the catwalk from the forward section. Gamay climbed onto the ladder, intending to go up it, but another man appeared above her, coming down.

Glancing downward, she noticed the guys from below coming out of their stupor and looking up.

"Great work," she told herself as she took off running. "Now they're all after you."

Gamay was not the type to panic, but the adrenaline of not wanting to get captured spurred her on. She raced ahead of her pursuers and made a right turn at the next spur. Rushing toward what seemed like a dead end, she threw herself off the edge and landed on top of one of the railcar-sized helium cells.

The landing was soft, and under different circumstances might have been fun. The bundle absorbed the weight of her impact and held its position thanks to the Kevlar straps. The only problem was, she was in plain sight and a sitting duck the second anyone came around.

She pushed to the side, her feet digging into the inflated membrane, and ultimately puncturing it, as she tried to jump from one cell onto the next.

As her foot pushed through the fabric, her launch was compromised. She made it halfway to the next bundle of cells and fell between them onto a lower bundle. Realizing the advantage to this, she allowed herself to slide down the side of this bundle and ended up on another group of cells. This time she held tight and squirmed in between two of the inflated bags.

Though they were strapped together, each of the helium cells were slightly underinflated. It was intentional, to leave room for them to expand when the airship rose.

As she fit herself in between the two cells, Gamay felt a sense of claustrophobia that she didn't know she possessed.

This is what I get for making fun of Paul, she told herself.

She slowed her breathing and closed her eyes, trying to remind herself of the calm feeling she'd had in the tank. It did the trick. The fear vanished. She held still. The men ran past her without stopping.

As the chamber grew quiet, she inched outward until she was in a spot where she could breathe more easily. She was alone again, but as trapped as ever.

52

Kurt woke up feeling as bad as he could remember. No post-marathon exhaustion or any hangover he'd ever suffered could compare to what he was experiencing. He felt like he'd been kicked by a mule and dragged across a pile of rocks after chugging a bottle of tequila. Mercifully, the pain was receding as the tranquilizing drug left his system.

His senses came back in stages. First, he became aware that he was alive and breathing. Then he realized he was lying face up on a firm surface with only the thinnest of padding. Then he began to hear sounds, which at first seemed odd and nonsensical, but gradually co-alesced into spoken words.

"What do you want me to do with Solari?" one voice asked.

"Clean him up and get him on the *Eagle* before his sedation wears off," someone replied.

Kurt recognized the second voice as Colon's.

"You want me to dust him again?" the first man asked.

"No," Colon said. "At this point I want him to be his own random self."

Listening intently, Kurt noticed his vision returning. A blur of light on the periphery, which slowly seeped inward from the edges. As focus returned, he discovered he was in a medical bay, strapped to an examination table with plastic zip ties on both ankles and wrists.

They needn't have bothered, Kurt thought. The effort to move even one finger was beyond him at the moment.

"What about these three?"

Kurt squinted, trying to bring the man into focus. He recognized the forward-brushed hair and the rectangular glasses of the man who'd shot him with the tranquilizer gun. He was now wearing a lab coat.

"Treat them with the dust," Colon replied. "I may want to use them in the future."

"Shouldn't we just get rid of them?" the man in the lab coat asked.

Colon sounded disappointed. "Listen to me, Yago. These three are assets. The number one rule in this business is never get rid of an asset before you have to. They may come in handy as hostages or prove useful as puppets. If not, we'll dispose of them later. To ensure they give us no trouble, I need you to treat them . . . fully."

Somehow, Kurt didn't think that "treatment" was going to be a nice massage and a hot towel. He figured it was time to go and tried to move, attempting to pull one arm free. Despite intense concentration, he managed only the slightest twitch in his thumb.

Across the medical bay, Colon glanced at his watch. "I need to get on board the *Condor* with the replacement crew. Finish up here and get Solari onto the *Eagle*. Once you have these three indoctrinated, take the plane to Havana. Lorca will meet you at the airport. Make sure you keep a low profile until the chaos at the base is over."

Colon didn't bother waiting for an acknowledgment, he simply turned and went out the door. As he walked out, a technician entered.

"Get the stim ready," Yago directed, pointing toward an electrical device.

Kurt now found he was able to turn his head. Moving it slightly, he tracked the new arrival as the man went over to a shelf, switched on a power pack, and then picked up a headband that was connected to multiple colored wires.

For a moment, Kurt thought this was part of his threatened treatment, but then Yago pulled a curtain back, revealing Solari lying on a gurney.

The technician checked Solari's eyes and pulse. "He's still under the sedation."

"Good," Yago said. "Let's get to it. Colon wants him back on the *Eagle* before he wakes up. I don't want to have to give him another dose."

The technician slid the wired band over Solari's head, adjusting a strap and making sure it fit snugly across his temples. That done, he closed the circuit.

Solari's body jumped as the current hit, drawing involuntary grunts, but leaving him unconscious. The next cycle arrived with a more powerful surge of energy and Solari's muscles tightened as if he were fighting to break free of his straps. A third burst produced a less noticeable effect, and soon the machine was humming quietly and Solari was lying still.

"Let it run the full cycle," Yago said. "And get me a syringe of the dust for the first one."

A sense of urgency welled up inside Kurt, a spike of adrenaline that cleared some cobwebs. He watched as they wheeled Joe past and propped him up. Joe appeared to be unconscious. His eyes were closed, his body limp.

With Joe's upper half tilted at a forty-five-degree angle, the technician slipped a pair of headphones over his ears and plugged them into a laptop.

Joe moved a bit and seemed like he might be coming around.

"Good," Yago said. "This works better if you're awake."

He tapped the syringe, grabbed Joe's arm, and injected the dust directly into a vein.

Joe reacted to the needle and began to fight, twisting and wrenching his body one way and then the other. It was no use. Like Kurt, he was strapped to the gurney.

"Easy there," the technician joked. "You might strain something."

Yago put the empty syringe down on a tray and sidled over to another machine. Flipping a switch, he initiated the harmonic signal.

Joe twitched for several seconds and then began to shake as the radio waves flowed through his brain. His eyes sprang open at one point, and he tried to speak, but couldn't get the words out.

"Don't talk," Yago admonished Joe. "Just listen."

Glancing at his watch, Yago counted off the seconds. When a half minute had elapsed, he turned to his assistant. "Play the tones."

The technician tapped a key on the laptop and stood back.

Kurt watched helplessly as an image on the screen displayed frequencies rising and falling, like an equalizer in a music studio. He could hear no sound escaping the headphones, but he remembered Colon saying the first voice heard after being infected with the dust imprints on the subject's mind. He figured it was Colon's voice speaking softly and creating the hypnotic state for Joe. It doubled his determination to get out.

He twisted in the straps, trying to bust free, but all he did was draw attention to himself.

Yago turned and regarded Kurt with an evil grin. "Don't worry, you'll get your turn."

Kurt felt a growing rage inside him. He curled his arm like a man lifting a heavy dumbbell. He kicked his legs. Each move pumped more blood and life into his muscles, but he remained trapped. At least he could speak. "Fight it, Joe. Block it out."

Yago laughed derisively and turned up the volume.

Across from him, Kurt saw Joe relaxing. The hypnosis was taking effect. Before long, Joe went still, his eyes open, staring upward.

Yago checked his watch again. No more than ninety seconds had passed. The job was done. He pulled the headphones off. He glanced Kurt's way. "You can say whatever you want now."

Kurt didn't bother. Joe's eyes were glassy, his face blank.

Yago performed a few tests on Joe and, once he was satisfied, he picked up a second syringe and stepped toward Kurt.

Kurt began to thrash around once again, thinking he might be able to break the needle off in his arm and prevent the injection. It almost worked.

"Hold him still," Yago shouted.

The technician grabbed Kurt's arm with both hands and put all his weight on it. The syringe went in a second later.

Kurt felt the metal slurry entering his veins. It was like fire shooting through his arm and into his shoulder. The headphones came next, placed firmly over his ears. When the frequency generator came on, it felt like an ice pick surging through Kurt's mind.

Yago stood back, counting the seconds once more. Kurt knew what would happen next: the harmonic signal would grow, his brain waves would begin to align, slowing down into the theta and gamma bands, and then the voice on the headphones would speak and it would seem like the words were coming from his own mind.

To hell with that.

Kurt twisted one way and then the other, thrashing about wildly and trying to scrape the headphones off his ears. He banged his head on the side rail and rubbed his face against the table. One of the cups slid up, but Yago rushed over and shoved it back into place. He grabbed Kurt by the chin to keep him from repeating the performance.

As the frequency became harmonic, Kurt sensed a wave of pressure growing in his head, similar to what he felt when he was diving.

"Start the tones," Yago snapped, fighting to keep Kurt steady.

The technician went to the laptop and hit the key. Kurt heard bells and then a set of oddly descending frequencies. He felt dizzy for a moment.

A voice started counting backward. "Fifteen . . . Fourteen . . . Thirteen . . ."

He sensed that the countdown was just the preliminary intonation. He didn't want to hear the rest. He strained once more, and the zip ties stretched and discolored, but didn't snap.

He needed more strength. More power. He began to talk to himself, shouting at himself inside his own mind. *Break the straps and get up! You have the strength of a bull! Break the straps and get up!*

His heart pounded and sweat poured from his face. The voice over the headphones continued to count down, but Kurt didn't hear it.

"Get up," he shouted aloud. "Break the straps and get up!"

With a surge of power that could scarcely be described, Kurt's entire body flexed. He pulled his right arm back, wrenching it inward, and twisting with his core.

The plastic tie snapped in two and his arm came free. He swung wildly and clubbed Yago, sending the man into the wall.

The headphones slipped off and all that was left were Kurt's own commands. He was disoriented and raging, but he kept enough of his mind to tell himself what to do. "Break these men," he shouted. "Beat them into submission and use the stim."

As Yago was getting to his feet, the technician rushed in. He lunged at Kurt with a scalpel, trying to stab him. Kurt deflected the attack, receiving a new gash on his arm. He pulled a leg free and extended it with a powerful thrust, kicking the technician in the chest. The man went flying backward, crashing into a stack of equipment and ending up on the floor.

The remaining straps offered little resistance. Kurt broke free with ease and jumped off the table.

"Sleep," Yago shouted. "Sleep!"

Kurt didn't hear it. He didn't hear anything except the thoughts he'd programmed into his own mind.

Realizing the commands were having no effect, Yago reached for the double-barreled tranquilizer gun. As he picked it up, Kurt shoved the gurney toward him, pinning him against the wall and trapping him in a way that the weapon couldn't be brought to bear.

At this point the technician had rejoined the fight, grabbing Kurt around the neck and trying to pull him back. An elbow to the gut doubled the man over and broke his grasp. Kurt turned, grabbed him by the shoulders, and rammed him headfirst into the cinder-block wall. He fell to the ground and stayed there.

By now Yago was desperate. He couldn't pull the gun up and couldn't fight Kurt off. He looked to Joe and began to say something—no doubt a command word that would be followed by orders telling Joe to attack his friend—but Kurt flung the gurney aside and finished Yago off with a right cross to the jaw.

The two men were down. Kurt needed to make sure they stayed that way. He picked up the tranquilizer gun and methodically fired one dart into the technician and another into Yago. The room went silent.

Kurt looked around. He could hardly explain the state he was in or the level of energy flowing through him. On the one hand he saw everything. Every twitch of his enemies, every flashing light on the equipment, every shadow in the room. He saw Joe and Commander Wells on their gurneys. He saw Solari hooked up to the electrical stimulator. And yet, he had no concept of anything beyond the walls. He had no thoughts of airships, or Colon's dangerous plans, or even NUMA. A single obsession occupied his mind: to follow the commands that he'd given himself. The first part was done, he'd beaten Yago and his associate into submission. Now he needed to use the generator.

He moved to the device, his gait stiff and halting. Switching the power off, he removed Solari's headband and slipped it over his own head. He adjusted the straps until it fit snugly and then switched the power back on.

A surge of electricity raced through his body, dropping Kurt to his knees.

The system cycled, releasing him for an instant, then sending the next jolt. This one felt worse, like a bolt of lightning. His arms and legs went numb, then filled with pins and needles. He bit his tongue. A short respite let him breathe before the third surge came through.

With each shock he began to feel more like himself. Conscious decision-making was returning. The theta wave in his mind was breaking down and the alpha state of regular thinking taking over.

He knew it was working when he actively considered when to shut the system off. But Kurt was never a man to use three nails when he could use seven. He preferred to overdo things. He let the next wave hit and the next after that. Only when his hands and feet were trembling did he reach up and shut off the machine.

53

Unlike Kurt, Joe woke up feeling rested and refreshed. It was as if he'd just had a great night of sleep plus an afternoon nap. He felt energized and ready for action. Even the sore shoulder that had been nagging him over the past few days was gone.

To his surprise, Kurt was standing over him, looking . . . well, looking like Kurt. He had a new abrasion on his face, bloodshot eyes, and a hastily wrapped bandage on his forearm, through which blood was already seeping.

Kurt looked like this often enough on their adventures that Joe thought nothing of it. The only thing he found odd was Kurt's hair. It was volumized and sticking out in all directions, as if he'd joined a punk rock band.

"What happened to you?"

"I stuck a paper clip in the light socket," Kurt said.

"Paper clip?" Joe wasn't following.

Kurt pulled back, revealing the bundle of wires and the band of electrodes in his hand.

Joe sat up. "Easy, Dr. Frankenstein. I don't need my neurons re-arranged."

"Too late," Kurt said. "I zapped you while you were sleeping. Consider yourself lucky. It wasn't a fun thing to go through wide awake."

Joe felt a tingling sensation on the side of his head and realized one eyelid was fluttering. He looked past Kurt to Commander Wells, who seemed to be guarding the door in case anyone tried to enter. "Did you get this same treatment?"

"Tranquilizer dart, yes. Electroshock therapy, no. According to Kurt, you and he got dosed with the microchips, but they didn't get around to me."

"Lucky you."

Joe looked around. It started coming to him. They were in the Ostrom complex, deep underground somewhere. He remembered the submarine simulation, the shoot-out, and then getting hit with the tranquilizer dart. He spied the two men Kurt had battered to the ground, now tied together and gagged. "Guess I missed the party."

"Save your strength for the next one," Kurt said. "We still have to get out of here."

Joe swung his legs off the table, grabbing the rail as he fought a spell of dizziness. "What's the plan?"

"Yeah," Commander Wells asked. "What's the plan?"

Kurt didn't disappoint. "I overheard Colon saying the replacement crew was going aboard the *Condor*. He's going to use that airship to deliver those men to whatever submarine he's targeted. We need to stop it from taking off, even if we have to drive a truck into its side to do so."

"Can't do that from down here," Joe said.

"Which is why we're going topside as soon as you can stand," Kurt replied.

"And how do we do that without getting spotted, caught, or shot?" Commander Wells asked.

Kurt handed her a white jacket and a stethoscope, then pointed to Solari. "You're the doctor, he's the patient. Joe and I are a couple of gray-shirts here to help you."

"To help me with what?"

"Solari is supposed to be put on the other airship," Kurt said. "The one that's headed for Paris. Colon wanted him taken aboard before the sedation wore off. If we put him in a wheelchair and throw a blanket over him, we can walk out of here without anyone giving us a second look."

They left the medical bay wearing white coats and surgical masks. They pushed Solari along in a wheelchair, making their way to the elevator without any interference.

Stepping into the elevator, they rode up to the tunnel level. The tug was waiting right where they'd left it. Kurt removed his mask. "Please tell me you still have the key?"

Joe pulled the key from a pocket and climbed on board.

"Nice," Kurt said. "Let's go."

With Kurt and Commander Wells holding Solari, they drove back through the tunnel and into the underground warehouse. The guards recognized Solari and raised the gate, letting them pass.

From there, they went to the exit ramp, with its mild curve and slope. After a full turn they emerged from the underground complex into the warm, humid night. From where they were, they could see most of the SkyPort, including both landing pads. One look was enough to reveal a problem.

"Bad news," Joe said. "We've missed our flight."

Kurt saw it too. The *Condor* was already airborne. A subtle shimmer of heat distorted the landing pad as the impellers created a wave of thrust. They watched as it rose gently and pivoted to the west, climbing away from the island in what seemed like slow motion.

"So much for plan A," Kurt said wistfully.

Commander Wells suggested a plan B. "Maybe we should get out of here, contact your people, and turn this thing over to the military. It shouldn't take them long to find that thing and shoot it down."

"There are three hundred innocent people on that airship," Kurt said. "Including a couple of our friends and your man Walker."

"I didn't think about that," Commander Wells said.

"No worries, it's been a long night," Kurt said. "Truth is, even if they weren't on board, sending this up the chain of command will get us nothing but gridlock. It took the government a week to shoot down an unmanned Chinese spy balloon. Asking them to knock a billon-dollar Brazilian airship out of the sky would tie the decision-makers in knots that no human could undo."

"Agreed," Joe said. "But we can't stay here. Every minute we stand around doubles the chances we get caught."

Kurt wasn't sure about Joe's math, but the principle was correct.

"We could go for the Jeep," Commander Wells said.

"I wouldn't count on it being undiscovered at this point," Kurt said.

"We could sneak out with the night shift," Joe said, pointing to a line of people heading for the gate.

That seemed more promising. But Colon's people might spot them, and they certainly couldn't bring Solari, who was as much a victim as anyone else.

Kurt's gears turned furiously. Truth was, they needed a way to do multiple things at the same time and find a way off the SkyPort grounds that wouldn't get them caught or killed, or force them to leave Solari behind. A way to intercept the *Condor* that wouldn't require an act of Congress to implement. And—since the *Eagle* had a target of its own—a way to kill two airships with one stone.

And that was the answer.

"It's simple," Kurt said eventually. "All we have to do is hijack the *Eagle* and use it to force the *Condor* into the sea."

54

The *Eagle*'s preparations for launch were nearly finished by the time Kurt and company reached the landing pad. Incredibly, the airship was now pointed thirty degrees to the right of where it had been aimed when they'd last seen it.

Driving across a small gap revealed the secret. "This whole surface is a turntable," Joe said.

Kurt was impressed by the ingenuity, but more interested in the goings-on at the stern. The cargo ramp was still down, but nothing new was being put on board. They could see a member of the flight crew was directing vehicles down the ramp and off.

"Load-out is finished," Kurt said. "This ship is ready to go."

"Can't take off without the boss," Commander Wells replied.

"How is your patient?"

"Still out cold," she said. "Other than that, I haven't a clue."

Joe drove the tug alongside the airship, rumbling down its length and passing a number of gangways in the process of being pulled in. Up ahead, a well-lit ramp used by the officers and any passengers who'd debarked the ship was being unhooked. Below and behind it, a less important-looking ramp remained in place. Kurt saw a number of crewmen milling about and loading supplies for the transatlantic flight. "That's our ticket right there."

Joe turned toward the lower ramp, arriving as a forklift came down out of the airship and picked up what appeared to be cases of beer. As the forklift turned and went up the ramp, Joe attempted to follow.

A crewman stopped them at the threshold. "Where do you think you're going?"

Joe looked at Kurt, who looked back at Commander Wells. She had the stethoscope in her ears and the bell on Solari's chest. "Colon wants Solari in his quarters before he wakes up," she said. "You have a problem with that?"

Uttering Colon's name within Ostrom was like dropping the moniker of a high-ranking Gestapo leader in Nazi Germany: it made people get out of your way. These men did just that, though as they weren't gray-shirts, they didn't look particularly happy about it.

Joe pulled in and parked the tug. Kurt got the wheelchair and helped Commander Wells lift Solari out of the tug. As they wheeled him away, Commander Wells shouted back to the crewman. "Tell the captain that Solari is aboard, but that he's not to be disturbed."

"Fine," the crewman said. "But this ramp is getting pulled. You want off this ship you'll have to leave through the stern, with the rest of your crowd."

"We'll make our own way out," Kurt said.

"I bet you will."

With Joe leading the way and Commander Wells walking beside him, Kurt pushed Solari through the storeroom until they found an elevator. "Let's find Solari's quarters and get him all tucked in."

⸻

Solari's cabin was every bit as luxurious as the Presidential Suite on the *Condor* that he'd given to Paul and Gamay. It included a reclining chair covered in white leather, a separate sitting room, and a bed that was pushed up against the glass so he that could lie awake and look down at the world passing by.

It also included personal touches, like a first-class liquor collection, a closet of Solari's own clothes—which had been transferred from the *Condor*—and some personal items and knickknacks that were of negligible monetary value, but must have had sentimental importance to the Brazilian industrialist.

Kurt found a strange-looking rubber dragon that appeared to have been through the ringer a time or two. Nearby was a faded picture of two conservatively dressed older people with a little boy between them. He assumed it was a photo of Solari and his parents.

"Feel kind of bad for Solari at this point," Kurt said. "Colon has been using him this whole time. Stole his company and his dream."

Joe nodded. "Pretty sure he's setting Solari up to take the blame when all is said and done too."

Kurt placed the photo back on the desk and realized the airship had begun to move. The soft rise was almost imperceptible, but a glance though the windows revealed the lights of the SkyPort dropping below them.

When the airship was a hundred feet off the landing pad, it began pivoting to the east. A deep thrumming sound reverberated through the floor as the thrust came on. It was not unlike the feeling of an ocean liner building speed as the screws began to turn.

The last of Providencia's lights passed beneath them and the airship traveled out over the water, climbing into the night sky.

As if he were drawing power from the flight itself, Solari began to stir.

"Um, Kurt," Joe said, getting his attention. "We might want to get out of here."

That had been the plan, but seeing Solari's cabin and feeling the disdain of the regular crewman toward Colon's name had changed

Kurt's mind. He'd come to believe Solari's cabin was the best place they could possibly be. Especially once the CEO had come to his senses.

"What is . . . Where . . . Where am I?" Solari asked groggily. Still in lab coats, Kurt, Joe, and Commander Wells appeared like doctors.

"You're in your cabin on the *Eagle*," Kurt said quietly.

"I see," Solari said, propping himself up. "Colon made sure I got here. At least he's good for that."

"He made sure you got here, all right," Joe said.

"Did I have another seizure?" Solari asked.

Kurt took a deep breath and sat down across from Solari. "No," he said. "And you've probably never had a real seizure in your life."

"What are you talking about?" Solari asked. "They've been constant for the last two years. They're getting worse."

"That's what Colon wants you to think," Kurt said.

From Solari's perspective the situation was odd. Odder than usual even. He was now coherent enough to study them. One man, tall and lanky with wavy silver hair, the other shorter, stockier, with broad shoulders and short black hair. One woman, with blond hair and a serious look on her face. He didn't think they carried themselves like doctors. And he'd never seen them before, even when he'd previously had a spell on Providencia.

Looking closer, he noticed abrasions on the tall man's face. That they had gray coveralls on underneath their lab coats. That they all looked a little worse for the wear. And that, so far at least, they'd been exceedingly polite, something Colon's people never were—even to him. "What do you people want?"

"Your help," the taller man said. "And in return, we offer you ours."

Solari was intrigued. "To what end?"

"Stopping Colon. Saving your company. And preventing a war."

The words were spoken without a hint of jest. And Solari began to wonder if this was another dream or hallucination. If so, at least it was an interesting one.

He asked for a hand up and stood with help. "I expect this will take a great deal of explanation on your part. And plenty of questions on mine. There's an unopened bottle of Opus One Red in my wine fridge. Perhaps we should lubricate our vocal cords before we commence the conversation."

The silver-haired man grinned. "Best offer I've had all day."

55

Kurt started at the beginning, explaining who they were and why they were looking into the drone attacks. How that had led to Ostrom, and ultimately to Providencia and their encounters with Colon.

Kurt trod carefully around the notion of mind control, asking Solari about his experiences and allowing him to explain the seizures and episodes of missing time he'd experienced over the past two years.

"Did these things ever happen to you before you met Colon, or only after?"

A long pause ensued. "After."

Kurt nodded softly. He shared with Solari the background info they had on Colon, hitting the Cuban Intelligence angle as squarely as possible.

"He was forced on me," Solari explained. "Part of the deal for cheap helium. I never quite trusted him, but it's hard to think he's capable of what you're suggesting."

Kurt figured he had to play it straight. "He's been using your airships to launch drone attacks against container ships and other freighters far out at sea. He's been stealing cargo and abducting crewmen as part of his plan. Now he wants to go after a military vessel, an American nuclear submarine."

"Preposterous," Solari insisted.

"Do you carry drones on these airships?"

"Yes," Solari admitted. "Several kinds. So what?"

Joe chimed in. "Do you have any that are donut shaped? With a single large fan in the center?"

"Yes, I saw . . ." Solari stopped mid-sentence. "No, we have nothing like that . . . Except . . ."

Solari seemed to freeze as he sorted through his jumbled memories. Kurt let him have the time he needed.

"I'm almost certain I've dreamed of something exactly that shape," Solari admitted finally. "At one point I was considering designing one as my next engineering project, but I . . ."

"Most likely you've already designed and built just such a machine," Kurt said. "And Colon stole it from you."

"How could that be? You can't steal an idea from a man's mind."

"No," Kurt admitted. "But you can erase it from his memory."

Solari cut his eyes at Kurt.

"Might as well rip the Band-Aid off," Commander Wells said.

She was right. Kurt raised his hands as if cautioning Solari to allow him some leeway. He explained about the microchips, the hypnosis, and the effects on the brain.

Solari took it in, appearing dumbfounded, but not rejecting it.

Kurt could tell he was on the precipice. He would soon fall one way or another, either into belief or angry denial.

Kurt raised a hand and brushed his own hair back, revealing narrow rectangular marks like oddly shaped sunburn scars. "I'm guessing you have marks like these on your scalp somewhere."

"They're an epidermal infection," Solari replied tersely.

"In the shape of a perfect rectangle?"

"I'm treating it with antibiotic cream."

"It's no infection," Kurt said. "They come from electrodes used to shut down the tiny computer chips and reset your brain. Colon got us too."

Solari studied the marks on Kurt's temple and then looked into the mirror at his own. They were fresh and raw, although they'd almost been gone when he boarded the *Condor* the day before. "They always show up after I have an episode," Solari admitted. "And I always seem to have an episode around Colon."

"There's a reason for that."

Solari seemed to stop wondering. He began to look pleased. If this were true, then the blackouts and episodes of odd behavior were not his fault. It also meant they could be stopped. It meant the seizures didn't have to happen, perhaps ever again. Thinking this way, it seemed like the best news in years. "Tell me about this war Colon is going to start."

"He's trying to settle an old score with the United States," Kurt said. "He wants one of our nuclear submarines. That's the *Condor*'s mission. But this ship has a mission too. Colon's people loaded at least a hundred canisters of the mind-altering dust in your aft cargo hold. From what we know that's enough to infect a small city. I'm guessing we're going to fly over some metropolitan area and act like a crop duster."

"We don't fly over any cities," Solari said.

To prove it, he grabbed the remote control for the TV and switched it on. A blue screen appeared, followed by a highly detailed graphic of the airship. After selecting a menu, Solari clicked on the airship's navigation app. The screen came up showing the *Eagle*'s position as it flew across the Caribbean. As it zoomed out, its future course could be seen crossing the Atlantic all the way to France. The only landmass they even brushed against was Cuba.

For a brief instant Kurt wondered if Colon was going to dust his own country, maybe start a new revolution, but assuming the airship went on course, it would be far off the southern coast of Cuba for most of the transit, missing Havana and the more populated northern section by a hundred miles or more. Too far for the dust to drift without ending up in the sea.

"We could change course at some point," Commander Wells suggested.

"It would take a large diversion to hit Havana," Kurt said.

"Even longer to hit Miami or anything in the states," Joe said.

"Such a big move would be too obvious and too easy to stop," Kurt concluded.

"Can you zoom in?" Joe asked.

"Of course." Solari pressed a button on the remote and the view changed.

"Slide right."

Solari panned to the right, moving along the projected course.

"Stop there," Joe said. "Zoom one more time."

The more tightly focused map confirmed that the airship missed the vast majority of Cuba, only crossing land as it passed the southeastern tip. Seeing that, Joe knew instantly what the target was. "If this is the actual course we take, we'll go right over the top of Guantánamo Bay."

Kurt remembered Colon mentioning "chaos at the base" to Yago. Suddenly it made sense. "No wonder he thinks our military is going to be preoccupied with other things when he hijacks the sub. He's going to dust Guantánamo and cause some form of havoc. God only knows what he's actually planning, but you can bet it won't be pretty."

"Won't an airship crossing the base be suspicious?" Commander Wells asked.

Solari was ashen. "We won't cross the base, but we always cross the bay. Cubans retain the right of navigation across the water. When we set up the transatlantic routes, Colon insisted we fly as close to Guantánamo as legally allowed, to show the Americans that other countries in the hemisphere have technology too. I always thought it was foolish pride, but I figured it was harmless enough."

"It won't be harmless tonight," Kurt said.

Commander Wells added, "And having seen airships pass over dozens of times by now, no one will think anything of it as the *Eagle* approaches."

"Based on the chart," Joe said, "it looks like we'll cross the bay in the dark. Letting Colon's people spread that dust unseen where it can drift on the wind. The men and women on the base will breathe it in while they sleep."

Solari went for the phone. "I'll call the captain. We'll turn around immediately."

Kurt put his hand on the switch hook, pressing it down to make sure the line didn't connect. "Right now, we have the element of surprise. You turn this ship around and we lose that. In addition, Colon's got a bunch of people on board—a small army of those gray-shirts. He probably has a contingency plan ready should anyone try to divert the ship. Let's stay on course for now. We can turn the ship once we've secured it."

"How do you propose to do that?" Solari asked.

"A reverse mutiny," Kurt said. "Or a preemptive one. Take your pick."

56

As the *Eagle* continued on its current heading, Kurt, Joe, Commander Wells, and Solari began meeting with the oldest members of the crew, starting with Captain Bascombe, who was Solari's personal captain and had conducted the maiden flight on every one of Solari's airships.

Colon had pulled Bascombe and his crew off the *Condor* and put them on the *Eagle* to get his own people in place for the mission. The fact that Solari and his handpicked captain would be responsible for dusting the American base was only a secondary consideration.

And yet that had given Solari one ally he could absolutely trust.

Bascombe came to the cabin and listened to much the same speech Solari had been given. It took him no time at all to believe Colon was capable of such madness. In turn he brought four of his most loyal people to the suite and each of them tapped a couple of crew members they implicitly trusted. One of whom happened to be the quartermaster who had let Kurt and Joe and Commander Wells aboard. It took the man a little longer to trust what he was hearing, but Kurt figured he'd be a loyal ally in the fight that was about to go down.

All in, with Kurt, Joe, and Commander Wells included, they had a team of twenty.

"Any chance we could recruit a few more?" Joe asked.

Bascombe shook his head. "Not unless you want to risk adding newer personnel."

Kurt didn't want that. "Twenty will have to do. How many men are we likely to be facing?"

"Colon has placed eight members of his security team on board," the captain said. "And there are nineteen total among the cargo-handling teams."

That was more than Kurt was expecting. "That leaves us at a seven-man disadvantage."

"Not necessarily," the captain said. "Based on shift assignments, four members of the security team are off duty right now. While at least eight additional gray-shirts should be in their bunks or at least in their quarters, if they're not already asleep."

"We should take those groups first," Kurt said. "Put them out of action and then go for the cargo hold."

The captain agreed. "I'll take care of that. Then we'll join you at the stern. How do you intend to get into their strongholds without a frontal assault?"

"Good question," Kurt said.

They unrolled a schematic of the ship across Solari's coffee table.

"The hangar deck is here," Solari said, pointing to a large open space on the mid-deck, at the stern. "Directly below it is the cargo hold and the machinery room."

Joe studied the plans upside down, but that didn't stop him from spotting an unusual way in. He pointed to a series of braces running vertically through the aft section of the craft. "I assume this is the support brace for the vertical stabilizer."

"Correct," Solari said. "And?"

"The frame goes all the way to the bottom of the airship," Joe added.

"For rigidity," Solari replied, one engineer talking to another.

"What are the tolerances where it passes through the decks?"

"You want to climb down through it?" Solari realized.

"If possible," Joe said.

Solari hemmed and hawed. "It'll be a tight squeeze," he said, "but you should be able to make it."

"I'll take two volunteers along with me," Joe said. "And hopefully none of us will get stuck."

Several hands went up and Joe chose the smaller members of the group.

Kurt glanced at Joe, impressed by the plan. "You take the high road, I'll take the low road." He pointed to one of the thrust vectoring conduits that went directly under the cargo bay.

"Those conduits are sealed," the captain pointed out.

"There have to be inspection ports," Kurt noted.

"True," the captain said. He leaned on the schematic. "Here and here. This one is in the cargo bay. But it can't be opened from the inside."

"Not with a key," Kurt said, "but these conduits are designed to move high-volume, mid-pressure air, right?"

The captain nodded.

"I'm guessing they're made of lightweight material like everything else around here. Could they be forced?"

"Yes, of course," Solari said, jumping in. "The conduit walls and the inspection doors are made of 6000 series aluminum, extremely light and only an inch thick."

"I think I can bull my way through that," Kurt said.

"I'll go with you," Solari said.

"Sorry," Kurt said. "But I need you at the main door. The gray-shirts still believe you're under their master's spell. If you knock on the door, act like you're in a trance and insist that Colon wants you to check out the drones. They'll probably open the door and let you in. The captain's team can hide down the hall and rush the door behind you."

"You want a performance out of me?" Solari asked.

"All the world's a stage," Kurt replied.

"So it is," Solari said. "I'll do my best."

As the team got ready for action, Commander Wells came over to Kurt. "I noticed you left me out of the plan."

"Keep an eye on Solari," Kurt said. "I don't want him getting himself killed."

With the broad strokes in place, they discussed a few details, distributed the limited number of radios and the few weapons on board, and prepared to go to war.

"One last thing," Kurt said. "Think of this as an initiation of sorts, or a test of bravery and bonding ritual all rolled up together. It's also a method to make sure none of us are under Colon's control."

As Kurt produced a Taser that he'd asked the captain to procure, the crew lined up to take the electric shock. To prove he wasn't above them, Kurt zapped himself first. Joe, Commander Wells, and Solari went next. Once everyone had been given a shock and sufficient time to recover, the team moved out.

57

Rodrigo Bowin was brushing his teeth over the sink in the small cabin he shared with another member of the security crew when he heard a knock at the door. Irritated by the late-night interruption, he spit the toothpaste out, wiped his mouth with a hand towel, and stepped to the door. He was reaching for the handle when the door flew open and three men bulled their way in.

Taken by surprise, he was quickly subdued, tied up, and gagged. For extra security he was duct-taped to an electrical conduit and his computer and phones were confiscated.

No one explained what was happening or why. He was asked nothing. They just left him in the dark with his hands bound behind his back, his feet crossed at the ankles, and eight bands of the thick silver tape around his body. He tensed for a moment, but quickly gave up. The tape job was ruthless and precise, he couldn't move a muscle.

———

The captain's assault team performed the same routine five more times before encountering any resistance. In one cabin, they found three members of the cargo crew playing dominoes. A quick capture was impossible, and a tumbling brawl broke out. The fight left the compartment in shambles and the captain's men bloodied and bruised, but the end result was the same: the gray-shirts were tied up, taped together, gagged, and blindfolded.

The quartermaster, grinning through a busted lip, was the last to exit. He delivered a parting kick to one of the men before shutting the lights off. "That's for a friend of mine," he said. "A guy your people did a number on."

As the first stage of the operation was taking place, Joe and his two volunteers, a man named Gregorio and a woman named Irena, were moving along the central catwalk amid the inflated gas cells of the aft lifting chamber. They bypassed the first two ladders and reached the third.

"This is the one," Irena said.

Joe began the climb feeling as if the airship was rocking a bit. "Are we hitting some turbulence?"

"There are summer storms popping up here and there," Gregorio told him. "The captain gave orders to go between them, but we'll definitely feel some buffeting."

Joe continued up the ladder and came out on the upper catwalk. The lifting cells were below them now, with only the skin of the airship up above. For the first time since they came aboard, Joe could hear the wind and then the drumming of rain.

He moved along the catwalk until he reached the A-frame of the vertical stabilizer's support brace. By this point the roof above was sloping down toward them, and to Joe's surprise there was condensation and rivulets of water running down the side of the aluminum structure.

"Totally normal," Irena said. "The stabilizer is designed to allow water to enter, rather than have it pooling on the skin up above. It drains down to the hangar deck and out through a small pipe."

Studying the wet surface with his flashlight, Joe could see it would be a tricky climb down. Not only were all the braces wet and cold, but due to the size of the airship, he'd misjudged how far apart they were from one another.

"No time like the present," he said, clipping the flashlight to his belt. He began to climb down, with the two volunteers following him. They were halfway down when the first flash of lightning illuminated the airship from outside. Thunder rumbled a split second later, reverberating inside the airframe.

"Nothing like climbing down a wet metal surface in a lightning storm," Joe muttered.

"Theoretically," Irena said. "A lightning strike should just travel over the outside of the airframe and end up being discharged by small antennas underneath the ship."

"Let's hope theory holds," Joe said. Having already been zapped twice in the last few hours, he had no wish to undergo a larger, more powerful third round of such treatment.

        ———

From Kurt's perspective, a little rain to cool things down would be nice. He was crawling through a thruster tunnel only slightly wider than his body. At the moment—and for the foreseeable future, Kurt hoped—this particular thruster system had been disabled. Which meant the air inside was stagnant and hot.

As he crawled along, sweat was dripping down Kurt's face. He ignored it and continued forward. Passing several markers, he examined them with the flashlight in his hand and then crawled onward. By now he was underneath the cargo bay. A fact confirmed by a parade of hastily drilled holes in the thruster tunnel, through which brass metal nozzles had been pushed. Aluminum shavings on the floor of the tunnel told him this work had been recently done.

Kurt figured this was how they'd disperse the dust. Fly near the base, engage the thrusters, either automatically or manually, and open the nozzles. The dust would billow from the stern of the airship, invisible in the night sky, and then drift with the breeze while settling over the base. If they did it right, no one would even know what had occurred.

Shining his light ahead, he found he'd reached the divide where the tunnel split into two. The main inspection port was immediately before this divide. He aimed the flashlight forward until he spotted the indentation of the inspection port. Sliding toward it, he stopped just shy of the position.

He pulled the radio to his mouth and keyed the microphone. An earbud connected to a jack allowed him to hear any response. "Number one tunnel rat in position," he whispered.

"Copy," the captain's voice called back.

A slight grunting sound came over the radio next. "Team Big Top almost done with the monkey bars," Joe said. "Give us sixty seconds."

"Copy that," Commander Wells said. "Getting our fearless leader ready for his soliloquy."

"Make it Oscar worthy."

58

By this point in the flight, the gray-shirts in the operations team on the hangar deck were bored and tired. While they knew something was afoot, based on the load-out at Providencia, none of them were privy to the truth and most simply thought they were on another smuggling run.

With the airship underway and the compartment secured and locked down, there was little work to be done, other than some cleaning and minor maintenance. A radio was playing. A couple of mechanics were working on a larger drone. The rest of the night crew was organizing spare parts or just shooting the breeze.

As was often the case when the ship ran at low speed on a hot day or evening, they had the launch ramp down, giving them a wide letterbox view of the sky. With the hour past midnight there wasn't much to see, but the cool air was welcome in the compartment, which was otherwise climate-control free.

With the music playing and the attention levels low, the knock on the door went unnoticed at first. A second, louder bang was enough to get the attention of the nearest technician. He went to the door, glanced at the little screen that was connected to an exterior camera, and made a strange face. "It's Solari."

Other sections of the ship would have snapped to attention had the CEO arrived, but for obvious reasons there was little respect for the man among this group.

"What's he want?" the shift leader asked.

"How should I know?"

Solari banged on the door again, standing rigid and tall. He leaned toward the camera until his face was filling the screen. "I must speak to you. Colon sent me."

The men looked around at one another until Solari started banging again and the shift leader made a decision. "Let him in."

The door was opened. Solari walked stiffly in. "I need to speak with everyone."

"Now isn't a good time, Mr. Solari," the shift leader said.

Solari continued walking and looking straight ahead.

The technician who'd opened the door glanced out onto the catwalk, saw no one there, and closed the door.

"I have new instructions for you," Solari said, moving past the shift leader and then turning around.

His performance was more like a robot than a zombie or a hypnotized man. And it was odd enough that it raised a suspicious feeling among those who had seen how Colon's dust actually worked. But it was certainly captivating enough that every eye remained glued to him.

The lightning flickered outside, illuminating the compartment with a brief and blinding flash.

"What is this?" Solari asked, startled.

"This guy's off his rocker," someone said.

"Or his meds."

"It's just the storm," the shift leader said. "Let's get you back to your quarters."

He moved in to take Solari by the hand, but the flamboyant CEO raised his arm dramatically. "This is the message," he said, projecting his voice in full baritone. "Full fathom five thy father lies; / Of his bones are coral made; / Those are pearls that were his eyes; / Nothing of him that doth fade."

The crew was mystified. Some laughed to themselves. They'd seen Solari do weird stuff before, but this took the cake. Still, none of them looked away, his reputation for strange and ostentatious behavior working in his favor at this point.

Up above, Joe and his two volunteers had squeezed through the gap in the overhead and were now climbing down behind a row of parked drones. Joe could hear Solari's speech perfectly. "He's doing *The Tempest.*"

"Fine choice," Irena said.

Solari was swinging his arms about now, really getting into the character. "But doth suffer a sea-change; / Into something rich and strange; / Sea-nymphs hourly ring his knell: / Ding-dong. / Hark! Now I hear them—ding-dong, bell."

As Solari shouted the last word in a booming crescendo, the captain and his crew rushed in, busting open the thin aluminum door and charging across the deck. Colon's men turned to take the charge, while Joe and his partners climbed down behind them.

Half the gray-shirts were taken instantly, but they didn't go down without a fight, brawling and struggling even as they were outnumbered. At the same time, the shift leader and a small group of men closest to him managed to pull back. Some grabbed club-like weapons, while the shift leader produced a handgun and started firing.

Joe dropped to the deck behind the man. He clubbed the pistol to the deck and kicked it away. The shift leader lunged at him, but Joe dodged the attack, stunned the man with a jab, and then knocked him out with an uppercut.

While Joe was winning by a knockout, Gregorio tackled a second member of the gray-shirts, wrestling him to the ground and putting him in a half nelson. The third gray-shirt ended up on the receiving end of the Taser as Irena fired the prongs into his chest and shocked him into submission.

Solari had finished his speech and was watching with glee when one of the last gray-shirts rushed him and attempted to take him hostage.

Commander Wells intercepted the assault, throwing a shoulder into him like a cross-checking hockey player. He missed his mark and tumbled to the deck. Two of the regular crewmen subdued him before he could get up.

"My bodyguard," Solari said, putting his hands together. "I thank you."

The fight was over. While the captain and his men secured the survivors, Solari beamed.

"What did you think of my performance?"

"I see Broadway in your future," Commander Wells said.

"So do I," he replied. "Maybe I'll buy a theater or two."

"It'll have to wait until we're done," Joe added, tapping his foot on the metal plating of the floor. "We still have the cargo deck to deal with, down below."

A quick head count showed that ten of Colon's gray-shirts had been on the hangar deck, along with one member of the security detail. That left only three of his proxies still to fight, but as they were all security team members, there was a significant chance they'd be armed.

The captain's men checked the hatches that led to the cargo deck below. Both of them were locked down. "We've lost the element of surprise."

"Any other way down?" Joe asked.

The captain pointed to the aircraft carrier–style elevator in the middle of the hangar floor. "It's a slow ride," he warned. "Anyone on the platform will be a sitting duck."

"Can't leave Kurt to do it alone," Joe said.

Captain Bascombe nodded grimly. "I'll activate the controls."

59

Kurt heard nothing of the brawl, or Solari's speech, or anything aside from his own breathing. He'd dragged two items along with him as he crawled through the thruster tunnel. And the effort had been substantial.

The first and heaviest was a forty-eight-inch, powder-coated utility jack that was bright yellow. He set it up underneath the inspection port and began to work the lever, ratcheting the lifting pad up until it touched the door above.

Sweating profusely, he slowed his pace. After three more pulls on the rachet, the door had bent upward, but hadn't popped open.

Waiting to make his move, Kurt got a message from Joe via the earbud.

"Hangar deck secure. Based on the numbers up here, you should be facing three well-armed hombres down there. Wait till you hear the buzzing to make your move."

Kurt wasn't sure what that meant, but he would do as suggested. He reached back for the second item he'd dragged with him: Yago's double-barreled tranquilizer gun.

―――

The men on the cargo deck were indeed armed, but there were four, not three. And the fourth was a red-haired man with a beard who held only a collapsible baton.

For the moment they stood all together in a small open space between the stacks of metal cylinders that had been loaded aboard the ship. They looked at the ceiling, listening to the sound of boots pounding on the deck above. They heard the thuds and angry shouts as the *Eagle*'s loyal crewmen brawled with their comrades. By comparison, the sound of handguns being discharged was muted and sporadic.

"Should we go up?" one of the men asked.

Lobo considered it briefly, but the fight was already waning. Climbing the ladder and popping their heads out through the hatch would just get them picked off or captured. "No," he said. "Lock the hatches down tight and get Colon on the radio."

"We've been told to stay off the radio," one man said.

"And I'm telling you to get on it."

Stepping across the myriad snaking lines they'd used to connect the cylinders to the ship's exhaust ports, one of the men made his way to the sat comm unit that they used to communicate with Colon. He powered it up and waited for the confirmation signal and got nothing. "They've cut us off."

"How?" Lobo demanded.

"The unit transmits through the main dish on the top of the ship," the man said. "They must have broken the link."

There could be no doubt about it now: They were in a fight to the death for control of the ship. Winner take all.

So be it, Lobo thought.

He took charge of the men. "You," he said to the man at the comm station. "Guard the ladder. If anyone pries it open, you shoot them between the eyes."

The man nodded, checked his weapon, and moved to a spot where he could fire directly upward.

Lobo sent the second man to guard the door at the far end of the compartment, which led to the lower catwalk. He gave the same shoot-to-kill order.

With the obvious routes in now locked and covered, there was only one other way into the compartment: the elevator that was used to move large drones and other equipment between the cargo deck and hangar deck.

Lobo expected the attackers to use it. He was proved right as the sound of the hydraulic actuators kicked on.

"Kill the lights," he ordered.

The last of his men threw a switch on the bulkhead and the compartment went dark. At almost the same moment a horizontal crack of illumination appeared in the ceiling above. The crack widened and spread as the platform dropped slowly into the cargo hold and the light from the hangar deck spilled in.

Crouching behind one of the panels, Lobo stared at the descending platform. He saw no one riding it and was busy wondering what kind of trick was being played, when a pair of small drones roared to life with an instant high-pitched buzz.

The drones leapt off the platform and raced into the cargo bay with reckless abandon. Lobo ducked and spun as the dinner plate–sized machines zipped past them at high speed. They circled through the cavernous compartment, splitting off from one another, and then converging back toward Lobo and his group.

One of the men opened fire, blasting away at the nimble machines, his bullets ricocheting off the nearby walls.

"Stop," Lobo shouted. "You're only wasting ammunition."

The buzzing sound reached Kurt loud and clear. He hit the inspection door with the heel of his palm, punching it open. Popping his head out, he saw one of the drones whiz by, its green and red lights blinking as it passed.

Placing the tranquilizer gun on the deck, he climbed out of the exhaust tunnel and picked up the weapon. A quick scan revealed the three men Joe had told him about. Two to his left, watching the various entryways, and one to his right, gazing up and out through the opening to the hangar deck where the elevator had descended.

Kurt stepped forward, leveling the double-barreled tranquilizer gun and pulling the right-hand trigger. A soft pop sounded, and the first dart hit the man watching the main door. Kurt turned without waiting to see the man fall and fired the second dart. This one hit the man watching the ladder. The first man had already slumped to the deck in a heap, while the second was grabbing at the dart much as Kurt had done, an act he knew to be futile. The man swirled to the ground and lay there.

Kurt crouched and turned, looking toward the third man just as a drone zipped across the compartment and nailed the man in the side of the head.

The five-pound drone, traveling at thirty miles an hour, hit with the force of a major-league fastball. The man went over, dropped his pistol, and lay in the fetal position, groaning and shuddering.

Three men down, but no one had seen the fourth. Lobo suddenly appeared and lunged at Kurt from behind one of the canisters. He delivered a spinning kick that knocked the tranquilizer gun out of Kurt's hands. Next came the silver-tipped staff, which whistled through the air and grazed Kurt's cheek as he spun and dove out of the way.

Kurt backpedaled, but tripped over one of the cylinders. Tumbling backward, he rolled away and jumped up to his feet in time to block another strike from the baton. Up close, he saw who his opponent was. "So, we get round three after all."

"This will be the last round," Lobo promised.

"For you," Kurt said. "It's over. Drop the cane before you get yourself shot."

Lobo ignored the advice and pressed his attack, the staff slicing the air as he hacked and slashed at a retreating Kurt.

From up above, Joe sent another drone on a kamikaze run, but Lobo heard it coming, ducked, and then knocked it out of the sky with a powerful strike. The shattered machine tumbled out of control and smashed into the bulkhead.

The aerial threat dealt with, Lobo turned and rushed at Kurt, vaulting over the cylinder between them and swinging for Kurt's head. Kurt ducked and fired a punch into Lobo's midsection. Lobo grunted, spun, hooking Kurt's leg with the end of the staff and sweeping Kurt's feet out from under him.

Kurt fell hard, landing near the open inspection port. He rolled over and reached down into it.

"Slithering away like a snake," Lobo shouted.

"Bulls, snakes, wolves," Kurt grunted. "You guys have a lot of animal-related thoughts."

"You'll have no thoughts in a moment."

Lobo reared back, raising the staff like a sword. But Kurt rolled onto his hip and fired his leg forward, crushing in one of Lobo's knees and dropping him to the deck.

Lobo howled in pain, looking very wolflike for just a second. He dropped the staff and grasped his knee. With shaking hands and rage-filled eyes, he spotted a pistol that had been dropped by one of the tranquilized gray-shirts. He twisted his body and lunged for the weapon, using the pain to fuel his effort. He grasped the weapon, spun back toward Kurt, and was struck in the face by a solid-steel object coated in bright yellow paint.

The impact was mind crushing. Lobo fell like a sack of flour, landing on top of Kurt, the rectangular imprint of the utility jack visible across his forehead.

Kurt shoved him off, picked up the pistol, and looked around to see if there were any other foes to deal with. The compartment was still.

Getting up slowly, Kurt took a seat atop one of the cylinders, watching Joe and the captain's men shimmy down ropes from the deck above.

One of the crewmen turned on the lights, the second climbed up the ladder and locked the hatch from the inside. As they secured the compartment, Joe came over to where Kurt stood.

Joe pointed to more blood, this time oozing from Kurt's chin. "You're going to need a transfusion before this is over."

"I need to learn how to duck," Kurt replied.

Joe pointed to the man on the deck. "Is that Lobo?"

Kurt nodded. "I jacked him up."

Joe laughed. "I see what you did there. You're getting better at this."

By now Captain Bascombe had come down the ladder. He gawked at the number of cylinders Colon's people had stacked in the compartment. He was amazed by the number of lines snaking about. "All this to poison your servicemen at Guantánamo Bay?"

"It's rigged to spray out through the exhaust ports," Kurt said.

"But how did they expect to get away with it?"

"By pretending it wasn't them or blaming you, Solari, and the *Eagle*'s crew. A false flag operation that would've required your minds be altered, or maybe the crashing of this airship with all hands on board, so there'd be no one left to dispute the story."

Bascombe took in this thought with a grave look on his face. He'd had a distinguished career. He was glad to know it wouldn't end in infamy. "You've saved us from that, and from the guilt of false accusations. And you've risked life and limb to do it. Is there anything I can do to repay you for your efforts?"

"There is," Kurt said. "You can turn this ship around, run the engines up to full power, and chase down the *Condor*."

60

The *Eagle* leaned into a turn unlike any it had made since its original airworthiness test. Rolling to the right and using the thrusters to push the nose one way and the stern in the other direction, the huge ship thundered through a hundred-and-eighty-degree curve.

The crew held on tight, staring out from the bridge as the storms they had recently passed reappeared. In the dark, it was hard to tell precisely how far the ship had rolled, then the lightning flashed, and the sea, sky, and clouds looked as if they were aligned diagonally, sloping sharply downward to the left.

As they finished the turn, Captain Bascombe centered the All-Con with a satisfied grin on his face. He ordered maximum speed. "Close all outer ports, clean this ship up, and give me full power. One hundred and ten percent, if you can manage."

The chief engineer grimaced. "The engines can handle it, but drawing that much power will drain the batteries in a hurry. They're more than five years old, they're not what they used to be."

"Will they make it till dawn?" the captain asked.

"Perhaps," the engineer said. "If we run dark."

Bascombe nodded and offered Kurt a conspirator's grin. "I assumed we were going to do that anyway."

"It's the only way to fly," Kurt said.

The engineer went over to the main panel and began shutting off nonessential systems, flipping switches and tripping breakers. By the time he was done, the airship was blacked-out except for the bridge, the engineering spaces, and the emergency lights in both the corridors and passenger spaces.

An announcement was made over the PA system, requiring the passengers to remain in their cabins. Kurt would have preferred to drop them off somewhere, but they didn't have that kind of time.

"Captain," he said, "may we use your radio room?"

"Of course," the captain said. "Right this way."

He led Kurt to a small room just behind the bridge. Control units for several different communications systems were stationed there: high-frequency, low-frequency, and shortwave, along with dedicated satellite, cellular satellite—which was more like a satellite phone—and even a system called Data-Link Five, which was basically a prehistoric version of texting.

"Take your pick."

Kurt avoided the regular satellite system and went to the cellular unit, dialing up NUMA and ending up on the phone with the communications desk. After explaining who he was, he asked to be connected with Rudi Gunn. Expecting some pushback on a two a.m. call, Kurt tried to preempt the argument. "Sorry, but this is an emergency. Someone will have to wake him."

"Not necessary," Kurt was told. "He's been in the building since shortly after midnight."

Rudi sounded like he was on his third cup of coffee when he came on the line, but once Kurt launched into the narrative of events, Rudi held off interrupting him.

"Bottom line," Kurt said, "we've thwarted an airborne attack against Guantánamo, but there's no guarantee that Colon wasn't planning to back up his airdrop with clouds of dust launched from the bay itself."

"We'll make sure to inform the Navy," Rudi insisted.

"While you're at it, tell them to button up their nuclear subs," Kurt said. "We think that's the main target."

"Already told them," Rudi said.

Kurt paused, processing Rudi's statement. "Come again?"

"We already informed them of the threat," Rudi insisted. "We figured out the danger earlier this evening."

"And what hat did you pull that information out of?"

Rudi laughed. "Your friend Rolle sent us a report about Gerald Walker, which caused Max to reexamine what we knew about the hijackings," Rudi explained. "She put two and two together and realized an inordinate number of the missing crewmen were former sub-surface warriors from English-speaking countries. A further search revealed other missing persons connected with various nuclear missile programs, all of them retired, so their vanishings didn't raise any red flags. We found a missing engineer from the company that makes the Trident launch tubes, a missing guidance expert from the company that made the control systems, and a lost propellant engineer, who vanished on a hunting trip."

"Well done," Kurt said. "It would have saved us a lot of trouble if Max figured that out a few days ago."

"We still wouldn't have known about Guantánamo," Rudi countered. "So don't be too mad, you haven't been completely replaced by a computer . . . Yet."

"Yet being the operative word," Kurt said. "What kind of security measures are they putting on to protect the missile boats?"

"Every SSBN at sea has been ordered to run silent and run deep," Rudi told him. "The hulls that are docked have been secured and decrewed and are now being watched over by a triple guard of angry Marines in full chemical warfare gear."

It sounded impressive, but it was all too standard. An utterly predictable response. One Colon would have accounted for in his years of planning. "It couldn't be this easy."

"Come again?" Rudi asked.

"Colon has spent years setting this up," Kurt said. "He's been meticulous, resourceful, and visionary. There's no way he's gone through all that, just to leave the final hurdle to chance, hoping he's lucky enough to catch a nuclear submarine running on the surface. He has to have something planned. A way to force the issue. We're kidding ourselves if we believe otherwise."

Rudi paused before answering. "I know you like to the cover all the bases, Kurt. That's part of what makes you good at what you do. But this is over. Whatever Colon was planning, we beat him to the punch. Drones can't get at a nuclear submarine when it's beneath eight hundred feet of seawater. Neither can radio waves. Not the kind he's using anyway. And none of our boats are going to surface and come into port until this thing is handled and Colon is in custody."

Rudi paused for a second and then continued. "You've won, you've beat Colon and cut him off at the pass, or whatever metaphor you want to use. Now's the time to take a victory lap and let the rest of the world's agencies do their jobs."

It might have been lack of sleep, the accumulating aches and pains, or the self-administered shock therapy he'd received on Providencia, but Kurt had to fight the urge to snap at Rudi and tell him to wake up. Rather than get angry he changed his approach.

"Even if you're right, that still leaves the question of Colon. If he knows the game is over, he's not going to land in San Diego or Vancouver or anywhere else in the Western world. He'll go right back to Cuba and touch down out of our reach. And he'll be taking three hundred hostages with him, including Paul, Gamay, and Walker. He'll use the dust on them and trot them out in front of news cameras to confess to all kinds of crimes they've never committed."

Rudi sighed loud enough to be heard over the phone. "Not ideal," he admitted. "But there might not be anything we can do about that. You're not going to get the Pentagon or the White House to approve shooting down an airship with three hundred VIPs on board. Especially now that the sub fleet is secure."

"We don't have to shoot him down," Kurt said. "We can force him down. For all the technology in these things, they're still flying balloons with an outer skin made of fabric."

Rudi didn't dismiss the idea out of hand. "What are you thinking?"

"Target the top half of the *Condor*. Shred a few hundred lifting cells, just enough to force them down onto the water."

"You'll be a grandfather before anyone agrees to that," Rudi said.

"What if we do it ourselves?"

"Airship to airship?" Rudi asked, a slight change in his tone.

Kurt imagined Rudi's eyebrows going up, an expression that gave him an owl-like quality. "Something like that."

"Hmm . . ." Rudi said, pondering the idea. "I'm not going to advise you try such a stunt. But if you happen to run into them, I'm sure the Navy would be more than willing to assist with the rescue effort. If you get my drift."

Kurt understood implicitly. "I'll keep you posted."

After promising to report in later, Kurt made some plans with Captain Bascombe and his officers. Leaving the bridge, he went aft, navigating the darkened halls with a flashlight, until he arrived at the hangar deck, where Commander Wells had stood watch while Joe and Solari had taken apart one of the donut-shaped drones.

"What's the word?" Joe asked.

"We're on our own," Kurt said. "What are you finding back here?"

Joe pointed to the mess. "These are the systems of the attack drone."

"I was right," Solari announced. "I did design this version. I remember every detail now. Every detail except one," he corrected. He held up a lunch pail–sized box bristling with electronics.

"What is it?"

Joe answered. "The frequency generator they've been using against the cargo ships. In addition to the radio transmitter, it's equipped with a powerful speaker that operates at the very fringes of human hearing. Highest and lowest. Nothing in between. Play a song on this and you'll feel it and imagine it, but you'll never really hear it."

"That's how they transmit the orders," Commander Wells said.

"It's a form of subliminal messaging," Joe said. "But the poor infected sailors get overwhelmed by the ideas, as if they're coming from inside their own minds."

Commander Wells shook her head angrily, thinking of Lieutenant Weir.

Kurt put a hand on her shoulder and then turned back to Joe. "Good work. Box that thing up. We might be able to use it."

"Think we're going to catch them in time?" Joe asked.

Kurt had just come from the bridge. It all depended on where Colon was going to find a submarine. "We'll see."

61

USS *MARYLAND* (SSBN-738)

After a long day moving through the locks and across Gatun Lake, the *Maryland* had finished the transit and left the Panama Canal after nightfall. Submerging once, it was three miles off the coast and the submarine was now running quietly to the east at a depth of three hundred feet. It would go deeper soon, but not until the next watch.

In the meantime, Rear Admiral Wagner and Captain Lyle had met up in the captain's quarters. They talked about retirement, the misery of desk jobs, and the joy of their first commands, which seemed to have been given to them only yesterday.

"It goes by fast," Lyle said.

"You're damn right it does," Wagner said.

"Retirement won't be so bad, though."

"Come on, Bob," Wagner said. "It's a little early to start lying to ourselves. How about a drink first?"

The captain's quarters were large for a submarine, but still cramped enough that plenty of surfaces were set up to fold away and store in hidden sections of the wall. Work desks, cabinet doors, even the captain's bed.

"Second compartment on the right," Lyle said, pointing to one particular compact cabinet.

Wagner pulled on a latch, revealing a bottle of bourbon and pair of glasses. He took them out, set them up, and filled both glasses. Handing one to Lyle, he kept the second for himself.

"Let me tell you why Washington isn't the worst," Wagner said.

"Not this again," Lyle said. "At least let me get a buzz on before you hit me with the sales pitch."

They clinked glasses and knocked down the swigs of bourbon in short order.

"Another?" Wagner asked.

"Sure," Lyle said. "But only if you tell me the real reason you're here on my boat."

"Drones," Wagner said, refilling the captain's glass and topping up his own.

"What?" Lyle said.

"I'm here because of the drones," Wagner said, handing him the glass.

The captain had to laugh. He had another sip and leaned back in his chair. He felt a little odd, almost as if he were already drunk. "Strikes me that drones are more of a problem for the surface fleet," he said. "Reality is, nothing can touch us once we're down below."

"Which is why I'm here," Wagner said, sounding strangely serious and suddenly distant. "We have a mission to complete. A mission so secret that orders couldn't be sent by proper channels."

Lyle stared at his old friend, waiting for him to deliver the punch line. It never came. "Come on, Wags," he said, surprising himself by using the Rear Admiral's nickname to his face. "What the hell are you talking about?"

Wagner remained fully serious. His watch started chirping and he let it go. His eyes locked on to Lyle's and bored holes into his old friend. "This comes straight from the CNO," Wagner said, referring to the chief of naval operations. "Aside from the CNO, only the President, the secretary of the Navy, and the director of the CIA know what I'm about to tell you."

Lyle narrowed his gaze. Despite the annoyance of the chirping watch, Wagner had his full attention.

"They sent me to give you new orders," Wagner continued. "Orders that went active the moment we left the canal zone."

The captain's first thought was that this was highly irregular. Mixed in with that thought was the observation that Wagner wasn't smiling or laughing. In fact, his face had lost all expression. And he was the Navy's spy chief. "What new orders are you talking about?"

Even as he spoke, the captain felt a headache coming on. Damned bourbon must have been stronger than he thought.

"I have a new course for you," Wagner said. "It takes us to a rendezvous point, where we'll meet with another ship at dawn. That's all I can tell you for now. You'll receive additional information once we surface."

"Surface?" the captain said. "We just received orders to remain submerged until we reach Kings Bay."

"Which is why I had to be on this ship when those orders came in," Wagner said. "To countermand them."

The headache was rising in pitch, the damned watch was still chirping, and the captain was finding it harder and harder to think.

"Why . . . Why . . ." Lyle couldn't get the question out, the pain in his mind had grown, the sound of the watch chirping had become excruciating. "Why this boat?" he grunted. "Why me?"

"Because I trust you," Wagner said. "And because this is your last cruise. Other captains wouldn't be willing to take the risk I need you to take."

Of course.

And just like that it all made sense. The wall of pain fell away, the chirping watch seemed to go silent. Lyle could see it all clearly now.

Wagner and the boys on the Beltway needed him. His country needed him. It would obviously be a dangerous operation, but that's what he'd signed up for.

Suddenly, he felt empowered and energized. Instead of sailing to a dull and depressing retirement party that would see him off and forgotten, he stood a chance to do something of importance, to finish his career at its highest point, or if things went bad, to go out in a blaze of glory.

He looked at Wagner the way he'd looked at his first commander all those years ago. "Just tell me what you need, sir. The boat is at your disposal."

Wagner nodded, raised his glass, and drank down the last of the bourbon. "First things first," he said. "We need to talk to your chief engineer about the CO_2 scrubbers. I need to make sure they haven't been tampered with."

62

From the bridge of the *Condor*, Colon watched the sky turn from midnight blue to a dusky aquamarine color. Just then, the sun peeked over the horizon, painting the underside of the airship with streaks of orange and turning the surface of the Caribbean from black to a translucent green.

For the second time in a week, a strange bit of nostalgia hit Colon. He'd witnessed countless things from the drifting airship that could simply not be seen or appreciated from the cramped seats of streaking jetliners or the decks of ponderous steel vessels plowing across the sea. This dawn would be the last. Whatever happened today, he'd never set foot on one of the great ships again.

"Target sighted," Colon's handpicked captain said. "Due west. Range five miles."

Colon adjusted his gaze. A thin black line could be seen sitting motionless on the surface. He trained his binoculars on it, focusing and zooming. The outline of a ballistic missile submarine was easy to make out. The USS *Maryland* was right where she was supposed to be. And she was alone.

"Take us down to a thousand feet," he ordered. "Close to half a mile and then hold station."

The captain programmed the orders into the computer and allowed it to fly the ship to the required coordinates.

As they closed in on the submarine, Colon watched through the binoculars. Before long he could make out little orange dots, both fore and aft of the conning tower. Men in life jackets, standing around as if waiting for rescue. If Rear Admiral Wagner had done his job as programmed, they would all be infected with the dust, spread through the ship by its own air-scrubbing system. It would almost be a shame to kill Wagner at this point, but Colon didn't have time to even fake a rescue. He would send out the drones and order the *Maryland*'s crew to start jumping into the sea.

He brought a radio to his mouth. "Hangar deck, this is Colon. Launch the drones. When they get within five hundred feet of the sub, start broadcasting. And get the replacement crew loaded on board the shuttles. I want this done quickly."

At the stern of the *Condor*, Torres stood between three of the car-sized, donut-shaped drones. "Lower the doors and launch," he ordered.

A safety latch was unlocked, a hydraulic switch thrown. The wide hangar doors began to fold down. When they'd dropped far enough, the blinding glare of the sun poured in.

The *Condor* was heading nearly due west. The rising sun was directly behind it, so intensely powerful that even the darkest sunglasses were no match for its brilliance.

Torres threw up an arm to cover his eyes. Even then he saw large swaths of green where the sun had blazed across his retinas. The other men in the compartment were doing the same or looking away completely.

"Launch the drones," he ordered again.

The drone operator to his right hit the command switch and the big fans in the center of the donut-shaped craft powered up. They lifted off in perfect formation, oriented themselves, and then tilted their rotors and began to move forward. They left the hangar in a single file, picking up speed while slowly falling behind the airship.

"Commence turn and approach," Torres ordered.

The drone operator typed the command and hit enter. The drones tilted their fans to the left, swung out wide, and began to track for the submarine. They'd covered perhaps a thousand yards when a shape appeared out of the sun's glare. It grew rapidly, blocking the light and revealing itself.

Torres shuddered in terror at what he saw: another airship bearing down on them from behind, charging at flank speed and approaching as if it were going to ram directly into the *Condor*'s hangar deck. He shouted something unintelligible and ducked, bracing for impact, though he knew it was a futile gesture.

But the airship didn't hit them. It thundered by, no more than sixty feet to the right. It passed with such speed and fury that the *Condor* was shoved violently aside from the air displaced.

Torres held on and watched it race by, studying the dimpled anti-drag coating on the forward third of the ship, the field of solar panels, and the glass-domed SkyDeck, and then finally the vertical tails, which sliced through the air like the fins of a monstrous shark.

He saw it was the *Eagle*, but his mind couldn't fathom what it was doing here. The answer came when the onrushing ship barreled through the swarm of drones at top speed, obliterating them like a flight of tiny birds.

———

On the bridge of the *Eagle*, Kurt was gripping a safety bar and staring out the window. He saw debris falling and fluttering to the sea. As far as he could tell, there were no drones left in the sky.

"Got 'em," he said to Captain Bascombe. "Three birds with one very large stone."

The captain was pulling back on the All-Con, staring at the approaching sea. They'd been traveling full-speed as they came up on the *Condor*, approaching their sister ship from out of the sun like a World War I fighter plane. But upon the launch of the drones, Kurt had directed the captain to change plans and take out the drones first.

The captain rolled the *Eagle* to the right and dove under the *Condor*, instead of passing over it and attacking the upper section of the ship as originally planned. Now, as they tried to pull out of the dive, the helm was very slow to answer.

"Come on," he urged his trusty machine. "This is no time to dip our feet in the pond."

Leaning back as if that would help, the captain held the controls full aft. The green water and the waves grew larger and closer until that was all that could be seen.

"Vertical thrusters," Bascombe ordered.

One of the helmsmen diverted full thrust to vents beneath the airship, and it gave the settling craft a boost at just the right time. They leveled off at a hundred feet, raced by the submarine—and the astonished and disoriented men standing on her deck—and then began to climb once again.

Kurt let go of the safety bar and looked over at the captain. "Never a doubt," he said. "Now let's get above them, take out their lifting cells, and call it a day."

"Coming around," the captain said to his crew. "Someone find me the *Condor*."

63

It stood to reason that spotting a thousand-foot vessel in a cloudless sky would be child's play. As simple as looking up. The problem was—with the exception of the rooftop observation deck—everything on the airship was designed to offer views of the sea or the ground down below.

And as the *Eagle* wheeled around, neither Kurt, nor the captain, nor anyone else on the massive craft could put eyes on their adversary.

"She's up above us somewhere," the captain barked. "If we're not careful, she'll do to us what we planned to do to her."

Kurt grabbed a radio. "Joe, can you see anything behind us?"

Joe was still on the hangar deck, having slept there to be ready for action in the morning. "Nothing in our wake," he replied. "Can't see up due to the overhang."

Kurt hit the talk switch again. "Jodi," he called out. "Anything from where you are?"

Commander Wells had rounded up a small group of the crewmen and distributed the weapons they'd found aboard. After moving the passengers to the port side of the ship, she'd assembled her rifle brigade along the starboard balconies.

"We passed it on the wrong side," Commander Wells radioed back. "Can't see anything from here."

Nothing like a plan that was going wrong right out of the gate. Kurt turned back to the captain. "Head away from the sub at full speed, see if you can draw them off and climb if you can. I'll go up top and give you a report."

Solari jumped at the chance to help. "I'll show you the way."

As Kurt and Solari left the bridge, the captain guided the airship to the south. He kept the engines at full power, but a warning light on the number three battery pack told him they didn't have much time.

"At least the sun's up," one of the officers suggested hopefully.

"Won't help us much while it's still on the horizon," the chief engineer replied.

"How much time do we have?" Bascombe asked.

As the engineer performed some rough calculations, a warning light for the number four battery pack turned yellow as well. "Five or six minutes. No more unless you throttle back."

The captain wasn't going to do that, not until they were above the *Condor* and blasting her into the sea. He kept the craft going all out and started a silent count in his head.

———

Kurt and Solari climbed up to the main passenger deck, encountering a few passengers who'd left their staterooms against orders.

"What's happening?" one of them demanded.

"Are we crashing?" another asked.

"Please return to your quarters," Solari urged. "Things are bound to get rough."

"Rougher than this?"

With no more time to explain, they raced through the central lounge toward an elevator bank amidships. The elevator took them up to the SkyDeck, its doors opening to reveal a pool deck with multiple levels of chairs and tables, all covered by a retractable clear dome.

As Kurt stepped from the elevator, a vast shadow passed over them. The *Condor*.

He snapped the radio to his mouth. "Break left! *Condor* is directly above us and coming down."

The *Eagle* rolled hard once more. The tables and chairs slid across the SkyDeck, a flood of water surged out over the edge of the pool and swept toward Kurt and Solari.

"I guess your passengers have their answer," Kurt said.

Solari went to a microphone and dialed up the main circuit, making an announcement.

"All passengers remain in your cabins," he ordered. "We are involved in an emergency situation."

That was an understatement, Kurt thought. He ran to the highest point on the deck—a spot where he had lines of sight in all directions—and scanned the blue sky for the *Condor*. The sudden turn separated the two ships, but the *Condor* was coming about hard and trying to get above them once more.

"Joe," Kurt said into the radio, "we've got a bird of prey swooping in for the kill. If you can do anything with those drones, now would be a good time."

Back on the *Eagle*'s hangar deck, Joe was ready for action. He launched one of the donut-shaped drones. Working off a computer screen that relayed video from the drone's camera system, he adjusted course and allowed the drone to trail out behind them before aiming it at the *Condor*, which was still stalking them from above.

"If I was the criminal mastermind type," Joe asked himself, "where would I be right now?"

The answer was obvious. Zeroing in on the bridge, Joe zoomed the camera until he could see the main windows. With the location locked in, he set the drone to full speed and put his finger on the command key for the illumination.

The drone sped away from the *Eagle*, rising upward and back. Joe tapped the light switch until full brightness had been achieved and then sat back.

"Fastball, right down the pike," he said, pleased with himself.

The drone raced toward the *Condor*'s bridge, closing the gap rapidly. Joe imagined the men inside spotting the glowing orb and trying to dodge it. In fact, the *Condor* did begin to turn, but it was like a blue whale trying to dodge a flying fish. It was never going to happen.

The orb smashed into the bridge glass, but the impact blew the drone apart. It fell along the hull in a rain of plastic confetti.

"Fouled that one off, did you?" Joe said. "Maybe you'd like a taste of my curveball."

He launched the second drone, sending it at the bridge on a slightly different arc. This one came in from the side, blazing orange-white as it raced up.

The *Condor* adjusted course earlier this time, as the pilots were obviously on the lookout for another attack. Once again, the brightly lit drone smashed into the windows. And once again the near-indestructible polymer panels held.

———

Up on the top deck, Kurt saw both impacts. He noticed the maneuvers of the *Condor* each time. When Joe sent the third drone into the fray, Kurt got on the radio. "Hard to port," he advised. "Maximum climb."

Bascombe followed the directions precisely, and as the *Condor* rolled to starboard to avoid the third impact, the *Eagle* turned to port.

The brief divergence in headings allowed the *Eagle* to get out from under its larger sibling and it pitched upward until its lower deck was even with the *Condor*'s upper third. As the ships came even, the *Condor* appeared on the *Eagle*'s starboard side.

"Run out the guns," Kurt ordered, as if he were commanding a sailing ship with fifty cannons. "Fire at will."

64

The "guns" were not cannons, or mortars, or anything capable of delivering a devastating broadside, but Commander Wells had scrounged every weapon that Colon's people had brought on board, including a crate of assault rifles, which they'd been unable to access during the surprise attack of the reverse mutiny.

While shouting directions to her men, she cradled a rifle herself. "Aim high," she said. "You need to account for the bullet's drop as it crosses the space between our ship and theirs."

She raised the barrel of her assault rifle ten degrees and opened fire. Her teams did the same, concentrating their attack against the very top of the *Condor*'s fuselage. Commander Wells was proficient enough on the rifle range that she knew the bullets were flying straight and true, even without tracers to zero things in. But even as they exhausted entire magazines of 7.62mm ammo, they saw nothing to suggest they'd had any effect. So vast was the target, and so minute the initial effect of the bullets, that even as dozens of lifting cells were getting shredded, no one on the *Condor* even realized they were under attack.

"Reload," she told her charges, then grabbed the radio. "First volley away," she reported. "No sign of damage. Get us in closer. We'll concentrate on the aft compartment."

With Bascombe's deft touch, the *Eagle* moved closer, near enough that Commander Wells thought she might be able to jump from one airship to the other.

Her team opened fire once more, this time unloading everything they had at the compartment just ahead of the twin tails. The barrage was more focused and intense. The gunfire more constant. The target unmissable.

Just before the ships veered away, a pair of the harpoon-shaped, rocket-propelled anchors were fired. They arced upward and then down like artillery shells, puncturing the side of the *Condor* and vanishing as if they'd been absorbed by a cloud.

Kurt watched it all from the SkyDeck.

"How are we doing?" Solari asked.

Kurt couldn't tell. "It's like throwing pebbles into a tidal wave."

The attack had at least come to the attention of the men on the *Condor*. It broke away, climbing and turning toward the west. The *Eagle* turned east, circling and rising, as the two ships partook in a desperate race to get above one another.

As it turned out, neither would win. They came full circle at nearly the same altitude and began approaching each other head-on. Both ships moved slower now, having lost speed with all the twists and turns. It made them seem larger and more ponderous, instead of the sleek and nimble craft they'd been just a moment ago.

They closed the gap toward each other like ships of the line ready to exchange broadsides. To keep its opponent to starboard, the *Eagle* offset to one side. The *Condor* shifted to the other, as if they were engaged in some chivalrous contest with rules agreed upon in advance.

This time, the *Condor*'s side was teeming with armed men. They opened fire with their own weapons: fifty-caliber machine guns and AK-47s. The onslaught was directed not at the inert gasbags up above, but at the center of the *Eagle* itself.

Shells tore into the crew quarters, the engineering spaces, and a large number of passenger cabins. Two glass panels on the bridge were scarred by bullets that didn't penetrate. Several of Commander Wells's men were shot as they crouched on the balconies.

One man fell backward into the cabin, safe but injured. At the same time his valuable weapon dropped over the railing, twirling as it plunged to the sea.

"Return fire," Kurt ordered. "Give it everything you've got."

The *Eagle*'s outgunned crew held their ground and did just that, exhausting their ammunition and launching two more of the harpoon-like anchors.

Kurt watched closely, hoping the onslaught would have some effect, but the *Condor* rumbled on by as if unaffected by the barrage.

———

Inside the *Condor*, more was happening than Kurt could see. The rifle bullets were taking a toll, with many of the shots cutting through multiple helium cells in one pass and exiting through the far side of the airship. But because the holes were small, the helium was venting slowly. Lift was being lost, but not all at once.

The gunfire had another effect, chasing Colon's men from the lifting chambers.

Gamay took this as a positive, though she had no idea what was going on.

One minute she'd been in hiding, desperate to quelch hunger pangs that were so strong she thought her growling stomach might give her away, the next she was being thrown about as the huge ship swung itself from side to side.

When bullets started whistling through the compartment, she'd sought cover and had hidden behind a large structural beam. There she'd crouched as the gunfire raged and the ship turned.

Just as she was wondering whose military was attacking the airship, an arrow-shaped projectile plunged through the outer hull, tore into a nearby bundle of lifting cells, and embedded itself into the very support beam she was hiding behind. It's carbide tip poked through, its barbed edges locking it into place. She recognized the object as one of the rocket-propelled anchors Solari had joked about.

She knew instantly that the military wouldn't be launching anchors at the airship. The only people she could imagine coming up with a scheme like that were Kurt and Joe.

"About time you guys showed up," she whispered.

To her surprise, her voice was pitched high like Mickey Mouse. Then again, despite all the vents and gashes in the outer skin, there was a lot of helium flowing around the compartment.

Gamay instantly understood what Kurt and Joe were attempting. They were trying to bring the ship down by turning the lighter-than-air craft into one that was heavier than air.

"Let me give you boys a hand," she said aloud.

Grasping a sliver of the aluminum brace that had been nearly separated by the anchor, she worked it back and forth until it broke free. It wasn't an elegant weapon, but it was two feet long and jagged.

She used it to stab the nearest gas cell, grinning as the punctured airbag collapsed. She stabbed the ones beside it to the same effect.

Feeling the airship turn, she got up and began to move along the catwalk, slashing and cutting every cell she could reach. There seemed to be countless numbers of them, but Gamay was determined not to rest until she'd punctured them all.

On the SkyDeck of the *Eagle*, Kurt studied the enemy vessel. It had finished the pass and appeared unharmed, but as it trundled away, he could tell it was down at its stern, like a car with an overloaded trunk.

And yet it banked into a turn, angling to make at least one more pass.

Kurt got on the radio to share the good news. "She's coming back around," he said. "But she's losing lift at the tail end. Get us up above her and we can finish this. It's now or never."

For a moment there was no reply. Kurt keyed the mike. "Captain?"

When Bascombe finally radioed back, Kurt heard the sound of alarms and warning bells in the background.

"Sorry, lad," the captain replied. "The batteries are going. We've had to throttle back. We'll be a sitting duck if we waste the rest of the juice trying to get above them."

Kurt swore under his breath. They were a sitting duck either way. He cocked his head to the right. The *Condor* was bearing down on them. And this time it was coming in for the kill.

Aboard the wounded *Condor*, Martin Colon was having the very same thought. "I want to finish them on this pass," he shouted. "Use one of the Needles."

The Needles were antiaircraft missiles, a Russian version of the American Stinger. Colon had put his hands on a half dozen of the rockets months ago, intending to load them aboard the submarine in case the boat was attacked by American aircraft before he and his replacement crew could submerge.

On the hangar deck of the *Condor*, Colon's men unpacked the missiles with all possible haste. The first rocket was readied and hefted onto a burly shoulder. The man carrying it moved toward the open doors.

Torres watched this with great concern. "We're in position," he reported. "Missile ready."

"Stand by," Colon replied. "Wait until we've passed them."

The man with the launcher stood his ground, waiting for the order to fire. As he gazed out though the open doors, he noticed the stern was dipping lower and lower.

His train of thought was broken as a wave of turbulence hit the airship. They were passing the *Eagle* now and turning away. The *Eagle* appeared out behind them, huge and slow. A sitting target.

The man looked through the viewfinder, unsure what to aim at on a vessel so large. He chose the center of the ship and squeezed the handles.

The missile launched in a cloud of white smoke, the orange flame of the booster visible as it crossed the gap, rose upward, and smashed into the *Eagle*'s solar array.

———

Kurt saw the missile coming and braced himself. It hit fifty yards ahead of the roof deck. The explosion wasn't exactly massive—the missile carried only a three-pound warhead—but shrapnel from the missile and unused but burning rocket fuel doubled and tripled the damage.

Kurt soon felt the airship nosing over.

"That's it," Bascombe radioed. "We're done for. All we can do now is put down and hope we don't sink."

The blast had taken out too many gas cells in the same location. The airship had become nose heavy, forcing Bascombe to vent gas from the aft compartment for balance.

Kurt looked back at the *Condor*, waiting for the inevitable. She was wounded and lumbering, but still the last fighter standing. But instead of returning to finish off her foe, she continued to pull away, bending her course back to the north.

"Are they giving up?" Solari asked hopefully.

"No," Kurt said. "They're going back for the *Maryland*. They still plan on taking the sub."

65

Colon kept an eye on the smoking hulk of the *Eagle* even as he ordered the *Condor* to reverse course. The older airship was settling slowly. There was nothing to suggest it had any fight left. The missile had done its job.

"How far are we from the *Maryland*?" he asked, turning his thoughts back to the submarine.

"Six miles," the captain replied.

The battle had drawn them off to the south, but as they came about, Colon could see the nuclear vessel through the binoculars. It was still sitting idle on the surface. It hadn't moved. He couldn't see the sailors from this range, but the signal Wagner was using must have been holding them in their trance or the sub would have been crash-diving to safety. There was only one problem. As Colon scanned the waters below them, they appeared to be traveling ever more sluggishly. "We need to go faster."

The captain pointed to a systems screen. Blinking numbers showed the status of the gas cells. "We've taken a lot of damage. We're venting large amounts of helium from the aft compartment. There's not enough lift to keep us in the air. To compensate, the flight control system is vectoring most of our thrust downward. That leaves only a minimal amount for propulsion."

"How soon till we're over the sub?"

"At this rate, ten minutes," the captain said. "But shouldn't we be heading back to Providencia, before the Americans send jets to shoot us down?"

An hour ago, Colon would have labeled that idea as fanciful or even ludicrous. They had three hundred human shields aboard the ship. A fact he'd believed would make them invulnerable to attack. But whoever had taken over the *Eagle*—and there was only one person he imagined it could be—had circumvented that wall of human shields by firing upon the uninhabited, upper reaches of the ship.

A grudging feeling of respect crept into his mind. He'd bloodied and wounded the bull over and over, only to see it rise up again after each stumble. He wondered just how they'd done it. How had they escaped, and unraveled his perfectly orchestrated plan?

The bull is cunning, he told himself. *And that is why we respect it.*

Still, it would be only a moral victory for Austin and the Americans. The attack on Guantánamo was primarily intended as a diversion. Something to occupy their forces while he spirited the Trident missiles from the hijacked submarine to secret locations around Cuba. And that was still going to happen.

Once he had the submarine, he could force the Americans to leave Guantánamo whenever he wanted. And if they tested him, he would nuke one of their cities and leave it glowing, just to teach them a lesson.

"Continue toward the submarine," he ordered. "To keep the American military at bay, we must gain control of that ship."

Two miles away, the V-shaped bottom of the *Eagle*'s hull creased the shimmering green water of the Caribbean. The landing was relatively smooth, cushioned by the vertical thrust from the fans and the lift from the remaining helium cells, but even with the pontoons extended—and the crew frantically shoving cargo and ballast out every door and hatchway—the freeboard was nearly used up before the airship's downward momentum ceased and she began to rise.

After an oscillation or two, the *Eagle* settled like a duck and held steady with a gap of only three feet between the crests of the passing swells and the sections of the airship that were not watertight.

"Thank god we have calm seas," Bascombe announced. "Damage control teams to the lifting compartments. Inflate all emergency cells. Engineering, continue to release all ballast, we need to lighten the ship."

By the time these orders went out, Kurt was running along the upper catwalk and heading toward the stern. He'd left Solari to help with the damage control and was on his way to the hangar deck.

Reaching the mid-level catwalk, he continued aft, calling Joe on the radio as he did so. "Looks like we're down safely," he said. "Can you see the *Condor* from where you are?"

"Looking at her right now," Joe said. "She's limping away but still headed for the *Maryland*. Seems to be struggling, though."

Finally, a bit of good news. "Think we can catch her?"

"If you hurry."

"You boys aren't going without me," Commander Wells insisted.

"Meet us in the hangar bay," Kurt said. "Train leaves in sixty seconds. Don't be late."

By the time he reached the hangar deck, Joe had one of the shuttle drones charged up and ready to go. They were designed to take six people, but Kurt, Joe, and Commander Wells were going on this mission alone. The rest of the *Eagle*'s crew was needed to keep her afloat and assist the passengers into the inflatable lifeboats if the airship started sinking.

Kurt climbed into the drone as Commander Wells came running. Joe handed Kurt the Taser they'd used the night before and then lowered a heavy backpack into the center seat.

"Is that what I think it is?" Kurt said.

Joe nodded. "Let's hope it works."

Commander Wells climbed aboard and strapped herself in, still carrying the AK-47. "It's just for show," she admitted. "Used every bullet we had during the fight."

At the touch of a button, the fans surrounding them spun up to full power. Seconds later the shuttle was accelerating across the threshold and out into the mild Caribbean air.

"Hang on," Joe said, pushing the shuttle to its maximum speed.

They closed on the limping airship relatively quickly with the airship doing thirty knots and the drone more than twice that.

"Guessing they won't give us permission to land," Commander Wells said, shouting to be heard above the wind noise.

"Probably not," Joe said. "No matter how nicely we ask."

"Take us up top," Kurt replied. "Acres of room to land up there."

"And then?"

"We find Colon and finish this."

Joe kept the drone at full power, climbing until they were well above the struggling airship. By now it was obvious that the *Condor* was tail heavy and almost stationary.

Kurt was surprised. "Didn't think we'd done that much damage." He turned to Commander Wells. "Good job, you."

"Never count out a few lucky shots," she replied.

"I'll take whatever luck we can get," Kurt said. "Fly us between the vertical tails and land next to the SkyDeck. Do your best to set us down on a rib or spar, otherwise this thing will go right through the skin."

Joe would have preferred to land on the SkyDeck itself, but the clear dome hadn't been retracted. He eased the drone down in front of it, trying his best to touch down softly. Even so, the right-hand skid punctured the airship's skin, and their chariot began to tilt and slide through.

"Last stop," Joe announced. "Everyone off."

Kurt was already moving. He grabbed the backpack and leapt out of the seat. Commander Wells was right behind him.

Joe followed, scrambling across the rapidly fraying fabric, his feet—and then hands and knees—sinking into the material as it gave way beneath them.

They reached the safety of a carbon fiber rib in time to see the drone tilt precariously and then vanish into the interior of the airship. Through the fluttering fabric, they saw the gas cells and framework of the aft lifting compartment.

"You seem to have found the way in," Kurt said.

"Just like I planned," Joe said.

Handing the backpack to Joe, Kurt crawled along the strut until he found a spot where they could drop in. He slid his legs over and lowered himself down until he was hanging from his fingertips. From there, he dropped onto the upper catwalk. Commander Wells landed next to him and raised the assault rifle as if to sweep their path. Joe pulled the backpack over his shoulders and followed suit, catching up with them a few seconds later.

Moving along the catwalk, they passed dozens upon dozens of deflated lifting cells. But there was something odd. While many of the ruptured cells were sagging and losing gas from bullet holes, the ones closest to the catwalk were shredded and flat, hanging like plastic bags caught on a tree limb. A close inspection revealed that they'd been ripped open with long jagged slashes.

Joe looked closely. "This was done by hand. It's sabotage."

Kurt grinned. "Paul and Gamay."

Following the trail of damaged cells, they came to a vertical ladder. A commotion could be heard down below.

They slid down the ladder and followed the sound, arriving at a spur that went off to one side. There they discovered the source of the turmoil: a tall woman with wine-colored hair who was swinging a jagged metal weapon at a trio of gray-shirts who'd cornered her.

"We'll make you eat that blade, you little witch," one man said.

As they closed in on her, Gamay swung the weapon from side to side as if it were a flaming torch keeping wild animals at bay.

One man seemed to think he'd spied an opening to attack and charged. Gamay caught him with a backhand strike that would have made any tennis coach proud. The man tumbled sideways and off the catwalk, crashing through the gas cells below.

Kurt and Joe pounced before the other men could move on their friend. Joe spun one of the men around, coldcocking him, while Kurt jabbed the second man with the Taser and zapped him until he dropped to his knees. At which point Gamay kicked him in the face.

The two men gave up the fight when Commander Wells coughed loudly and aimed the rifle in their direction.

Gamay sighed in relief. "Good to see you," she said, hugging Kurt. "And whoever your friend is."

Introductions were made. The situation discussed.

"You have no idea what I've been through on this flight," Gamay insisted. "I'll never complain about lost luggage at the airport again."

"I'm just glad you're still as feisty as ever," Kurt said. "We thought you and Paul might have been co-opted."

"They got to Paul," she said sadly. "But not completely." She pulled out the syringe. "He was supposed to jab me with this, but he handed it over instead."

"Good old stubborn New Englander," Kurt said. He offered her the Taser. "Trade you."

Gamay took the device. "What do you want me to do with this?"

"Find Paul and zap him with it," Kurt said. "It should reset his brain waves and get him back to normal."

"I get to zap my husband and be the hero," she said. "It's every wife's dream. Where are you three going?"

"The only place Colon can go if he hopes to escape: the hangar bay."

66

Colon stared hopelessly out the bridge windows. The *Condor*'s pace had grown ever slower even as they approached. Now it had come to a halt. With the submarine less than a mile away.

The bridge itself was a room of chaos. Red and amber warning lights were flashing everywhere, men were scrambling about to do what they could, a computer voice was interspersing system failure warnings with announcements regarding the initiation of the automated landing procedure.

"Do something," Colon demanded.

"I can't," the captain replied. "Lift has dropped below minimum required for flight. Even with thrust fully diverted to vertical we can't stay airborne. We're going to hit the water. And we're going to stay there."

At that very moment, Torres called over the radio. He sounded panicked. "Our cameras picked up a drone landing on the roof deck. At least three people climbed out of it. And there's a ship on the horizon steaming this way. Can't tell if it's military or not, but it's coming on fast."

It was all falling apart, Colon thought. And with the submarine so close. Colon had no doubt who had climbed out of that drone, but it gave him an idea. If Austin could use a drone to cover the gap between the airships, Colon could use it to reach the submarine. "Get the replacement crew into the shuttle drones," he said. "I'm heading your way."

"Where are we going?"

"The submarine."

The *Condor* hit the water less gracefully than the *Eagle*. Because the damage from the *Eagle*'s guns and Gamay's makeshift sword was so heavily concentrated in the aft lifting compartment, it became impossible to trim the ship correctly. It smacked the water tail-first, causing a whiplash effect that slammed the front half of the ship down even harder. An eruption of spray flew up around it, while an artificial swell surged outward across the water, pushing in all directions. As the craft settled, its large tails caught the wind, turning it like a weather vane, until its stern was pointed toward the motionless submarine.

Gamay had just reached the passenger deck when the impact occurred, and she was thrown forward into the corridor leading to the Presidential Suite. It was now full of passengers with life jackets on. The *Condor* was in trouble, and everyone knew it.

Gamay pushed through the crowds of people, most of whom were running in the opposite direction. At one point a pair of gray-shirts rushed past her, but they took no notice. At this point, survival was on everyone's mind.

At the end of the hall, she found the Presidential Suite. Not bothering to look for her key, she slammed her shoulder into the door. It flew open.

Paul was there. Standing at the window, staring out it. He turned at the sound of her entrance but said nothing.

"Come on," she said. "We have to get to a lifeboat."

He stepped forward, then stopped. "Can't leave," he said. "I have to stay."

She clenched her teeth. He was still under the hypnotic spell.

Suddenly, he reverted to the original instructions. "I have to give you something," he said.

She gulped hard. "I have something for you as well."

As Paul reached into his pocket for the syringe that was no longer there, Gamay brought up the Taser, jabbed it into Paul's side, and pressed the discharge switch. Paul stiffened and fell back.

"I have something I have to give you," he said angrily.

This time she fired the prongs. They hit him in the chest, allowing the full course of the electrical charge to go through his body. He shook with the current and then dropped to his knees, stiff as a board.

She crouched beside him. "Paul, are you okay? I had to do it. I'm so sorry."

He was breathing hard and wincing in pain, but when he looked at her, he was himself again. "Don't be. I needed that. My, what a miserable experience."

"The Taser or the hypnosis?"

"Both," he replied. "Now, what was that you said about lifeboats?"

She helped him up. "I'm not sure this thing is going to stay afloat. Let's grab our life jackets and get out the door."

67

Martin Colon pushed his way onto the hangar deck with the ship in full chaos. The gray-shirts were gone. He saw them out behind the airship in bright yellow lifeboats, rowing with gusto. Rats abandoning a sinking ship.

Only Torres and the replacement crew remained. Torres was sitting in the lead drone by himself, while the false crew sat in the shuttle drones behind him, all of them waiting for Colon to arrive. The discipline instilled by the dust had always impressed him. When this was over, he decided, he'd find other uses for it.

Colon made his way for the lead craft, climbing in beside Torres. "Let's go," he snapped.

Torres just sat there staring blankly ahead. Tracking his gaze, Colon noticed a man standing directly in their way, on the threshold of the launch bay.

The man had his back to Colon and Torres. His pose suggested he was watching the gray-shirts paddling like mad in their yellow lifeboats. "Have to admire their effort," the man said, "but I don't see them making it all the way to Cuba."

The figure turned around. It was Kurt Austin. He was unarmed, but blocking their path like a traffic cop on the street of some one-horse town.

"Run him over!" Colon ordered.

Torres remained still. His unblinking eyes continued staring straight ahead. Only now did Colon see the syringe sticking out of his leg. The dust.

Colon grew angry, but he could pilot the drone himself. First, he would finish Austin once and for all. He pulled out the handheld frequency generator, which never left his possession. Pressing the button and holding it, he issued a command to the replacement crew. "*Maryland* crew," he shouted, pointing to Kurt. "Rip that man apart! Tear him limb from limb!"

He expected movement, expected to enjoy watching the men in U.S. Navy uniforms maul Austin like a pack of dogs, but they never even flinched.

He pressed the button again, his eyes on the green lights that lit up when the signal went out. He gave the same order. He got the same result. His eyes grew wide in anger.

Austin stood his ground, unafraid and unharmed, a smug grin firmly in place. "They don't listen to you anymore," Austin insisted. "They've given themselves over to a higher power."

Colon looked up. Perched in the support beams was the other thorn in his side, Zavala. He was tapping away at a laptop computer, which was connected to an emitter that Colon recognized as coming from inside one of the mind-control drones.

Cocking his head, Colon could just make out the command. "*Stand down . . . Stand down . . . Stand down . . .*"

Zavala turned up the volume and it became that much clearer.

Austin explained. "Like you said, they obey the first voice they heard. This is the computerized voice you used to abduct them from their ships. It's their prime recollection."

Colon fumed, trapped and desperate for an option. He looked around in vain, eventually coming back to gaze upon Austin's grinning face.

"Sometimes the bull wins," Austin said.

Colon slammed his fist down in a rage, hitting the control panel. The fans surrounding the drone spun up with a near instant whirr. As the craft rose off the deck, Colon grabbed the control stick and shoved it. The drone surged toward Kurt, who drew a pistol, fired a snap shot, and then dove out of the way.

Colon didn't bother to take another run at him. He was free. Out past the threshold and cruising across the water. He held the control stick cautiously, pulling back to get a little more altitude.

As the craft came up, he felt an odd pain in his side. He reached down and touched his abdomen. His hand came back wet with red blood. Austin had shot him as he escaped.

Grunting and checking the wound again, Colon wondered how bad it was. The blood was red and not dark. It meant his liver had been spared. It changed nothing, he told himself. There were medical personnel on the *Maryland*. All he had to do was get to the sub. He still had the transmitter. He could still use it to control Wagner, and through him, command the rest of the crew.

The submarine and its missiles would still be his. And if the Americans tried to find him and sink him, he would surface and launch every missile he could, just to burn them in spite.

Gritting his teeth, he turned his gaze forward. The submarine was less than a mile away, directly in front of him. All he had to do was reach it and land. Austin hadn't won. He had failed after all.

Back on the *Condor*, Kurt might have thought the same thing. But he knew better. A few feet away, Commander Wells had unboxed one of the Russian missile launchers. Hefting it up onto her shoulder, she locked in on the fleeing craft.

"Pull the trigger," Kurt said.

She nodded, squeezing the handles and launching the missile. The Needle erupted from the tube, its engine bursting to life in a glow of orange flame as it went. The rocket flew straight and true, leaving a smoke trail behind it as it tracked the fleeing machine. It closed the gap in a matter of seconds, blasting through the lightweight craft and obliterating it upon impact. Plastic parts fluttered and fell from the sky.

Kurt saw two bodies windmilling downward. They dropped two hundred feet, hitting the surface in a pair of muted splashes.

The fight was over.

Kurt looked up at Joe with triumph, then he walked over to Commander Wells, who was lowering the launch tube wearily. "You okay?"

She'd been through it longer than any of them. The toll seemed to appear on her face even as the weight was lifted from her shoulders. "I've felt better, but I'm not angry anymore."

Kurt smiled. This was good news on multiple levels. "Come on," he said. "We need to make sure this ship isn't going to sink."

68

Kurt Austin wore NUMA dive gear as he swam alongside the hull of the *Eagle*, looking for bubbles. Inside the airship, teams of men were using compressed air to force water out of the flooded compartments. The high-pressure air forced itself through tiny cracks, allowing Kurt to find the holes.

Discovering a trail of escaping air, he alerted Joe. "Pinholes in section fifteen, and at least one fifty-caliber puncture. Give me a few minutes and I'll have them sealed up."

"How much spackle you got left?" Joe asked.

Kurt wasn't using spackle, of course, but a thick rubbery goo that he smeared onto a thin sheet of aluminum tape, which could then be pressed against the hull, where it would quickly meld itself to the airship despite it being immersed in the water. "Enough for one more repair and then I'm coming up for lunch. Someone order me a pizza."

"Sure," Joe said. "We'll fly one in from Pepe's in New Haven."

Kurt knew Joe was kidding, but that sounded spectacular.

Finishing the patch job, he waited thirty seconds and then had the team inside restart the pumps. As the pressure test commenced, not a single trail of bubbles appeared.

"Section fifteen clear," Kurt said. "Coming aboard."

Kurt swam to the pontoon and then climbed a ladder that had been rigged for the divers. Shedding his tanks and other gear he crossed a jerry-rigged gangway and entered the *Eagle*. Going up two decks he found a group of men and women in what had been the airship's main lounge. It was now filled with salvage equipment, everything from compressors, generators, and welding gear to endless rolls of the aluminum tape, which were stacked up against the wall. Different crews were working on different parts of the ship. Kurt and Joe were handling the subsurface work, while Solari's men repaired the lifting cells and the damage done by the missile strike up above.

At the center of everything a small pyramid of prewrapped sandwiches covered the grand piano at the center of the room. Not exactly five-star luxury, Kurt thought, but as hungry as he was, it would do.

With a ham and cheese in one hand and a turkey on wheat in the other, he left the lounge and stepped out onto the balcony, where he found Joe setting up a NUMA communications dish.

He tossed Joe the ham and cheese and then stepped to the rail. The view was one he would not soon forget.

Forty-eight hours after they'd battled in the skies over the Caribbean, the two airships remained afloat and drifting and surrounded by a small fleet of ships. Two research vessels from NUMA lay in close, along with an American guided-missile destroyer. A pair of charter boats heavy with members of the press lay farther off, circling constantly as photographers angled for the perfect shot. In between sat the nuclear submarine the *Maryland*, which remained on the surface, buttoned-up and empty and guarded by a trio of patrol boats filled with U.S. Marines. Last but not least, he spied Rolle's sailboat, which spent most of its time moored to the *Condor* as Rolle used his expertise in carbon fiber and composites to help inspect the ship and determine if it could be saved.

Kurt smiled as he recalled Rolle's negotiations with Solari. Rolle had driven such a hard bargain that by the end of the week he might be the billionaire and Solari the workingman. From the way Solari had taken control of the repair work, Kurt thought that role reversal might suit the Brazilian just fine.

"Good to work with my hands again," Solari had insisted. "And to know my mind is my own. If I do anything crazy now, you know it's just the real me."

Kurt hoped they wouldn't see anything crazy, and so far, they hadn't.

The bigger surprise was that Ostrom remained a going concern, instead of falling into bankruptcy and receivership. The incident had become worldwide news, playing on every network and internet terminal in an endless loop. Talk of a conspiracy within Ostrom was bad enough, and even Kurt knew that a pair of airships engaging in a dogfight and then crashing into the ocean could not be good publicity.

But when both ships remained afloat, and neither burned, as the *Hindenburg* once had, Solari began using the incident as a testament to the strength and dependability of the airships. He pointed out that the *Eagle* had even taken a missile strike and landed safely. And that not a single passenger had died.

Then, with four hundred people needing a way back to shore ASAP, Solari had pulled another marketing coup out of his hat, diverting a third airship, named the *Osprey*, to come pick everyone up.

The survivors had been lifted from the sea in front of a hundred TV cameras and then flown to Miami in great style and world-class comfort. Solari even invited a few dozen reporters to go along. By some estimates, the airtime had been a hundred million dollars in free advertising.

Realizing it would have taken an entire squadron of large

helicopters to pull off the same trick, the Coast Guard had contacted Solari about the availability of his next craft. As had an unnamed internet billionaire and at least one major cruise line. According to the financial pages, investors were flooding Solari with offers to buy part, or even all, of the airship line.

Good for Solari, Kurt thought. He was certainly the type who made his own luck.

"All set," Joe said, popping up from behind the screen.

A few moments later they were linked up with Commander Wells, who'd traveled back to the States with Rear Admiral Wagner, Gerald Walker, and both crews of the *Maryland*—the real one and their hypnotized replacements.

While the initial treatments of electrical stimulation had rid the hypnotized men of the dust, those who'd been indoctrinated longest were requiring extensive deprogramming.

As the image cleared, Kurt could see that Commander Wells was at a hospital. "You getting your tonsils out?" he asked. "There are easier ways to get free ice cream, you know."

"Just here to support the troops," she said. "They hit Walker with a lot of that stuff. He's dealing with a lot of physical issues. Rear Admiral Wagner is on the other end of it. Struggling to deal with what they made him do. Turns out they got to him before I even went to Cuba. Once he was programmed, they checked in with him repeatedly using the posthypnotic method and some chimes on his watch that put him back under. He's feeling a heavy load of responsibility about the operations that were blown and the people we lost."

Kurt understood that. He figured it would be a long road for Wagner. "Remind him that he supported you when you went rogue. And that stopping Colon would have been impossible if you and Walker weren't out there off the reservation."

"I have," she said. "And I'll keep telling him."

"Good work, Commander," Kurt said.

"Thanks," she replied. "And you can call me Jodi now. I resigned my commission yesterday. Soon I'll just be another civilian looking for a job."

Kurt offered a subtle smirk. "I know a place you might want to apply."

She smiled back. "Funny, Dr. Pascal suggested the same thing."

Someone redirected the phone and Dr. Pascal appeared.

"Hey," Joe said, waving excitedly.

"Hey, yourself," the doctor replied.

"What are you doing up there?"

Dr. Pascal looked hurt. "I'm the world's foremost expert in treating people who've been affected by this dust. Where else would I be?"

Joe, who was always so cool with women, stumbled over his words. "I meant . . . um . . . How lucky are they to have you."

Dr. Pascal tilted her glasses down and bent her head toward the screen as if examining Joe more closely. "I'm worried about you, Zavala. You need to finish up down there and get back to the States for a full physical examination."

She winked and Joe smiled. "First thing on my list, once I get home."

Kurt coughed to make sure the flirting was done. The sound of a boat coming over from one of the NUMA ships told Kurt it was time to sign off. They said their goodbyes, wolfed down the sandwiches, and met Rudi Gunn on the dock beside the pontoon.

"Surprised to see you here," Kurt said. "Are they fumigating your office this week or something?"

"I had to come down," Rudi said, stepping onto the airship. "I just had to see it with my own eyes."

"See what?"

"The two of you actually doing salvage work," Rudi explained. "You know that's officially what we pay you for. And yet, I can't remember the last time you did any."

"Well," Kurt said, "next time there's a big crisis out there in the world, you can find someone else to fix it. I'll be busy salvaging an inflatable raft in someone's pool."

"And I'll be using some of the two hundred and fifty-three accrued sick days that I never get around to," Joe insisted.

"Sure you will," Rudi said. "And all I have to do is say something doesn't add up here and you two will be on the job like a shot."

Kurt laughed. He couldn't argue with that.

"Any word from Paul and Gamay?"

"Doing fine and resting," Rudi said. "Strange how things work out. Paul says he's no longer afraid of heights and Gamay insists she's never flying again."

"Go figure," Kurt said. "What about the guys on Providencia?"

"A joint American and Colombian team raided the complex yesterday," Rudi said. "They seized the machinery and shipped it back to the States. A few of Colon's people got caught up in the net, but the rest might have flown the coop back to Cuba. The State Department is alerting certain reasonable members of the Cuban government to the possibility that Colon and his crew might have some undue influence in the party. We'll see what comes of it."

Kurt doubted anything would happen, but one could never be too sure. "Maybe this will start a thaw in our relations. I know a few people who'd like to go down there and check out the food and the cars."

Rudi nodded and then changed the subject. He was tired of talking, he wanted to see something happen. "Any chance we're going to get lucky here? Or are these two monstrosities a pair of lost causes?"

Kurt pointed across the water to the other airship. "*Condor* won't fly again," he said. "At least not without major work. It hit the water too hard, causing significant structural damage. Solari is trying to shore things up and then have it towed to Panama. They'll either strip her for parts or try to rebuild her there."

"A shame," Rudi said. "What about this bird?"

Joe answered. "New lifting cells are being installed and inflated now. Once we finish sealing up the holes and pumping the water out of the bilge, she'll be taking to the skies . . . and hopefully staying there."

"Well," Rudi said, "it's not exactly raising the *Titanic*, but impressive nonetheless."

It would be another twenty-four hours before the salvage work was done. By then the *Condor* had been towed off and the *Maryland* re-crewed with legitimate U.S. Navy personnel, who took the ship toward Florida without submerging. The patrol boats and the guided-missile destroyer traveled alongside, escorting her the entire way.

With the *Condor* gone, Rolle checked in, wished Kurt and Joe well, and then sailed off for the Bahamas, but only after making a pass in front of the press boats while flying a sail emblazoned with an advertisement for Performance Sailing and the link to his website.

As Rolle left, Solari reboarded the *Eagle*, inviting Kurt and Joe to join him on the bridge as guests of honor. It was time to fly once more.

Without enough helium to go straight up, they would have to skip their way into the sky. Captain Bascombe handled the controls, bringing the power up slowly. The craft began to inch forward, gaining speed as it rode the swells, but proving unable to free itself from the grip of the sea.

Solari commanded a second attempt be made and then a third, but each time the craft shuddered and shook as it crossed the swells, threatening to undo all the repair work that had been done. Kurt began to wonder if they would have to impersonate a boat all the way back to Rio.

After the third run, Bascombe and Solari discussed the situation privately. They decided they would try once more. With everyone in position, Bascombe gave the type of order all captains want to at one time or another. "Damn the waves," he cried out. "Full speed ahead."

The airship began another run, pushing into the swells and picking up speed. The vibration came on, quickly turning into a repetitive jarring as the top of each swell banged against the V-shaped hull.

Kurt felt every hit in his legs. Joe held on, wondering how much the ship could take. And then, all of sudden, the shaking ceased, and the *Eagle* pulled free of the water. It leapt into the air, shedding the water that clung to its sides in a shower of droplets and spray.

The bridge crew shouted with joy.

Kurt nodded in satisfaction.

Joe pumped his fist.

"Airborne at last," Solari shouted. He turned to Kurt. "You're the man of the hour. Where should we go from here?"

Kurt grinned. There was only one answer worth giving. "To wherever the next adventure begins."

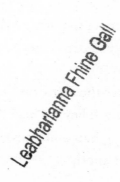